The Master Sniper

The
Master
Sniper

Stephen Hunter

WILLIAM MORROW AND COMPANY, INC.

New York   1980

Library of Congress Cataloging in Publication Data

Hunter, Stephen, 1946-
    The master sniper.

    1. World War, 1939-1945—Fiction. I. Title.
PZ4.H9484Mas [PS3558.U494]   813'.5'4   79-26065
ISBN 0-688-03591-4

Book Design by Michael Mauceri

Printed in the United States of America

For Jake Hunter
and Tolka Zhitomir

Marksmen are not limited to the location of their unit and are free
to move anywhere they can see a valuable target. . . .

—*Instructions for use of S.m.K.
cartridges and rifles with tele-
scopic sights, 1915*

Death is a gang-boss *aus Deutschland* his eye
  is blue
he hits you with leaden bullets his aim
  is true

—PAUL CELAN, *"A Death Fugue"*

The
Master
Sniper

Part One

Schützenhaus

(Shooting Gallery)

January-April 1945

I

The guards in the new camp were kinder.

No, Shmuel thought, not kinder. Be precise. Even after many years of rough treatment he took pride in the exactness of his insights. The guards were not kinder, they were merely indifferent. Unlike the pigs in the East, these fellows were blank and efficient. They wore their uniforms with more pride and stood straighter and were cleaner. Scum, but proud scum; a higher form of scum.

In the East, the guards had been grotesque. It was a death factory, lurid, unbelievable, even now eroding into fantastic nightmare. It manufactured extermination, the sky above it blazed orange in the night for the burning of corpses in the thousands. You breathed your brothers. And if not selected out in the first minutes, you were kept caked in your own filth. You were *Untermensch*, sub-human. He had survived in that place for over a year and a half and if a large part of his survival was luck, a large part also was not.

Shmuel came by the skills of survival naturally, without prior training. He had not lived a hardy physical life in the time he thought of as Before. He had in fact been a literary type, full of words and ideas, a poet, and believed someday he would write a novel. He had written bold commentaries for *Nasz Przeglad*, Warsaw's most influential Yiddish newspaper. He'd been the friend of some real dazzlers too, Mendl Elkin, Peretz Hirschbein, the radical Zionist poet Uri Zvi Greenberg, Melekn Ravitch, to name but a few. They were great fellows, talkers, laughers, great lovers of women, and they were probably all dead now.

Shmuel had not thought of literature since 1939. He rarely thought at all of Before, knowing it the first sign of surrender. There was only now, today. Perhaps tomorrow as well, but one could never be too sure. But he persisted in his literary habits in just one way: he insisted on looking into the center of things. And he'd been puzzling over this strange new place for days now, ever since he'd arrived.

They'd been trucked in; that in itself was an astonishment, for the German way was to herd Jews through forests and if some—

or many—died along the way, well, that was too bad. But a truck had bounced them in cold darkness for hours, and Shmuel and the others had sat, huddled and patient, until it halted and the canvas blanketing its back was ripped off.

"Out, Jews, out! Fast, fast, boys!"

They spilled into snowy glare. Shmuel, blinking in the whiteness of it, saw immediately he was at no *Konzentrationslager*. He knew no German word for what he saw: a desolate forest setting, walls of pine and fir, sheathed in snow, looming beyond the wire; and within the compound just three or four low wooden buildings around a larger one of concrete. There were no dogs or watch-towers either, just laconic SS boys dressed in some kind of forester's outfit, dappled in the patterns and shadows of deep trees, with automatic guns.

More curiosities became evident shortly and if the other prisoners cared merely for the ample bread, the soup, the occasional piece of sausage that it had become their incredible good fortune to enjoy, Shmuel at least would keep track.

In fact he and his comrades, he quickly came to realize, were still another oddity of the place. Why had the Germans bothered to gather such a shabby crew of victims? What do we have in common, Shmuel often wondered, we Jews and Russians and Slavic types? There were twenty-five others and in looking at them he saw only the outer aspects of himself in reflection: small, wiry men, youngsters many of them, with that furtive look that living on the edge of extinction seems to confer. Though now it was a fact they lived as well as any German soldier. Besides the food, the barrack was warm. Other small privileges were granted: they were allowed to wash, to use latrines. They were given the field gray flannels of old Wehrmacht uniforms to wear and even issued the great woolen field coats from the Russian front. Here Shmuel experienced his first setback. He had the bad fortune to receive one that had been hacked with a bayonet. Its lining was ripped out. Until he solved this problem, he'd be cold.

And then the labor. Shmuel had had the SS for an employer before at the I. G. Farben synthetic fuel factory—the rule was double-time or die. Here, by contrast, the work was mostly listless digging of defensive positions and the excavation of foundations for concrete blockhouses under the less-than-attentive eye of a pipe-smoking SS sergeant, an amiable sort who didn't seem to care if they progressed or not, just as long as he had his tobacco and a warm coat and no officers yelling at him. Once a prisoner had dropped his shovel in a fit of coughing. The sergeant looked at him, bent over and picked it up. He didn't even shoot him.

One day, as the group fussed in the snow, a young corporal came out to the detail.

"Got two strong ones for me? Some heavy business in Shed Four," Shmuel heard the young man ask. "Hans the Kike."

The sergeant sucked reflectively on his pipe, belched out an aromatic cloud of smoke, and said, "Take the two on the end. The Russian works like a horse and the little Jew keeps moving to stay warm." And he laughed.

Shmuel was surprised to discover himself "the little Jew."

They were taken over to some kind of warehouse or supply shed just beyond the main building. Boxes were everywhere, vials, cans. A laboratory? wondered Shmuel uneasily. A small man in civilian clothes was already there. He did not glance at them at all, but turned to the corporal and said, "Here, those, have them load them up and get them over to the Main Center at once."

"Yes, Herr Ingenieur-Doktor," said the corporal, and when the civilian fellow left, the corporal turned to Shmuel and said quite conversationally, "Another Jew, you know. They'll come for him one day." Then he took them to the corner of the room, where two wooden crates were stacked, and with a wave of the hand indicated to the prisoners to load them onto a dolly.

Each crate weighed around seventy-five kilos and the prisoners strained to get them down and across the room to the dolly. Shmuel had the impression of liquid sloshing weightily as he and the Russian crab-walked the first one over, yet there was nothing loose about the contents. The twin runes of the SS flashed melo-dramatically in stencil across the lid, and next to them, also stamped, was the mighty German eagle, clutching a swastika. The designation *WVHA* also stood out on the wood and Shmuel wondered what it could mean, but he should not have been wondering, he should have been carrying, for the heel of his boot slipped and he felt the crate begin to tear loose from his fingers. He groped in panic, but it really got away from him and his eyes met the Russian's in terror as the box fell.

It hit the cement floor with a thud and broke apart. The Russian

dropped to his knees and began to weep piteously. Shmuel stood
in fear. The room blurred in the urgency of his situation. Askew
on the cement, a great fluffy pile of excelsior spewing out of it
like guts, the box lay broken on the floor. An evil-smelling fluid
spread smoothly into a puddle.

The civilian returned swiftly.

"You idiots," he said to them. "And where were you while
these fools were destroying valuable chemicals? Snoozing in the
corner?"

"No, sir, Herr Ingenieur-Doktor," lied the young corporal. "I
was watching closely. But these Eastern Jews are shifty. I just
wasn't fast enough to prevent—"

The civilian cut him off with a laugh. "That's all I get from
the Waffen SS is excuses. Have them clean it up and *try* not to
drop the other crates, all right?"

"Yes, Herr Ingenieur-Doktor. My apologies for failing at—"

"All right, all right," said the civilian disgustedly, turning.

When the civilian left, the SS corporal hit Shmuel across the
neck, just above the shoulder, with his fist, a downward blow. It
drove him to the floor. The boy kicked him, hard, in the ribs. He
knew he was in a desperately dangerous situation. He'd seen a KZ
guard in '44 knock down an elderly rabbi in much the same way.
The man, baffled, glasses twisted, raised his hands to ward off
other blows; this insolence so enraged the stupid young soldier that
he snatched out his pistol and shot the man through the forehead.
The body lay in the square for three days, head split apart, until
they'd removed it with tongs.

"You stinking kike pig," screamed the boy. He kicked Shmuel
again. He was almost out of control. "You piece of Jew shit."
Shmuel could hear him sobbing in anger. He bent over and grabbed
Shmuel by the throat, twisting him upward so that their faces were
inches apart.

"Surprises ahead for you, Jew-shit. *Der Meisterschuster*, the
Master Shoemaker, has a nice candy delight for you." His face
livid and contorted, he drew back. "That's right, Jew-shit, a real
surprise for you." He spoke in a clipped Prussian accent hard and
quick, that Shmuel, whose basic Yiddish was a derivation of the
more languid Bavarian German, had difficulty understanding when
spoken so quickly.

The corporal backed off, color returning to his face.

"All right, up! Up!" he shouted.

Shmuel climbed up quickly. He was trembling badly.

"Now get this mess cleaned up."

Shmuel and the Russian gathered the excelsior into a wad of newspaper and mopped the floor dry. They also retrieved the broken glass and then, carefully, finished loading the cart.

"Bravo! Fine! What heroes!" said the boy sarcastically. "Now get your asses out of here before I kick them again!"

Shmuel had been playing for this second for quite some time. He'd seen it from the very first moments. He'd thought about how he'd do it and resolved to act quickly and with courage. He took a deep breath, reached down and picked up the wad of newspaper and stuffed it into his coat.

With the bundle pressing against his stomach, he stepped into the cold. He waited for a call to return; it didn't come. Keeping his eyes straight ahead, he rejoined the labor detail.

Not until late that night did Shmuel risk examining his treasure. He could hear steady, heavy breathing; at last he felt safe. You never knew who'd sell you for a cigarette, a sliver of cheese. In the darkness, he opened the paper carefully, trying to keep it from rattling. Inside, now matted and balled, the clump of excelsior was still damp from the fluid. The stuff was like mattress ticking, or horsehair, thick and knotted. Eagerly, his fingers pulled tufts out and kneaded them, until he could feel the individual strands.

There was no question of knitting; he had no loom and no skill. But he spread it out and, working quietly and quickly in the dark, began to thread it into the lining of the greatcoat. He kept at it until nearly dawn, inserting the bunches of packing into the coat. When at last there was no more, he examined what he had made. It was lumpy and uneven, no masterpiece; but what did that matter? It was, he knew, significantly warmer.

Shmuel lay back and felt a curious thing move through his body, a feeling long dead to his bones. At first he thought he might be coming down with a sickness and the feeling might be fever spreading through his body. But then he recognized it: pleasure.

For the first time in years he began to think he might beat them. But when he slept, his nightmares had a new demon in them: a master shoemaker, driving hobnails into his flesh.

* * *

A week or so later, he was in the trench, digging, when he heard voices above him. Obeying an exceedingly stupid impulse, he looked up.

Standing on the edge, their features blanked out by the winter sun, two officers chatted. A younger one was familiar, a somewhat older one not. Or was he? Shmuel had been dreaming all these nights of the Master Shoemaker and his candy delight. This man? No, ridiculous, not this bland fellow standing easily with a cigarette, discussing technical matters. He wore the same faded camouflage jackets they all had, and baggy green trousers, boots with leggings and a squashed cap with a skull on it. Quickly Shmuel turned back to his shovel, but as he dropped his face, he felt the man's eyes snap onto him.

"*Einer Jud?*" Shmuel heard the man ask.

The younger fellow called to the sergeant. The sergeant answered Yes.

Now I'm in for it, Shmuel thought.

"Bring him up," said the officer.

Strong hands clapped onto Shmuel instantly. He was dragged out of the trench and made to stand before the officer. He grabbed his hat and looked at his feet, waiting for the worst.

"Look at me," said the officer.

Shmuel looked up. He had the impression of pale eyes in a weathered face which, beneath the imprint of great strain, was far younger than he expected.

"You are one of the chosen people?"

"Y-yes, sir, your excellency."

"From out East?"

"Warsaw, your excellency."

"You are an intellectual. A lawyer, a teacher?"

"A writer, most honored sir."

"Well, you'll have plenty to write about after the war, won't you?" The other Germans laughed.

"Yes, sir. Y-yes, sir."

"But for now, you're not used to this hard work?"

"N-no, sir," he replied. He could not stop stuttering. His heart pounded in his chest. He'd never been so close to a German big shot before.

"Everybody must work here. That is the German way." He had lightless eyes. He didn't look as if he'd ever cried.

"Yes, most honored sir."

"All right," the officer said. "Put him back. I just wanted the novel experience of taking one of them *out* of a pit."

After the laughter, the sergeant said, "Yes, Herr Obersturmbannführer," and he knocked Shmuel sprawling into the trench. "Back to work, Jew. Hurry, hurry."

The officer was gone quickly, moving off with the younger chap. Shumel stole a glimpse of the man striding off, calm and full of decisiveness. Could this simple soldier be the Master Shoemaker? The face: not remotely unusual, a trifle long, the eyes quick but drab, the nose bony, the lips thin. The overall aspect perfunctorily military. Not, Shmuel concluded, an unusual fellow to find in the middle of a war.

And yet because he seemed so easily in command and it was so clear that the others deferred to him, Shmuel took to thinking of the man as the Shoemaker.

Then a day came when the Germans did not fetch them for work. Shmuel awoke at his leisure, in light. As he blinked in it, he was filled with dread. The prisoners lived so much by routine that a single variation terrified them. The others felt it too.

Finally the sergeant came by.

"Stay inside today, boys, take a holiday. The Reich is rewarding you for your loyal service." He grinned at his joke. "Important people crawling about today." And then he was gone.

Late in the afternoon, two heavy trucks pulled into the yard. They halted next to the concrete building and hard-looking men with automatic guns dismounted and deployed around the entrance. Shmuel caught a glimpse and stepped away from the window. He'd seen their type before: police commandos who shot Jews in pits.

"Look," said a Pole, in wonder. "A big boss."

Shmuel looked again, and saw a large black sedan parked next to the truck; pennants hung off it limply; it was spotted with mud, yet shiny and huge.

A prisoner said, "I heard who it is. I heard them talking. They were very nervous, very excited."

"Hitler himself?"

"Not that big. But a big one still."

"Who, damn you? Tell."

"The Man of Oak."

"What? What did you say?"

"Man of Oak. I heard him say it. And the other—"

"It's crazy. You misunderstood."

"It's the truth."

"You *shtetl* Jews. You'll believe anything. Go on, get out of here. Leave me in peace."

The car and the police commandos remained until after dark, and later that night, a crackling rang in the distance.

"Somebody's shooting," said a man.

"Look! A battle."

In the distance, light sprayed through the night. Flames glowed. The reports came in the hundreds. It didn't look like a battle to Shmuel. He recalled the sky over the crematorium, shot with sparks and licks of flame. The SS was feeding the Hungarian Jews into the ovens. The smell of ash and shit filled the sky. No bird would fly through it.

Abruptly the shooting stopped.

In the morning the fancy vehicles were gone. But things did not return to normal. The prisoners were formed into a column and marched off along a heavily rutted road through the forest. It was February now, and much of the snow had melted, but patches of it remained; in the meantime there had been rain, and the road was mud which congealed on Shmuel's boots. The woods on either side of the road loomed up, dense and chilly. To Shmuel they were the woods of an ugly German *Märchen*, full of trolls and dwarves and witches, into which children disappeared. He shivered, colder than he should have been. These people loved their dark forests, the shadows, the intricate webs of dark and light.

A mile or so away, the woods yielded to a broad field, yellow and scaly with snow. At one end of it, the earth mounted into a wall and at the other, the nearer, a concrete walkway lay and a few huts huddled in the trees.

"Boys," said the sergeant, "we had a little show out here last night for our visitor and we'd like your help in cleaning up."

The guards handed out wooden crates and directed the prisoners to harvest the bits of brass that showed in the mud alongside the walkway. Shmuel, prying the grimy things out—they were, it turned out, used cartridge cases—felt his knees beginning to go

numb in the cold, his fingers beginning to sting. He noted the
Gothic printing running across the box in his hand. Again, the
melodramatic bird and the double flashes of the *SS*. He wondered
idly what the next gibberish meant: "7.92mm X 33 (Kurz)" read
one line; under it "G. C. HAENEL, SUHL," and under it still
a third, "STG-44." The Germans were rationalists in everything;
they wanted to stick a designation on every object in the universe.
Maybe that's why he'd walked around marked JUD the last year
or so.

"He certainly fired enough of the stuff," said the pipe smoker
to one of the other guards.

"We could have used some at Kursk," said another man bitterly.
"Now they shoot it off for big shots. It's crazy. No wonder the
Americans are on the Rhine."

This exercise was repeated several times in the next few weeks.
Once, several prisoners were jerked from their sleep and marched
out. The story they told the next morning was an interesting one.
After they'd picked up the spent shells, the Germans had been
especially hearty to them, treated them like comrades. A bottle
had even been passed around to them.

"German stuff."

"Schnapps?"

"That's it. Fiery. An instant overcoat. Takes the chill out of
your bones."

The Big Boss—Shmuel knew it was the Shoemaker—was there
too, the man said. He'd walked among them, asking them if they
were getting enough to eat. He handed out cigarettes, Russian
ones, and chocolates.

"Friendly fellow, not like some I've seen," said the man. "Looked
me square in the eye too."

But Shmuel wondered why they'd need the shells back in the
night.

A week, perhaps two, passed, though without reference to
clock or calendar it was hard to tell. Rain, sun, a little snow one
night. Was there more activity around the concrete building?
More night firings? The Shoemaker seemed everywhere, almost
always with the young officer. Shmuel had never seen the civilian
—the one they said was a kike—again. Had he been taken away
like the boy said? And he began to worry about this "Man of

Oak." What could it mean? Shmuel started to feel especially uneasy, if only because the others were so pleased with the way things were going.

"Plenty to eat, work's not so bad, and one day, you'll see, the Americans'll show up and it'll be all over."

But Shmuel began to worry. He trusted his feelings. He worried especially about the night. It was the night that frightened him. Bad things happened in the night, especially to Jews. The night held special terrors for Jews; the Germans were drawn to it unhealthily. What was their phrase? *Nacht und Nebel.* Night and fog, the components of obliteration.

Light flashed through the barrack. Shmuel, dazed out of his sleep, saw torch beams in the darkness, and shadows. The SS men got them awake roughly.

"Boys," the pipe smoker crooned in the dark, "work to do. Have to earn our bread. It's the German way."

Shmuel pulled the field coat around him and filed out with the others. His pupils were slow in adjusting and he had trouble making out what was occurring. The guards trudged them through the mud. They had left the compound. Guards with automatic guns prowled on either side of the column. Shmuel peered up through the fir canopy. Cold light from dead stars reached his eyes. The dark was satiny, alluring, the stars abundant. A wind howled. He pulled the coat tighter. Thank God for it.

They reached the firing range. Fellows were all about, a crowd. Everybody was there. Shmuel could sense their warmth, hear them breathing. All the SS boys; the Shoemaker himself, smoking a cigarette. Shmuel thought he saw the civilian too, standing a little apart with two or three other men.

"This way, lads," said the sergeant, leading them into the field. "Brass all over the place. Can't leave it here, the General Staff'd kick our ass for sure. Hot coffee, schnapps, cigarettes for all when the job's done, just like before."

There was no moon. The night was dark and pure, pressing down. The prisoners spread out in a line and faced back toward the Germans.

"It's in front of you boys, brass, tons of it. Have to get it up before the snow."

Snow? It was clear tonight.

Shmuel obediently worked his fingers over the frozen ground, found a shell. He found another. It was so cold out. He looked around. The guards had left. The prisoners were alone in the field. The trees were a dark blur in the far distance. Stars towered above them, dust and freezing gas and spinning firewheels. Far off, unreachable. The field was another infinity. It seemed to stretch forever. They were all alone.

"Hey, he's sleeping," said someone, laughing.

Another man slid himself carefully on the ground, shoulders flat to the earth.

"You jokers are going to get us all in trouble." The same voice laughed.

Another lay down.

Another.

They fell relaxed, turned in slightly, tucking the knees under, seeming to pause at the waist then gently lurching forward.

Shmuel stood.

"They're shooting us," somebody said quite prosaically. "They're shoo—" The sentence stopped on a bullet.

Prayers disturbed the night; there was no other sound.

A bullet struck the man closest to him in the throat, driving him backward. Another, slumping, began to gurgle and gasp as his lungs flooded. But most perished quickly and silently, struck dead center, brain or heart.

It is here. The night has come, Shmuel thought. *Nacht, nacht,* pressing in, claiming him. He always knew it would come and now it was here. He knew it would be better to close his eyes but could not.

A man ran until a bullet found him and punched him to the ground. A man on his knees had the top of his head blown off. Drops landed wet and hot on Shmuel.

He alone was standing. He looked around. Someone was moaning. He thought he heard some breathing. It had taken less than thirty seconds. The shooting was all over now.

He stood in the middle of the field, surrounded by corpses. Now he was really alone.

A shape in the dark moved. Then others. Shmuel could see soldiers picking their way toward him in the darkness. He stood very still. The Germans began to kneel at the bodies.

"Right in the heart!"

"This one in the head. That Repp fellow really can shoot, eh?"

"Hold that noise down, damn you," cried a voice Shmuel recognized as the pipe smoker's. "The officers will be out here soon."

A soldier was standing six feet from him.

"What? Say, who's that?" the man said in bewilderment.

"Hauser, I said keep the noise down. The offi—"

"*He's alive!*" bellowed the soldier, and began to tear at his gun.

Shmuel willed himself to run. But he couldn't.

Then he was fleeing blindly across the field.

"Damn, I saw a prisoner."

"Where?"

"Stop that fellow. Stop that man."

"Shoot him. Shoot him."

"Where, I don't see a damned thing."

Other voices mingled in confusion. A shot rang out, loud because it was so close. More shouts.

Shmuel had just made it into the trees when the lights came on. The Germans were pinned in a harsh, white glare, losing more seconds. Shmuel caught a glimpse of the Shoemaker moving fast into the light, automatic gun in one hand. A whistle shrilled. More lights flickered on. There was a siren.

It was at this moment, as he seized a moment's rest, that a revelation hit him. A moment of perfect, shimmering lucidity enveloped him and a truth that had these many months been just beyond knowing at last stood revealed. His heart tripped in excitement.

But no time now. He turned and lurched into the forest. He began to run. Branches cut at him like sabers. Once he tripped. He could hear Germans behind him, much commotion and light; the glare of heavy arc lamps filled the sky. He thought he heard airplanes too, at any rate some kind of heavy engine, trucks perhaps or motorcycles.

Then the lights were out, or gone. He was utterly confused and quite frightened. How long had he been gone and how far had he traveled? And where was he going? And, would he be caught? Miraculously, his feet seemed to have found a path in the heavy undergrowth. He wanted badly to rest but knew he couldn't. Thank God the food and labor had given him strength for all this, and the coat the warmth. He was a lucky fellow. He plunged on.

The sun was just up when Shmuel finally lay down in the silence of the great forest. He lay shuddering convulsively. He seemed to have come to a vault in the trees, a cathedral of space formed by interlocking branches. The silence was thunderous in here; he interrupted it only with his breathing. He felt himself at last escaping into sleep.

His final thought was not for his deliverance—who could question such caprices?—but for his discovery.

Meisterschuster, master shoemaker, he heard, or thought he'd heard. But the boy was a North German, he spoke fast and clipped and the circumstances of the moment were intense. Now Shmuel realized the fellow had said something just a syllable shy of *Meisterschuster*. He'd said *der Meisterschütze*.

The Master Sniper.

II

Caparisoned in elegant damp Burberry, imperially slim, impossibily dapper, with just the faintest smudge of ginger moustache to set off his boyish though firm features, a British major named Antony Outhwaithe bore down on a large target that hunched behind a typewriter in an upper-story office.

"Hello, chum," called the major, knowing the American hated the chum business, which by now, winter of '45, had in London become quite tiresome, "greetings from Twelveland."

The American looked up; a bafflement fell across his open features, just the merest foreboding of confusion.

His name was Leets and he was a captain in the Office of Strategic Services. He wore brown wool and gold bars and looked unhappy. His crew cut had grown out thatchily and his face had accumulated pockets and wattles of fat. He had just been typing the final draft of what was certain to be the most unread document in London that month, a report on the new grip configuration of the *Falschirmjaeger-42*, the German short-stroke paratroop carbine.

"Something right up your alley," the major sang out gleefully, and without fear of retribution. He enjoyed considerable advantage over the bloke: he was smaller and a few years older to begin with, cut on roughly half the scale. He was quicker, wittier, more ironic, better connected. His employers, the Special Operation Executive of MI-6, were a better bunch than Leets's; and finally, he'd once upon a time saved the American's life. That was back in the shooting war, in June of '44.

Leets, a beat behind already, queried in his reedy Midwestern voice, "Small arms, you mean?"

"That *is* what you do in the war, is it not?" asked Tony.

Leets ignored the sarcasm and received from Tony's briefcase a tatty-looking scrap of yellow paper, almost the texture of parchment, as though it had passed through many hands.

"Been around, huh?" Leets said.

"Yes, lots of chaps have seen it. It's not terribly interesting. Still, since it is guns and bullets, I thought you might care to have a look."

"Thanks. Looks like a—"

"It's a telex."

"Yeah, some kind of shipping order or something." He scanned the thing. "Haenel, eh? Funny. STG forty-fours."

"Funny, yes. But significant? Or not? You'll give us your evaluation, of course."

"I may have some things to say about it."

"Good."

"How fast?"

"No rush, chum. By eight tonight."

Swell, Leets thought. But he had nothing to do anyway.

"Okay, let me dig out the specs on the thing and—" But he was talking to air. Outhwaithe had vanished.

Leets slowly drew out a Lucky, lit it off his Zippo and went to work.

Leets was a biggish man, not slobby fat, but ample, with a pleasantly open American face. He was far into his twenties, which was old for the rank of captain he wore in two bars on his collar, especially in a war in which twenty-two-year-old brigadier generals led thousands of airplanes deep into enemy territory.

He looked like a studious athlete or an athletic scholar and now that he limped, compliments of the Third Reich, and occasionally went white as the pain flashed unexpectedly across him, he'd acquired a grave, almost desperate air. His many nervous habits—unpleasant ones, licking his lips, muttering, gesturing overtheatrically, blinking constantly—half suggested dissipation or indolence, though by nature he was an austere man, a Midwesterner, not given to moodiness or mopery. Yet lately, as the war roared by him, someone else's invention, he'd been both moody and mopey.

Now, alone in the office—another source of bitterness, for he'd been assigned a sergeant, but the kid, an energetic young beast, had a tendency to disappear on him at key moments such as this one—he brought the telex close to his eyes in an unselfconscious parody of bookish intellectual and, squinting melodramatically, attempted to master its secrets.

It was a pale carbon of a shipping order out of the Reich Rail Office, a part of the Wehrmacht Transport Command, authorizing the G. K. Haenel Fabrik, or factory, near Suhl, in northern Germany, to ship a batch of twelve *Sturmgewehr*-44's, formerly called *Maschinenpistole*-44's, cross-country to something called, if

Leets understood the nomenclature of the form, *Anlage Elf*, or Installation 11. The 44 was a hot assault rifle, tested in Russia, that had lately been turning up on the Western front in the hands of Waffen SS troops, paratroopers, armored-vehicle commanders—glory boys, hard cores, professionals. Leets had a memory of the thing too—he'd lain in high grass on a ridge above a burning tank convoy while Waffen SS kids from an armored division called "Das Reich" had poured heavy STG-44 fire into the area. He could still hear the cracks as the slugs broke the sound barrier just above his head. It fired a smaller bullet than the standard rifle—it hadn't the range—but at higher velocity; and it was lighter and tougher and could pump out rounds at full automatic. Leets shivered in the memory: lying there, his leg bleeding like sin all over the place, the men near him dead or dying, the smell of burning gas and summer flowers heavy in his nose and the thatchy figures of the camouflaged SS men moving up the slope, firing as they came. His throat was dry.

Leets lit a butt. He had one going, but what the hell? It was another habit gone totally out of control.

Okay, where was I?

Curious, yes, quite curious. STG-44's went out from Haenel all the time, but in larger quantities. They came off the assembly line in the hundreds, the thousands, but distribution was always through normal channels, ultimately in the hands of local commanders. Why bother to make a big deal of *shipping* rifles across a Germany whose railway network was one huge target of opportunity for fighter-bombers? What's more, he realized that the form had the top rail priority, *DE*, and *Geheime Stadatten*, top secret, and the magenta eagle of state secrecy pounded onto it.

Wasn't *that* an odd one?

They were cranking these things out by the thousands—that was one of the charms of the 44, for unlike the MP-40 or the *Gew*-41, it could be quickly assembled from prestamped parts, without any time-consuming milling. Their ease of manufacture was part of their appeal. So all of a sudden they were top secret? Goddamnedest thing.

Leets drew back from the yellow sheet and squirmed at the effort of trying to apply his thoughts to these matters. It was a big mistake, because a chip of German metal deep in the core of his leg rubbed the wrong way, flicking against a nerve.

Pain jacked up through his body.

Leets rocketed out of his seat and yelped. He felt free to let it take him because he was alone. Among others, he simply clenched and clammed up, whitening, looking at his feet.

The pain finally passed, as it always did. He limped back to his chair and gingerly reclaimed it. But his concentration had been seriously damaged, more and more of a problem these recent days, and he knew if he didn't act fast the whole fucked-up scenario of that one battle would unreel before his eyes. It was no favorite of his.

So Leets grabbed back into his mind for something to put between himself and the day Jedburgh Team Casey caught it. He came up with football, which he'd played at Northwestern, '38, '39 and '40. He had been an end, and ends didn't do much except knock people down, a task made significantly easier because he'd played next to NU's all-American tackle Roy Reed, and Reed, in the '40 season, had picked up the nickname "Nazi" after the *Blitzkrieg* of the spring, because of the way he crashed through and laid people out. But Leets had once caught a touchdown pass— perhaps the happiest moment of his life—and now he resurrected the glory of that moment as a shield against the panic of this one.

He remembered an object coming wobbling out of the dusk of a Dyche Stadium afternoon; it was way off the true, a lumbering, ungainly thing that seemed far gone if it could reach him at all through the gauntlet of flailing arms he saw it must travel. The only reason the ball was coming at Leets was that a hand-off to the right halfback who was supposed to follow Reed into the end zone for a winning touchdown had somehow missed connections, and the quarterback, a big, stupid boy named Lindemeyer, a Phi Delt, had taken his only available option, which was to toss the thing to the first guy in purple he saw.

Leets saw it bending toward the earth, miraculously untouched by the half a dozen hands that had had a shot at it, and he had no memory of catching, only the sensation of clasping it to his chest while people jumped on him. Later, he'd figured that he must have been in midair when he made the grab, defying gravity, and that his normally unwilling fingers, clumsy, blunt things, had acquired in the urgency of the instant a physical genius almost beyond his imagination. But in the exultation, none of this was clear: only sensation, as joy flooded through him, and people pounded him on the back.

Leets took another stab on the Lucky. He readjusted his reading lamp—he must have knocked it askew when he popped up—and looked for an ashtray amid a clutter of pencils, curling German weapons instruction charts, sticks of gum, assorted breech parts, cups of cold tea, and cough drops—Roger, his sergeant, had had a cold a few weeks back. What was I looking for? Ashtray, ashtray. He slid it out from the pile that had absorbed it just as a worm of ash on the end of his cigarette toppled off into gray haze and settled across the table.

The office was on the upper floor of an undistinguished building on Ford's Place near Bloomsbury Square, a cold-water flat converted to commercial use sometime in the Twenties by knocking down most of the interior walls and adding an elevator—lift, lift, *lift!*, he was always forgetting—which never worked anyway. The roof leaked. There was no central heating and Roger never remembered to keep the coal heater stoked so it was always cold, and every time a V-2 or a doodle touched down anywhere within ten square miles, which was frequent these days, a pall of dust drifted down to coat everything.

Leets squinted again at the German document, as if drawing a bead on it. Its bland surface revealed nothing new. Or did it? Holding it at an angle into the light, he could make out two faint impressions on the paper. Someone had stamped the original with a great deal of zeal; down here on the bottom carbon only a trace of the stamper's enthusiasm remained, fainter than a watermark. Surely the Brits would have some sort of Scotland Yard hocus-pocus for bringing up the impressions. Still, he laid the thing out and, remembering some Boy Scout stuff, ran the flat of a soft lead pencil across the ridges just as gently as he knew how, as if he were stroking the inside of a woman's thigh. Susan's thigh, to be exact, though thoughts of her were of no use now—but that was another problem.

Two images revealed themselves in the gray sheen of the rubbed lead, one familiar, one not. The old friend read simply *WaPrüf 2*, which Leets knew to be the infantry weapons department of the *Heereswaffenamt Prüfwesson*, the Army testing office. These were the boys who'd cooked up the little surprises of late that had made his job so interesting: that junky little people's machine pistol, the *Volksturmgewehr*, manufactured for a couple of dimes' worth of junk metal, it fired 300 nine-mills a minute; and they also had an imitation Sten out, for behind-the-lines operations, or after the war; and a final dizziness, something called a Krummlauf modification, a barrel-deflection device mounted on the STG-44, which enabled it to fire around corners. The line on German engineering had always been that it was pedantic and thorough; but Leets didn't think so. A wild strain of genius ran through it. They were miles ahead in most things, the rockets, the jets, the guns. It made him uneasy. If they could come up with stuff like that (a gun for shooting round corners!), who knew what else they were capable of?

Leets was by profession an intelligence officer; his specialty was German firearms. He ran an office—obscure to be sure, not found in any of the mighty eight-hundred-page histories—called the Small Weapons Evaluation Team, which in turn was part of a larger outfit, a Joint Anglo-American Technical Intelligence Committee, sponsored in its American half by Leets's OSS and in its Anglo half by Major Outhwaithe's SOE. So SWET worked for JAATIC, and Leets for Outhwaithe. That was Leets's war now: an office full of dusty blueprints. It was no-SWET, as Roger was so fond of pointing out (Leets's joke actually; Roger was a great borrower).

But here was *WaPrüf 2* involved in a shipment of twelve rifles across Germany. Now what could be so fascinating about those particular twelve rifles? It bothered him, because it was so un-German. Twelveland, as the Brits called the place in their intelligence jargon, was a maze of intricacies: bureaus, departments—*Amts*, the Germans called them—desks, subdesks—not at all unlike London in this respect—but the place was in its way always tidy, ordered. Even with the bombs raining down, most of her cities wrecked, millions dead, Russian armies squeezing in from the East, American and British ones poised in the West, no food, no fuel, still the paper work moved like clockwork. Except, all of a sudden, here was this obscure little agency that nobody except himself probably and some two or three others in this town had ever even *heard* of, involved in some goofy business.

It bothered him; but what bothered him more was the other stamp he'd brought out: WVHA.

Now what the hell was WVHA?

Another bureau presumably, but one he'd never heard of; another tidy little office buried away in downtown Berlin.

An idea was beginning to grow in Leets's mind, dangerously. He lit another cigarette. He knew somewhere in the files he had a real good breakdown on the STG-44. It was an ingenious weapon, a *Sturmgewehr*, assault rifle, cross between the best parts of a submachine gun, firepower and lightness, and a rifle, accuracy, range. He supposed he'd have to dig the goddamned stuff out himself; he remembered how when they'd gotten their hands on one they'd broken it down to the pins and put it together again, taken it out to the range and shot up a battalion of targets, and put together an absolutely brilliant technical profile which had been shipped up to JAATIC and routinely ignored.

Leets went over to the files and began to prowl. But just as he got the report out, another thought came flooding over him.

Serial numbers.

Goddamn, serial numbers.

He rushed back to the telex. Now where the hell was it?

A stab of panic but then he saw the yellow corner sticking out from under a dog-eared copy of Bill Fielding's *Tournament Tennis and the Spin of the Ball*—Roger's bible—and he knocked the book aside and seized the telex.

Serial numbers.

Serial numbers.

Leets stood at the window with the lights out, even though the blackout was officially over and London was now into a phase called dim-out. He looked over the skyline, drawn not long ago by the impact of a V-2. Sometimes they burned, sometimes they didn't. This one had come down to the north a half a mile or so, beyond, Leets hoped, the Hospital for Sick Children on Great Ormond Street, maybe as far off as Coram Fields. But there'd be nothing to burn if it went down in that rolling meadow and he could see a smudge—orange thumbprint—on the horizon; so clearly there was fire. Thing must have hit even farther out, beyond Gray's Inn Road and the Royal Free Hospital. He'd have to walk out there sometime and see.

The rockets were a curious phenomenon for Leets. They were big bullets really; even the Germans acknowledged this. The V-2, technical designation A4, was a Wehrmacht project, administered by the SS, interpreted as artillery. A bullet, in other words. The doodles, V-1's, were Luftwaffe, aircraft.

Consider: a bullet as big as a building fired from a rifle in Holland or Twelveland itself at a target in London. Jesus; Leets felt a shiver run through him. It *was* different from being bombed or shelled randomly; some fucking Kraut sniper was scoping in on you through the dark and the distance, this feeling of *being watched*, strange; a weirdness traveled his spine, a chill, but he realized that it was only a draft and a split second later that the door had been opened.

"Should have knocked, sorry," said Tony.

"I wanted to see where they parked their freight tonight. Looked like it went down near the hospital, the one for kids."

"Actually, it went down much farther out, in Islington. Could we, chum, do you mind?" Gesturing Close-the-curtains while he turned on the switch.

"You're early," said Leets. It was half past seven.

"Bit ahead of schedule, yes."

"Okay," Leets said, taking his seat and pulling out the telex and assorted other items, "this is funny."

"Make me laugh."

"They're shipping a special consignment of rifles across Germany. Now our best estimate is that maybe eighty thousand of the things have been built since Hitler gave 'em the green light in '43. Most of the eighty thousand came off the Haenel line at Suhl, although the Mauser works at Oberndorf did a run of ten thousand before we bombed out the line. The markings are different, and the plastic in the grip was cheaper, chipped more easily."

Outhwaithe, in Burberry, collar upturned, hair slicked wetly back, face calm, eyes dead-fish cold, studied him in a way his class of Briton had been perfecting for seven hundred years.

Leets absorbed the glare unshaken, and went on. "The serial numbers run eight digits, plus the manufacturing designation. Do you follow?"

"Perfectly, dear fellow."

"Now they always use two dummy numbers. So you've got two dummy numbers, then the five viable ones which indicate which part of the run it was, then another dummy, then the manufacturing code. The point of the dummy integers is to make us think they're manufacturing them in the millions. They do it on all their small stuff, it's so stupid. Are you with me? Am I going too fast?"

"I'm making a manful effort to stay abreast."

"According to this order"—he held up the telex—"here you've got no digits at all. The serial-number blank has been crossed out."

"If that is supposed to be a Major Intelligence Breakthrough, I'm afraid I rather miss the thrust of it."

"The Germans keep records. Always. I can show you orders on stuff going back to the Franco-Prussian War. The whole stamping process is built into their manufacturing system, in their assembly lines. You see it everywhere, Krupp, Mauser, ERMA, Walther, Haenel. It's part of their mentality, the way they organize the world."

"Yes, I quite agree. But you were going to explain to me the significance of all this." Tony did not at all look impressed.

"These twelve rifles: they're handmade. There is no serial number. Or at least the barrel and breech, the key components, the numbered parts."

"Which means?"

"For a production-line piece, the forty-four is great. Best gun in the war. Can cut a horse in two at four hundred meters. In Russia you could get three PPSH's for a forty-four. But because it's a production-line piece, you can't get a real tight group. You're shooting a small seven-point-nine-two-millimeter bullet, *kurz*, their word for short. It's not a rifle that offers a great deal in the way of precision."

"Until now."

"Until now. Taking into consideration this is a high-priority project, taking into consideration *WaPrüf 2* is cooperating with this outfit WVHA that I've never heard of, and taking into consideration they're shipping the guns to some secret location down south, this Anlage Elf, I would say it's obvious."

"I see," said Tony, but Leets could tell his presentation was not having the desired effect.

He played his trump card.

"They're going to try and kill *someone*. Someone big, I'd say. They're going to snipe him."

But Tony, once again, topped him.

"Rubbish," he said.

III

Shmuel was totally of the forest now. He was part of it, a sly, filthy animal, nocturnal, quick to panic, impelled into motion by ravenous hunger, shivering himself to sleep each morning in small caves, tufts of brush, against rocks. He ate roots and berries and wandered almost helplessly through the deep stillness, guided by only a primitive sense of direction. His journey was bounded by mountains. He was terrified of their bare slopes. What would he do up there on those rounded humps, except die? So he skirted them, threading his way through the densely wooded highlands at their base. Ten days now, twelve, maybe two weeks.

But it was a losing proposition and he knew it. He lost too much each day and the disgusting stuff he made himself eat could never replace it. He was running down, the fat and fiber and muscle he'd picked up in the camp melting away. The forest would win. He'd known it always. He'd pass out from weakness, die in wet leaves next to an obscure German stream.

His clothes had shredded, though into German tatters, not Jewish ones. The boots had disintegrated partially. The trousers were frayed and shiny. The coat was the only thing left. Stuffed with excelsior, it kept enough of the cold out and enough of the wet off. It forestalled sickness. Sickness was death. If you were too weak to move, you died. Motion was life, that was the lesson here. You kept moving. God would show you no pity.

One night rain came, a full storm. Shmuel cowered and could not move. Lightning bounded across the horizon behind the screen of trees, and the thunder was mighty, a roar that rose and fell and never went wholly away.

The next day, and the next, he smelled a tang to the air, sulfurous almost. And once he came upon an opening in the trees, where the open space seemed to fill with light; but this abundance of perspective filled him with horror and he lurched ahead, deeper into the wet trees.

I hope it doesn't freeze, he thought. If it freezes I die. If I run into soldiers, I die. If I sleep too long, I die.

There were many, many ways to die, and he could not think of a single one to survive.

Several times he crossed roads and once he found himself on the grounds of some hotel or inn or something, but the thought of a caretaker or soldiers terrified him, and again he ran deeper into the forest.

But his strength was fleeing quickly now. It had held for so long, augmented by berries and roots and lichens, but in the last day or two his weakness seemed to have increased enormously.

Finally he crawled from sleep knowing he was doomed. He was too weak. There'd been no food he could hold down, the forest here was a thicket of old bones, clacking in the wind. Leafless trees white and knuckled like gripping hands, millions of them.

I am the last, he thought, the last Jew.

The ground here was matted with dead leaves into a kind of cold scum; it was not even dirt.

He lay on his back and looked up into the trees. Through the canopy he could make out chinks of blue. He tried to crawl, but could not.

At last they got me. How long did I last? Almost three weeks. I'll bet that German would never have thought I could last three weeks. I must have come nearly a hundred kilometers. He tried to think of a death prayer to say, but he had not said prayers in years and could think of none. He tried to think of some poetry to recite. This was a monumental occasion, was it not? Certainly a poem was called for. But his mind was empty of words. Words were no good, that was their trouble. He knew lots of words, how to string them together and make them do all kinds of fancy tricks, and they had not done him one bit of good since 1939 and now, when he needed them most, they let him down.

He was at last *in extremis*, a matter of great curiosity to all writers. It was said that if you had the answers to certain questions posed by these final moments, you could write a great book. Conrad for one had tried; no surprise it was a Polish specialty. But Shmuel did not find his own imminent destruction particularly interesting. As a phenomenon it lacked resonance. The sensations, though extreme, proved predictable; almost anybody could imagine them. A great melancholy, chiefly; and pain, much pain, though not so bad now as earlier, pushing ahead though hungry and exhausted. Indeed, this last aspect of the ritual was proving quite pleasant. He at last began to feel warm, though perhaps it was rather more numb. It occurred to him that the body died in degrees, limbs first, mind last; and how horrible to lie alive in brain but dead in body for days and days. But the mind would be kind; it would fog and blur, sink into a kind of haze. He'd seen it at the camps.

He began to hallucinate.

He saw a man of oak, giant, sprouts and twigs and green fronds springing from a wooden face, old and desiccated. Something pagan, loamy, fairy-tale quality. The fantastic was everywhere. Imps and goblins whirred about. And he saw the head German, the big shot, the Master Sniper: yet it was any face, tired, altogether un-interesting. He tried to conjure up his own past, but lacked the energy. What of the people he loved? They were gone anyway; if he regretted his death, it was only that their memories would no longer live. But certain things could not be helped. He thought maybe God had had a purpose in sparing him by miracle back there in the black field when the shooting happened. But this was another jest. .

As if to drive home this idea, the last seconds of the scene of the death he should have had began to unreel before his eyes. He could almost see soldiers moving toward him, out of the shadows. They came with great caution, without rush.

An image filled the sky above him.

A man stood with a rifle.

Shmuel waited for the bullet.

Instead, he heard words in a language he knew: English.

"Freeze, fuckface."

Other forms swirled above him.

"Jesus, pitiful," somebody said.

"Hey, Lieutenant. Nelson caught the sorriest-looking Kraut I ever saw."

And someone else said, "Another fucking mouth to feed."

IV

T-5 Roger Evans, Leets's nominal assistant, counseled practicality.

"Forget it," he advised. He was an insouciantly handsome teenager who quite naturally assumed arrogant postures and spoke in a voice cold with an authority he in no way possessed. The kid also knew how to dress: his shiny paratrooper boots rested against an edge of a table, propelling him outward, on the back two legs of a chair, delicately poised. His Ike jacket, cut tight, emphasized his athletic frame, and his service cap perched snidely on an angle down across his forehead. Leets had loathed him at once but in the months they'd worked together—"work" was an entirely inaccurate word, in Roger's case—he'd come finally to accept the kid as basically harmless.

Rog threaded his hands together on the back of his neck, and continued in his instruction, bobbing all the while.

"That's all, Captain. Forget it. No skin off your nose." Nothing was ever skin off Roger's nose. What Leets found especially irritating this midwinter morning was that Roger was probably right.

Leets said nothing. He fiddled with some papers at his desk: a field report on the double-magazine feed system *WaPrüf 2* had improvised for the MP-40 submachine gun, giving it a sixty-round capacity, to match the Soviet PPSH's seventy-one-round drum. Now these gadgets were showing up in the West.

What irked Leets was Tony Outhwaithe's—and, by extension, all official London's—rejection of his brainstorm.

"I do not think," Tony had said imperially, "our analysts—yours, for that matter, although they are quite the junior at the game—will agree with you, chum. Frankly, it's not the Nazi style. They tend to kill in larger numbers, and are quite proud of it."

"We got Yamamoto in the Pacific, '44," Leets argued. "You guys sent some commandos after Rommel. There were rumors the Krauts had a mission on Roosevelt in Casablanca. And just a couple of months ago, when the Bulge started, that stuff about Skorzeny going after Eisenhower."

"Exactly. An unpleasant rumor that caused a great deal of discomfort in all kinds of circles in this town. Which is precisely why we'll not be calling up the guards on the basis of a scrap of paper. No, it's this simple: you're wrong."

"Sir," Leets had pulled himself to full attention, "may I respectfully—"

"No, you may not. Our intent in handing you this slight job was to take advantage of your somewhat specialized knowledge of German small arms technology. We thought you might provide some insight as to what pressures their industrial nut was undergoing. Instead you check in with a rather odd tale out of James Hadley Chase. Very disappointing."

And he was dismissed.

But Leets let his enthusiasm get the best of him. In a frenzy of zeal, he dashed off a batch of memos one afternoon to various bodies whose support he hoped to enlist in his crusade—SHAEF, CIC, Army Intelligence, the OSS counterintelligence outfit called X-2, OSS German Desk over at Grosvenor Square, and so forth. The results were depressing.

"It's 'cause I don't know anybody. They're all buddy-buddy, Eastern. Clubby. Harvard-Oxford-Yale," he claimed.

Rog, old Harvard man at nineteen, tried to dissuade him from this concept.

"It's not *like* that up at Harvard, Captain. It's just a bunch of guys having a good time, like anywhere. Reason you're not getting anywhere is simply that the clowns running the show don't know what they're doing, no matter what school they went to. This war's the best thing they've got going; it sure beats working for a living. Once it's over, they're back jerking sodas." Rog spoke with the brilliant assurance of a man who'd never jerk a soda in his life. His education entitled him to sit in the office with his paratroop boots on the table and dispense homilies of sociology to Leets.

"Aren't you supposed to be *doing* something?" Leets said.

Airily, Roger continued with his analysis, now reaching cross-discipline into psychology. "I know what's eating you, Jim. You want back in it." He was genuinely amazed at this. "Boy, between us we got this war *solved*. Now why you'd want to—"

Leets knew in many ways he baffled the young tennis player. He of late had been baffling himself. Now why, all of a sudden, was he off on a crusade? Upstairs had said No; then No it would be.

But Leets kept thinking: Yes. It's got to be Yes.

* * *

Several days later, Leets appeared at Tony's office.

"Back again?" Tony asked.

"Yes," Leets replied, unsmilingly.

"And so soon."

"I was trying to sell it around town. No takers."

"No. Thought not. Simply won't wash, is why. Surely you can see that. No convincing dope."

Leets concentrated on remaining pleasant. He explained politely, "The reason there's no convincing dope is that I can't get any. I can't get any because the word's out."

"Whatever can you mean?"

Leets explained as if to a schoolboy: "Someone's stamped me 'Crank,' 'Nut.' I dropped in on some of the other sections, thinking maybe I could round up some help, and suddenly I'm getting pitched in the street. You can tell from the way they look at you and whisper. You're out, you're dead."

"I'm sure," Tony said primly, "you exaggerate."

"I figure it was you *put* the word out. Sir."

Tony did not look away. There was not a fiber in his body capable of showing embarrassment. He looked at Leets evenly, his gaze richly amused, and said, "I'll allow that's a possibility. Even a probability."

"I thought so," said Leets.

"Nothing personal. I'm quite fond of you. You're my favorite American. Unlike most of them, you are not madly obsessed with yourself. You do not tell me stories of growing up on a farm in Kansas and the name of your wife and children. Still, there are limits."

"Major Outhwaithe."

"Please. Tony is fine."

"Major Outhwaithe, I'm asking you to take me out of the freezer."

"Absolutely not." He gazed calmly at him. Pity registered in his eyes; he was about to reveal a Major Truth, some elemental rule of the game that the thick Yank hadn't caught on to. "Because you've got a *real* job to do. I know, I gave it to you. I'm responsible for it. I am exec officer of this little clown show JAATIC; directly under which is *your* little clown show, SWET. Not everybody can have a big job in the war, Captain Leets. Some of us—you, me—must do the little jobs, the boring jobs in safe offices five hundred miles from the front."

Leets sighed. "Sir, it's not a question of—"

"I shall tell you what it's a question of. It's a question of maturity. You had your time playing Indian, so did I. All over now. We're desk chaps, you and I. See that attractive girl. Enjoy the flicks. Do your job. Thank God you didn't get your nose or jaw shot off. Rejoice in the coming Triumph of Our Way of Life. The war's almost over. Weeks, months perhaps. Unless a rocket lands on your skull, you've made it. See that girl. Her name—"

"Susan. I don't. See her, that is. Anymore."

"Pity. But the town's full of them. Find another."

"Sir. A few words from you and—"

"You mad fool. Go back to guns, to blueprints. Forget murder plots, assassinations. It's London, February, 1945, not Chicago, 1926."

Leets couldn't afford anger and anyway wasn't sure he had the strength; and he knew the Brits hated scenes. It's what they hated most about Americans. And what he needed he'd have to get from Tony Outhwaithe sooner or later, one way or the other, for in this town Tony knew all the right ears to whisper into. If Tony'd frozen him, then only Tony could unfreeze him.

"Major Outhwaithe," Leets began again, in a voice he imagined was sweet with reason, "I'd merely like an opportunity to locate additional intelligence. I need more evidence than a Wehrmacht Transpo Command order, even a damned strange one. I need access to other sources, other distributions. The archives, the reading lists. Your technical people. The—"

"Leets, old man, I'm quite busy. We all are, except you. You're becoming dreadful, you and that bratty boy of yours. You're turning into Jews, with your own private patch of persecution, as though the war was a special theater for you and you alone. Who chose you, old man? Eh? Who chose you?"

Leets had no answer. The British major glared at him, ginger moustache bristling. The eyes were cold as dead glass.

"Be off!" He flicked insolently with his wrist, Noel Coward in the khaki of King and country, and brushed Leets, the bug, out.

Leets found himself exiled into the streets, disappointed. He stood a second on the pavement in front of the Baker Street headquarters, a nondescript joint called St. Michael House, No. 82. He was one American among crowds of the brutes on the sidewalks of the old city, all of them healthy, shoving, yakky types, many

squiring girls. It was chilly and gray—typical London midwinter—
but the fresh American flesh seemed to warm the old city's streets
and fill them with human color and motion. Next to the ruddy
Yanks, the Brits were pale and thin, but not too many of them
were in evidence. Whose city was this, anyway? Leets felt as if
he were lost in a football crowd—Homecoming perhaps, some kind
of rite. Everybody seemed happy, pink, party-bound. London was
a party if you were American, had reasonable chances at survival
and pounds in your pocket.

Triumph was in the air, self-congratulation. The soon-to-come
victory would be moral as well as tactical. A way of life, a civilization, had been tested and vindicated. Looking about, Leets saw
how glad these guys all were to be American, and how glad, in
turn, the pale girls were to have latched onto them. The war was
almost all gone. It was feeble and far off. Only the bomber crews,
by their paradoxical youth, called it up. They were all over the
place now, Eighth Air Force teen-agers, in for a desperate day or
two between missions, recognizable by their three gunner's chevrons
on their Air Corps sleeves, unable yet to shave, toting guidebooks
and cameras and asking stupid questions in loud voices. They were
too young to be scared, Leets thought.

He shivered, pulling his coat tighter. Not a Chicago winter, but
cold, just the same. It had the subsidiary effect of drying out
London's normally damp air and this in turn seemed to prevent his
wound from suppurating painfully.

He went down Baker Street until it became Orchard Street—
crazy Brit streets, they just turned into *other* streets on the next
block without warning and if you had to ask you were dumb—
and took a left up Oxford Street toward Bloomsbury. He walked
with no particular hurry, knowing nothing urgent awaited him
in the office. It did occur to him he was just a block or two
off Grosvenor Square—all he had to do was follow Duke Street,
upcoming here—where the OSS headquarters were. A fleeting
thought sped through his head of crashing the place, making a
scene, demanding to see Somebody Important. It was said Donovan
bought anything presented with enthusiasm; he could sell Wild Bill
Donovan. But more likely he'd run into the patrician colonel who
ran the place, the OSS head of London Station, prime Eastern
snoot, or one of his neckless, nameless Brit-licking assistant heads
of Station, sure conspirators with Tony O.

Leets reached Oxford Circus, way past Duke Street, and realized he'd given up on Somebody Important. Not his style, after all.

At the Circus, the traffic whirled about, small, strange black cars, like planets out of control, headed for doom. Shouts, honks, the bleat of motors, blue fumes from their exhaust pipes, rose and enveloped him. Where'd they get the fuel? In the mechanical whirligig he insisted on seeing a metaphor of futility: all the metal going round and round and nowhere.

Forget it, okay?

They're right.

You're wrong.

An American sergeant—B-17 gunner, probably—walked by drunkenly, throwing him a wobbly salute.

"Sir." The boy grinned brokenly. His arm lay across the shoulder of a tart, a shriveled, frizzy, titless, tough-looking girl; quite a picture, the two of them.

Leets answered the kid's salute with one equally limp and watched him and his cutie stagger away. Night was falling. Leets felt none of the triumph of the streets. These crowds of corn-fed heroes, of whom the boy and girl were prime examples, so sure, so full of life, so ready for the next day. Heroes.

Yet the Germans were going to kill one of them. Leets knew it. There was a man, perhaps in this city, who right now, four hundred miles to the east, in a shattered Germany, sinister minds were planning to kill. He alone knew it.

Who would the Germans kill? And why was it so different? A V-2 might land that second and turn out the lights on three hundred: pure random stroke, an accident, a function of applying so much industrial power to such and such a technological problem.

The sniping was different. They knew a man, a special man, so vile to them, such an insult to their imaginations, that even as they were themselves about to become extinct, they would kill.

Churchill? Had the speeches angered them so much? Ike? That smiling Kansas face, bland and seemingly guileless. Patton, for beating the Panzer geniuses at their own game? Montgomery, who was as ruthless as any of them?

Leets knew it didn't add up. Maybe Tony was right: maybe the freeze was good and just.

He felt drained of energy. A soft dark had fallen on Oxford Circus. There was not so much traffic, and now the cars moved more slowly. What am I going to do? he wondered.

He wished he weren't so far from his office or billet; he wished he weren't so tired; he wished there was a little piece of the war left over for him; he wished he could get somebody to listen to him. But chiefly he wished he could park his ass someplace soft, hoist a mug of that thin stuff the Brits called beer, and forget 1945 for a while.

Even as he walked through the anonymous maze of the city in the deepening dark, he knew he'd secretly changed course several blocks back, though he'd lied to himself, refused to acknowledge it at the moment of decision.

But when he reached the flats in which she was quartered, he was unable to maintain the fiction of coincidence. He was going to see Susan.

She was not there, of course; Mildred, one of the roommates, was vague but remotely optimistic about her return, and so Leets sat idiotically in the living room and waited, passing the time with Mildred's date for the evening, a B-24 pilot, another captain, while Mildred made ready in the john.

The pilot was not so friendly.

"One of my buddies got killed in some crazy OSS thing," he told Leets.

"Sorry," Leets said mildly, hoping to end the conversation there.

"Low-level agent drop, nobody came back at all," the pilot declared, fixing Leets in the black light of a glare.

And what about all the agents spread to hell and gone by panicked pilots who dumped them like freight twenty miles off the drop zone? His own operational jump had been handled by a British crew, who'd been in the business since 1941; they'd put him and his two companions right on the mark. But he'd heard horror stories of poor guys coming down in enemy territory miles from their contacts, to wander about stupidly until nabbed.

"People get killed in a war," Leets said. "Even Air Force pilots."

"Yeah, sure, in the *war*," the pilot said. "What I want to know, is that crazy stuff you do, is it part of the *war*? Or is it some game for rich kids? Is it *real*?"

An interesting question. Leets had no answer. He looked steadily at the other man and saw that the fellow wasn't really angry with him but at the war and its waste and stupidity and ignorance.

"It varies," he finally said, and as he spoke he heard the door opening in the hallway.

Mildred, coming out of the john, ran into her first.

"Suse, guess who's back?"

"Oh, Christ," Leets heard Susan say.

He felt himself rising as she came into the room.

Her starches were wilted and her hair was a mess. She held her white shoes in her hand. Her face was tired and plain.

"Well, here I am again, ha, ha," Leets said, grinning sheepishly, uncomfortably aware of the hostile bomber pilot watching him.

"Suse, we're going now," Mildred called, as she and the grumpy pilot got ready to leave.

Susan still had not said anything. She looked him over, ruthlessly, as if he were another patient on the triage list. She was a first lieutenant in the Army Nurse Corps, in plastic surgery; she was a pale, bright, pretty girl from Baltimore; Leets had known her forever, meaning from that magical period only remotely remembered as Before the War. She'd gone to Northwestern too, where she'd dated and, incidentally, married a friend of his who was now on a ship in the Pacific. Leets had run into her six months earlier in the hospital, where his leg had put him.

"Guess I can't stay away," he confessed. "I had my mind all made up; it was set. No more Susan. Best for her. Best for me. Best for Phil. But here I am again."

"This must be the twentieth time you've pulled this routine. When you get it just right, you can do it on 'Jack Benny.'"

"It is pretty funny, I admit."

"You don't look so hot," she said.

"I'm not. You don't have a date, or anything?"

"Date? I'm married, remember."

"You know I do."

"But I do have something later. I said I'd—"

"Still going?"

"Still."

"They give the Nobel peace prize during a war? You deserve one."

"How's the leg, Jim?"

"I should love it; it brought us together." He'd first seen her with his leg hanging on a line off the ceiling like a prize fish.

"But it's not so good," he said to her now, "the goddamn thing still leaks and when it leaks, it really *aches*."

"There's still metal in there, right?"

"Real small stuff."

"Too small for the X-rays. And they keep infecting on you. They've got you on penicillin, right?"

"A ton a day."

"Nobody'll catch the clap from you, that's for sure."

"Hear from Phil?"

"His ship took one of those crazy Jap kamikazes in the bridge. Fifteen guys got killed. He's all right. He made lieutenant commander."

"Phil'll do fine. I know he will. He'll come out an admiral."

"Hear from Reed?"

"No, but I got a note from Stan Carter. He's still in Washington. He says Reed's a major, shooting down Japs left and right. *Major!* Christ, and look at me."

"You never were the ambitious one."

"Say, let's go get something to eat. I need something to cheer me up. Tough one at the office. They've all decided I'm a crank. The jerks. So anyway, okay?"

"Jim, I don't have time. Really. Not tonight."

"Oh. Yeah, sure, I see. Well, listen, I just stopped by to see how you were, you know, see if you'd heard from anybody."

"Don't go. Did I say go?"

"No, not in so many *words*. But—"

"Damn you. I wish you'd make up your goddamned mind."

"Susan," he said.

"Oh, Leets," she said. "What are we going to do? What in hell are we going to do?"

"I don't know. I really have no idea."

She stood up and began to unbutton her uniform.

Later, in the dark, he lit a cigarette.

"Listen, darling, put that cigarette out. It's time to go," she said. "The Center."

"Yes. Walk me over, all right? It's not far."

"Okay. You sure know how to keep yourself depressed."

"Somebody's got to go. From our side, I mean. I promised my father—" She turned on the light.

"I know. I know all that. But it's such a waste of time. They don't *own* the war, you know. We get part of it too, you know."

"I'm sure there's enough to go around," Susan said. Naked, she walked to the dresser. She was beautiful to him. Her hips were slim and he could see her ribs. She had small, fine breasts, with just enough a sense of density to them, roundness without bulk. He felt another erection begin to swell. The center of his body warmed. He reached and turned out the light.

"No," she said, disinterestedly. "Not now. Please. Come on."

He turned it on again, and climbed out of bed into his GI underwear. The Jews. The fucking Jews came first.

"They're a pain in the ass," he said. "The Jews."

"Their part of the war is special."

"Special! Listen, let me tell you something. Everybody who somebody's trying to kill is special. When I was in France getting shot at, was I ever special!"

"No, it's different. Please, let's not go over this again, all right? We always come back to it. Always."

She was right. They always did. Sooner or later.

He grunted, putting on his uniform. Susan, meanwhile, stepped into a civilian dress, a shapeless, flowered thing, dowdy. It made her look forty and domestic.

"Look," he suddenly said, tightening his tie, "I'll tell you who's special. Who's *really* special."

"Who? Reed?"

"No. You. Divorce Phil. Marry me. All right?"

"No," she said, trying to get a necklace fastened. "First, you don't mean it. You're just a lonely boy from the Midwest in a big European city. You think you love me. You love my—well, we both know what you love. Second, *I* don't love you. I love Phil Isaacson, which is why I married him, even if he is six thousand miles away on a ship and I feel guilty as hell. Third, you're what we call a Goy. No offense. It doesn't mean inferior, but it means different. It would make all kinds of problems. All kinds. And fourth— well, I don't remember number four." She smiled. "But I'm sure it's a great one."

"They're all great," he said, smiling himself. "I ask you every time. When we started you had ten reasons. Then eight. Now it's down to four, three really, because you don't remember the last one. I feel like I'm making some kind of progress." He leaned over and gave her a kiss on the cheek.

* * *

"Turn here?" Leets thought he remembered, even in the fog.

"Right. Good memory," she said.

He'd been there once before and was not overwhelmed at the prospect of returning. He knew he didn't belong.

"Funny the stuff that sticks in your mind. I remember the kid."

"The kid?"

"The little boy. You know, the one in the picture they've got there."

"Oh, yes. That's Michael Hirsczowicz. At fifteen months. In pleasanter times. Warsaw, August, 1939. Just before it all began."

"You'll laugh at this. Tony called *me* a Jew today."

"That's not very funny."

"No, I suppose it's not. Here, right?"

"Yes."

They turned in a dark doorway and began to climb some dim stairs.

"You don't think of the Jews having a government in exile," Leets said.

"It's not a government in exile. It's a refugee agency."

"Everybody knows it's political."

"It's powerless. How can that be political? It's to try and keep people alive. How can that be political? It's funded by little old ladies in Philadelphia. How can that be political?"

The sign on the door said something in that squiggly funny writing and beneath it ZIONIST RELEIF AGENCY.

"Jesus, they can't even spell."

"It *is* pitiful, isn't it," Susan said bitterly.

She'd been coming for months now, three, four nights a week. First it was a joke: her father had instructed her in a letter not to forget who she was, what she came from, and though she blithely said she was an American, from Baltimore, she dropped in that first time only because she recognized Yiddish on the door. But gradually, it began to get under her skin.

"What the hell do you get out of it?" Leets had wondered.

"Nothing," she said.

Still, she kept it up, until it became almost obsessive.

But it wasn't as if she could do any good, any real good. That was the bitter joke beneath it all, though for Leets it wasn't a joke anymore, merely a bitterness. They were so pathetic: from the old man Fischelson on down, the girls in the office, all hysterics, scared, most of them. They needed so much help and Susan did what she could, with paper work, and telephones, small things like dealing with the landlord, making sure the place stayed heated, proofreading the news releases, even in their fractured, East Side Yiddish-English. She knew all along that nobody was listening.

"It's Communist, isn't it?" he said.

"It's Jewish. Not quite the same thing. Anyway, the man whose money started it was a rich, conservative land- and factory-owning aristocrat. A banker. What could be further from communism?"

Still, Leets had his doubts. "I don't know," he said.

"It's his kid. In the hall. Josef Hirsczowicz: he's the father. One of the richest men in Europe. That's his child. Or was."

"They're dead?"

"They didn't get out. That little boy, Jim. Think of that. The Germans killed him, because he's Jewish."

"They're trying to kill a lot of little boys. They tried to kill *this* little boy. Religion has nothing—" but he stopped. He didn't want to get back into it.

They reached the door at the end of the stairway.

"You're wasting your time," he cautioned.

"Of course I am," she said. The Zionists hoped to communicate to the indifferent Western world what they maintained was happening in Occupied Europe. Susan had monstrous tales, of mass executions and death camps. Leets told her it was propaganda. She said she had proof. Pictures.

"Pictures don't mean a thing," he'd instructed her brutally weeks ago. "Pictures can be faked. You need a goddamned witness, someone who's been there. That's the only way you'll get anybody to listen to your stuff. Listen, you're going to get in trouble. You're an officer in the United States Army. Now you're hanging around with a group of—"

She'd put a finger to his lip, ending his sentence. But later she talked of it. Nobody would believe, she said. The Zionist leaders sat in the offices of great men in London, she explained with great bitterness, who'd listen earnestly, then shoo them out after a polite moment or two.

Now, standing in the outer office, about to lose her, Leets felt the beginning of a headache. The headaches always ended in rage.

Christ, what a hole! All that peeling paint and those blinky, low-watt bulbs that almost looked like candles. It smelled like a basement up here, and was always chilly, and all the other people seemed pallid and underfed and would not look at him in his uniform.

"Thanks for walking me over, Jim," she said. "I appreciate it. I really do." She smiled, and stepped away.

"Susan." He grabbed her arm. "Susan, not tonight. Come on, we'll do the town."

"Thanks, Jim, but we had our fun."

He didn't mind losing her to Phil—he knew he would in the end anyway—but he hated losing her to this.

"Please," he said.

"I can't. I've got to go."

"It's just—"

"Just Jews, Leets," she said. "Me too." She smiled. "Believe it or not."

"I believe, I believe," he protested. But he did not believe. She was just an American girl, who'd invented her membership in this fossil race.

"No, you don't," she said. "But sometimes, I love you anyway."

And she disappeared behind the door.

The next morning, in the office, Leets's headache still banged away. He stood looking across the gray skyline.

And where was Roger? Late as usual, he came crashing in, uniform a mess.

"Had trouble finding a *cab*," he said. He'd once pointed out that he was probably the only enlisted man in any army who took a cab to World War II each morning.

"Sorry," he continued.

Leets said nothing. He stared grumpily out the window.

"Guess who I met last night? Go on. Guess, Captain."

Leets complained instead. "Rog, you didn't sweep up last night. This place isn't the Savoy, but it doesn't have to look like Hell's Kitchen either."

"Hemingway."

"You could at least empty the wastebaskets once in a while."

"Hemingway. The writer. Over from Paris, from the Ritz. Met him at a party."

"The writer?"

"Himself. In the flesh. Big guy, mustache, steel glasses. You should have seen him pour the booze down."

"You travel in flashy circles."

"Only the best. I go to all the good parties. Don't let my stripes keep me out of anything. After Bill Fielding, he's about the most famous man in the world."

The door flew open; Tony Outhwaithe swirled in as if the star of the play.

"Captain Leets, send this boy out to hit balls against a wall or something," he commanded.

"Roger, out."

Roger was off in a flash. "I'll be at the squash club, you need me."

Tony turned to Leets. "The news is bad. Bad for you. Rather good for me." He smiled with great satisfaction.

"You love to top me, don't you?" Leets said.

"Yes, but there are tops and tops, and this is a true top."

Leets braced; was he being shipped to Burma to hunt Japs in jungles?

"Are you still banging away on that assassin matter?"

"Sort of. Not getting any—"

"Excellent. I can now prove you wrong. New data."

"What?" Leets sat up, his heart beginning to excite a bit.

"My, interested so soon."

"What?"

"All right. Last night I happened to run into a donnish sort from PWE. Know what that is?"

"Your Political Warfare Executive. Sort of like—"

"Yes. Anyway, it seems he can identify your phantom acronym. WVHA."

"Yeah?"

"Yes." Tony was richly satisfied. He was enjoying every minute of all this. "It has nothing to do with us. It doesn't even concern the war. It's not related to intelligence or espionage or the racket at all. You're out of luck, I'm afraid."

"What is it?" Leets demanded. Why was his heart going, why did he have so much trouble breathing?

"It's a part of the administrative section of dear old SS. *Wirtschafts- und Verwaltungshauptamt*. Obscure, easy to miss among the more flamboyant organizations in Twelveland."

Leets translated prosaically. "Economic and Administrative Department," he said glumly, "that's all. They do the payrolls. Clerks."

"Yes. Not the sort of lads to go gunning after generals, eh?"

"No, no, suppose not."

"They've got other concerns at the moment. Those clerks run one of the more interesting phenomena of the Third Reich, old bun," Tony said, smiling brightly. "They run the concentration camps."

V

Vollmerhausen not only knew that it wasn't his fault the prisoner had escaped, he knew whose fault it was. It was Captain Schaeffer's fault. The man was incompetent. Schaeffer was involved in most things that went wrong at Anlage Elf. He'd seen the type before, a real SS fanatic, sullen and stupid, a brutal, suspicious Nazi peasant. Vollmerhausen had explained this very carefully to anybody who cared to listen, though not many of them did.

Now he was going to explain it to Repp.

"If," he began, "if Captain Schaeffer's men had been adequately trained, had reacted quickly, had treated this whole enterprise as something other than a holiday rest camp, then the prisoner could never have escaped. Instead they blunder about like comedians in a farce, shooting at each other, screaming, turning on lights, hooting and tooting. A disaster. I thought the Waffen SS, especially the famed *Totenkopfdivision*, had a reputation for efficiency. Why, the most inept conscriptees—old men and youngsters—could have performed better." He sat back smugly. He'd really told them. He'd really let them have it.

Repp sat, toying with something at his desk. He did not appear particularly impressed. He certainly could be a cold chap.

But Schaeffer, there too, rose to his own defense.

"If," he replied, talking straight to Repp, "there had been no" —he pronounced the next words with special precision, knowing how they hurt—"*machine failure*, if Herr Ingenieur-Doktor had been able to get his gadget to do its job—"

Gadget?

"Slander! Slander! I will not be slandered! I will not be slandered." He rose, red-faced, from the chair.

Repp waved him down.

"So that the *Obersturmbannführer* had been able to take out his targets as the mission specifications call for—"

"There was no machine failure," screamed Vollmerhausen hysterically. He was always being slandered, lied about. He knew people called him a kike behind his back. "I deny, deny, deny. We checked the equipment until we were blue in the face. It had integrity. Integrity. Yes, problems, we work around the clock, the Waffen SS should work half so hard, problems with weight, but the machine works. Vampir works."

"The fact remains," insisted the young captain—some men just could not accept defeat gracefully—"the fact remains, and no Yid argument is going to change it, that Vampir displayed twenty-five targets and there were twenty-six subhumans out there."

It was obvious. "He slipped away before, don't you see?" said Vollmerhausen. "He slipped out on your men before. I'm told he was a Jew, an educated fellow. He must have realized something was up and in the moments—"

"He was seen leaving the field, Herr Ingenieur-Doktor," Repp said quietly. "And fired upon."

"Yes, well," Vollmerhausen sputtered, "he'd obviously, well, it's clear that he separated himself before and so he wasn't within the range of the mechanism."

"Herr Obersturmbannführer, the men swear he was standing *among* the corpses."

"The main question must be," Vollmerhausen bellowed, corkscrewing insanely out of his seat, "why wasn't the area fenced? My people slave into the night over Vampir, yet the Waffen SS is unable to construct a simple fence to hold a Jew in."

"All right, Herr Ingenieur-Doktor," said Repp.

"A simple fence to stop a Jew who—"

Repp said, "Please."

Vollmerhausen had several points yet to make and he'd just thought of five or six of them when Repp's stare fell across him. Something quite frosty in it. Extraordinary. The eyes cool, almost blank. The demeanor so perfectly calm, almost unnaturally calm. Repp had an incredible talent for stillness.

"I was simply—but no matter," Vollmerhausen said.

"Thank you," said Repp.

Another silence. Repp was masterful with silences, and he let this one drag on for several seconds. The air in the room was dead. Vollmerhausen shifted in his chair uneasily. Repp kept it so hot in here; in the corner the stove blazed away merrily. Repp, in faded camouflages, made them wait while he took out and, with elaborate ceremony, lit one of those Russian cigarettes he smoked.

Then finally he said, "Of the Jew, I have decided to let the matter drop. He's somewhere in the forest, dead. They are not a hearty, physical race. They have no will to survive. Doom is their

natural fate, and in the forest he'll locate his own quickly. Therefore, I'm recalling the patrols."

"Yes, Herr Obersturmbannführer," said Captain Schaeffer. "Immediately."

"Good. Now as for Vampir." He turned to Vollmerhausen.

Vollmerhausen licked his lips. They were dry. His mouth was
dry. He returned to a familiar, discomfiting litany: What am I
doing here, locked up in a wild forest with SS lunatics? It was a
long way from the *WaPrüf 2* testing ground outside Berlin.

"As for Vampir, I'm afraid I must require another test, Herr
Ingenieur-Doktor."

Vollmerhausen swallowed. So that was it, then. Another load of
Jews would be brought in, fattened up, shot down.

"More prisoners, Herr Obersturmbannführer?" he asked.

"That's all finished, I'm afraid," said Repp. "Which I'm sure
makes you happy, Herr Ingenieur-Doktor."

"It was unpleasant, yes, killing—"

"You must have a hard heart for these hard times," said Repp.
"You'd lose your uneasiness around death in a day in the East.
But the *Reichsführer* informs me that the camps are no longer
in the disposal business."

"Animals, then," said Vollmerhausen. "Pigs would do it. Or
cows. About the—"

"I think not. Vampir must locate people, not animals, at four
hundred meters' range. And it must not weigh more than forty
kilos. Those are the limits."

Vollmerhausen moaned. Back to weight again. "I don't know
where I'm going to get ten more kilos. We've taken off all the
insulation, we've got the lead sulfide down to a minimum without
sacrificing resolution." He looked desperate. "It's that damn battery."

"I'm sure you'll find a way. After all, you've got the best men
and equipment in the Reich. Far better than up at Kummersdorf."
As he spoke he'd begun to tinker again with a piece of metal or
something on his desk, an innocent, entirely reflexive habit.

"We've tried everything. A smaller battery won't put out the
necessary current. A—"

"I'm sure a great miracle will happen here," Repp said, taking
great pleasure in the phrase.

Vollmerhausen, fascinated, could see the thing he worked in his fingers. It was a small black cube, metallic, with a spindle through it. But that's all.

"Miracles cannot be requisitioned like machine pistols, Herr Obersturmbannführer."

"You'll do your best, I'm certain."

"Of course, sir. But forty kilos is so little."

"I just want to explain the importance here. I want to emphasize it. Our actions are only part of a larger campaign, involving agents in other countries even. Still, we are the most important; we are the *fulcrum*. Do you understand? Great and heavy responsibilities have descended upon us. This is a privilege rarely given soldiers. Think about it."

He paused, to let the grave information sink in.

"And so for the test," he said.

"Yes, Herr Obersturmbannführer," Vollmerhausen said.

"I think I've found an unlimited supply of targets for you. A whole world full of targets. I've just had word from Berlin. One hundred miles north of here, the Americans have crossed the Rhine. They're on our soil, Herr Ingenieur-Doktor. It seems that I must demand that you quickly find a way to knock those ten kilos off Vampir. And then you and I are going hunting."

The asshead Schaeffer snickered.

Repp was smiling.

After they were gone, Repp reached into his desk and removed a silver flask. He was not a drinking fellow by habit but this night he felt a need. He unscrewed the cap and poured a few ounces of schnapps into a glass, and sipped it. He savored the fiery fluid.

The hour was late, time was slipping away, time, time, time the real enemy. Pressures from Berlin were mounting, that crazy goose the *Reichsführer* himself calling twice a day, babbling of what his astrologer and his masseur and his secretary and the little birdies in the sky were telling him. What had General Haussner said? "He has both feet planted firmly three feet above the ground." Something like that.

Repp first met the *Reichsführer* in the 1942 season in Berlin, shortly after Demyansk, when he was the hero of the hour. Himmler had worn cologne that smelled like mashed plums and wanted to know about Repp's ancestors.

Repp knew what to say.

"Common people, Reichsführer."

"Very good. Our strength, the common people. Our mystic bond with the soil, the earth." These words were delivered with unblinking sincerity in the middle of an opulent party in an industrialist's mansion. Beautiful women swirled about—Margareta was one, he remembered. The room was filled with warmth and light. Sex was in the air and wealth and power and not seventy-two hours earlier Repp had been in the tower.

"Yes, the people," the Reichsführer had said. He looked like an eggplant wearing glasses.

But Repp didn't want to think about the Reichsführer right now. He took another sip of the schnapps and called Margareta up into his mind.

She'd been so beautiful that year. He was not moved by many things but he'd allowed himself to be moved by her. How had she ended up there? Oh, yes, she'd come with some theatrical people. He'd seen her before, back when he was a young lieutenant and too frightened to speak. But this time he walked up boldly and took her hand. He saw her eyes go to the Iron Cross he now wore.

"I'm Repp," he said, bowing slightly.

"At least you didn't snap your heels together like so many of them."

He smiled. "I've been told anything in the city is mine. I choose you."

"They meant hotel rooms. Restaurant tables. Seats at the opera. Invitations to parties."

"But I don't want those things. I want you."

"You're very forward. You're the fellow in the tower, is that it? It seems I read something."

"Three days ago I killed three hundred and forty-five Russians in the span of eight hours. Now doesn't that make me rather special?"

"Yes, I suppose it does."

"May I present you to the Reichsführer? He's now a patron of mine, I believe."

"I know him. He's dreadful."

"A little pig. But a powerful patron. Come, let's leave. I was in a very pleasant restaurant last night. I believe they'll treat me nicely if I return. I even have a car and driver."

"My first lover was killed in Poland. My next died in an air fight over London. Another was captured in the Western Desert."

"Nothing will happen to me. I promise. Come, let's go."

She looked at him narrowly. "I came with a fellow, you know."

"A general in the Waffen SS?"

"No, an actor."

"Then he's nothing. Please. I insist."

She'd paused just a second, then said, "All right. But, please. No talk of war, Captain Repp."

Pleasant. Yes, pleasant.

Repp finished the schnapps. He was tempted to take another, but a principle of his was to never yield to temptations.

He knew the *Reichsführer* could call at any moment; and he knew he needed his strength for what lay ahead.

He sealed the bottle.

VI

Susan and Leets were wedged tight against the Claridge bar. It was late on a Friday night in mid-March, wall-to-wall uniforms, no V-2's had fallen for a couple of days, and after a lot of trying he'd finally talked her into an actual date. They'd had dinner at the Hungaria and, on Roger's recommendation, had dropped by this bright spot, where all the London beauties and big shots were said to camp out. So far Susan had seen two movie stars and a famous radio broadcaster. Leets had noticed instead other OSS officers in the smoky crowd and had fancied himself already slighted a couple of times, and once had even made a move toward one snide aristocratic profile, but Susan had tugged him back.

"No trouble. Remember. You promised."

"Yeah, yeah," he mumbled.

Now, several whiskies down him, he was feeling sweeter, the friend to all men. He had her to himself: no Phil, no Jews.

"Barkeep," he hailed, trolling in one of the red-jacketed boys behind the mahogany bar, "two here, old bun."

"No wonder they hate us," she said.

Around them the talk was of the new offensive. Beyond the Rhine! It would be over by the blooming of the flowers, the coming of spring. This optimism had the effect of depressing Leets.

"You're supposed to be enjoying yourself," she said. "For God's sakes, smile a little. Relax."

"You're damned cheerful," he said with surprise. It was true. The whole evening, she'd bubbled. She was especially beautiful, even in the severe cut of the brown uniform; some women looked good in anything. But it was something else. Susan seemed to be her old self: sly, mocking, mildly sarcastic, full of mischief.

"You've decided to make a career of Army nursing. Congrats!" he said.

She laughed.

"You're divorcing Phil. Right? Am I right?"

Again, laughter. "It's a long story," she said. "A long story."

But before she could tell it, an elegant Brit voice crooned to them. "Darlings."

It was Leets's turn to make a face.

But Tony came ahead confidently, until he seemed to embrace the two Americans.

"One more of what these chaps are having," Tony commanded the barman, and turned to press an icy smile on Leets.

"Sir," Leets said evenly.

"Rather a long Thursday, eh?" Tony asked.

Leets didn't say a thing.

"What, three, four hours? Or was it five?"

"Jim? What—" Susan said.

Leets looked bleakly off into the crowd.

"The captain had a rough go of it, I hear. Trying to get in to see—ah, who was it this time? Yours or ours?"

"Yours," Leets finally admitted.

"Of course. Knew it all the time. Major General Sir Colin Gubbins, was it not?"

"Yes."

"Thought so. Head of SOE. Pity he couldn't see you."

"I'm on the list for Monday, the girl said."

"I'll put in a good word for you tomorrow at lunch," Tony said, smiling maliciously.

"You bastard," Leets said.

"Now stop that kind of talk," Susan commanded.

"Susan, would you care to accompany me to lunch with General Sir Colin Gubbins tomor—"

"Goddamn it, Major, knock it off," Leets said.

Tony laughed. "You're getting a rather peculiar reputation in certain circles," he cautioned. "You know, he tells *any*one this mad scheme he's dreamed up. Jerry snipers. Quite strange."

Leets now felt fully miserable.

"It wouldn't hurt a bit to listen to him," Susan said. "You people have been told things all during the war you wouldn't listen to. You never listen until it's too late."

Tony stepped back, made a big show of shock. "Dear girl," he said theatrically, "of course we make mistakes. Of course we're old fuddy-duddies. That's what we're paid for. Think how dangerous we'd be if we knew what we were doing." He threw back his head and brayed.

Leets realized the man was quite drunk and beyond caring what he said, and to whom. But, surprisingly, there seemed to be in his act some affection for the miserable American and his girl.

"Listen, I know where there are some marvelous gatherings tonight. Care to come along? Really, I can offer Indian nabobs, Communist poets, homosexual generals, Egyptian white slavers. The relics of our late empire. It's quite a show. Do come."

"Thanks, Major," Leets said. "I'd really rather—"

"Tony. *Tony.* I've taken to the American habit. *You* call *me* Tony and *I'll* call *you* Jim. First names are such fun."

"Major, I—"

"Jim, it might be kind of fun," Susan said.

"What the hell," Leets said.

Presently, they found themselves in a cavernous flat in a splendidly fashionable section of London, along with a whole zoo of curiosities from all the friendly nations of World War II. Leets, pinned in a corner of the room, drank someone's wonderful whisky and exchanged primitive pleasantries with a Greek diplomat, while he watched as across the room Susan deflected, in rapid succession, an RAF group captain, a young dandy in a suit and tie, and a huge Russian in some sort of Ruritanian clown suit.

"She's smashing," Tony said to him.

"Yes, she's fine, just fine," Leets agreed.

"Is good very, no?" the Greek said, somewhat confusingly to Leets, but he merely nodded, as though he understood.

But after a while he went and got her, fighting his way through the mob.

"Hello, it's me," he said.

"Oh, Jim, isn't it wonderful? It's so *in*teresting," she said, beaming.

"It's just a party, for Christ's sake," he said.

"Darling, the most wonderful thing happened today. I can't wait to tell you about it."

"So tell."

"I say, guess who's here now?" Tony said suddenly, at his ear.

"It's Roger," shrieked Susan. "My God, look who he's got with him!"

"Indeed," said Tony. "An authentic Great Man! That is the hairy-chested novel writer who kills animals for amusement, is it not? Thought so."

"All we need is Phil," said Susan.

"Phil who?" said Leets, as his young sergeant drew near, his eyes crazy with glee, pulling in drunken tow the great writer himself. The two of them weaved brokenly across the crowded floor, Roger guiding the blandly smiling bigger man along. The fellow wore some kind of safari-inspired variation on the Air Corps uniform, open wide at the collar so that a thatch of iron-gray hair unfurled.

"The famous chest, for all to see," said Tony.

The writer had a pugnacious mustache and steel-frame glasses. He was big, Leets could see, big enough for Big Ten ball, but now he had a kind of drunken, horny benevolence, dispensing good fortune on all who passed before him. Several times in his journey, the writer stopped, as though to establish camp, but at each spot, Roger'd give a yank and unstick the fellow and pull him yet closer.

"Mr. Hem," Roger declared when he got the big fellow near enough, "Mr. Hem, I want ya ta meet the two best friggin' officers in World War Two."

"Dr. Hemorrhoid, the poor man's piles," the writer said, extending a paw.

Leets shook it.

"I adored *The Sun Actually Rises*," said Tony. "Really your best. So *feminine*. So wonderfully *feminine*. Delicate, pastel. As though written by a very sweet lady."

The writer grinned drunkenly. "The Brits all hate me," he explained to Susan. "But I don't let it bother me. What the hell, Major, go ahead and hate me. It's your bloody country, you can hate anybody you goddamnwellfucking choose. Nurse, you're beautiful."

"She's married," Leets said.

"Easy, Captain, I'm not moving in. Easy. You guys, do the fighting, you have my respect. No problems, no sweat. Nurse, you are truly beautiful. Are you married to this fellow?"

Susan giggled.

"She's married to a guy on a *ship*. In the *Pacific*," said Rog.

"My, my," said the writer.

"Hem, there's some people over here," Rog said.

"Not so fast, Junior. This looks like a most promising engagement," the writer said, grinning lustfully, putting a hand on Susan's shoulder.

"Hey, pal," said Leets.

"No fighting," Susan said. "I hate fighting. Mr. Hemingway, please take your hand off my shoulder."

"Darling, I'll put my hand anywhere you *tell* me to put it," Hemingway said, removing his hand.

"Put it up your ass," said Leets.

"Captain, really, I have nothing but respect. You're the guy putting the hun in his grave. Putting Jerry to ground, eh, Maj? Any day now. Any bloody day. Junior, how 'bout getting Papa a drink? A couple fingers whisky. No ice. Warm and smooth."

"War is hell," Leets said.

"How many Krauts you kill?" Hemingway asked Leets.

Leets said nothing.

"Huh, sonny? Fifty? A hundred? Two thousand?"

"This is a terrible conversation," Susan said. "Jim, let's get out of here."

"How many, Cap? Many as the major here? Bet he's killed jillions. That Brit special-ops group, goes behind the lines. Gets 'em with knives, fucking *knives*, right in the gizzard. Blood all over everything. But how many, Captain? Huh?"

Leets said he didn't know, but not many. "You just fired at vehicles," he explained, "until they exploded. So there was no sense of *killing*."

"Could we change the subject, please," Susan said. "All this talk of killing is giving me a headache."

"There is no hunting like the hunting of man, and those who have hunted armed men long enough and liked it, never care for anything else thereafter," recited Hemingway.

"I wouldn't know about that," said Leets. He remembered bitterly: the tracers spraying through the grass, kicking spurts out of the earth, the sounds of the STG-44's, the universe-shattering detonations of the 75's on the Panzers. "It was just a fucking mess. It wasn't like hunting at all."

"Really, I'm not going to let this nonsense ruin my evening. Come on, Jim, let's get out of here," Susan said, and hauled him away.

They walked the cold, wet London streets, in the hours near dawn. An icy light began to seep over the horizon, above the blank rows of buildings that formed the walls of their particular corridor. Again, fog. The streets were empty now, except for occasional cruising jeeps of MP's and now and then a single black taxi.

"They say at High Blitz Hitler never even stopped the cabs," Leets said abstractedly.

"Do you believe in miracles?" Susan, who'd been silent for a while, suddenly said.

Leets considered. Then he said, "No."

"I don't either," she said. "Because a miracle has to be sheer luck. But I believe certain things are meant to happen. Meant, planned, predestined."

"Our meeting again in the hospital?" he said, only half a joke.

"No, this is serious," she said.

He looked at her. How she'd changed!

"You're generating enough heat to light this quarter of the city. I hope there're no Kraut planes up there."

"Do you want to hear about this, or not?"

"Of course I do," he said.

"Oh, Jim, I'm sorry," she said. "I know you're feeling awful. Outhwaithe was very cruel."

"Outhwaithe I can handle. I just know something and I can't get anyone to believe me. But don't let my troubles wreck your party. Really, Susan. I'm very happy for you. Please, tell me all about it."

"We have one. Finally. One got out. A miracle."

"Have one what? What are you—"

"A witness."

"I don't—"

"From the camps. An incredible story. But finally, now, in March of 1945, a man has reached the West who was in a place called Auschwitz. In Poland. A murder camp."

"Susan, you hear all kinds of—"

"No. He was there. He identified pictures. He described the locations, the plants, the processes. It all jibes with reports we've been getting. It's all true. And now we can prove it. He's all they have. The Jews of the East. He's their testament, their witness. Their voice, finally. It's very moving. I find it—"

"Now just a minute. You say this camp was in Poland? Now, how the hell did this guy make it across Poland and Germany to us? Really, that's a little hard to believe. It all sounds to me like some kind of story."

"The Germans moved him to some special camp in a forest in Germany. It's a funny story. It makes no sense at all. They moved him there with a bunch of other people, and fed them—fattened them up, almost like pigs. Then one night they took him to a field and . . ."

"It was some kind of execution?"

"A test. He said it was a test."

And Susan told Leets the story of Shmuel.

And after a while Leets began to listen with great intensity.

VII

Vampir would work; of that Vollmerhausen had little doubt. He had been there, after all, at the beginning, at the University of Berlin lab in 1933 when Herr Doktor Edgar Kutzcher, working under the considerable latitude of a large *Heereswaffenamt* contract, had made the breakthrough discovery that lead sulfide was photoconductive and had a useful response to about three microns, putting him years ahead of the Americans and the British, who were still tinkering with thallous sulfide. The equation, chalked across a university blackboard, which expressed the breakthrough Herr Doktor had achieved, realized its final practical form in the instrument on which Vollmerhausen now labored in the research shed at Anlage Elf, under increasing pressure and difficulty.

It was a business of sorting out dozens of details, of burrowing through the thickets of technical confusions that each tiny decision led them to. But this is what Vollmerhausen, a failed physicist, liked about engineering: making things work. Function was all. Vampir would work.

But would Vampir work at forty kilos?

That was another question altogether, and although his position officially demanded optimism, privately his doubts were deep and painful.

Under forty kilos?

Insane. Not without radically compromising on performance. But of course one didn't argue with the SS. One smiled and did one's best and hoped for luck.

But forty kilos? Why? Did they plan on dropping it from a plane? It would shatter anyway, and shock absorption hadn't been tied into the specifications. He'd gone to Repp privately:

"Surely, Herr Obersturmbannführer, if you could just give me some reason for this arbitrary weight limit."

Repp, frosty, had replied, "Sorry, Herr Ingenieur-Doktor. Tactical requirements, that's all. Someone's going to have to carry the damned thing."

"But certainly there are vehicles that—"

"Herr Ingenieur-Doktor: forty kilos."

Lately Hans the Kike had been having nightmares. His food

bubbled and heaved in his stomach. He worked obsessively, driving his staff like a tyrant, demanding the impossible.

"Hans the Kike," he heard one of them joke, "rather more like Attila the Hun."

But he had come so far since 1933, and the journey was so complex, so full of wrong starts, missed signs, betrayals, disappointments, unfair accusations, plots against him, credit due him going to others. More than ever now, 1933 came to haunt him. The last year I was ever truly happy, he told himself, before all this.

A year of beginnings—for Vampir, for Kutzcher, for Germany. But also one of endings. It had been Vollmerhausen's last year with physics, and he'd loved physics, had a great brain for physics. But by the next year, '34, physics was officially regarded as a *Jewish* science, a demi-religion like Freudianism, full of kabala and ritual and pentagram, and bright young Aryans like Vollmerhausen were pressured into other areas. Many left Germany, and not just Jews either; they were the lucky ones. For the ones who stayed, like Vollmerhausen, only melancholy choices remained. Dietzl went into aerodynamics, Stossel back to chemistry; Lange gave up science altogether and became a party intellectual. Vollmerhausen too felt himself pressed into an extraordinary career shift, a daring, uncharacteristically bold one—and one he hated. He returned to the Technological Institute and became a ballistics engineer, rather than an exalted *Doktor* of Science. It hadn't the challenge of physics, the sense of unlocking the universe, but everybody knew there'd be a war sooner or later, and wars meant guns and guns meant jobs. He threw himself into it with a terror, succeeding on sheer determination where once there'd been talent. It began to look as though he'd made the right decision when he was invited to join Berthold Giepel's ERMA design team. ERMA, the acronym for *Erfurter Maschinenfabrik B. Giepel GmbH, Erfurt*, was at that moment in history the most fertile spot in the world in arms design, and from all over the world acolytes swarmed, young engineers out of the technical institutes, or off apprenticeships at the *Waffenfabrik Mauser* at Oberndorf, or for Walther AG in Munich, even a Swiss lad from SIG and an American from Winchester. All were turned down. For the brilliant team that Giepel had assembled was up to nothing less than revolutionizing automatic weapons theory by building a *Maschinenpistole* off the radical open-bolt straight-blowback principle, which made for greater manu-

facturing simplicity, lightness and reliability, yet at the same time
permitted air circulation through breech and barrel between rounds
with subsequent temperature reduction, jacking the rate of fire up
to about 540 per minute cyclical. They were inventing, in short,
the best submachine gun in the world, the MP-40, until it became
better known under a different name.

These should have been extraordinary days for Vollmerhausen,
and in a way they were. But his physics background, like a whiff
of the Yid, clung to him. He could never shake it; the others
gossiped behind his back, played small pranks, teased him un-
mercifully. They hated him because he'd once aspired to be a
scientist; what scientists he now came in contact with hated him
because he was an engineer. He grew into a somewhat twisted
personality, with a tendency toward surliness, bitterness, self-pity.
He was grumpy, gloomy, a great self-justifier and blamer of others.
His head was full of imaginary compliments that he felt he deserved but that he never received, because of course the others
were jealous of his brilliance. Out of all this was born the name
Hans the Kike.

So when in 1943 he was offered a position at the *WaPrüf 2*
testing facility at Kummersdorf, he jumped at it. A new project
was under way. The army had learned in Russia of the terrors of
the night and had let a contract for *Vampir 1229 Zeilgerät*, the
Vampire sighting device, Model 1229, based on the data that Herr
Doktor Kutzcher, now dead, had developed back in '33. Vollmerhausen had an extraordinary background for the undertaking:
he knew both the physics of the project and the ballistics. It was
a job made for him.

In its wisdom, *Waffenamt* had decided that the weapon best
suited to mount Vampir was none other than the prototype
Sturmgewehr on which Hugo Schmeisser was so furiously laboring,
then designated the MP-43. Thus Ingenieur-Doktor Vollmerhausen
and Herr Schmeisser (for old Hugo had no degrees) found themselves uneasily collaborating on the project at the dictates of the
Army bureaucracy.

From the start, Hugo was undercutting him.

"Too bulky," the old fool claimed. "Too sensitive. Too complicated."

"Herr Schmeisser," Hans began, suffering the immense strain of
having to deal politely with a fool, "a few design modifications and

we can join your assault rifle and my optics system and achieve the most modern device of the war. No, it'll never be an assault weapon, or for the parachutists, but in the years ahead will come battles of a primarily defensive nature. The great days of rapid expansion are over. It's time to concentrate on protecting what we've got. In any kind of stable night tactical situation, Vampir will make our enemies totally vulnerable." And as he spoke, he could watch the old man's eyes frost over with indifference. It was a most difficult situation, especially since in the background was another under-current: Hans the Kike was from the ERMA team that had built the wonderful MP-40; but, strangely, that weapon had picked up the nickname "Schmeisser," though the old goat had had nothing to do with it. But he'd never disavowed the connection either, mad as he was for fame and glory.

With Schmeisser against him, he was doomed. The STG modifications were never approved, funds began to vanish, tech-nicians were siphoned off to other projects, the Opticotechna people had difficulty with the lenses—Schmeisser's influence?—and much gossip and vicious humor raged behind Hans the Kike's back. He had no connections, nothing to match the might of the adroit Schmeisser, who didn't want his assault rifle associated with some strange "wish-machine" invented by an obscure scientist and supervised by a disreputable ERMA veteran.

Vollmerhausen, under pressure, felt himself becoming more repellent. Whatever chances he had as an advocate for Vampir disappeared when he ceased shaving and bathing regularly, when he began denouncing the secret cabal that conspired behind his back. Vampir never went beyond prototype, despite some promising initial test results. It failed to meet certain specifications in its field trial, though Vollmerhausen asserted that "the cabal" had stacked the test against him. In May of '44 the *Waffenamt* contract was canceled, and Vollmerhausen was ordered sharply back to Kum-mersdorf to a meaningless job. He was let go shortly afterward.

They let him dangle for a bit, nudging him closer and closer to despair. Worries on top of worries. His career in total collapse. Questions were asked. People began to avoid him. Nobody would look him in the eye. He thought he was being watched. The Army called him up for a physical exam and pronounced him fit for combat duty, despite fallen arches, a bronchial infection, bad ears and severe nearsightedness. He was advised to get his affairs in order, for the notice would arrive any day. It appeared his final fate might be to carry a "Schmeisser" on the *Ostfront*.

One day he happened to run into a friend in a disreputable café where he'd taken to spending his days.

"Have you heard, is Haenel still taking on people? I'd do anything. Draftsmanship, apprentice work, modeling."

"Hans, I don't think so. Old Hugo, you know. He'd stand in your way."

"That old fool."

"But, Hans, I did hear of something." The friend was extremely nervous. It was the first time Vollmerhausen had seen him since he'd been fired. Hans had in fact been startled to see him in this place.

"Eh, what?" Vollmerhausen squinted, rubbed his hands through his hair and across his face, noticing for the first time that he hadn't shaved in quite some time.

"Well, they say some fellows in the SS are going to let a big contract soon. For Vampir. They may revive Vampir."

"The SS. What do they care about—"

"Hans, I didn't ask. I-I just didn't ask. But I hear it has to do with . . ." He trailed off.

"What? Come on now, Dieter. What on earth? I've never seen you quite so—"

"Hans. It's just another job. Perhaps the Waffen SS wants to put Vampir into production. I don't—"

"What did you hear?"

"It's a special thing. A special mission. A special most secret, mot important effort. That's all. It's said to originate from—from high quarters."

Vollmerhausen pursed his lips disgustingly, puzzled.

"I think they're interested in you. I think they're quite interested in you. Would you be willing? Hans, think about it. Please."

The SS filled him with dread. You heard so much. But a job was a job, especially when the alternative was the *Ostfront*.

"Yes. Yes, I suppose I—"

A day or so later he found himself in conversation with a pale officer at Unter den Eichen, the underground headquarters of the SS administrative and economic section, in Berlin.

"The *Reichsführer* is anxious to let a contract on an engineering project, sited down in the Schwarzwald. Actually, I may as well be frank with you, he believes this Vampir thing you worked on might have applications with regard to the duties of the SS and he's anxious to pursue them."

"Interesting," said Vollmerhausen.

The man then proceeded to discuss with surprising precision the history and technology of Vampir, especially as linked to the STG-44. Vollmerhausen was stunned to realize how carefully the project had been examined by—what was it?—WVHA, of which up until a day or so ago he'd not even heard.

"There's no question of funding," the man explained, "we have access to adequate monies. A subsidiary called *Ostindustrie GmbH* produces quite a lot of income. Cheap labor from the East."

"Well, the budget would certainly be a factor in such a project," said Vollmerhausen noncommittally.

"Do you know this fellow Repp?"

"The great Waffen SS hero?"

"Yes, him. He's a part of it too. He'll be joining the project shortly. We've given it a code name, Nibelungen. Operation Nibelungen."

"What on earth—"

"The *Reichsführer*'s idea. He likes those little touches. It's a joke, actually. Surely you can see that?"

But Vollmerhausen was baffled. Joke?

The officer continued. "Now, Herr Ingenieur-Doktor, here"—he shuffled some papers—"Vampir's chief liability, according to the field results—"

"The test was planned for failure. They treated it like a piece of cookware. It's a sophisticated—"

"Yes, yes. Well, from our point of view, the problem is weight."

"With batteries, insulation, wiring, precision equipment, a lens system, energy conversion facilities, what do you expect?"

"What does the Vampir weigh?"

Vollmerhausen was silent. The answer was an embarrassment.

"Seventy kilos." The man answered his own question. "At the very limits of movability."

"A strong man—"

"A man at the front, in the rain, the cold, hungry, exhausted, is not strong."

Vollmerhausen was again silent. He glared off into space. It was not safe to show anger toward the SS; yet he felt himself scowling.

"Herr Doktor, our specifications call for forty kilos."

Vollmerhausen thought he had misheard. "Eh? I'm not sure I—"

"Forty kilos."

"That's insane! Is this a joke? That's preposterous!"

"It can't be done?"

"Not without compromising Vampir out of existence. This is no toy. Perhaps in the future, when new miniaturization technologies become available. But not now, not—"

"In three months. Perhaps four, even five, difficult to say at this point."

Vollmerhausen almost leaped from his chair again; but he saw the man fixing him with a cool, steady glare.

"I—I don't know," he stammered.

"You'll have the best facilities, the top people, the absolute green light from all cooperating agencies. You'll have the total resources of the SS at your disposal, from the *Reichsführer* on down. I think you know the kind of weight that carries these days."

"Well, I—"

"We're prepared to go all the way on this. We believe it to be of the utmost importance to our Führer, our Fatherland and our Racial Peoples. I don't see how you can say No to the *Reichsführer*. It's an honor to be chosen for this job. A fitting climax to your service to the Reich."

Vollmerhausen deciphered the threat in this, more vivid for remaining unspecified.

"Of course," he finally ventured, with a weak kike smile, "it would be an honor," thinking all the time, What am I doing? *Forty kilos?*

The forty kilos now, months later, were within ten kilos; they'd picked and peeled and compromised and teased and improvised their way down, gram by painful gram. Vollmerhausen could almost measure the past days in terms of grams trimmed here and there, but these last ten kilos seemed impossible to find. After steady progress, the staff had stalled badly and another of Vollmerhausen's concerns was whether or not Repp had noticed this.

It was a typical career development for him, he thought. He'd done so much good work, so much brilliant work, and never gotten any real credit for it. Meanwhile, once again, everything was coming unraveled over some nonsense that he had no control over.

Tears of black bitterness welled up in his eyes. Bad luck, unfair persecution, unlucky coincidences seemed to haunt him.

For example, *for example*, what thanks, what respect, had he gotten for his modifications thus far to the STG-44? He'd taken a clever, sound production rifle, albeit one with a hand-tooled breech and barrel, but still just another automatic gun, and turned it into a first-class sniper's weapon. He solved the two most pressing problems—noise and accuracy at long range—in one stroke, devising a whole new concept of ballistics. The mission specs called for thirty rounds to be delivered silently and devastatingly to a target 400 meters out. So be it: now Repp had his thirty chances, where before he had nothing.

And what had been the response?

Repp had merely fixed those cold eyes on him and inquired, "But, Ingenieur-Doktor, how much does it weigh?"

Today's meeting was not going well: a bitter squabble between the optics group, most of them from the Munich Technological Institute, and the power group, the battery people: natural antagonists in the weight business. Meanwhile, the people from Energy Conversion remained silent, sullen.

All at once the complexities seemed overwhelming. An incredible restlessness stirred through his limbs, as the eyes of his staff pressed into him, demanding answers, guidance, adjudication. Beyond them, more threatening, he could see Repp. His misery was intense, fiery.

"Gentlemen, please. I believe—" He halted, absolutely no idea what he'd meant to say when he began to speak. That had been happening often too, sentences that began in confidence, then somewhere in the middle veered out of control and trailed off into silence, the ideas they had sought to express vanishing. He felt the impulse to flee mounting in him; it fluttered in his chest like a live thing.

"I believe," he continued, and was as amazed as they at the finish, "that I'm going to go for a walk."

They looked at him in bafflement. He'd always been so driven, trying to beat the problem down by sheer intensity of will, flatten it with his energy, his doggedness. He read in several sets of eyes the suspicion that Hans the Kike was finally cracking on them.

"It'll do us all some good," he argued. "Get away from the problem for a few hours, get a fresh perspective on it. We'll meet again at one."

He rushed from them into the out-of-doors and felt a burst of clean spring air and the heat of the sun. It's spring, he thought with surprise. He'd lost all sense of time and season, shut off in his exotic world of microns and heat curves and power sequences. Then he noticed how the installation had changed, having become now almost a fortification. He nearly stumbled into a trench that ran between cement blockhouses that were surely new since the last time he'd come this way. He picked out a path around sandbagged gun emplacements and maneuvered through trellises of barbed wire. Were the Americans close by? It frightened him suddenly. Must remember to ask Repp.

But he wanted green silence, blue sky, the touch of the sun; not this vista of war, which merely stressed his problems. He rushed through the gate and headed down the road to the range a mile or so away; it was the only available openness in the surrounding woods. The journey wasn't pleasing; the trees loomed in on him darkly, sealing off the sky, and there were spots after an initial turn where he felt completely isolated in the forest as the road wound through it. Not another living creature seemed to stir; no breeze nudged the dense overhead branches, which sliced the sun into splashes at his feet. But then a patch of yellow appeared at the end of the corridor after another turn. He almost ran the remaining distance.

The range was empty, a yellow field banked on four sides by the trees. He walked to the center of it, felt the sun's warmth again build on his neck. It *was* March, after all, April next, then May, and May was said to be especially nice in these parts, on a clear day one could make out the Alps one hundred kilometers or so away to the south. He twisted suddenly in that direction, seeking them as one would seek a hope. Above the trees was only haze and blur. He looked about for symbols of life reviving, for buds or birds or bees, and shortly picked out a flower, a yellow thing.

He bent to it. An early fellow, eh? It was a spiky, not too healthy-looking creature, stained faintly brown. Vollmerhausen had never felt much for such displays, had never had the time for them, but now he thought he had a glimmer into the simple pleasures so many of his countrymen had crooned about over the years. He plucked the flower from the soil and held it close to study it: an interesting design, the petals really slivers of a disk sectioned to facilitate easy opening and closing, a clever notion for capturing maximum sunlight, yet not sacrificing protection from the night cold. A little sun machine composed of concentric circles, efficient, elegant, precise. Now *there* was engineering! As if to confirm this judgment, the sun seemed to beat harder on the back of his neck.

He felt extraordinarily pleasant. He really felt as though he'd discovered something. He must remember to find a book on flowers. He knew nothing about them but was filled with a sudden overwhelming curiosity.

These soothing thoughts deserted him abruptly when he realized he stood in the middle of the killing ground.

A memory of that night came quickly over him. When had he known they were going to shoot them? He couldn't remember exactly, the knowledge evolved slowly, over the first few months. He could not identify an actual moment of awareness. It just seemed they all knew and didn't find it remarkable. Nobody was upset. Repp seemed to think it quite unexceptional. He had no involvement in it in any way; it would simply happen, that's all, when the prototype Vampir reached a certain stage. But the whole business left Vollmerhausen queasy, uncomfortable.

He remembered the beginning best, the double line of men standing listlessly in the dark cold. He could hear them breathing. They seemed so *alive*. He was wildly excited, nervous, his stomach so agitated that it actually hurt. The Jews stood in their ranks, waiting to die. He could see no faces; but he noticed at this penultimate moment a curious thing.

They were so small.

They were all small. Some mere boys, even the older men wiry and short.

After that, it moved clinically. The Jews were marched away and when he could not see them he no longer thought of them.

The preparations were laconic, calm. Repp fussed with the weapon, then dropped behind it and drew it to him, arranging himself into a strained pose, all bone beneath the rifle, no flesh, no muscle, nothing but a structure of bone to hold the weight.

"You have power, sir," someone said.

"Ah, yes," said Repp, his voice somewhat muffled in the gunstock, "quite nice, quite nice."

"Sir, the guards are clear," somebody called. "The targets are at four fifty."

"Yes, yes," said Repp, and then his words vanished in the thumping of the burst, one fast, slithering drum roll, the individual reports fusing in their rush.

It was just seconds later they realized a man had survived, and just seconds after that that all hell broke loose, the lights flashed on, two American fighter-bombers roaring down into the bright zone, spitting bullets into the field, running their earth-splitting hemstitches across the field, and the lights flashed out.

"Fuckers," somebody said, "where the hell did *they* come from?"

Vollmerhausen shuddered. He stood now in the grass where the mangled bodies had lain. The Vampir rifle's slugs had torn huge chunks in the flesh. Blood had soaked the earth that night, but now there was only grass, and sun, blue sky, a little breeze.

Vollmerhausen began to walk toward the trees. He realized the sun was behind a cloud. No wonder it felt cool all of a sudden.

The sun came out; he felt its heat across his neck again.

Yes, warm me.

Soothe me.

Clean me.

Yes, purify me.

Forgive me.

Then he knew where his ten kilos were coming from.

VIII

They made an odd pair: Susan in her dumpy civilian dress, and Dr. Fischelson, dressed in the fashion of the last century, fussy and ancient in wing collar, spats, a striped suit, goatee and pince-nez. We look like a picture of my grandparents, she thought.

She had him calmer now, but still was uncertain. He could go off dottily at any moment, ranting in an odd mixture of Polish, Yiddish, German and English, his eyes watering, licking his dry lips, talking crazily of obscure events and people. He was not an effective man, she knew; but when it came to one thing, his will was iron: the fate of the Jews. He seemed to carry it around with him, an imaginary weight, bending him closer to earth each day, making him more insane.

But now he was calmer. She'd soothed him, listening, nodding, cajoling, whispering. They sat on two uncomfortable chairs in an antiseptic corridor of a private clinic in Kilburn, a London suburb, outside the door behind which the Man from the East—Fischelson's portentous phrase—rested.

The crisis of the evening was now over. It seemed that late in the afternoon some investigators had shown up at the clinic and asked rude questions. Fischelson had panicked. A rough scene had ensued. In frenzy, he'd called her. She'd begged off late duty and gotten out there as fast as she could—only to find them gone and Fischelson shaking and incoherent.

"Now, now," she calmed. "I'm sure it was nothing. Emigration people probably, or security. That's all. They have to check these things."

"Rude. So rude they was. No respect." How could she make this man see how armies—modern nations, for that matter—worked?

"It's nothing, Dr. Fischelson. Nothing at all. They have to check these things." She stole a glance at her watch. Christ, it was getting late: near midnight. She'd been here with the old bird since eight. She was due in at six tomorrow. "Perhaps we ought to leave. Everything's quiet now."

"Sure, leave. You leave. Me, an old man, I'll stay here." The old Jews; they were all alike. Now he sounded like her mother.

Manipulation with guilt. Most effective. Jesus, how long would this go on?

"All right. We'll stay a little longer." How could you get rough with Fischelson? He wasn't some jerk who was pawing at you. But she was exhausted. They had the witness, curious man in the back room—an incredible story. A story that would be told now, at last. Even if it was too late. No, it wasn't too late. In the camps were still many, near death. If the authorities could at last be convinced, who knew what was possible? Armored attacks driving toward the KZ's, with doctors and medicine: thousands could be saved. If only the proper people could be convinced.

The doctor sat with hands folded, breathing heavily. Then he took off his pince-nez and began to polish the lenses in his lapel. He had long, bony fingers. In the yellow light of the corridor, he looked as if he were made of old paper, parchment. Our Jewish general, she thought: half insane, half senile, furiously indignant. It would be funny if it weren't so sad.

Fischelson had been here since '39. When the philanthropist Hirsczowicz had converted to Zionism late in that year, his first act had been to establish a voice in the West. He was very shrewd, Hirsczowicz: he knew the fate of the Jews rested in the hands of the West. He'd sent Fischelson over first, a kind of advance guard, to set things up. But Fischelson became the whole show when the war broke out and Hirsczowicz disappeared in a Nazi execution operation. The old man proved to be horribly unsuited to the task: he was not delicate, he had no tact, no political sensibility; he could only whine and rant.

"His papers is good," Dr. Fischelson said, in his heavy accent.

"Pardon?" she said.

"His papers is good. I guarantee. I guarantee. He has release from prison war camp. Our peoples find him in DP hospital. Sick, very sick. They get him visa. Jews help Jews. Across France he comes by train. Then the last by ship. Lawyers draw up papers. All good, all legal. This I tell you. So why investigators? So why now investigators?"

"Please, please," she said, for the old man had begun to rise and declaim. A vein pulsed beneath the dry skin of his throat. "It's some kind of mistake, I'm sure. Or a part of the routine. That's all. Look, I have a friend in the intelligence service, a captain."

"A Jew?"

"No. But a good man, basically. A decent man. I'll call him and—"

She heard the doors at the end of the corridor swing open and at first could not recognize them. They were not particularly impressive men: just big, burly, a little embarrassed. Susan's sentence stopped in her mouth. Who were they? Dr. Fischelson, following the confusion in her eyes, looked over.

They came silently, without talking, four of them, and the fifth, a leader, a way back. They passed Susan and Fischelson and stepped into Shmuel's room.

My God, she thought.

"What's this, what's going on?" shouted Fischelson.

Susan felt her heart begin to accelerate and her hands begin to tremble. She had trouble breathing.

"Easy," said the leader, not brutally at all.

"Miss Susan, what's going on?" Fischelson demanded.

Say something, you idiot, Susan thought.

"Hey, what are you guys doing?" she said, her voice breaking.

"Special Branch, miss. Sorry. Just be a moment."

"Miss Susan, Miss Susan," the old man stood, panic wild in his eyes. He began to lapse into Yiddish.

"What's going on?" she shouted. "Goddamn you, what's going on?"

"Easy, miss," he said. He was not a brutal man. "Nothing to concern yourself with. Special Branch."

The first four came out of the room. On a stretcher was the swaddled form of the survivor. He looked around dazedly.

"I'm an American officer," she said, fumbling for identification. "For God's sake, that man is ill. What is going on? Where are you taking that man?"

"Now, now, miss," the leader soothed. It would have been easier to hate him if he hadn't been quite so mild.

"He's ill."

The doctor was denouncing them in Polish. "Please don't get excited," the man said.

"*Where is your authority?*" she shouted, because it was the only thing she could think of.

"Sorry, miss. You're a Yank, wouldn't know, would you? Of course not. Special Branch. Don't need an authority. Special Branch. That's all."

"He's gone, *mein Gott*, is gone, is gone." The doctor sat down.

Susan stared down the hall at the swinging doors through which they'd taken the Jew.

The leader turned to go, and Susan grabbed him.

"What is happening? My God, this is a nightmare. What are you doing, what is going on?" Her eyes felt big and she was terrified. They had merely come in and taken him and nothing on earth could stop them. There was nothing she could do. She and an old man alone in a corridor.

"Miss," the leader said, "please. You are supposed to be in uniform. The regulations. Now I haven't taken any names. We've been quite pleasant. Best advice is to go away, take the old man, get him some tea, and put him to bed. Forget all this. It's a government matter. Now I haven't taken any names. Please, miss, let go. I don't want to take any names."

He stood back. He was ill at ease, a big, strong type, with police or military written all over him. He was trying to be kind. It was a distasteful business for him.

"Who can I see?" she said. "Jesus, tell me who I can see?"

The man took a nervous look around. Outside, a horn honked. Quickly, his hand dipped into his coat, came out with a paper. He unfolded it, looked it over.

"See a Captain Leets," he said. "American, like you. Or a Major Outhwaithe. They're behind it all." And he was gone.

"The Jews," Dr. Fischelson was saying, over on the chair, looking bleakly at nothing, "who'll tell about the Jews? Who'll witness the fate of the Jews?"

But Susan knew nobody cared about the Jews.

Leets, alone in the office, waited for her. He knew she'd come. He felt nervous. He smoked. His leg ached. He'd sent Roger out on errands, for now there was much to do; and once Tony had called, urgent with a dozen ideas, with several subsidiary leads from the first great windfall. But Leets had pushed him off.

"I have to get through the business with Susan."

Tony's voice turned cold. "There is no business with Susan. You owe her nothing. You owe the Jews nothing. You owe the operation everything."

"I have to try and explain it," he said, knowing this would never do for a man of Tony's hardness.

"Then get it over with quick, chum, and be ready for business tomorrow. It's first day on the new job, all right?"

Leets envied the major: war was simple for the Brits—they waged it flat out, and counted costs later.

He heard something in the hall. Susan? No, something in this ancient building settling with a groan.

But presently the door opened, and she came in.

He could see her in the shadows.

"I thought you'd be out celebrating," she said.

"It's not a triumph. It's a beginning."

"Can we have some light, please, goddamn it."

He snapped on his desk lamp, a brass fixture with an opaque green cowl.

Because he knew he was dead to her, she seemed very beautiful. He could feel his cock tighten and grow. He felt a desperate need to return to the past: before all this business, when the Jews were little people in the background whom she went to see occasionally, and his job was simple, meaningless, and London a party. For just a second he felt he'd do anything to have all that back, but mainly what he wanted back was her. Just her. He wanted to have her again, all of her—skin, her hands and legs. Her mouth. Her laugh. Her breasts, cunt.

She wore full uniform, as if at a review. Army brown, which turned most women shapeless and sexless, made Susan wonderful. Her brass buttons shone in the flickery English light. A few ribbons were pinned across the left breast of her jacket. A bar glittered on her lapels, and a SHAEF patch, a sword, upthrust, stood out on her shoulder. One of those little caps tilted across her hair. She was carrying a purse or something.

"I tried to stop you, you know," she said. "I tried. I went to see people. People I know. Officers I'd met in the wards. Generals even. I even tried to see Hemingway, but he's gone. That's how desperate I was."

"But you didn't get anywhere?"

"No. Of course not."

"It's very big. Or, we think it's big. You can't stop it. Ike himself couldn't stop it."

"You bastard."

"Do you want a cigarette?"

"No."

"Do you mind if I smoke?"

"I was there when they came and took him. 'Special Branch.' There was nothing we could do."

"I know. I read the report. Sorry. I didn't know it would work out that way."

"Would it have made any difference?"

"No," Leets said. "No, it wouldn't have, Susan."

"You filthy bastard."

She seemed almost about to break down. But her eyes, which had for just a flash welled with tears, returned quickly to their hard brilliance.

"Susan—"

"Where is he?"

"In another hospital. A British one. He'll be fine there. He'll be all right. If it's a matter of worrying about him, then please don't. We'll take good care of him. He's quite important."

"You have no idea what that man's been through."

"I think perhaps I do. It's been very rough on him, sure, we realize—"

"You have no idea, Jim. You can't possibly begin to imagine. If you think you can, then you're fooling yourself. Believe me."

Leets said nothing.

"Why? For Christ's sakes, *why*? You kidnap a poor Jew. Like Cossacks, you come in and just take him. Why?"

"He's an intelligence source. An extraordinary one. We believe he's the key to a high-priority German operation. We believe we can work backward from the information he gives us and track it down. And stop it."

"You bastard. You have no idea of the stakes involved, of what he means to those people."

"Susan, believe me: I had no choice. I was walking down a London street a few nights ago with a woman I love. All of a sudden she unreels a story that struck right at the heart of something I'd been working on since January. You needed a witness? Well, I needed one too. I had no way of knowing they'd turn out to be the same man."

"You and that bastard Englishman. You were the officers that came by the clinic yesterday. I should have known. Dr. Fischelson said investigators. I thought of cops. But no, it was you and that Oxford creep. You'd do anything for them, won't you, Jim?

Anything! To get in with the Oxford boys, the Harvard boys. You've come a long way from Northwestern, goddamn you."

"I'm sorry. I didn't send the Jew to Anlage Elf in the Schwarzwald. I didn't set him among the Waffen SS and the Man of Oak and Obersturmbannführer Repp. The Germans did that. I've got to find out why."

"You bastard."

"Please. Be reasonable."

"That's what you people always say. That's what we've been hearing since 1939. Be reasonable. Don't exaggerate. Stay calm. Keep your voice down."

"Yell then, if it makes you feel better."

"You're all the same. You and the Germans. You're all—"

"Shut up, Susan. You've got no call to say that."

She stared at him in black fury. He'd never seen so much rage on a human face. He swallowed uncomfortably, lit a cigarette. His hands were shaking.

"Here, I brought you something." She reached into her purse. "Go ahead. Look. Go ahead, you're brave. I insist."

It was a selection of photographs. Blurry, pornographic things. Naked women in fields, standing among German soldiers. Pits jammed with corpses. One, particularly horrible, showed a German soldier in full combat gear, holding a rifle up against the head of a woman who held a child.

"It's awful," he said. "Jesus, of course it's awful. What do you expect me to say? It's awful, all of it. All right? Goddamn it, what do you want? I had a fucking job to do. I didn't ask for it, it just came along. So get off my back, goddamn it."

"Dr. Fischelson has an interesting theory. Would you like to hear it? It's that the Gentiles are still punishing us for inventing the conscience five thousand years ago. But what they don't realize is that when they kill us, they kill themselves."

"Is that a theory or a curse?"

"If it's a curse, Jim, I extend it to you. From the bottom of my heart, I hope this thing kills you. I hope it does. I hope it kills you."

"I think you'd better go now. I've still got work to do."

She left him, alone in the office. The pictures lay before him on the desk. After a while, he ripped them up and threw them into the wastebasket.

* * *

Early the next morning, before the interrogations began, Leets composed the following request and with Outhwaithe's considerable juice got it priority circulation as an addendum to the weekly Intelligence Sitrep, which bucked it down as far as battalion-level G-2's and their British counterparts ETO-wide.

> JOINT ANGLO–AMERICAN TECHNICAL INTELLIGENCE COMMITTEE PRIORITY ONE
>
> REQUEST ALL–LEVEL G-2/CIC STAFFS FORWARD THIS HDQ ANY INFO IN RE FOLLOWING FASTEST REPEAT FASTEST FASTEST
>
> 1. UNUSUAL ENEMY SMALL ARMS PROFICIENCY, ESP INVOLVING WAFFEN SS UNITS
> 2. HEAVILY DEFENDED TEST INSTALLATIONS ENCOMPASSING FIRING RANGE FACILITIES
> 3. RUMORS, UNCONFIRMED STORIES, INVOLVING SAME
> 4. PW INTERROGATION REPORTS INVOLVING SAME

"Jesus, the crap we're going to get out of *that*," complained Roger.

IX

It was clear the Jew was trying to accommodate them. He answered patiently their many questions, though he thought them stupid. They kept asking him the same ones again and again and each time he answered. But he could only tell them what he knew. He knew that Repp had killed twenty-five men at long distance—400 meters Leets had figured—in pitch dark, without sound. He knew that a mysterious Man of Oak had come to visit the project at one point or other during his time there. He knew that he'd been picked up near Karlsruhe, which meant he'd traveled the length of the Black Forest massif, a distance of one hundred or so kilometers, which would put the location of Anlage Elf at somewhere in that massive forest's southern quadrant.

Beyond that, only details emerged. One day he identified the collar patches of the SS soldiers at the installation: they were from III Waffen SS *Panzergrenadierdivision Totenkopf*, the Death's Head division, a group of men originally drawn from the pre-war concentration camp guard personnel that had since 1939 fought in Poland, France, Russia and was now thought to be in Hungary. Another day he identified the kind of automobile the mysterious Man of Oak had arrived in: a Mercedes-Benz twelve-cylinder limousine, thought to be issued only to *Amt* leaders, or department heads, in the SS bureaucracy. But as to the meaning or identity of this strange phantom, he had no idea. He did not even have much curiosity.

"He was a German. That's all. A German big shot," he said laconically in his oddly accented English.

Another day he correctly identified the STG-44 as the basic weapon of the *Totenkopf* complement. Another day he discussed the installation layout, fortifications and so forth. Another day he created to the best of his ability a word-picture of the unfortunate civilian called Hans the Kike, whose chemicals he'd tried to move.

Leets smiled at how far they'd come and how fast. From that first meeting in the hospital to now, no more than a week had passed. Yet a whole counter-espionage operation had been mounted. SWET effectively no longer existed; it had been given over entirely to the business of catching Repp . . . and he, Leets, would run the show, reporting only to Tony. He would have first priority in all matters of technical support: he could go anywhere anytime, spend any amount of money, as long as Tony didn't scream too loud, and Tony wouldn't scream at all. He had the highest security clearance. More people in this town knew of him than ever before, and he'd been asked to three parties. He had a car, though only Rog as driver. There was talk of a Majority. He knew he could get on the phone and call up anybody short of Ike; and maybe even Ike.

Yes, it was quite a lot.

But it was also very little.

"He can only get us so far. We are helpless until we find this place," Tony said.

But Leets pressed ahead. It was his hope that somewhere in the Jew's testimony a hidden clue would be uncovered, yielding up the secrets of Repp and his operation.

Black Forest? Then consult with botanists, hikers, foresters, geographers, vacationers. Look at recon photos. Check out library books—*Tramping the German Forests*, by Maj. H. W. O. Stovall (Ret.), D.F.C., Faber and Faber; *The Shadowy World of the Deciduous Forest*, by Dr. William Blinkall-Apney. And do not forget that trove of intelligence: Baedeker.

Man of Oak? Scan the British Intelligence files for German officers with wooden arms or legs or even jaws—it had happened to Freud, had it not? Check out reputations, rumors, absurd possibilities. Could a fellow walk stiffly? Could he be extremely orthodox? Very conservative? Slow-moving, losing his leaves, deep-rooted, dispensing acorns?

"It's rather ridiculous," Tony said. "It sounds like something out of one of your Red Indian movies."

Leets grunted. Man-of-Oak? Jesus Christ, he moaned in disgust.

And what about equipment?

Hitting twenty-five targets dead center from 400 meters in the dark? Impossible. Yet here was the crucial element that had convinced Tony to call upstairs and make noise. For in a mob of dead Jews he could easily see dead generals or dead ministers or dead kings.

But ballistics people said it was impossible. No man could shoot so well without being able to see. There must have been some kind of secret illumination. Radar? Unlikely, for radar, though still primitive, worked best in the air, where it could see only airplanes and space. There was some kind of sound business the Navy had—sonar, someone said. Perhaps the Germans had worked out a way to hear the targets. Supersensitive microphones.

"Maybe the guy can just see in the dark," Rog suggested.

"Thanks, Rog. You're a big help," Leets said.

But even if he could see, how could he hit? Four hundred meters was *a long way*. If he was going to hit at that range, he had to be putting out a high-velocity round. And when it sliced through the sound barrier, *krak*! Leets could himself remember. And he knew the guy was firing a very quick 7.92-millimeter round. Could they silence it? Sure, silence the gun, no problem; *but not the bullet*! The bullet made the noise.

How the hell were they doing it?

It terrified him.

Who was the target?

Now there was the big one. With the who, everything else would come unraveled. Leets's guesses went only to one con- clusion: it had to be a group. Else why would this Repp practice up on a group, and why would he use a weapon like the thirty-shot STG-44, as opposed to a nice five-shot Kar '98 rifle, the bolt-action, long-range instrument the Germans had been building in the millions since the last century?

Yet killing *anyone* would not seem to gain them much, except some hollow vengeance. Sure, kill Churchill, kill Stalin. But it wouldn't change the outcome of the war. Kill the two houses of Parliament, the Congress and the Senate, the Presidium and the Politburo: it wouldn't change a thing. Germany would be squashed at the same rate. The big shots still rode the rope.

Yet, goddamn it, not only were they going to kill someone, the SS was going to an immense effort, an effort that must have strained every resource in these desperate days, to kill a few more.

What could it matter? Millions were already dead, already wasted. Who did they hate enough to kill even as they were dying?

Who were they trying to reach out of the grave to get?

And that is where Shmuel's information left them. Except for one thing.

Leets was alone in the office, working late into the night. That day's work with the Jew had not gone well. He was beginning to balk. He did not seem to care for his new allies. He was a grim little mutt, grumpy, short of temper, looking absurd in new American clothes. He'd been returned to the hospital now, and Tony was off in conference and Rog was hitting balls against a wall and Leets sat there, nursing the ache in his leg amid crumpled-up balls of paper, books, junk, photos, maps, and tried not to think of Susan. He knew one thing that could drive Susan from his mind.

Leets opened the drawer and drew out a file. It was marked "REPP, first name ?, German SS officer, Le Paradis suspect," and though its contents were necessarily sketchy, it did contain one *bona fide* treasure. Leets opened it and there, staring back at him through lightless eyes, was this Repp. It was a blow-up of a 1936 newspaper photo: a long young face, not in any way extraordinary, hair dark and close-cropped, cheekbones high.

The Master Sniper, the Jew had called him.

Leets rationed himself in looking at the picture. He didn't want to stare it into banality, become overfamiliar with it. He wanted to feel a rush of breath every time he saw it, never take it for granted. To take this guy for granted, Leets knew, would be to make a big mistake.

They'd showed the picture to Shmuel.

He'd looked at it, given it back.

"Yes. It's him."

"Repp?"

"Yes. Younger, of course."

"We think he was involved in a war-crimes action against British prisoners in 1940 in France," explained Outhwaithe, who'd brought the file by. "A wounded survivor gave two names. Repp was one of them. A researcher then went through the British Museum's back files and came up with this. It's from the sporting-news section of *Illustrierter Beobachter*, the pre-war Nazi picture rag. It seems this young fellow was a member of the German small-bore rifle team. The survivor identified him from it. So we've a long-standing interest in Herr Repp."

"I hope you arrest him, or whatever," Shmuel had said. He had to be pressed into pursuing the topic of Repp, but finally said only, "A soldier. Rather calm man, quite in control of himself and others. I have no insights into him. Jews have never understood that sort. I can't begin to imagine what he's like, how his mind works, how he sees the world. He frightens me. Then. And now, in this room. He has no grief."

Though Shmuel had no interest in knowing Repp, that was now Leets's job. He stared hard at the photo. Its caption simply said, "Kadett Repp, one of our exemplary German sportsmen, has a fine future in shooting competitions."

Another day passed, another interrogation spun itself listlessly out. Leets felt especially sluggish, having spent so much time the night previous with the picture of the German. Another researcher had been dispatched at Tony's behest through the back issues of all German periodicals at the British Museum; perhaps something new would surface there. Whatever, that aspect had passed momentarily out of Leets's hands; before him now, instead, sat the Jew, looking even worse than usual. He had rallied in his first days among the Allies, bloated with bland food, treated with unctuous enthusiasm; perhaps he'd even been flattered. But as the time wore on, Leets felt they were losing him. Lately he'd been a clam, talking in grunts, groans. Leets had heard he sometimes had nightmares and would scream in the night—"*Ost! Ost!*" east, east; and from this the American concluded things had been rough for him. But what the hell, he'd made it, hadn't he? Leets hadn't been raised to appreciate what he took to be moodiness. He had no patience for a tragic view of life and when he himself got to feeling low, it was with an intense accompanying sense of self-loathing.

Anyway, not only was the Jew somewhat hostile, he was sick. With a cold, no less.

"You look pretty awful," said Rog, in a rare display of human sympathy, though on the subject of another man's misfortune he was hardly convincing.

"The English keep their rooms so chilly," the man said.

"Roger, stoke the heater," Leets said irritably, anxious to return to the matter at hand, which this day was another runaround on the topic of the Man of Oak.

Roger muttered something and moped over to the heater, giving it a rattle.

"A hundred and two in here," he said to nobody.

Shmuel sniffled again, emptied his sinuses through enflamed nostrils into a tissue, and tossed it into a wastebasket.

"I wish I had my coat. The German thing. They make them warm at least. The wind gets through this." He yanked on his American jacket.

"That old thing? Smelled like a chem lab," Roger said.

"Now," Leets said, "could there be some double meaning in this Oak business? A pun, a symbol, something out of Teutonic mythology—"

Leets halted.

"Hey," he said, turning rudely, "what did you mean, chem lab?"

"Uh." Roger looked up in surprise.

"I said, what did you mean—"

"I heard what you said. I meant, it smelled like a chem lab." It was as close as he could get. "I had a year of organic in high school, that's all."

"Where is it?"

"Um," Roger grunted. "It was just an old Kraut coat. How was I to know it was anything special? I uh . . . I threw it out."

"Oh, Jesus," said Leets. "Where?"

"Hey, Captain, it was just this crappy old—"

"Where, Sergeant, *where?*"

Leets usually didn't use that tone with him, and Rog didn't like it a bit.

"In the can, for Christ's sake. Behind the hospital. After we got him his new clothes. I mean I—"

"All right," said Leets, trying to remain calm. "When?"

"About a week ago."

"Oh, hell." He tried to think. "We've got to get that thing back." And he picked up the phone and began to search for whoever was in charge of garbage pickup from American installations in London.

The coat was found in a pit near St. Saviour's Dock on the far side of the Thames from the Tower of London. It was found by Roger and it *did* smell—of paint, toast, used rubbers, burnt papers, paste, rust, oil, wood shavings and a dozen other substances with which it had lain intimately.

"And lead sulfide," Leets said, reading the report from the OSS Research and Development office the next day.

"What the hell is that?" Roger wanted to know. Shmuel did not appear to care.

"It's a stuff out of which infrared components are built. It's how they could see, how Repp could see. I find out now we're working hard on it in ultra secrecy, and the English as well. But this would tend to suggest the Germans are at the head of the class. They've got a field model ready, which means they're years ahead of us. See, the thing converts heat energy to light energy: *it sees heat.* A man is a certain temperature. Repp's gadget was set in that range. He could see the heat and shoot into it. He could see them all. Except—" he paused—"for him."

He turned to Shmuel.

"You were right," he said. "God did not save you. It was no miracle at all. The stuff absorbs heat: that's why it's photo-conductive. And that's why it's such a great insulator. It's why the thing kept you so warm, got you through the Schwarzwald. And why Repp couldn't see you. You were just enough different in temperature from the others. You were invisible."

Shmuel did not appear to care. "I knew God had other worries that night," he said.

"But the next time he shoots," Leets said, "the guys on the other side of the scope won't be so lucky."

X

Vollmerhausen is visibly nervous, Repp noticed with irritation. Now why should that be? It won't be his neck on the line out there, it'll be mine.

It was still light enough to smoke, a pleasant twilight, mid-April. Repp lit one of his Siberias, shaggy Ivan cigarettes, loosely packed, twigs in them, and they sometimes popped when they burned, but it was a habit he'd picked up in the Demyansk encirclement.

"Smoke, Herr Ingenieur-Doktor?" he inquired.

"No. No. Never have. Thanks."

"Certainly. The night will come soon."

"Are you sure it's safe here? I mean, what if—"

"Hard heart, Herr Ingenieur-Doktor, hard heart. All sorts of things can happen, and usually do. But not here, not tonight. There'll only be a patrol, not a full attack. Not this late. These Americans are in no hurry to die."

He smiled, looked through the glassless farm window at the tidy fields that offered no suggestion of war.

"But we are surrounded," said Vollmerhausen. It was true. American elements were on all sides of them, though not aggressive. They were near the town of Alfeld, on the Swabian plain, in a last pocket of resistance.

"We got in, didn't we? We'll get back to our quiet little corner, don't worry." He chuckled.

An SS sergeant, in camouflage tunic, carrying an MP-40, came through the door.

"Herr Obersturmbannführer," he said in great breathless respect, "Captain Weber sent me. The ambush team will be moving out in fifteen minutes."

"Ah. Thank you, Sergeant," said Repp affably. "Well," turning to the engineer, "time to go, eh?"

But Vollmerhausen just stood there, peering through the window into the twilight. His face was drawn and he seemed colorless. The man had never been in a combat zone before.

Repp hoisted the electro-optical pack onto his back, struggling under the weight, and got the harness buckled. Vollmerhausen made no move to help. Repp lifted the rifle itself off its bipod—it rested on the table—and stepped into the sling, which had been rigged to take most of the weight, made an adjustment here and there and declared himself ready. He wore both pieces of camouflage gear tonight, the baggy tiger trousers along with the tunic, and the standard infantry harness with webbed belt and six canvas magazine pouches and, naturally, his squashed cap with the death's-head.

"Care to come?" he asked lightly.

"Thanks, no," said Vollmerhausen, uneasy at the jest, "it's so damned cold." He swallowed, clapped his hands around himself in pantomimed shiver.

"Cold? It's in the forties. The tropics. This is spring. See you soon. Hope your gadget works."

"Remember, Herr Obersturmbannführer, you've only got three minutes—"

"—in the on-phase. I remember. I shall make the most of them," Repp replied.

Repp left the farmhouse and under his heavy load walked stiffly to a copse of trees where the others had gathered. Frankly, he felt ridiculous in this outlandish rig, the bulky box strapped to his back, the rifle linked to it by wire hose, the sighting apparatus itself bulky and absurd on top of the weapon, which itself was exaggerated with the extended magazine, the altered pistol grip and the bipod. But he knew they wouldn't smirk at him.

Tonight it was Captain Weber's show. It was his sector anyway, he knew the American patrol patterns. Repp was along merely to shoot, as if on safari.

"Sir," said Weber. "*Heil Hitler!*"

"*Heil, Schutzstaffel,*" responded Repp, tossing up a flamboyantly casual salute. The young men of XII *Panzergrenadierdivision* "Hitlerjugend" jostled with respect, though the circumstances seemed to prevent more elaborate courtesies. This pleased Repp. He'd never been much for ceremony.

"Ah, Weber, hello. Boys," nodding to them, common touch, nice, they could talk about it after the war.

"Sir," one of the worshipers said, "that damned thing looks heavy. Do you need a man—"

It was heavy. Even with Vollmerhausen's last stroke of genius, the one he'd been laboring on like a maniac these last few days, Vampir, the whole system, gun, rack, scope, light source, weighed in at over forty kilos, 41.2, to be exact, still 1.2 kilos over, but closer to the specs than Repp ever thought they'd get.

"Thanks, but no. That's part of the test, you see, to see how well a fellow can do with one of these on his back. Even an old gent like me."

Repp was thirty-one, but the others were younger; they laughed.

Repp grinned in the laughter: he liked to make them happy. After it had died, he said, "After you, Captain."

There was a last-second ritual of equipment checks to be performed, MP-40 bolts dropped from safe into engagement, feeder tabs locked into the machine gun, harnesses shifted, helmet straps tightened; then, Weber leading, Repp somewhere in the center, they filed out, crouched low, into the fields.

Vollmerhausen watched them go, silent line of the ambush team edging cautiously into the dark. He wondered how long he'd have to wait until Repp returned with the happy news that it had gone well and they could leave. Hours probably. It had already been a terrible day; first the terrifying flight in from Anlage Elf in the Stork, bobbing and skimming, over the trees. Then the long time among the soldiers, the desultory shellings, and the worry about the weather.

Would the sun hold till twilight?

If it didn't they'd have to stay another day. And another. And another. . . .

But it had held.

"There, see: your prayers have been answered, Herr Ingenieur-Doktor," Repp had chided him.

Vollmerhausen smiled weakly. Yes, he had prayed.

Displaying a dexterity that might have astounded his many detractors, Hans the Kike had prepared Vampir for its field test. He quickly mounted the scope and the energy conversion unit with its parabola-shaped infrared lamp to the modified STG receiver, using a special wrench and screwdriver. He locked in the power line and checked the connections. Intact. He opened the box and gave it a quick rundown, tracing the complex circuitry for faulty wiring, loose connections, foreign objects.

"Best hurry," Repp said, leaning intently over the engineer's shoulder, watching and recording his rundown, "we're losing it."

Vollmerhausen explained for what must have been the thousandth time, "The later we charge, the later it lasts."

Finally, he was finished. Sun remained, in traces: not a fiery noontime's blaze—of furnaces or battles—but a fleeting late-afternoon's version, pale and low and thin, but enough.

"It's not the heat, it's the light," he pointed out.

Vollmerhausen yanked a metal slide off a thick metal disk spot-welded crudely to the top of the cathode chamber, revealing a glass face, opaque and dense. Its facets sparkled in the sunlight.

"Fifteen minutes is all we need; that gives us eight hours of potency for an on-phase of three minutes," he said, as if he were convincing himself.

The problem with infrared rays, Vollmerhausen had tried to explain to Repp, was that they were lower in energy than visible light—how then could they be made to emit light rays of a higher value, so that images might be identified and, in this case, fired upon? Dr. Kutzcher had found a part of the answer at the University of Berlin those many years ago: by feeding high-tension electricity across a cathode tube, he'd caused the desired rise in energy level, producing the requisite visibility. But Vollmerhausen, improvising desperately at Anlage, had not the latitude of Kutzcher. His problem was narrowly military—he was limited by weight, the amount a man could carry efficiently on his back over rough terrain. When all the skimming and paring and snipping was done, he found himself a full ten kilos distant from that optimum weight; no further reduction was possible without radically compromising Vampir's performance. And the mass of the unbudgeable ten kilos lay in the battery pack and its heavy shielding, the source of the high-tension electricity.

His stroke of inspiration—it took the form of the blisterlike dial welded to the scope, no, not pretty at all—was a solar unit. No less a power than the sun itself would provide Vampir with its energy; not an inexhaustible supply, but enough for a few minutes of artificial, invisible daylight at high midnight. Vollmerhausen could not totally abandon a battery, of course; one was still needed to provide juice for the cathode ray tube, but not nearly so much juice, for the phosphors in the chamber had been selected for their special property to absorb energy from sunlight and then, when bombarded by infrared rays, to release it. Thus instead of a 10-kilo 30-volt battery, Vampir could make do with a 1.3-kilo 3-volt battery, a net savings of 8.7 kilos while maintaining the intensity and brilliance of image within the specified limits. But not for long:

for the phosphors had a very brief life in their charged state, and once exposed to the infrared lost their powers quickly. But for a good three minutes, Repp could peer through the eyepiece and there, wobbling greenly before him, magnified tenfold by a specially ground Opticotechna lens, undulated targets, visible, distinct, available, 400 meters out.

Vollmerhausen had checked his watch, snapped the face of the solar disk closed.

"There. It's done. You've got your power now, until midnight."

"Just like a fairy tale," Repp had said merrily.

"And you've got the special ammunition?"

"Of course, of course," and he had clapped the magazine pouch on his belt.

Now, in the farmhouse, Vollmerhausen looked out into a darkness that was total. Repp was somewhere out there, in his element. The night belonged to him.

I gave it to him, Vollmerhausen thought.

Repp slid into position behind the rifle, which rested on its bipod. His shoulders and arms ached, and the strap had cut deeply across his collarbone. The damned thing *was* heavy, and he'd come but three or four kilometers, not the twenty-three kilometers he'd be traveling the day of Nibelungen. He felt his breath coming unevenly, in sobs and gasps, and fought to control it. Calm was the sniper's great ally, you had to will yourself into a serenity, a wholeness of spirit and task. He tried hard to relax.

Four hundred meters beyond him the tidy fields fell away into a stream bed, where a stand of trees and thicker vegetation grew, and here the land delivered up a kind of fold, a natural funnel that men moving over unfamiliar territory, scared probably, wishing themselves elsewhere, would be surely drawn to.

"There, Herr Obersturmbannführer, do you see it?" asked Weber, crouching beside him in the darkness.

"Yes. Fine."

"Four nights out of five they come through there."

"Fine."

Weber was nervous in the great man's presence, talked too much.

"We could move closer."

"I make it four hundred meters, about right."

"Now we've flares if you—"

"Captain, no flares."

"I've the machine-gun team over on the right for suppressing fire if you need it, and my squad leader, a sound man, is on the left with the rest of the patrol."

"I can see you learned your trade in the East."

"Yes, sir." The young captain's face, like Repp's own, was dabbed with oily combat paint. His eyes shone whitely in the starlight.

"They usually come about eleven, a few hours off. They think this is the great weakness in our lines. We've let them through."

"Tomorrow they'll stay away!" Repp laughed. "Now tell your fellows to hold still. No firing. My operation, all right?"

"Yes, sir." He was gone.

Good, so much the better. Repp liked to spend these moments alone, if possible. He considered them very much his own minutes, a time for clearing the head and loosening the muscles and indulging in a dozen semiconscious eccentricities that got him feeling in touch with the rifle and his targets and himself.

Repp lay very still and warm, feeling the wind, the rifle against his hands, studying the dark landscape before him. He felt rather good, at the same time remembering that things had not always been so pleasant. A frozen February's memory floated up before him, a desperate month of a desperate year, '42.

Totenkopfdivision had been pushed into a few square miles of a pulverized city named Demyansk, in the Valdai Hills between Lake Ilmen and Lake Seliger in northern Russia—the Winter War, they later called it. In the city, all rudiments of military organization had broken down: the battle had become one huge alley fight, a small-unit action repeated on a vast scale, as groups of men stalked each other through the ruins. Young Repp, a *Hauptsturmführer*, as the Waffen SS designated its captains, was the champion stalker. With his Mannlicher-Schoenauer 6.5-millimeter mounting the 10× Unertl scope, he wandered from gunfight to gunfight, dropping five, ten, fifteen men at a throw. He was a brilliant shot, and about to become famous.

The morning of the twenty-third found him squatting wearily in the ruins of a factory, the Red Tractor Plant, sipping tepid ersatz, listening to the soldiers around him grouse. He didn't blame them. The night had been one long fruitless countersniper operation: the Popovs were curiously silent. He was tired, tired down to his fingers; his eyes were swollen and they ached. As he examined the thin swirl of liquid in the tin cup, it was not hard for him to imagine other places he'd rather be.

Yawning, he glanced around the interior of the factory, a maze of wreckage, twisted girders, heaps of brick, a skeletal outline showing against a gray sky that promised more snow; the damned stuff had fallen again yesterday, must be six feet of it now, and all about the factory fresh white piles of it gleamed brightly against the blackened walls, giving the place a strange purity. It was cold, below zero; but Repp was past caring of cold. He'd gotten used to it. He wanted sleep, that was all.

The firing opened gradually. Shots always rattled around the city as patrols bumped into each other in alleyways; one grew accustomed and did not even hear them, or the explosions either, but as the intensity seemed to mount after several minutes, when contact might ordinarily be measured in seconds, some of the men around him perked up out of their whiny conversations.

"Ivan's knocking again," someone said.

"Shit. The bastards. Don't they sleep?"

"Don't get excited," someone cautioned, "probably some kid with an automatic."

"That's more than one automatic," another said. And indeed it was, Repp could tell too, for the firing then churned like a thunderstorm.

"All right, people," said a calm sergeant, "let's cut the shit and wait for the officers." He hadn't seen Repp, who continued to lie there.

After several minutes a lieutenant came in, fast, looked about for the sergeant.

"Let's get them out, huh? A big one, I'm afraid," he said laconically. Then he saw Repp, was taken aback by another officer.

"Oh? Say, what the hell, who the hell are—"

"Repp," said Repp. "Damn! I needed sleep bad. How many? Big, you say."

"It's not clear yet. Too much smoke and dust at the end of Groski Prospekt. But it sounds big."

"All right," said Repp, "these are your boys, you know what to do."

"Yes, sir."

Repp picked himself up wearily. He flicked the ersatz out and paused for a moment. Men scurried by, clapping helmets on, drawing parkas tighter, throwing Kar '98 bolts, rushing into the street. Repp checked the pocket of his snow smock, then tightened it. He was loaded with ammo, not having fired a round the night before. The Mannlicher-Schoenauer fired from a clever spool magazine, almost like the cylinder of a revolver, and Repp had a pouchful of the things.

He stepped into the street finally, with the rifle. Outside, the glare was fierce and the panic unleashed. He felt at storm center. At the end of Groski Prospekt an armored car blazed. Small-arms fire kicked up spurts of dust and snow along the pavement. The noise was ugly, careening. SS *Panzergrenadiers* came racing down the corridor from the wall of smoke, one of them dropping when a shot took him. As they fled by, Repp snagged one.

"No use. No use. They've broken through. Hundreds, thousands, oh, Christ, only a block—"

A blast drowned him out and a wall went down nearby, filling the air with smoke and dust. The panicked man squirmed away and disappeared. Repp saw the young lieutenant placing his men in the wreckage along the street. They all looked scared but somehow resigned. *Totenkopfdivision* had a reputation for staying put. Repp knew that reputation was to be tested again. Smoke shielded the end of the street from his eyes. Nothing down there but haze.

"Herr Repp," someone yelled, for he already had a reputation, "kill a batch of the fuckers for us, it looks like we won't be around to do it ourselves."

Repp laughed. Now that was a man with spirit. "Kill them yourself, sonny. I'm off duty."

More laughter.

Repp turned, headed back into the factory. He was tired of Ivans and wreckage and filth from blown-up sewers and rats the size of cats that prowled the ruins and crawled across your belly while you slept and he never expected to survive anyway, so why not go out today? It was as good as any day. A stairway left freakishly standing in one corner of the room caught his eye. He followed it up through the deserted upper floors of the factory. He heard men crashing in below. *Totenkopf* people, falling back on the factory. So that was it then, the Red Tractor Plant. He was twenty-eight years old and he'd never be another day older and he'd spend his last one here in a place where Bolshevik peasants built tractors and, more recently, tanks. Not the end he'd have picked, but as numbness settled over him, he began to feel it wouldn't be so bad at all. He was in a hurry to be done.

At the top he found himself in a clock tower of some kind, shot out, of course, nothing up there but snow and old timbers, bricks, half a wall blown away, other gaps from rogue artillery rounds. Yet one large hole opened up a marvelous view of the Groski Prospekt—a canyon of ragged walls buried in smoke. Even as he scanned this landscape of devastation, it seemed to come alive before him. He could see them, swarming now, Popovs, in those white snowsuits, domed brown helmets, carrying submachine guns.

Repp delicately brought the rifle to his shoulder and braced it on a ledge of brick. The scope yielded a Russian, scurrying ratlike from obstacle to obstacle. He lifted his head warily and flicked his eyes about and Repp shot him in the throat, a spew of crimson foaming down across his front in the split second before he dropped. The man was about 400 meters out. Repp tossed the bolt—a butter-knife handle, not knobby like the Kar '98—through the Mann-licher's split bridge, keeping his eye pinned against the cup of the absurd Unertl ten-power scope, which threw up images big and clear as a Berlin cinema. Its reticule was three converging lines, from left, right and bottom, which almost but did not quite meet, creating a tiny circle of space. Repp's trick was to keep the circle filled; he laid it now against another Red, an officer. He killed him.

He was shooting faster, there seemed to be so many of them. He was wedged into the bricks of the tower, rather comfortably, and at each shot, the rifle reported sharply with a slight jar, not like the bone-bruising buck of the Kar '98, but gentle and dry. When he hit them, they slid into the rubble, stained but not shattered. A 6.5-millimeter killed with velocity, not impact; it drilled them and, failing deflection at bone or spine, flew on. Repp was even convinced they felt no pain from the way they relaxed. He didn't even have to move the rifle much, he could just leave it where it was, they were swarming so thickly. He'd fired five magazines now, twenty-five rounds. He'd killed twenty-five men. Some looked stupefied when he took them; others angry; still others oblivious. Repp shot for the chest. He took no chances. Nothing fancy.

They had spotted him of course. Their bullets thunked and cracked around him, chipping at the bricks, filling the air with fine dust or snow, but he felt magical. He kept dropping them. The white bodies were piling up.

Behind him now sprang a noise, and Repp whirled. A boy crouched at the head of the stairs with a pack.

"Your kit, sir. You left it down below."

"Ah." Yes, someone'd thought to bring it to him. It was packed with ammunition, six more boxes, in each fifty specially loaded rounds, 180 grains behind a nickle-tip slug. Berdan primers—the best—with twin flash holes.

"Can you load those for me? It works same as with your rifle, off the charger," Repp said mildly as a Degtyarev tracer winked through and buried itself in the wall. He pointed to the litter of empty spool magazines lying amid spent shells at his boots. "But stay low, those fellows are really angry now."

Repp fired all that morning. The Russian attack had broken down, bottled up at Groski Prospekt. He'd killed all their officers and was quite sure that had been a colonel he'd put down just an instant ago. He thought he'd killed almost a hundred. Nineteen magazines, and three rounds left in this one; he'd killed, so far, ninety-eight men in just over two hours. The rifle had grown hot, and he'd stopped once or twice to squirt a drop or so of oil down its barrel. In one two-minute period, he ran his ramrod with patch vigorously in the barrel and the patch came up black with gunk. The boy crouched at his feet, and every time an empty spool dropped out, he picked it up and carefully threaded the brass cartridges in.

The Popovs were now coming from other directions; evidently, they'd sent flanking parties around. But these men ran into heavy fire from down below, and those that survived, Repp took. Still, the volume of fire against the Red Tractor Plant was building; Repp could sense the battle rising again in pitch. These things had their melodies too, and he fancied he could hear it.

The grimy lieutenant from that morning appeared in the stairwell.

"You still alive?" Repp asked.

But the fellow was in no mood for Repp's jokes. "They're breaking through. We haven't the firepower to hold them off much longer. They're already in a wing of the factory. Come on, get out, Repp. There's still a chance to make it out on foot."

"Thanks, old man, think I'll stay," Repp said merrily. He felt *schussfest*, bulletproof, but with deeper resonations in the German, connoting magic, a charmed state.

"Repp, there's nothing here but death."

"Go on yourself," said Repp. "I'm having too much fun to leave."

He was hitting at longer ranges now; through the drifting pall of smoke he made out small figures several blocks away. Magnified tenfold by the Unertl, two Russian officers conferred in a doorway over a map. The scene was astonishingly intimate, he could almost see the hair in their ears. Repp took one through the heart and the other, who turned away when his comrade was hit, as if in hiding his eyes he was protecting himself, through the neck.

Repp killed a sniper seven blocks away.

In another street Repp took the driver of a truck, splattering the windscreen into a galaxy of fractures. The vehicle bumped aimlessly against a rubble pile and men spilled out and scrambled for cover. Of seven he took three.

Down below, grenades detonated in a cluster, machine pistols ripped in a closed space which caught and multiplied their noise.

"I think they're in the building," Repp said.

"I've loaded all the rounds left in the magazines now," the trooper said. "Nine of them. That's forty-five more bullets."

"You'd best be getting on then. And thanks."

The boy blushed sheepishly. Maybe eighteen or nineteen, handsome, thin face.

"If I see you afterward, I'll write a nice note to your officer," Repp said, an absurdly civil moment in the heat of a great modern battle. Bullets were banging into the tower from all angles now, rattling and popping. The boy raced down the stairs.

At the end of Groski Prospekt, the Ivans were organizing for another push before nightfall. Repp killed one who stupidly peeked out from behind the smoldering armored car. The rifle was hot as a stove and he had to be careful to keep his fingers off the metal of the barrel. He had touched it once and could feel a blister on his skin. But the rifle held to the true; those Austrians really could build them. It was from the Steyr works near Vienna, double trigger, scrollwork in the metal, something from the old Empire, hunting schlosses in the Tyrolean foothills, and woodsmen in green lederhosen and high socks who'd take you to the best bucks in the forest.

Blobs of light floated up to smash him. Tracers uncoiled like flung ropes, drifting lazily. Some rounds trailed tendrils of smoke. The bullets went into the brick with an odd sound, a kind of clang. He knew it was a matter of time and that his survival this far, with every Russian gun in the city banging away, was a kind of statistical incredibility that was bound to end shortly. Did it matter? Perhaps this moment of pure sniper war was worth his life. He'd been able to hit, hit, hit for most of the day now, over three hundred times, from clear, protected shooting, four streets like channels to fire down, plenty of ammunition, a boy to load spools for him, targets everywhere, massing in the streets, crawling through the ruins, edging up the gutters, but if he could see them he could take them.

Repp killed a man with a flamethrower on his back.

Forty-four bullets.

By thirty-six, it had become clear that the men below had either fallen back or been killed. He heard a lot of scuffling around below. The Russians must have crept through the sewers to get in; they certainly hadn't come down the street.

Twenty-seven.

Just a second before, someone at the foot of the stairs had emptied a seventy-one-round drum upward. Repp happened to be shielded, he was standing in a recess in the brick wall, but the slatted floor of the tower was ripped almost to slivers as the slugs jumped through it. Wood dust flew in the air. Repp had a grenade. He pulled the lanyard out the handle and tossed the thing into the stairwell, heard it bouncing down the steps. He was back on the scope when the blast and the screams came.

Eighteen.

Tanks. He saw one scuttle through a gap between buildings several blocks away. Why didn't they think of that earlier, save themselves trouble and people? Then he realized the Stalins had the same trouble the Panzers had had negotiating the wreckage-jammed streets. To get this far into the ruins at all, Russian engineers must have been working frantically, blowing a path through to him.

Eleven.

Repp heard voices below. They were trying to be silent but a stair gave. He stepped back, took out his P-38 and leaned into the stairwell. He killed them all.

Five.

One magazine. The first tank came into view, lurching from around the corner at the Groski intersection. Yes, hello. Big fellow, aren't you? A few soldiers crept behind it. Repp, very calm and steady, dropped one, missed one. He saw a man in a window, shot him, high in the throat. One of the men he'd dropped behind the tank attempted to crawl into cover. Repp finished him.

One.

The turret was revolving. Not a Stalin at all, a KV-1 with a 76-millimeter. He fixed with fascination on the monster, watching as the mouth of the gun lazed over, seeming almost to open wider as it drew toward him. They certainly were taking their time lining up the shot. The tank paused, gun set just right. Repp would have liked at least to get rid of his last bullet. He didn't feel particularly bad about all this. The hatch popped on the tank, someone inside wanted a better look, and the lid rose maybe an inch or two. Repp took him, center forehead, last bullet.

There was nothing to do. He set the rifle down. This was an execution. As if by signal, Russian troops began to file down Groski Prospekt. Repp, firing since 0930, checked his watch. 1650. An eight-hour day, and not a bad one. He chalked up the score in the seconds left him. Three hundred and fifty rounds he had fired, couldn't have missed more than a few times. Make it ten, just to be fair. That was 340 men. Then the three on the stairway with the pistol. Perhaps two more in the grenade blast. Three hundred and forty-five kills, 345. Three hundred and fo—.

The shell went into the tower forty feet below Repp. The Russians had gotten fancy, they wanted to bring the tower down with Repp inside it, poetic justice or some such melodramatic conceit. The universe tilted as the tower folded. The line of the horizon broke askew and dust rose chokingly. Repp grabbed something as gravity accelerated the drop.

The tower toppled thunderously into Groski Prospekt in a storm of dust and snow. But its top caught on the roof of the building across the way and was sheared neatly off. Repp found himself in a capsule of broken brick deposited there, untouched, baffled. It was as if he'd walked away from a plane crash.

He walked across the flat roof of the building, waiting to get nailed. Artillery started up but the shells landed beyond him. There was smoke everywhere but he was alone. Across the roof, a shell had blown open a hole. He looked down into almost a museum specimen of the Soviet Worker's apartment, and leapt down into it. He opened the door and headed down a dark hallway. Stairs. He climbed down them, and left through a front door. There were no Russians anywhere, though far off, he could make out small figures. Taking no chances, he headed down an alley.

That night he had schnapps with a general.

"The world," the sentimental old man intoned, "will know you now." Dr. Goebbels stood ready to make this dream come true.

"Sir," somebody whispered.

"I see them," said Repp.

Scope on. The screen lights. He saw the first one, a wobbling man-shaped blotch of light, against green darkness. Then another, behind him, and still another.

Germs, Repp thought. They are germs, bacilli, disease. They are filth.

He drew back the bolt and squirmed the black cross of Vampir's reticule against the first of the shapes.

"Filth," he repeated.

He took them.

XI

"Vampir did quite well, I thought," said Repp. He abstractedly counted off the reasons for his pleasure, each to a finger. "No sight picture breakup, good distinct images, weight not a factor. In all, easy shooting."

Vollmerhausen was astonished. He certainly wasn't expecting praise. Though he knew the shooting had gone well, for he'd heard two enlisted men chattering excitedly over it.

But Repp was not yet finished. "In fact," he elaborated, "you've performed extraordinarily well under great pressure. I wish it were possible to arrange for some kind of official recognition. But at least accept my congratulations." He was toying with the blackened metal cube Vollmerhausen had noticed earlier, a charm or something. "A great miracle has happened here." He smiled.

"I—I am honored," stuttered Hans the Kike. They were back at Anlage Elf, in the research facility, safe in the Schwarzwald after another harrowing flight.

"But then sometimes the most important assignments are those nobody ever knows about, eh?" said Repp.

Vollmerhausen felt this was a strange comment for a famous man, but merely nodded, for he was still stunned at Repp's sudden burst of enthusiasm. And a sudden, still-resentful part of him wished that the asshead Schaeffer were here to listen to *Der Meisterschütze* himself heap on the praise. Yet, he acknowledged, he deserved it. Vampir represented an astonishing feat in so small a time, under such desperate pressure. Though even now it was hard to believe and take real pleasure in: *he'd done it.*

Still, certain details and refinements remained to be mastered, as well as some after-mission checks and some maintenance, and it was this problem he now addressed, aware at the same time how modest he must have seemed. "May I ask, Herr Obersturmbannführer, how soon you expect to go operational? And what preparations will be necessary on my part?"

"Of course," Repp said smartly. "Certain aspects of the mission remain problematical. I've got to wait on intelligence reports: target confirmations, strategic developments, political considerations. I would say another week. Perhaps even more: a delicate job. It depends on factors even I can't control."

"I see," said Vollmerhausen.

"I should tell you two things further. The weapon and I will leave separately. Vampir will be taken out of here by another team. They are responsible for delivery to target area. Good people, I've been assured."

"Yes, sir."

"So you'll have to prepare a travel kit. Boxes, a trunk, I don't know. Everything should be lashed down and protected against jolts. It needn't be fancy. After what you've handled, I shouldn't think it would be a problem."

"Not at all."

"Now, secondly—look, relax. You look so stiff."

It was true. Though seated, Vollmerhausen had assumed the posture of a Prussian *Kadett*.

"I've noticed that I make people nervous," Repp said philosophically. "Why, I wonder? I'm no secret policeman. Just a soldier."

Vollmerhausen forced himself to relax.

"Smoke, if you care to."

"I don't."

"No, that's right. I think I will." He drew and lit one of the Russian things. He certainly was chipper this morning, all gaudy in his camouflages. "Now, may I be frank with you?" He toyed again with the black cube Vollmerhausen had noticed earlier.

"Germany is going to lose the war. And soon too. It's the third week in April now; certainly it'll all be over by the middle of May. You're not one of those fools who thinks victory is still possible. Go ahead, speak out."

Again, Repp had astonished him. He realized it showed on his face and hurriedly snapped his mouth shut.

"Yes, I suppose. Deep down. We all know," Vollmerhausen confirmed.

"Of course. It's quite obvious. They know in Berlin too, the smart ones. You're a practical man, a realist, that's why we chose you. But I tell you this because of the following: Operation Nibelungen proceeds. No matter what happens in Berlin. No matter that English commandos and American tanks are inside the wire here. In fact especially in those cases. You weren't in Russia?"

"No, I—"

"No matter. That's where the real war is. This business here with the Americans and the British, just a sideshow. Now, in Russia, four million fell. The figure is almost too vast to be believed. That's sacrifice on a scale the world's never seen before. That's why the mission will go on. It's all that generation will ever have. No statues, no monuments, no proud chapters in history books. Others will write the history; we will be its villains. Think of it, Vollmerhausen! Repp, a villain! Incredible, isn't it?"

He looked directly at the engineer.

"Unbelievable," said the engineer.

Vollmerhausen realized Repp was not giving a speech. He had none of the orator's gifts and little of his zeal; he spoke tiredly, laconically, only in facts, as if an engineer himself, reading off a blueprint.

Another thought occurred to Vollmerhausen: the man is quite insane. He is out of his mind. It's all over, still he talks of monuments, of consecrations. It's not survival for him, as it is for me. There is no after-the-war for Repp; for Repp, there'll always be a war. If not in a shell hole or on a front line, then in a park somewhere, at a pleasant crossroads, in a barn or an office building.

"Y-yes, unbelievable," Vollmerhausen repeated nervously, for he was just beginning to realize how dangerous Repp was.

XII

"They're calling him, even here, right afterward, *der Meister-schütze*, not, I say again, not *der Scharfschütze*, the technical German for sniper. Which of you brilliant Americans will now explain the significance of this?"

Tony held in hand his scoop of the week: the March 5, 1942, issue of *Das Schwarze Korps*, the SS picture magazine, which the burrower who'd been sent to the British Museum's collection of back-issue German periodicals had uncovered. Its lead story was Repp at Demyansk.

Leets cleared his throat.

"*Meisterschütze*: master shot. Literally."

"Ah, see, chum, you haven't *entered* it. You don't *feel* it. However can you hope to track a man whose nickname you cannot fathom?"

"I wasn't finished, goddamn it," Leets snarled.

"*Meisterschütze*, yes, master shot, and since the context is clearly military, one may indeed say, as did the Jew, master sniper. A nice turn of phrase: the man has some talent. He is a writer though, is he not? At any rate, it's a higher form of rhetoric, more formal, playing on the long Germanic tradition of guilds, apprentices and journeymen. It's more, shall we say, *resonant*."

His cold smile drove the heat from the room. Clever bastard: a Bloomsbury wag, only-my-genius-to-declare amusement smug on his face.

But the lesson was unfinished.

"It's not hard to see why they made such a hero of him, *is* it?"

"It's part of another war," Leets explained. He was ready for this one. "Waffen SS against the Wehrmacht. Nazis against the old boys, the Prussians who run the army. Repp is perfect. No aristo, just a country boy who can kill anything he can see. The prize is first place in line—Hitler's line—for the new-model Panzers coming out of the shops, the Tigers. They were in the market for heroes, right?"

"Right, indeed," admitted Tony.

"But more to the point: from this we can see how important Repp will be to the SS. That is to say, from here on in, he's not just one of them. He *is* them. That is to say, he becomes their official instrument, the embodiment of their will. He's—" he struggled for language in which to make this concept felt, "—he's an idea."

Tony scowled. "You're talking like a don. Dons don't win wars."

"You've got to see in this a higher reality. A symbolic reality." Leets himself wasn't sure what he was saying. A voice from inside was doing the talking; somewhere a part of his mind had made a leap, a breakthrough. "When we crack it, I can guarantee you this: it will be pure Nazi, pure SS. Their philosophy, given flesh, set to walking."

"Wow, Frankenstein," called Roger, across the room.

"You Americans have too much imagination for anybody's good. You go to too many films."

But Tony had more.

"I have found," he announced, "the Man of Oak."

Leets turned. He could not read the Englishman's face. It was impassive, imperial.

"Who?" Leets demanded.

"It occurs to me that we knew all along. We knew, did we not, that our phantom WVHA has an address in eastern Berlin. A suburb called Lichtenfelde; but the place itself goes by an older, more traditional name. It is called Unter den Eichen."

He paused, allowing the information its impact.

"Translate it literally," he advised some seconds later when he saw the befuddlement on Leets's face.

Leets worked it out into English.

" 'Under the Oaks,' " he said.

"Yes."

"Goddamn it!," Leets said.

"Yes. And this Jewish chap presumably heard reference to a man from 'Under the Oaks,' as one would say 'A Man from Washington,' or 'A Man from London,' meaning a man of authority. But his knowledge of the language was imperfect, since his Yiddish only allowed him access to the most basic German. He garbled it, perhaps inflated it somewhat for rhetorical effect. Thus, Man of Oak, as Shmuel overheard him say."

"Goddamn it," Leets said again. "It must have been some officer, some supervisor. But it tells us nothing."

"No, nothing: Another disappointment. It tells us only what we know."

It was true. During the hot week with Shmuel, information had seemed to surge in on them. There had been so much to *do*. A powerful illusion of progress made itself felt. But in the very act of mounting, it had peaked. Leets saw this rather sooner than the others; now Tony had caught on: that, though all kinds of context and background were being assembled, the real nut of the problem had not yet been cracked. They knew Repp, and of his rifle, rudimentary facts, but compelling nonetheless. But they had no idea of more crucial matters. Who would the German shoot? When? Why?

"Your idea that somewhere in his testimony was a clue has gone up in smoke," Tony said.

"We've got to find Anlage Elf, that's all. Could we increase air recon of that area? Aren't there French armored units closing in? Could they be directed to penetrate the forest, in hopes of—"

"No. Of course not. It's huge, over and over we've remarked on how huge it is."

"Goddamn it. We need something. A break."

It arrived the next morning.

> IN REF JAATIC REQUEST 11 MAR 45 THIS HQ
> ADVISES 3D SQD 2ND BN 45 INF DIV TOOK HEAVY
> CASUALTIES ON RECON PATROL 15 APRIL APPX
> 2200 HRS VICINITY ALFELD INTELL SUGGEST 11
> ROUNDS 11 HITS IN DARK AND SILENCE ARMY
> GRP G-2 CONFIRMS WAFFEN SS UNIT HITLER-
> JUGEND THIS AREA PLS ADVISE
>
> RYAN
> Maj Inf
> 2nd Bn G-2

"Well," said Leets, ending the silence, "the fucking thing's operational. They've worked out the bugs."

"Rather," said Tony.

"They can go anytime they want."

Leets and Outhwaithe flew into the 45th Division's sector early the next morning, landing in a Piper Cub not far from Alfeld, the divisional headquarters. Ryan's shop, though, was farther toward the front. And here there was a front, in the classical sense: two armies facing each other warily across a bleak, crater-scaped gulf of no-man's land, after the configuration of the last war. The Americans had gone across this raw gap many times, and each time, bitterly, they were driven back by the *Panzergrenadiers* of "Hitler-jugend." So when Leets and Outhwaithe, in strange new combat gear they'd picked up for their trip to the line, approached the blown-out farmhouse in which Ryan's G-2 outfit hung out, they were not surprised by the sullenness with which they were greeted. Outsiders, fresh, strange officers, one a foreigner, an exotic Brit, rear-echelon types: they expected to be hated, in the way locals always hate tourists; and they were.

"I never saw anything like it," Major Ryan, a sandy-haired freckled man whose nose ran constantly, told them. "Center chest, one shot each. No blood. Patrol that found them thought they were sleeping."

"And at night? Definitely at night?" Leets pushed.

"I said at night, *didn't* I, Captain?"

"Yes, sir, it's just that—"

"Goddamn it, if I *say* at night, I mean at night."

"Yes, sir. Can we get up there?"

"This is a combat zone, Captain. I don't have time to take people on trips."

"Just point us in the right direction. We'll find it."

"Jesus, you guys are eager. All right, but goddamn it, get yourselves a helmet. It's right smack in Kraut country."

The Jeep could only get them so close; after that it was a walk in the sun. A sign in a shattered tree announced the sudden change in climate tersely and without fanfare: "YOU ARE UNDER OBSERVED ARTILLERY FIRE THE NEXT 500 YARDS" in standard GI stenciling, all the letters split neatly in two; but a wit had edited an improvement into the copy, replacing the word "artillery" with "sniper" in bold child's scrawl. The war was everywhere up here, in the wary quick stares of the men who were fighting it, the hulks of burnt-out armor that littered the landscape, in the haze of smoke, heavy and lazy, that adhered to everything, and beneath it another odor that infiltrated the nostrils.

Leets sniffed.

"Ever been in a combat zone, Captain?" asked Ryan.

"Nothing stable like this. I did some running around behind the lines last summer."

"I recognize the odor," said Tony. "Bodies out there. Beyond the wire."

"Yeah," confirmed Major Ryan. "Theirs. Just let 'em try and come out and bury 'em."

"My father," said Outhwaithe, "mentioned it in his letters. The Somme, all that, '14 to '18. I read them later."

They began to encounter the infantrymen here, just behind the line, relaxing around cooking fires, or simply dozing in the shadows of half-tracks and Jeeps. The still landscape actually teemed with men, though if there was a principle of organization behind all this casual cluster, Leets missed it. Who was in charge? Nobody. Who knew what they were doing? Everybody. But Leets did not feel himself the object of curiosity as he scurried along, self-consciously clean and unaccustomed to the crack of bullets aimed his way. Nobody cared. He was not German; he was not an officer who could send anybody out on patrol or launch an attack; therefore he was not significant. A couple of tired-looking teen-agers with BAR's twice their size looked at him stupidly. It did not occur to them to salute, or to him to require it. Farther on, some wise man cautioned, "Keep your asses low."

A final hundred yards had to be covered belly-down, without dignity, across a bare ridge, through a farmyard, to a low stone wall.

Here, settled in cozy domesticity, had gathered still more GI's. Weapons poked through holes punched in the wall or rested on sandbags in the gaps of the wall, and a scroll of barbed wire, jagged and surreal, unreeled across the stones; yet for all these symbols of the soldier's trade, Leets still felt more as if he'd crashed a hobo's convention. Unshaven men, grousing and farting, clothes fetid, toes popping hugely out of blackish OD socks, lay sprawled about in assorted poses of languor. A few peered intently out through gaps in the wall or Y-shaped periscopes at what lay beyond; but most just loafed, cheerful and uncomplicated, enjoying the bright moment for what it was.

The platoon leader, a young lieutenant who looked tireder than Ryan, crawled over, and a meeting convened in the lee of the wall.

"Tom," said Ryan, "these fine gents flew in special from London; they're after a big story." Newspaper lingo seemed to be Ryan's stock in trade. "Not their usual beat at all, but here they are. And the story, in time for the late editions, is Third Squad."

"Never knew who turned the lights out on 'em," said Tom.

More precisely, thought Leets, who turned the lights *on*.

A sergeant was soon summoned who'd been at the wall the night of the patrol, evidently pulled from sleep, for the flecks of crud still clotted in his eyes. He affected the winter-issue wool-helmet cap, called a beanie and useless except for decoration in this warm weather, and he yanked hard on a dead cigar. All these men who lived in the very smile of extinction insisted on being characters, vivid and astonishing, rather than mere soldiers. They looked alike only for the second it took to categorize their eccentricities.

"Not much to tell, sir," he said, not knowing which of the four officers to address. "You can see if you're careful." He gestured.

Leets took off his borrowed helmet, and eased a dangerous half a head up over the wall. Germany, tidy and ripening in the spring, spilled away.

"Just to the left of those trees, sir."

Leets saw a stand of poplars.

"We sent 'em out looking for iron," explained Ryan, not bothering to explain that in the patois, iron meant armor. " 'Hitlerjugend' is technically a Panzer division, though we're not sure if they've got any operational stuff. We didn't run into it on our trips over there, but who had time to look? I just didn't want any Bulge-type surprises coming into the middle of my sector."

"Sir," the young sergeant continued. "Lieutenant Uckley, new guy, he took 'em down that hill, then across the field, long way to crawl. They were okay there, we found chewing gum wrappers. When they got to those trees, they went up that little draw."

Leets could see a fold in the earth, a kind of gully between two vaguely rising landforms.

"But you didn't hear anything? Or see anything?"

"No, sir. Nothing. They just didn't come back."

"Did you recover Third Squad's bodies?" asked Outhwaithe.

"Yes, sir," piped the lieutenant. "Next day. We called in smoke and heavy Willie Peter. Went out myself with another patrol. They'd been dropped in their tracks. Right in the ticker, every last one. Even the last guy. He didn't have time to run, that's how fast it was."

Leets turned to Ryan. "The bodies. They'd be at Graves Registration?"

Ryan nodded. "If they haven't been shipped out to cemeteries yet."

"I think we ought to check it out."

"Fine."

"Sir," asked the sergeant.

Leets turned. "Yeah."

"What did he hit 'em with?"

"Some kind of night vision gear. It was broad daylight for him."

"You're looking for this guy, right?"

"Yeah."

"Well," said the sergeant, "I went looking for him too." A tough kid, made his stripes at what, eighteen, nineteen? Good man in a fire fight, natural talent for it. "Had me a BAR and twenty clips."

"But no luck," said Leets.

"Nah, uh-uh."

You did have luck, kid: you didn't run into Repp; you're still alive.

"I had friends in that squad, good people. When you catch this guy, burn him. Huh? Burn him."

The Graves Registration section took the form of a forty-cot hospital tent some miles behind the front lines, and into this tent sane men seldom ventured. Leets, Outhwaithe, Major Ryan and an Army doctor stood in the dank space with the dead, rank on rank of them, in proper order, awaiting shipment, neatly pine-boxed. Everything possible had been done to make the location pleasant, yet everything had failed and the odor that had paused at Leets's nostrils on the line hung here pungent and tangible, though one adjusted to it quickly.

"Thank God it's still coolish," said Outhwaithe.

The first boy was no good to them. Repp had hit him squarely in the sternum, that cup of bone shielding, however ineffectively, the heart, shattering it, heart behind and assorted other items, but also shattering, most probably, the bullet.

"Nah," said the doc, "I'm not cracking this guy. You won't find a thing in there except tiny flakes cutting every which way. Tell 'em to look some more."

And so the Graves Registration clerks prowled again through the stacked corridors of the dead, hunting, by name off the list 45th Division HQ had provided, another candidate.

The second boy too disappointed. Repp was less precise in his placement, but the physician, looking into the opened body bag in the coffin, judged it no go.

"Nicked a rib; that'll skew the thing off. No telling where it'll end up—foot or hip. We don't have time to play hide-and-seek."

A success was finally achieved on a third try. The doctor, a stocky, blunt Dartmouth grad with thick clean hands and the mannerisms of an irritated bear, announced, "Jackpot—between the third and fourth ribs. This guy's worth the effort."

The box was dollied into the mortuary tent.

The doctor said, "Okay, now. We're gonna take him out of the bag and cut him open. I can get an orderly over here in an hour or so. Or I can do it now, this minute. The catch is, if I do it now, somebody here'll have to help. You've seen battle casualties before? You've seen nothing. This kid's been in the bag a week. You won't recognize him as human."

The doctor looked briefly at each of them. He had hard eyes. How old? Leets's age, twenty-seven maybe, but with a flinty glare to his face, pugnacious and challenging. Guy must be good, Leets thought, realizing the doctor was daring one of them to stay.

"I'll do it," he said.

"Fine. Rest of you guys, out." The others left. Leets and the doctor were alone with the bagged form in the box.

"You'd best put something on," the doc said, "it's going to be messy."

Leets took his coat off and threw on a surgical gown.

"The mask. The mask is most important," the doctor said.

He tied the green mask over his nose and mouth, thinking again of Susan. She lives in one of these things, he thought.

"Okay," the doctor said, "let's get him onto the mortuary table."

They reached in and lifted the bagged thing to the table.

"Hang on," the doctor said, "I'm opening it."

He threw the bag open.

"You'll note," he said, "the characteristics of the cadaver in the advanced state of decomposition."

Leets, in the mask, made a small, weak sound. No words formed in his brain. The cadaver lay in rotten splendor in its peeled-back body bag on the table.

"There it is. The hole. Nice and neat, like a rivet, just left of center chest."

Swiftly, with sure strokes, the doctor inscribed a Y across the chest, from shoulder down to pit of stomach and then down to pubis. He cut through the subcutaneous tissue and the cartilage holding skin and ribs together. Then he lifted the central piece of the chest away and reflected the excess skin to reveal the contents.

"Clinically speaking," the doctor said, looking into the neat arrangement, "the slug passed to the right of the sternum at a roughly seventy-five-degree angle, through the anterior aspect of the right lung"—he was sorting through the boy's inner chest with his gloved fingers shiny—"through the pericardial sac, the heart, rupturing it, the aorta, the right pulmonary artery—right main-stem bronchus, to be exact—the esophagus, taking out the thoracic duct and finally—ah, here we are," cheerful, reaching the end of his long shuffle, "reaching the vertebral column, transecting the spinal cord."

"You got it?"

The doctor was deep inside the boy, going through the shattered organs. Leets, next to him, thought he was going to be sick. The smell rose through the mask to his nostrils, and pain bounded through his head. He felt he was hallucinating this: a fever dream of elemental gore.

"Here, Captain. Your souvenir."

Leets's treasure was a wad of mashed lead, caked with brown gristle. It looked like a fist.

"They usually open up like that?"

"Usually they break apart if they hit something, or they pass on through. What you've got there is a hollow nose or soft point or something like that. Something that inflates or expands inside, I think they're illegal."

The doctor wrapped the slug in a gauze patch and handed it over to Leets.

"There, Captain. I hope you can read the message in it."

Eager now with his treasure, Leets insisted on adding one last stop to the tour of the combat zone. He'd learned from Ryan that the divisional weapons maintenance section had set up shop in the town of Alfeld proper, not far from Graves Registration, and they headed for it.

Leets entered to find himself in a low dark room lined with workbenches. Injured American weapons lay in parts around the place, a brace of .30-caliber air-cooled perforated jacket sleeves, several BAR receivers, Garand ejector rods, Thompson sling swivels, carbine bolts, even a new grease gun or two. Two privates struggled to dismantle a .50-caliber on a tripod, no easy task, and in the back another fellow, a T-5, hunched over a small piece, grinding it with a file.

Leets, ignored, finally said, "Pardon," and eventually the tech looked up.

"Sir?"

"The CO around?"

"Caught some junk last week. Back in the States by now. I'm pulling the strings for now. Sir."

"I see," said Leets. "You any good on the German stuff?"

"Meaning, Can I get you a Luger? The answer is, Can you get me thirty-five bucks?"

"No, meaning, What's this?"

He held out the mashed slug.

"Outta you, sir?" asked the tech.

"No. Out of a kid up on the line."

"Okay. That's that new machine carbine they've got, the forty-four model. You catch SS boys with 'em, right?"

"Right."

"Seven point nine-two millimeter *kurz*. Short. Like our carbine round."

He took it from Leets and held it close.

"All right," he said. "A hundred for the forty-four, five bucks apiece for any spare magazines you can get me."

Oh, Christ, Leets thought.

"One fifty," the tech upped his bid, "provided it's in good condition, operational, no bad dents or bends. You get me one with the barrel-deflection device, the Krummlauf, and I'll jump to two bills. That's top dollar."

"No, no," said Leets, patiently, "all I'm interested in is this slug."

"That's not worth a goddamned penny, sir," said the sergeant, offended.

"Information, not dollars, goddamn it!"

"Jesus, I'm only talking business," said the sergeant. "I thought you was a client, is all, sir."

"Okay, okay. Just look at the fucking bullet and tell me about it."

"Frank, c'mere, willya? Frank's our expert."

Frank untangled himself from the struggle with the .50 and loped over. Leets saw that if the tech was the business brain, Frank was the esthete. He had the intellectual's look of scorn; this was too low for him, he was surrounded by fools, more worthy ways of spending one's life could certainly be found.

He picked the piece up, looked at it quickly.

"Let's weigh it," he said. He took it over to the bench and balanced it on the pan of a microscale, fussed with the balances and finally announced, "My, my, ain't we got fun." He rummaged around on the bench and produced a greasy pamphlet, pale green, that read "ORDNANCE SPECIFICATIONS AXIS POWERS ETO 1944" and pawed through it.

"Yes, sir," he finally said, "usually goes one hundred and twenty grains, gilding metal over a soft steel jacket. Inside this jacket is a lead sleeve surrounding a steel core. A newer type of powder is used. But this here mother weighs in at one forty-three grains. And there ain't no steel in it at all. Too soft. Just plain old lead. Now that's no good against *things*. Won't penetrate, just splatter. But into something soft, meaning people, you got maximum damage."

"Why would they build a bullet out of pure lead in wonderful modern 1945?" Leets asked.

"If you're putting this wad through a barrel with real deep grooves, real biters, you can get a hell of a lot of revs, even on something moving slow. Which means—"

"Accuracy?"

"Yes, sir. The guy on the gun can put them on fucking dimes from way out if he knows what he's doing. Even if the bullet's moving real slow, no velocity at all. The revs hold her on, not the speed."

"So it's moving under seven hundred feet per second? That's slow, slower than our forty-five."

"Right. And at seven hundred fps or less, you're under the sound barrier."

"No pop. It's better than a silencer, isn't it?" Leets wanted to know.

"Yes, sir. Because any baffle system cuts down on feet per second, so you get a drop off in accuracy and range. Someone real smart figured all this out. I've never seen anything like it."

So that's how they did it, Leets thought.

"Hey, Captain, you get a line on this gun, you let me know," said the tech. "It sounds nice. I'd go a thousand for it."

* * *

When they got back to Ryan's shop to wait for the plane that would take them back to London, the major asked an innocent question.

"Hey," he said, "by the way, what's Anlage Elf?"

That got Leets's attention. He yanked up, staring hard, feeling the breath sucked from him.

"Your CO," said Ryan, baffled by the intense reaction, "he bumped a high-priority telex through. It's just down from Division."

"CO?" said Leets.

"Colonel Evans."

That son of a—

"He wants you back fastest. He says he found Anlage Elf."

Part Two

Gesamtlösung

(General Solution)

April-May 1945

XIII

Repp had a special request.

"Now, Herr Ingenieur-Doktor, if all goes well," he said one morning, "all your inventions will work wonderfully. It'll be like the tests, the targets out front, I'm shooting from a clear lane, protected. Eh? But suppose things get a little mixed up?"

"I'm not sure I—"

"Well, old friend, it's possible"—Repp was smiling—"there'll be some boys interested in stopping me. I might find myself in a ruckus with them, a close-in thing. Have you ever been in a fire fight?"

"No. Of course not," said Vollmerhausen.

Again Repp smiled. "The weapon you've given me is superb for distance and dark. But fire fights take place where you can see the other fellow's dental work, tell if he's still got milk on his tongue from breakfast."

Vollmerhausen saw immediately what Repp was driving at. Repp, equipped as no man ever had been for the special requirements of the mission, was in a more conventional engagement as good as unarmed. The heavy scope, with its cathode tube, energy converter and infrared light blocked out his view of the standard iron battle-sights.

"I can hit a germ at four hundred meters," Repp said, "at midnight. Yet a man with a fowling piece has the advantage at fifty meters. Can you help me out? I'd hate to have all this end up in disappointment because of some accident."

Vollmerhausen puzzled over the problem, and soon concluded that he could spot-weld still another piece, a tube or something, under Vampir, to serve crudely as a sight. It wouldn't be on the weapon's axis, however, but rather parallel to it, and thus it would have to be adjusted in its placement to account for this difference. He chose the carrying case of a K-43 scope, a nicely milled bit of tubing of acceptable weight and length; and he mounted at its rear rim a peephole just a trifle right of center and at its front rim a blade just a trifle left of center. Repp, his head a little out of position, would line the blade in the center of the peephole, and find himself locked into a target 100 meters out where the line of his vision intersected the flight of the bullet. Nothing fancy; crude in fact, and certainly ugly, grotesque.

The original outlines of the once sleek STG-44 were barely visible under the many modifications, the cluster of tubes up top, a reshaped pistol grip, the conical flash-hider, and the bipod.

"It's truly an ugly thing," said Repp finally, shaking his head.

"Or truly beautiful. The modern architects—not thought highly of by certain powerful people, I admit—" Vollmerhausen was taking a real risk but he felt his new kinship with Repp would allow such a radical statement—"say beauty is form following function. There's nothing very pretty about Vampir, which makes it beautiful indeed. Not a wasted line, not an artificial embellishment."

"Form follows function, you say. Tell me, a Jew said that, didn't he?" He was fiddling again with that curious black thing, that little metal cube.

Vollmerhausen wasn't really sure. "Probably," he admitted.

"Yes, they are very clever. A clever race. That was their problem."

It was not long after this unsettling conversation that another curious thing began to happen. Or rather: not to happen. Vollmerhausen began to realize with a distinct sensation of reluctance that he was done. Not merely done with this last modification, but done completely. Done with Vampir.

There was simply nothing to do until the team came for the gun.

In this involuntary holiday, Vollmerhausen took to strolling the compound or the nearby woods, while his staff fiddled away their time improving their quarters—technical people love to tinker, and they'd worked out a more efficient hot water system, bettered the ventilation in the canteen, turned their barrack into a two-star facility (a joke was making the rounds: after the war they'd open a spa here called Bad Anlage). Now that the pressure was off, their morale rose remarkably; the prospect of leaving filled them with joy, and Vollmerhausen himself planned to check with Repp as soon as possible about the evacuation. Once, in his strollings, he even passed his old antagonist Schaeffer, resplendent in the new camouflage tunic all the soldiers had brought back from a tank-warfare course they'd gone to for two days, but the SS captain hardly noticed him.

Meanwhile, rumors fluttered nervously through the air, some

clearly ridiculous, some just logical enough to be true: the Führer was dead, Berlin Red except for three blocks in the city center; the Americans and English would sign a separate peace with the Reich and together they would fight the Russians; Vienna had fallen, Munich was about to; fresh troops were collecting in the Alps for a final stand; the Reich would invade Switzerland and make a last stand *there*; a vast underground had been set up to wage war after surrender; all the Jews had been freed from the KZ's, or all had been killed. Vollmerhausen had heard them all before, but now new ones reached him: of Repp. Repp would kill the Pope, for not granting the Führer sanctuary in the Vatican. Absurd! Repp was after a special group that Himmler had singled out as having betrayed the SS. Repp would kill the English king in special retribution; or the Russian man of steel. Even more insane! Where could Repp get from here? Nowhere, except south, to the border. No, Vollmerhausen had no ideas. He'd given up wondering. He'd always known that curiosity is dangerous around the SS, and doubly dangerous around Repp. Repp was going to a mountain, that's all he knew.

It occurred then to Vollmerhausen, with a sudden jolt of discomfort:

Berchtesgaden was on a mountain. And not far. Yet the Führer was supposedly in Berlin. The reports all said he was in Berlin.

The engineer suddenly felt chilly. He vowed not to think on the topic again.

Vollmerhausen was out of the compound—a beautiful spring day, unseasonably warm, the forest swarming green, buzzing with life, the sky clear as diamond and just as rare, spruce and linden in the air—when the weapon team arrived. He did not see them, but upon his return noticed immediately the battered civilian Opel, pre-war, parked in front of Repp's. Later he saw the men himself, from far off, civilians, but of a type: the overcoats, the frumpy hats, the calm, unimpressed faces concealing, but just barely, the tendency toward violence. He'd seen Gestapo before, or perhaps they were Ausland SD or any of a dozen other kinds of secret policemen; whatever, they had an ugly sort of weariness that frightened him.

In the morning they were gone, and that meant the rifle too, Vollmerhausen felt. Twice before breakfast staff members had approached.

"Herr Ingenieur-Doktor? Does it mean we'll be able to go?"

"I don't know," he'd answered. "I just don't know." Not needing to add, Only Repp knows.

And shortly then, a man came for him, from Repp.

"Ah, Hans," said Repp warmly, when he arrived.

"Herr Obersturmbannführer," Vollmerhausen replied.

"You saw of course our visitors last night?"

"I caught a glimpse across the yard at them."

"Toughies, no? But sound men, just right for the job."

"They've taken Vampir?"

"Yes. No reason not to tell you. It's gone. All packed up. Carted away."

"I see," said Vollmerhausen.

"And they brought information, some last-second target confirmations, some technical data. And news."

Vollmerhausen brightened. "News?"

"Yes. The war is nearly finished. But you knew that."

"Yes."

"Yes. And my part of the journey begins tonight."

"So soon. A long journey?"

"Not far, but complicated. On foot, most of it. Rather drab actually. I won't bore you with details. Not like climbing aboard a Hamburg tram."

"No, of course not."

"But I wanted to talk to you about your evacuation."

"Evac—"

"Yes, yes. Here's the good news." He smiled. "I know how eager your people are to get back to the human race. This can't have been pleasant for them."

"It was their duty," said Vollmerhausen.

"Perhaps. Anyway, you'll be moving out tomorrow. After I've gone. Sorry it's so rushed. But now it's felt the longer this place stays, the bigger the chance of discovery. You may have seen my men planting charges."

"Yes."

"There'll be nothing left of this place. Nothing for our friends. No clues, no traces. Your people will return as if from holiday. Captain Schaeffer's men will return to the Hungarian front. And I will cease to exist: officially, at any rate. Repp is dead. I'll be a new man. An old mission but a new man."

"Sounds very romantic."

"Silly business, changing identities, pretending to be what one's not. But still necessary."

"My people will be very excited!"

"Of course. One more night, and it's all over. Your part, *Toten-kopfdivision*'s part. Only my part remains. One last campaign."

"Yes, Herr Obersturmbannführer."

"The details: have them packed up tonight. Tomorrow at ten hundred hours a bus will arrive. It's several hours to Dachau. From there your people will be given travel permits, and back pay, and be permitted to make their way to destinations of choice. Though I can't imagine many of them will head east. By the way, the Allies aren't reported within a hundred kilometers of this place. So the travel should be easy."

"Good. Ah, thanks. My thanks, Herr Obersturmbannführer." He reached over and on impulse seized Repp's hand.

"Go on. Tell them," Repp commanded.

"Yes, sir, Herr Obersturmbannführer," Hans shouted, and lurched out.

Tomorrow! So soon. Back into the world, the real world. Vollmerhausen felt a surge of joy as if he'd just glimpsed the sea after a trek across the Sahara.

It was in the general confusion of preparing for the evacuation that night that a thought came to him. He tried to quell it, found this not difficult at first, with the technicians rushing merrily about him, dismantling their elaborate comfort systems in the barrack, storing personal belongings in trunks, even singing—a bottle, no, *several* bottles appeared and while Vollmerhausen, teetotaler, couldn't approve, neither could he prevent them—as if the war were officially and finally over and Germany had somehow won. But later, in the night, in the dark, it returned to him. He tried to flatten it, drive it out, found a hundred ways to dispel it. But he could not. Vollmerhausen had thought of a last detail.

He pulled himself out of bed and heard his people breathing heavily—drunkenly?—around him. He checked his watch. After four, damn! Had Repp left already? Perhaps. But perhaps there was still time.

It had occurred to Vollmerhausen that he might not have warned Repp about the barrel residue problem. So many details, he'd forgotten just this one! Or had he? But he could not picture a conversation in which he properly explained this eccentricity of the weapon: that after firing fifty or so of the specially built rounds, the residue in the barrel accumulated to such an extent that it greatly affected accuracy. Though Repp *would* know, probably: he made it his business to know such things. Still . . .

Vollmerhausen drew a bathrobe around himself and hurried out. It was a warm night, he noticed, as he hurried across the compound to the SS barrack and Repp's quarters. But what's this? Stirrings filled the dark—a squad of SS troopers moving about, night maneuvers, a drill or something.

"Sergeant?"

The man's pipe flared briefly in the dark. "Yes, sir," he responded.

"Is Obersturmbannführer around? Has he left yet?"

"Ah—no, sir. I believe he's still in his quarters."

"Excellent. Thank you." Ebullient, Vollmerhausen rushed on to the barrack. It was empty, though a light burned behind the door of Repp's room. He walked among the dark, neat bunks and rapped at the wood.

No answer.

Was Repp off after all?

"Herr Obersturmbannführer?"

Vollmerhausen felt edgy, restless with indecision. Forget the whole silly thing? Go on in, be a bulldog, wait, make sure? Ach!

Hans the Kike pushed through the door. Room was empty. But then he noticed an old greatcoat with private's chevron across a chair. Part of Repp's "new identity"? He entered. On the desk lay a heap of field gear: the rumpled blanket, the six Kar '98 packs on the harness, the fluted gas-mask cylinder, a helmet, in the corner a rifle. Repp clearly hadn't left yet. Vollmerhausen began to wait.

But he again began to feel restless and uncomfortable. You didn't want to stand in a man's room uninvited. Perhaps he should slip out, wait by the door. Ah, what a dilemma. He did not want to do the wrong thing. He turned to stride out, but his sudden spin sent a spurt of commotion into the still air, and a single paper, as though magically, peeled itself off the desk and zigzagged dramatically to the floor. Vollmerhausen hurried over and picked it up to replace it.

It was hotly uncomfortable in the room. A fire blazed in Repp's stove and the smell of his Russian cigarettes filled the air. Vollmer-hausen's eyes hooked on the *GEHEIME KOMMANDOSACHE* stamped haphazardly across the page top. The title read " N I B E L U N G E N, " the exotic spacing for emphasis, and beneath the subtitle "LATEST INTELLIGENCE SITUA-TION 27 APR 45."

He read the first line. The language of the report was military, dry, rather abstract, ostentatiously formal. He had trouble under-standing exactly what they were saying.

Vollmerhausen was completely lost. Nuns? A convent? He couldn't make it out. His heart was pounding so hard he was having trouble focusing. So damned hot in here. Sweat oozed from his hairline. He knew he must put the report down instantly, but he could not. He read on, the last paragraph.

He felt a growth of pain in his stomach. I am part of this? How? Why?

Repp asked, "Find it interesting?"

Vollmerhausen turned. He was not even surprised.

"You simply can't. We don't make war on—"

"We make war on our enemies," said Repp, "wherever we find them. In whatever form. The East would make you strong for such a thing."

"You could bring yourself to *do* this?" Vollmerhausen wanted to cry. He was afraid he was going to be sick.

"With honor," Repp said. He stood there in the dirty tunic of a private soldier, hatless.

"You can't," Vollmerhausen said. It seemed to him a most cogent argument.

Repp brought up the Walther P-38 and shot him beneath the left eye. The bullet kicked the engineer's head back violently. Most of the face was knocked in. He fell onto Repp's desk, crashing with it to the floor.

Repp put the automatic back into the shoulder holster under the tunic. He didn't look at the body. He picked the report up from the floor—it had fluttered free from Vollmerhausen's fingers at the moment of death—and walked to the small stove. He opened the door, inserted it and watched the flames consume it.

He heard a machine pistol. Schaeffer and his people were bumping off Vollmerhausen's staff.

It occurred to Repp after several seconds that Schaeffer was doing the job quite poorly. He would have to speak to the man. The firing had not let up.

A bullet fractured one of Repp's windows. Firing leapt up from a dozen points on the perimeter. Repp had an impression of tracers floating in.

Repp hit the floor, for he knew in that second that the Americans had come.

XIV

Roger played hard to get at first, demanding wooing, but after five minutes Leets was ready to woo him with a fist, and Roger shifted gears fast. Now it was a production, starring himself, directed by himself, produced by himself, the Orson Welles, tyro genius, of American Intelligence.

"Get on with it, man," said Outhwaithe.

"Okay, okay." He smiled smugly, and then wiped it off, leaving a smirk, like a child's moustache of milk.

"Simple. In two words. You'll kick yourself." A grin split his pleasant young face. "The planes."

"Uh—"

"Yeah," he amplified. "So much on the route he took, so much on tracing it back, following it back to its source—all wrong. He said he thought he heard planes. Or maybe trucks or motorcycles. But maybe planes. *Now—*" he paused dramatically, letting an imitation of wisdom, solemn, furrow-browed, surface on his face, "I give this Air Corps guy lessons, colonel in Fighter Ops, once a week, little walking-around money. *Any*way, I asked him if some guys bounced some weird kind of night action—under lights, middle of wilderness—say in March sometime, maybe late February, any chance you'd have it on paper?"

Leets was struck by the simple brilliance of it.

"That's really good, Roger," he said, at the same time thinking that he himself ought to be shot for not coming up with it.

Roger smiled at the compliment. "Anyway," he said, handing over a photostatic copy of a document entitled "AFTER ACTION REPORT, Fighter Operations, 1033d Tactical Fighter Group, 8th Air Force, Chalois-sur-Marne."

Leets tore into the pilot's prosaic account of his adventures: two fighter-bombers, angling toward the marshaling yards at Munich for a dawn strike, find themselves above a lit field in the middle of what is on the maps pure wilderness. In it German soldiers scurry about. They peel off for one run, after which the lights go away.

"Can we track this?"

"Those numbers—that's the pilot's estimated position," Roger said.

"Thirty-two min southeast Saar, one eighty-six?"

"Thirty-two minutes southeast of the Saarbrücken Initial Point, on a compass heading of one eighty-six degrees."

"Can we get pictures?"

"Well, sir, I'm no expert but—"

"I can have an RAF photo Spitfire in an hour," said Tony.

"Roger, get over to R and D and pick up those mock-ups of Anlage Elf they were building, okay?"

"Check," said Roger.

"Jesus," said Leets. "If this is—"

"Big if, chum."

"Yeah, but *if*, if we can get a positive ID, we can . . ." He let the sentence trail off.

"Yes, of course," said Tony. "But first, the Spit. You'll see the Jew. He'll be important in this too, of course. He'll have to come in at some point. He's necessary."

"Yes, I'll see him."

"Then I'm off," Tony said.

"Hey," wondered Roger, disappointed that his brief instant in the spotlight had so soon vanished, "what are you guys talking about?"

Leets didn't seem to hear him. He looked strangely excited, and he was muttering distractedly to himself. He rubbed his lips, which had dried in the excitement, and for just one second Roger had the impression the captain was near breakdown, madly muttering to himself, full of private visions and prophecies.

"Sir," Roger repeated, louder, "what's going to happen now?"

"Well," said Leets, "I guess we have to close them down. Put some people in there."

People, thought Roger, swallowing dryly. He had to stop himself from asking, *Me too?*

The Gentile women treated him like some dreadful little wog, foreign and stinky, that they were helping out of great pity. In return they expected his love and when he would not give it they were enraged. They resented the private room when down the hall their own boys, wounded gallantly in battle, lay festering in huge public bays. He was not truly hurt either; he insisted on heathen protocols, the removal of the crucifix, for example; but most contemptibly of all, Somebody Important had an interest in him.

Shmuel lay back, alone. His head buzzed with pain. Luminous shapes entwined on the ceiling. A film of sweat covered him. He closed his eyes and saw smokestacks belching flame and human ash on the horizon, the glow orange and lurid. He opened them to an equally unsatisfactory reality: the English hospital room to which he'd been removed, a blank green chamber, pitiless, the odors of disinfectants rising. There were screams in the night. He knew people looked in on him at all hours. And the hospital merely symbolized a whole Western world he'd fled into—where else had there been to go, what other direction for a poor Jew? But in many ways it was as dreadful a place as the one from which he'd just escaped. There, at least, there were other Jews, a sense of community. Here, nobody cared, or would even listen. The Gentiles wanted him for something strange; he was not sure he trusted them.

It didn't matter. He knew he was nearing the end of the journey and he didn't mean the geographic journey from Warsaw to the death camp to Anlage Elf to the forest to London, but rather its inner representation—as though each step was a philosophical position that must be mastered, its truth grasped, before moving on. At last he was turning into one of the *Mussulmen*, the living dead who roamed the camps as pariahs, having accepted doom and therefore no longer suited for human contact. Death was no longer meaningful; it was mere biology, a final technical detail to be adjusted.

He accepted death; therefore he accepted the dead; therefore he preferred the dead.

For everyone was dead. Bruno Schulz was dead, killed in '42, in Drohobicz. Janucz Korczak was dead; Auschwitz. Perle, Warsaw. Gebirtig, Cracow. Katzenelson, the Vittel camp. Glick, Vilna. Shaievitz, Lodz. Ulianover, also Lodz.

The list was longer of course, longer a million times.

The last Jew longed for a ghetto, kerosene lamps, crooked streets, difficult lessons.

Good night, electrified, arrogant world.

He walked gladly to the window.

He was four stories up.

Shmuel stood at the window in bedclothes, looking out. His features, even in the dim light, seemed remote.

"Nothing much to see, huh?" called Leets as he swept in.

The man turned quickly, fixing a stare on Leets. He looked badly spooked.

"You okay?" Leets wanted to know.

He seemed to grab hold. He nodded.

Leets was running late. He knew he was coming on all wrong but he was nervous and he could never control how he acted when he was nervous. Also, he hated hospitals, even more now because they reminded him so of Susan.

"Well, good, it's good you're okay."

He paused, stalling. Only one way to do this. Only one way to do anything. He kept having to remind himself: full out.

"Look, we need more help. Big help."

He waited for the Jew to respond. The man just sat on his bed and looked back. He seemed quite calm and disinterested. He looked tired also.

"Two days from now—it would be sooner, but the logistics are complex, forty-eight hours is the dead minimum—a battalion of American airborne troops is going into the Black Forest. We found it—Anlage Elf, Repp, the whole shooting gallery. We'll go in a little after midnight. I'll tag along with the airborne people; meanwhile Major Outhwaithe will come up on the ground in a column of tanks from a French armored division operating in the area."

Leets paused.

"We're going to try and kill Repp. That's what it gets down to. But only one man has seen him. Sure, we've got that old picture. But we've got to be *sure*. So it would help if—if you came along." He was troubled over all this.

"This is how I figure it. Nobody's asking you to go into battle; you're not a soldier, it's what we get paid for. No, after we take the place, we'll get a message out fast. You'll be in a forward area with Roger, I suppose. We can get you in fast in a light plane, have you there in an hour or two. It's our best shot at him, only way to be sure." He paused again. "Well, that's it. Your part will be risky, but a good, safe calculated risk. What do you think?" He looked up at Shmuel and had the discomfiting sensation the man hadn't understood a word he'd said. "Are you all right? Do you have a fever or something?"

"You'll jump out of an airplane? In a parachute, in the night? And attack the camp?" Shmuel asked.

"Yeah," said Leets. "It's not so hard as it sounds. We've got some good pictures. We plan to go down on the target range, where you escaped. We make it three miles back to—" But again he saw Shmuel's eyes glaze over, disinterested.

"Hey, you okay?" he said, and almost snapped his fingers.

"Take me," Shmuel said suddenly.

"What? Take you? In the air—"

"You said you needed me there. Fine, I'll go. With you. From the plane in the parachute. Yes, I'll do it."

"You got any idea what you're letting yourself in for? I mean, there'll be a *battle*, people getting *blown up*."

"I don't care. That's not the point."

"What is the point?"

"The point is—you'd never understand. But I must go. It's either that or nothing. You've never understood. But I must go. It's either that or nothing. You've got to do this for me. I'm clever, I can learn the techniques. Two days, you say? Plenty of time."

Leets was all mixed up, tried to run through a dozen motives. Finally he just asked, "Why?"

"Old friends then. I'll have the best chance to meet old friends."

A screwy answer, Leets thought. But he said, not quite knowing why, "All right."

The paratroopers all seemed husky boys in their teens, dumbly, crazily eager, full of bravado and violence. They worked hard at glamour and costumed themselves after lessons they'd learned in movie theaters. They blackened their faces with burnt cork until they gleamed like minstrels with mad white eyes and pink tongues; they dangled junk from themselves until they clanked like men in armor, but not just any junk: pistols in shoulder holsters were first-prize items, symbols of special pizazz; another melodramatic improvisation was the knife and sheath taped upside down along the boot; then too pouches, grenades, tightly wound ropes, ammo packs, canteens beside the two lumpy chutes; and on their helmets most taped first-aid kits and many of them still wore, though non-regulation now, the D-Day American flag patch on their shoulders. A few of the really demented boasted Mohawk haircuts.

Leets, sitting mildly among them, felt he'd wandered into someone's high school pep rally. The varsity was revving itself up before the game. As an ex-football player himself, ex-Wildcat, he could appreciate and almost savor that feeling of hate and fear and sheer shit-thinning excitement that coursed savagely through these nervous boys. The paratroopers shoved and joshed, even sang now as they relaxed in the airfield staging area in these last minutes before embarkation. Earlier someone had even produced a football, and Leets had watched an exuberant game of touch unfold before his eyes. The officers had seemed not to mind this extravaganza of energy: they were slightly older men, but all had that same thick-wristed blunt athleticism that Leets recognized immediately, heavy bones and close-cropped hair and flat faces. And while all this was familiar to him, it was at the same time strange; for Leets associated war with lonely men climbing into Lysanders or huddling in empty bays of big British bombers, drinking coffee. That had been his war anyway, not this festival of the locker room.

He turned his wrist over. Twenty-two hundred hours, his Bulova announced in iridescent hands. Another fifteen, twenty minutes to go. He snapped out and lit a Lucky, and did another—about the fiftieth—rundown on his own collection of junk. Canteen for thirst, compass for direction, shovel for digging, chute for jumping and the rest for killing: three fragmentation grenades, a bayonet, ten 30-round magazines in pouches on a belt stiffly around his middle and, thrust at an awkward diagonal down across his belly under the reserve chute, a Thompson submachine gun, the Army model designated M-1, standard issue for a paratroop officer. He must have weighed five hundred pounds; perhaps like a medieval knight he'd need a crane to get him off his ass when, so shortly now, the jousting hour arrived.

Leets ran his tongue over dry lips. If I'm scared, he wondered, what about *him*?

Shmuel lounged on the grass next to him, similarly encumbered, yet lacking weapons, which he did not know how to operate anyway and which by principle he would not have, though Leets had tried to argue him into carrying at least a pistol.

Yet Shmuel seemed strangely composed.

"How are you doing?" Leets inquired, with effort, for all the stuff pressing into his gut.

No expression showed beneath the blackface; he could have been any other paratrooper, counting out the final quiet minutes of the night, eyes showing white against the darkness of face, mouth grim, nostrils flaring slightly in the effort of breathing.

He nodded briskly in reply to the question. "I'm fine," he said.

"Good, good," Leets said, wishing he could make the same claim. He himself was exhausted, while at the same confusing time churning with energy and dread. A most curious state; it had the one benefit of quieting his leg, which with fatigue tended to throb and leak. A man leaned over, too dark to recognize, and said, "Sir, Colonel says planes'll be cranking up in five, we'll be loading in ten."

"Gotcha, thanks," said Leets, and the trooper was gone.

Leets looked nervously around him. It was warm and dark and the men were lying about on the grass of the airfield, though they'd been organized into their Dakota groups three hours ago. Those three hours had dragged by, as the light faded to twilight and then darkness, the soft English fields beyond the air base perimeter growing hazier. The men were Second Battalion, 501st Parachute Infantry Regiment, a part of the more widely known 82d Airborne Division. Tough boys with drops in Italy and Normandy, a long bad spell in the Bulge and most recently—March—an op named Varsity in which they'd jumped beyond the Rhine behind them. They'd been off the line a month, growing fat and sluggish here at the rest camp in southern England, and when Tony Outhwaithe had convinced the right parties that a batch of hell-raisers was needed for a night of close-in dirty work in south Twelveland, Second of the 501st got the word.

It was cold in the airplane. Shmuel sat in the chill, his back against the slope of the fuselage, shivering. Yet he felt quite wonderful. His journey was finally nearing its completion. A matter of hours now. He was one of two dozen men in the underlit darkness of the airplane, and he was as isolated from any of them as they were from each other, cut off by the noise from the engines that made human contact, now that they needed it most, impossible. Shmuel could sense the tension, especially in Captain Leets, and he pitied him for it. A *Mussulman* need feel nothing. A *Mussulman* was cut off from human sensation, complete within himself. Yet he looked over at Leets and saw him hunched and absorbed, filthy face glowing orangely over the tip of a cigarette. The layer of cork had dried crustily on his skin, making the features abstract, unreadable. But the eyes, staring blankly at nothing, had a message: fear.

Yet it was a fear Shmuel refused to accept. He was all through with fear, he had discovered a new territory. Having accepted and even welcomed his death, nothing mattered, not even preposterous things like the half-a-day session at the American parachute school with the boy Evans, performing feats of athleticism, jumping off of ten-foot platforms into sawdust pits, rolling when he hit; or hanging fifty feet up from risers, the straps nipping into his limbs while someone yelled at him about adjustments he didn't understand and the ground rushed up to hit him.

"You'll be all right," Evans had said. "The static line'll pull the chute open for you. Really, it's easy. When you hit the ground, the captain'll come by for you. He'll take good care of you." The boy had grinned optimistically. He could afford optimism because he wasn't going.

Then they took him to a supply depot and issued him equipment. It occurred to him that he'd never been so well dressed though he felt like an impostor. The clothes were all big, but looking around he saw that bagginess was the American style. It seemed to sym- bolize their wealth, huge flapping garments made from endless bolts of material. In the warehouse they peeled these items off from huge piles, piles of pants that reached the sky! The crowning mon- strosity was the helmet, shaped like a Moscow dome, weighing six tons, pulling him left or right unless he fought against it.

He examined himself. Third uniform of the war and what a peculiar journey they charted: inmate's ticking to Wehrmacht flannels to thick crinkly American cotton, crowned in steel like a bell.

Now, sitting in the airplane that drew ever closer to Germany, Shmuel had to wonder at the jokes of fate.

I had to find a special way to die, the ovens weren't good enough for me, no, I had to jump out of an airplane with teen-age cowboys and Indians and gangsters from America.

He glanced over at Leets, and noticed the way he was sitting, one leg pushed out straight, his face tight, eyes still distant, whole being focused on deriving maximum pleasure from the cigarette.

Leets saw the ready light come on. He smashed out his cigarette with the foot of his good leg. The bad one ached dully. Motion- less, stretched, stiff in the cold plane, it had cramped on him. He massaged it, kneading it nervously with his fingers, working some life back into it. A touch to the knee came back wet. Leakage.

You fucker, he thought.

Just when I need you.

He thought of his first jump, first *real* jump, that is, with live Germans and guns and real bullets down below: completely different. A Lancaster, though bigger, felt less solid than a C-47, and there was a sense of actual loneliness in the big bomber's bay, with just the three of them besides the sullen jumpmaster. Here, a crowd, two whole football teams and change. And a door, a wonderful American door, triumph of Yank ingenuity. The Brits leaped out of a hatch in the bomber floor for some absurd reason, a public school sort of ordeal that had to be got through like a cold bath or fagging for the older boys. Leets focused all his terrors on getting through without breaking his head. For some baffling reason, Yanks had a peculiar tendency to look *down* as they stepped out, see where they were headed, and catch a faceful of hatch. Leets had seen it happen at one of the British secret training schools where he'd learned to jump Brit-style preparatory for going to war for the OSS. There was a saying at the place: you could always tell a Yank by the broken jaw.

Another light flicked on, red. Three minutes. Time to hook up.

Shmuel was standing now in the aisle. It reminded him of a crowded Warsaw trolley, the one that traveled Glinka Street, near the jewelry shops. He even had a strap to hang onto in the closeness and he could feel other men's breath washing over him. A moment of unexpected terror had just passed: the plane had yawed to the left; Shmuel, awkward in all the new gear, almost fell. He felt his balance and, with it, his control draining away. Nothing to grab for; he surrendered to the fall; then Leets had him.

"Easy," he muttered. A breeze pummeled through the corridor of the airplane, fresh and savage. A glint of natural light, not much, illuminated the end of the darkness. Door opened.

Then, like a theater queue at last admitted to the big show, the line began to move. It moved with great swiftness, almost as if some reasonable destination lay ahead.

Shmuel faced sky. An American strapped by the doorway hit him in the shoulder without warning and, surprised at his own lack of respect, he snarled at the man, a stranger, and as if to insult him, stepped out.

Gravity sucked the dignity from his limbs and he flapped like a scrawny *shtetl* chicken. The face of the tailplane, rivets and all, sailed by a few inches beyond him. He fell, screaming, in the great cold dark silence, the engines now mercifully gone, the noise too, only himself, beginning to tumble until—*Ah! Oh!* Something snapped him hard and he found himself floating under a great white parasol. He looked about and noticed first that the sky was full of apparitions—jellyfish, moving with underwater slowness, silky petticoats under a young girl's skirts, pillowcases and sheets billowing on a wash line—and secondly that for all the majesty of the spectacle the ground was coming up fast. He'd expected a serene descent, thinking himself thousands of feet up. Of course they'd jump at minimum height, less time in the air, less time to scatter, and already Shmuel felt below the horizon. The ground, huge and black, smashed up at him. Wasn't he supposed to be doing something? He didn't care. He saw in the rushing wall of darkness, coming now like an express train, his fate. He reached to embrace it, expecting no pain, only release, and he hit with stunning impact, knocking a bolt of light through his head and all his sense out of him.

I'm dead, he thought with relief.

But then a sergeant stood over him, cursing hotly in English. "C'mon, Jack, off yer butt, move it," and sprinted on.

Shmuel got up, feeling sore in a dozen places but broken in none. His legs wobbled under his weight, his brain still resonated with echoes of the landing. Gradually he realized the field was very busy. Men rushed about, seemingly without order. Shmuel tried to figure out what to do and it occurred to him that he was supposed to free himself from the chute harness. Suddenly a man materialized next to him.

"You okay? Nothing busted?"

"What? Ah. No. No. What a sensation."

"Great."

Shmuel tugged feebly with the harness, couldn't get his fingers to work and wasn't exactly sure what it was he was supposed to *do*, and then felt Leets grab the heavy clip that seemed to be the nexus of the network of straps that held him, and in the next second the straps unleashed him.

Shmuel took a quick look around. He made out men scattered across the dark field, and, beyond, a looming bank of pines. All was silence under the towers of stars. It was so different now. He looked for landmarks, for clues, for help. He felt suddenly useless.

"This way, c'mon," hissed Leets, unlimbering his automatic gun, trotting off. Shmuel ran after.

Yes, yes, it really was the firing range. The shed bobbed up ahead, and he reached the concrete walkway. Then he saw the lamps in the trees; he remembered: they'd almost killed him.

Leets joined a crowd of whispering men, while Shmuel stood off to one side. Other shapes rushed by. Groups were forming up, leaders gesturing to unattached people. Shmuel could hear guns being checked and cocked, equipment adjusted.

Then Leets returned.

"You feel okay?"

"It's so strange," Shmuel said. A half-smile creased his face.

"You stick with me. Don't get separated. Don't wander off or anything."

"Of course not."

"Any shooting, down you go, flat. Got it?"

"Yes, Mr. Leets."

"Okay, we're moving out."

The soldiers began to move down the road.

It looked familiar, like something luminous from childhood that, seen finally through an adult's eyes, revealed itself tawdry, fraudulent. A spring camouflage pattern had been added to the buildings so that now they showed the shadowy patterns of the forest, but otherwise Anlage Elf looked unchanged.

He was amazed more at the stillness of the composition than the composition itself: hard to believe those dark trees that circled the place concealed hundreds of squirming men.

Leets, beside him, whispered, "Research? The big one in the middle?"

"Yes."

"And SS to the left?"

"Yes." Shmuel realized Leets knew all this, they'd gone over it a hundred times; Leets was talking out of his own nervous energy or excitement.

"Any second now," Leets said, looking at his watch.

Shmuel guessed that meant any second till a circle was closed around the place, like a noose. All exits cut off, all guns in place.

Leets was rubbing his hands in excitement, peering into the dark. Shmuel could see the fellow fight hard to restrain himself.

The report of the first shot was so abrupt that it shocked Shmuel. He flinched at it. Or was it a shot? It sounded muffled and indistinct. Yes, shot, for Leets's intake of breath was sudden and almost painful, pulled in, the air held. Then came a clatter of reports, more shots. They all seemed to come from inside Anlage and Shmuel did not see why. Glancing around at the others in the trees, he made out baffled faces, men searching each other's eyes for answers. Curses rose, and someone whispered hoarsely, "Hold it, hold—!" cut by a loud *krak!* from nearby. "Goddamn it, hold your—" someone shouted, but the voice was lost in the tide of fire that rose.

All wrong. Even Shmuel, not by furthest reach of imagination a military man, could tell: volley all ragged and patchy, tentative. Bullets just streaking out into the dark, unaimed.

Yet it was beautiful. He was dazzled by the beauty in it. In the dark, the gunflashes unfolded like exotic orchids, more precious for their briefness at the moment of blossom. They danced and flickered in the trees and as they rose in intensity, pulling a roar from the ground itself, the air seemed to fill with a sleet of light, free-floating streaks of sheer color that wobbled and splashed through the night. He felt his mouth hang dumbly open in wonder.

Leets turned to him. "All fucked up," he said darkly. "Some bastard let go too early."

Nearby, an older man shouted into a telephone, "Crank 'em up, all sections, get those people in the assault teams in there!"

Shmuel understood that the battle had prematurely begun, and reached its moment of equipoise in the very first seconds.

Leets turned to him again.

"I'm going in there. Stay here. Wait for Tony."

The American raced off, into the blizzard.

Leets rushed in, not out of courage so much as to escape the rage and frustration. He ran out of sheer physical need because in not running there was more pain, because the neat surgical operation that he had envisioned as the fitting end to this drama, to Anlage Elf, to Repp, to the Man of Oak, was now lost forever, dissolving into a pell-mell of indiscriminate fire. Susan had wished him dead; he'd risk it then, her curse echoing in his mind.

He entered a terrible world, its imagery made even keener by the gush of his own adrenaline. He ran into a riot of angry pulsing light and cruel sounds and hot gusts of air and needles of stirred dust. His lungs soon ached from the effort of breathing, he began to lose control of the visions that came his way: it was all pure sensation, overwhelming. It made no sense at all. Smoke billowed, tracers hopped insolently around, screams and thumps filled the air without revealing their sources. He felt as if he were in the middle of a panoramic vista of despair, a huge painting comprised of individual scenes each quite exact, yet overall meaningless in their pattern. He found himself hunching behind a coil of barbed wire, watching a German MG-42—that high, ripping sound as the double-feed pawls and rollers in the breech-lock mechanism really chewed through the belt—knock down Americans. They just fell, lazily, slumping sleepily to the ground; you had to concentrate to remember that death was at the end of the tumble. He became aware of the taste and texture of the dirt on his tongue and lips as he tried to press even closer into the loam, tracers pumping overhead. He saw running Germans flattened one-two-three by teen-agers with wild haircuts and tommy guns. Men in flames zigged in their own terrible light, frenzied, from a burning building. He crawled frantically over cratered terrain, sprawling comically in a pit for safety and there found another sanctum-seeker, half a grin spilling ludicrously across half a face. If this battle had a narrative, or a point of view, he was not a reader of it. In fact, he really didn't take part in it. He hadn't fired his weapon, the only Germans he saw close up were dead ones and nobody paid him any attention. Again, he was a visitor. For him it was mostly rolling around in the dirt, hoping he didn't get killed. He did nothing especially brave, except not run.

At one point, after what seemed hours of aimless crawling, he found himself crouching with a group of shivering paratroopers in the shelter of a shot-out blockhouse. Fire clattered and jounced hotly off the wall, and from somewhere up ahead, an insane sergeant howled at them to come on up and do some shooting.

"You go," a boy near him said.

"No, you go," said his friend.

"Hey, lookit this neat German gun," someone said.

"Hey, that's worth some money."

"Fuck, yes."

Leets saw the man had an MG-42; he was crawling out of the blockhouse.

"Hey, it's broke," someone said.

"No," Leets said. "That gun fires so fast they change barrels on it. They were in the middle of a change. That's why it looks all fucked up."

The barrel seemed to be hanging out of a vent in the side of the cooling sleeve.

"Go on back in. There ought to be a leather case around in there somewhere. About two feet long, with a big flap."

The kid ducked in and came out again with it.

"Okay," said Leets. He took the barrel pouch and drew a new barrel out.

"Gimme the gun," he said. "I think I can fix it."

Leets threaded the new barrel down the socket guides, and locked it. Then he closed the vent, heard the barrel snap into place. He turned the weapon over. Dirt jammed the breech. He pried the feed cover open, brushed the bigger curds out of the oily action.

"Are there any bullets?" he asked.

"Here," someone said, handing over a bunched-up belt.

Leets fed it into the mechanism and closed the feed cover. Then he drew back the operating handle and shoved it forward.

"I'm going to do some shooting," he said. "How about one of you guys come and feed me the belt?"

They looked at him. Finally, a kid said. "Yeah, okay. But could I shoot it a little?"

"Sure," Leets said.

They squirmed forward until they came against the lip of a ridge. Peering ahead, Leets saw the SS barrack looming like a ship. Flashes leapt out from it. Bullets whined above.

"There's some still in there," a sergeant said. "They pushed us out. I don't have enough men or firepower to get back inside."

"Isn't there supposed to be a lieutenant around here?" Leets asked.

"He got it."

"Oh. Okay, I've got a German gun here. I'm going to shoot the place up."

"Go ahead. Goose 'em good. Really spray 'em."

Leets pushed the gun on its bipod out beyond him, and drew it into his shoulder. He could feel the young soldier warm next to him.

"Don't let the belt get tangled, now," he said.

"I won't. But you said I could shoot."

"You can have the goddamn thing when I'm done. Okay?"

"Hey, super," said the kid.

The building was a black bulk against a pinker sky.

You in there, Repp? Repp, it's me out here. I hope you're in there. I've got five hundred rounds of 7.92 mill out here and I'm hoping one of them's for you. And what about you, Man of Oak, you bastard?

"Who are you talking to?" the kid wanted to know.

"Nobody," said Leets. "I'm aiming."

He fired. Each third round was a tracer. He saw them looping out, bending ever so slightly, sinking into the building. Occasionally one would jag off something hard, and prance into the sky. It seemed a neon jamboree, a curtain of dazzle, the chains of light rattling through the dark. Cordite rose to Leets's nose as he kept feeding twenty-round bursts into the building and as the empty shells piled, they'd sometimes topple, cascades of used brass, warm and dirty, rolling down the slope, clinking.

"Goose it again," said the sergeant.

Leets stitched another burst into the place. He had no trouble holding the rounds into the target. He took them from one end of the building to another, chest-high. The building accepted them stoically, until at last a tracer lit it off and it began to burn. A man inside waited until he ignited before coming out and Leets fired into him, cutting him in two. The flames were quite bright by that time, and there was not much more shooting.

Shmuel lay on his belly among strangers for the whole night. Nobody paid him any attention, but nearby the parachutists established their aid station, and besides the flashes of the battle, he'd seen the wounded drifting back, ones and twos, an occasional man carried by buddies who'd drop him and always return to the fighting. There was much screaming.

With dawn, fires arose from Anlage—Shmuel knew the buildings were burning. And then in the morning, the tanks had come down the road, clanking, sheathed in dust. The wounded cheered as best they could but the vehicles which looked so potent when first he glimpsed them seemed sad and beaten-up as they rumbled by. He could imagine better saviors than this ragged caravan of smoking creatures, leaking oil, scarred. Major Outhwaithe perched behind the turret of the first one, black and grimy, like a chimney sweep.

The tanks rolled into Anlage and Shmuel lost sight of them in the pall of smoke. Then explosions, fierce as any he'd heard.

"They must be blowing 'em out of that last pillbox," one hurt boy said to another.

Then a soldier came for him.

"Sir, Captain Leets wants you."

"Ah," said Shmuel, embarrassed to be so clean among the dirty bleeding soldiers.

But soon his discomfort replaced itself with a sensation of befuddlement. He found it hard to relate what he encountered to what he remembered. He was appalled at the destruction. He saw a world literally eviscerated, ruin, smoky timbers, gouged earth, bullet-riddled buildings, all the more unbelievable for the small scenes of domestic tranquillity enacted against it by surviving American soldiers, lying about in the sun, cigarettes lazy in their mouths, writing letters, reading Westerns, eating cold breakfasts.

His guide took him to a pit, where the German dead lay in rows, flies collecting busily in black clouds on them. He'd seen corpses before, but a corpse was a certain thing: first, it was Jewish, but more importantly it was very skinny, white, shrunken, its terror contained in the fact that it looked so unreal, a puppet or chunk of wood. Here, reality was inescapable: bones and brains and guts, blue-black, black-red, green-yellow, ripe and full of gore. Shmuel could think only of meat shops and the ritual slaughterers on the days before holidays—hanging slabs of beef, steamy piles of vitals, tripe white and cold. Yet in the butcher shops there was neatness, order, purpose: this was all spillage, sloppy and accidental.

"Not pretty. Even when it's them," said Leets, standing glumly on the brink. "These are the soldiers, the *Totenkopfdivision* people. All of them, or what's left of them. Sorry. But it's time to go looking."

"Of course. How else?" said Shmuel.

He walked the ranks. Dead, the Germans were only their flesh:

hard to hate. He felt nothing but his own discomfort at the re-
volting details of violent death; the odor of emptying colons and
the swarming flies. It became easy after a while, walking among
them. They were arrayed in their brightly vivid camouflage jackets, the pattern precise and inappropriately colorful, gay almost,
brown-green dappling dun. Soon he saw an old friend.

Hello, Pipe Smoker. You've a hole the size of a bucket mouth
at your center and you don't look happy about it. This is how
the Gentiles kill: completely, totally. A serious business, the manufacture of death. Us, they starve, or gas, saving bullets. They tried
bullets on us, but considered the practice wasteful. Their own
they kill with bullets and explosives, Pipe Smoker, spend millions.

Next came the boy who'd struck him in the storeroom. You
were a mean one, called me Jew-shit, kicked me. The boy lay
blue and halved on the ground, legs, trunk missing. What could
have done such a dreadful thing? He was surely the most mu-
tilated. You struck me, boy, and in that instant if this scene could
have been projected to you, Shmuel the Jew in an American uniform, all warm and whole, standing dumbly over only half your
body, you'd have thought it a joke, a laugh. Yet there you are
and here I am and by the furious way your eyes stare, I believe
you know. Ah, and Schaeffer, Hauptsturmführer Schaeffer, almost untouched, certainly unmussed, did you die of fright there
in your crisp and bright camouflage coat; no, there's a tiny black
hole drilled into your upper lip.

"No," he said, after the last, "he's not here."

Leets nodded and then took him to the bullet-riddled hulk of
barrack that had once housed Vollmerhausen's researchers. The
door was off its hinges and the roof had fallen in at one end,
but Shmuel could see the bodies in the blood-soaked sheets in the
cots.

"The civilians," Shmuel said. "A shame you had to kill them."

"It wasn't us," Leets said. "And it wasn't by accident either."
He bent to the floor and came up with a handful of empty shells.

"These are all over the place in there. Nine-millimeter. MP-
forty cases. The SS did it. The ultimate security. Now, one more
stop. This way, please."

They walked across the compound, avoiding shell craters and
piles of rubble, to the SS barrack. It still smoldered and had fallen
in on itself sometime after sunrise. But one end stood. Leets led

him to the side and pointed through a window that had been shot out.

"Can you see? On the floor. He's burned and most of his face is gone. He's in a bathrobe. That's not Repp, is it?"

"No."

"No. You'd never catch Repp in a bathrobe. It's the engineer, isn't it? Vollmerhausen?"

"Yes."

"Well, that's it then."

"You missed him."

"Yeah. He made it out. Somehow. The bastard."

"And the trail ends."

"Maybe. Maybe. We'll see what we can dig out of the rubble. And there's this." He held something out to Shmuel.

"Do you know what it is?" he asked.

Shmuel looked at the small metal object in Leets's upturned palm. He almost laughed.

"Yes, of course I know. But what—"

"We found it in there. Under Vollmerhausen. It must have been on the desk, which he seemed to hit on the way down. That's Yiddish on it, isn't it?"

"Hebrew," Shmuel corrected. "It's a toy. It's called a *draydel*. A top, for spinning." He'd done so a hundred, a thousand times himself when a boy. "It's for children. You make small wagers, and spin the top. You gamble on which of the four letters will turn up. Played on Hanukkah chiefly." It was like a die with an axis through the center, the inscribed letters almost rubbed out by so many small fingers. "It's very old," Shmuel said. "Possibly quite valuable. An heirloom at the very least."

"I see. What is the significance of the letters?"

"They are the first letters of the words in a religious phrase."

"Which is?"

"A Great Miracle Happened Here."

XV

Repp paused, hungry. Should he eat the bread now, or later? Well, why not now? He'd been moving hard half the night and most of the day, pushing himself, and soon he'd be out of forest and onto the Bavarian plain. Good progress, he reckoned, ahead of schedule even, a healthy sign considering the somewhat, ah, *hasty* mode of his departure.

He sat on a fallen log in a meadow. He was at last out of the coniferous zone, in a region of elm and poplars. Repp knew his trees, and poplars were a special favorite of his, especially on a fine spring afternoon such as this one, when the pale sun seemed to illuminate them in an almost magical way—they glowed in the lemon light, translucent, mystical against the darker tracings of the limbs which displayed them. The still, austere beauty of the day made the spectacle even more remarkable—a clean beauty, pure, untainted, uncontrived—and Repp smiled at it all, at the same time pleased that his own sensitivity to such matters hadn't been blunted by the war. Repp appreciated nature; he felt it important to good health, soundness of body and clearness of mind. Nature was particularly meaningful to his higher instincts in hard times like these, though it was rare that such natural beauty could be savored in and of itself, without reference to more prosaic necessities, fields of fire, automatic weapons placement, minefield patterns and so forth.

He tore into the bread. Dry, tough, it still tasted delicious. A good thing it had been in the pack when the Americans had come. Time only to grab the pack, throw it on and head for the tunnel. He'd made it after a long crawl across the open ground, American fire snapping into the ground around him. He curled in a gully by the tunnel entrance.

There were, in fact, six of them. Repp had insisted. He was a careful man who thought hard about likelihoods, and he knew no place in Germany in the late spring of 1945 that might not be assaulted by enemy troops, and if such an assault came, he had no intention of being trapped in it. He removed the camouflaged cover and squirmed down into the narrow opening. He slithered along. The space was close, almost claustrophobic, room for one thin man. Dust showered down on him as his back scraped the roof and the darkness was impenetrable. A great loneliness fell over Repp. He knew that even for a brave man panic was an instant away in a sewer like this. And who knew what creatures might be using it to nest in? It was damp and smelled of clay. Vile place: a grave. The world of the corpse.

He warned himself to be careful. Too much imagination could kill you just as quickly as enemy bullets. But Repp was used to working in the open, with great reaches beyond him. Here there was nothing except the dark. He could hold a hand to his face an inch in front of his eyes, and see nothing, absolute nothingness.

He pulled himself mechanically along, thinking this surely the worst moment in his long war, yet trying, desperately, to concentrate on the physical—the thrusts of his arms, the push of his legs, the slide of his torso. The roof pressed against his shoulders. At any moment it could come down. Repp wiggled along. Just a few more feet.

After what seemed years in the underground, he'd at last come to the end. He pulled himself the remaining few feet, but here the panic flappity-flapped through him; he thought of it as an owl, its wings unfurling frenziedly. The cool air came like a maddening perfume, rich and sensuous. The temptation to crash from the hole and dance for glee was enormous; he fought it. He edged back to the surface cautiously, without sudden movements. He emerged a few feet beyond the tree line. The fight still raged, mostly indistinct light and sound from here, but Repp hadn't time to consider it. He continued his crawl through the trees, dragging the pack and rifle with him. Once or twice he froze, sensing human activity nearby. When he was finally certain he was alone, he pulled himself up. He quickly consulted the compass and set off.

His route took him past the firing range. He skirted it, unwilling to risk its openness even though it was still dark. A voice came suddenly, brazen and American. He dived back instantly and lay breathing hard. Americans? This far out?

He pushed back the brush and stared into the dark. He saw men moving vaguely. Must be some kind of patrol, an extra security measure way out here. But his eyes began to adjust and he could see the men gathering up long white shrouds. He had trouble making sense out of this and—

Parachutes.

He knew then that this was not some accident of war, an American reconnaissance in force blundering into his perimeter.

The parachutists had come after a specific objective.

They had come after him.

Repp knew he was being hunted. He felt a weight in his stomach. If it were just shooting, his skill against theirs, that would be one thing. But this business was far more complex and his own path only one route to the center. In at least a thousand other ways he was vulnerable. He could move perfectly, do all things brilliantly, and still fail.

He was ahead of them, but by what margin? What did they know? What remained in the ruins of Anlage Elf? Had they seen the documents from Financial Section? Had they learned the secret of the meaning of Nibelungen, the *Reichsführer*'s pet name, the joke he delighted in?

The worst possibility of all was that they had come across Nibelungen's other half—the Spanish Jew, for whom all these arrangements had been made.

He stuffed what was left of the bread back into his pack, and walked on.

XVI

Leets was a man with problems. He had no Repp and not one idea in hell where the German was headed; worse, he had no idea where he himself was headed. His archeological expedition through the ruins of Anlage had come up bust—nothing but burnt files and shattered, blackened equipment. And corpses. In all this there was not one shard of pottery, not one scrap, one flake of debris that pointed to another step. The trail was stone cold.

Now he was reduced to hoping for luck. He sat by himself in front of an improvised table within the installation compound. Before him were what remained of several thousand 7.92-mm Kurz cases he'd had the paratroopers collect before they'd moved out.

Leets picked one up, and examined it with a sublimely ridiculous Sherlock Holmes magnifying glass. The shell in his huge grimy fingers glinted like the purest gold; Leets revolved it, studying its bland, flecked surface. He was looking for a gouge, a fracture mark, indicative of reloading, which in turn would be indicative of modification into one of the hand-tooled long-range custom jobs Repp had taken the patrol with. If he can find one, he can prove at least to himself Repp was here; he is not going insane. But nope, this shell holds no secrets; disgustedly, he tossed it into the pile at his feet, and plucked up another. He'd been at it now for hours, not exactly the sort of thing Army officers are expected to do at all, but what the hell, somebody's got to do it.

At first it was Roger's job, but the kid began wandering off. Roger had returned with special orders and presented them to Leets without one shred of embarrassment. The great Bill Fielding is putting on an exhibition in Paris ostensibly for the wounded boys, a morale builder, and Roger'd wangled his way into it. The OSS Harvard faction was keen to have the outfit represented, and Roger'd been anointed champion. He'd be taking off soon, and now he wasn't worth a damn, off screwing around somewhere with his racquets.

But that left Leets alone with the headache and a tableful of shells and a sinking conviction he was getting nowhere. It was spring, full spring now, almost May. The Black Forest was turn-

ing green, and the air was pleasant, even if still heavy with the
tang of ash. Leets returned to another shell. He was working
slowly, because he wasn't sure what the hell he'd do when he got
finished.

A shadow fled across the table, then returned and paused, and
Leets looked up from his collection and saw the Jew, Shmuel.

"Captain Leets?" the man said, looking absurdly American in
his uniform, a white spiffy triangle of cotton undershirt showing
above the top button of his wool OD shirt. Leets didn't have the
heart to tell him he was wearing the undershirt backward.

"A thought came to me. Maybe a help for you. Maybe not."

Shmuel had never volunteered before, except in that frantic
moment in the hospital when he insisted on making the jump.
But now he was calm and composed. Or maybe it was only the
weight he'd picked up since chowing with the Americans these
last weeks.

"So go ahead," Leets said. He still wasn't sure what to call the
man.

"Do you remember the bodies? The SS men? Before they were
shoveled into the pit?"

"Yes, I do," Leets said. Hard to forget.

"Something then bothered me. Now I can say it. It came to me
in a dream."

"Yes," Leets said.

"The jackets. The ones with the spots."

"The Tiger coats. Standard SS issue. You see them all over
Europe."

"Yes. Here's the curiosity. They were all new. Every single
one of them. It's what made the dead so vivid. In January the
coats were ragged and faded. Patched."

Leets took all day before cooking up a response. "So?" he
finally asked, confessing, "You've lost me."

"So, nothing. I don't know. But it struck me—strikes me—as
peculiar."

"Yeah, well, the Krauts got a batch of new coats. How about
that? Hmm." He turned it over in his mind several times, slowly,
looking past the Jew, looking hard at nothing as he picked at this
curious bit of info. A truckload of jackets, over one hundred of
them: quite a chunk of weight. Hard to believe the Germans
would haul it up from the plains, over that muddy road. Trucks

must have come in there all the time, of course, keep the place supplied. But all those coats . . .

"Thanks," he eventually said. "Something to think about, though I'm not just sure what the significance is."

The more he thought about it the more fascinating it seemed. Here it was, late in the war, very very late, two minutes to midnight, the Reich shattered, the supply system, like all systems, broken down. Yet they were shipping clothes about.

No, a more likely situation would be that the reinforced *Totenkopfdivision* company *went* somewhere to pick up the coats, someplace where piles and piles of the things were available—these were the March, 1944, model now, *coats*, not tunics, camouflaged, the four-pocket model with the snap buttons and the sniper's epaulets: a new item in their battle-dress collection.

"Damnedest thing," he said aloud.

The Jew still stood there. "I happen to know about these coats," he said. "A little. Not a lot."

"What?" Leets asked.

"One of the other prisoners told me he'd worked on them. In the factory as a laborer. He'd been a tailor and the SS sent him to work in their factory. In the plant. It's a place where there'd be a lot of them. Not so far from here. No rail travel would be involved."

"What place?" asked Leets.

"The SS *Konzentrationlager* Dachau," said Shmuel.

XVII

In an otherwise quite pleasant ash tree, the deserter swayed heavily at the end of the rope, face blue, neck grotesquely twisted. He'd been stripped of gear and boots but boasted a sign: I'M A PIG WHO LEFT MY COMRADES!

"Poor devil," said the man next to Repp. "Those SS bastards must have caught him."

Repp grunted noncommittally. He'd picked up this platoon of drifting engineers a few miles back and with them he was making his way across the Bavarian plateau in the southern lee of the Swabian Jura.

"They get you and your papers are wrong and it's—" Lenz made a comical imitation of a man choking in a noose.

Occasionally a vehicle would roll down the dusty road, a half-track once, a couple of Opel trucks, finally a staff car with two colonels in the back.

"They ride, we walk," said Lenz. "As usual. They'll get away, we'll go to a PW camp. Or Siberia. That's always the way it is. The little fellow catches—"

"Lenz, shut up," called back Gerngoss, the fat Austrian platoon sergeant.

The platoon continued to move down the road, through an empty landscape. Ostensibly, they were headed for the town of Tuttlingen, several kilometers ahead, to blow up a bridge before the Americans arrived. But Repp knew this was a pretext; actually they were just moping around enough to pass the time until the Amis showed and they could surrender. They were not *Totenkopf-division* boys, that was for sure.

Repp tuned out the chatter and plowed on. It was farming country, smoother here west of the River Lech, near the Lake of Konstanz. The Alps could be seen, especially the 9,000 feet of the Zugspitze, far to the south, unusual since it was not September or October. To the west, the Black Forest massif, off of which Repp had come, glowered smudgily against the horizon.

"Perfect hunting weather for Jabos. You'd think they'd be thick as flies, the bastards," said Lenz.

"Oh, Christ," said somebody.

Repp looked up.

It was too late to turn back, or fade off into the fields. They'd just rounded a bend in the road and there in the trees was a self-propelled antitank gun, huge thing, dragon on treads, riveted body, dun-colored. SS men in their camouflage tunics lounged about it, their STG's slung. Repp could tell from the flashes they were from the Field Police regiment of SS "Das Reich."

"Watch yourselves," muttered Gerngoss, just ahead. "Don't do anything stupid. These pricks mean business."

The young officer in the open pulpit of the gun mount leaned forward and with an exaggerated smile said, "You fellows going to Switzerland?" He wore a metal plaque with an embossed eagle on a chain around his neck; it hung down on his chest like a medieval breastplate.

"A joker," muttered Lenz.

"No, sir," replied Gerngoss, trying to sound casual but speaking over dry breaths through a dry mouth, "just going on down the road to a job."

"Oh, I see," said the young officer affably, though his eyes were metallic. "And which one might that be?" As he spoke one of the other SS men climbed down off the hull, unslinging his rifle.

"We're engineers, Lieutenant," explained Gerngoss, his voice rising suddenly. "Headed toward Tuttlingen. A bridge there to be blown before the Americans get to it. Then we'll rejoin our unit, Third Brigade of the Eighteenth Motorized Engineer Battalion, south of Munich. Here, I have the orders here." He held them out. Repp could see his hand tremble.

"Bring them here, Sergeant Fatty," the young officer said.

Gerngoss waddled over fretfully. In the shadow of the armored vehicle, he handed them up to the young officer.

"These orders are dated May first. Two days ago. It says you're traveling by truck."

"I know, sir," said Gerngoss, a weak smile bobbing on his lips. "We were hit by Jabos yesterday. A bad day. The truck was crippled, some people hurt, had to find a field hospital—"

"I think you're stalling." He smiled. "Dawdling. Waiting for the war to end." The SS lieutenant laid an arm across the MG-42 mounted before him. In his peripheral vision, Repp saw the SS man flanking off to the right, STG loose and ready.

"Oh, shit," Lenz muttered tensely next to him.

"S-sir," insisted Gerngoss, "w-we're doing our jobs. Our duty." His voice was small, coming from such a big man.

"I think," said the lieutenant, "you're a Jew-pig. A deserter. It's because of swine like you that we lost the war. Fat anushole Austrian, can't wait to get home and fuck Jew-cunts and eat pastries in the Vienna cafés with Bolsheviks."

"Please. Please," whimpered Gerngoss.

"Go on. Get out of here, you and your Army scum. I ought to hang you all." He spoke with angry contempt. "Drag your fat asses out of here."

"Yes, sir," mumbled Gerngoss, and shambled away.

"Thank Christ," muttered Lenz. "Sweet Jesus, thank Christ," and the squad began to shuffle forward humbly under the sullen gaze of the SS men.

"Ah, one second, please," the smiling lieutenant in the turret called out. "You, third from the end. Thin fellow."

Repp realized the man was talking to him.

"Lieutenant?" he inquired meekly.

"Say, friend, I just noticed that the piping on your collar is white," the smiler announced. He seemed quite joyful. "White— infantry. The others have black—engineers."

"He's not with us," announced Lenz, stepping away quickly. "He straggled in yesterday."

"He said he was trying to find his unit," Gerngoss called. "Second Battalion of Eleventh Infantry. It sounded fishy to me."

"I have papers," Repp said. He realized he was standing alone on the road.

"Here. Quickly."

Repp scurried over, holding the documents up. The young officer took them. As he read, his eyebrows rose. He was freckled and fair, about twenty years old. A lick of blond hair hung down from under his helmet.

"I was separated from my unit," Repp said, "in a big attack, sir. The Americans came and bombed us. It was worse than Russia."

The young lieutenant smiled.

"I'm rather afraid these papers aren't any good. Waffen SS field regulations supersede OKW forms. As of May first, on the order of the *Reichsführer* SS. For the discipline of the troops. You don't

have LA/fifty-three-oh-four, or its current stamp. A field ID. It
has to be stamped every three days. To keep"—the smile broadened
—"deserters from mingling with loyal troops."

"Most of them just stayed. Waiting for the Americans. I went
on. To find the rest of my unit. I was wounded in Russia. I have
the Knight's Cross."

"A piece of shit," the officer said.

"I have a note from my captain. It's here, somewhere."

"You're a deserter. A swine. We've run into others like you.
You're going where they are now. To a dance in midair. Take the
pig."

Repp felt the muzzle of the STG pressing hard into his back
and at the same moment his own rifle was yanked off his back.
Someone shoved him and he fell oafishly to the ground.

"You stinking fucker," a teen-aged voice behind him cursed.
"We'll hang you till your tongue's blue." He hit Repp in the lower
spine with his rifle butt. The pain almost crippled Repp. He yelped,
lurching forward, and lay in agony, rubbing the bruise through
his greatcoat.

The young soldier grabbed him roughly by the arm, pulling
him up with great disgust, the STG momentarily lowered in the
effort, and as Repp was twisted upward he laid the P-38 barrel
against the youth's throat and shot it out; then, as the boy fell back,
very calmly Repp pivoted, steadying the pistol with the other hand
under the butt, and shot the young officer in the face, disintegrating
it. He shot two other men off the hull of the self-propelled gun
where they sat, paralyzed, and dropped the pistol. He stood and
pried the STG from the tight fingers of the first soldier, who lay
back behind sightless eyes, slipping into coma, his throat spasming
empty of blood. He wouldn't last long.

Repp's finger found the fire-selector rod of the assault rifle just
above the trigger guard and he rammed it to full automatic, at the
same time palming back the bolt. Three more SS men careered from
behind the vehicle. He shot from the hip without thinking, one
long burst, half the magazine, knocking them flat in a commotion
of dust spurts. He ran another burst across the bodies just in case,
the earth puffing and fanning from the strike of the bullets.

Repp stood back, the weapon hot in his hand. The whole thing
had taken less than five seconds. He waited, ready to shoot at any
sign of motion, but there was none.

What waste, what sheer waste! Good men, loyal men, doing their jobs. Dead in a freak battleground accident. He was profoundly depressed.

Blood everywhere. It speckled the skin of the self-propelled gun, swerving jaggedly down to the fender, where it collected in a black pool. It soaked the uniforms of the two men who lay before the big vehicle, and puddles of it gathered around the three he'd taken in the last long burst. Repp turned. The boy he'd shot in the throat lay breathing raspily.

Repp knelt and lifted the boy's head gently. Blood coursed in torrents from the throat wound, disappearing inside the collar of his jacket. He was all but finished, his eyes blank, his face gray and calm.

"Father. Father, please," he said.

Repp reached and took his hand and held it until the boy was gone.

He stood. He was alone in the road, and disgusted. The engineers had fled.

Goddamn! Goddamn!

It made him sick. He wanted to vomit.

They would pay. The Jews would pay. In blood and money.

XVIII

Ugh!

Roger sat in his Class A's on the terrace of the Ritz. Before him was a recent edition of the New York *Herald Tribune*, the first page given to a story by a woman named Marguerite Higgins, who had arrived with the 22d Regiment, some motorized hot shots, at the concentration camp of Dachau.

Roger almost gagged. The bodies heaped like garbage, skinny sacks, ribs stark. The contrast between that place and this, Paris, Place Vendôme, the ritzy Ritz, the city shoring up for an imminent VE-Day, girls all over the place, was almost more than he could take.

Leets and Outhwaithe were there, poking about. Roger was due back in a day or so.

But he had come to a decision: he would not go.

I will not go.

No matter what.

He shivered, thinking of the slime at Dachau. He imagined the smell. He shivered again.

"Cold?"

"Huh? Oh!"

Roger looked up into the face of the most famous tennis player of all time.

"You're Evans?" asked Bill Fielding.

"Ulp," Roger gulped spastically, shooting to his feet. "Yes, sir, yes, sir, I'm Roger Evans, Harvard, '47, sir, probably '49 now, with this little *interruption*, heh, heh, number-one singles there my *freshman* year."

The great man was a head taller than Roger, still thin as an icicle, dressed in immaculate white that made his tan seem deeper than burnished oak; he was in his late forties but looked an easy thirty-five.

Roger was aware that all commerce on the busy terrace had stopped; they were looking at Bill Fielding, all of them—generals, newspapermen, beautiful women, aristocrats, gangsters. Fielding was a star even in the exotic confines of the Ritz. And Roger knew they were also looking at *him*.

"Well, let me tell you how this works. You've played at Roland Garros?"

"No, sir."

"Well, we'll be on the *Cour Centrale* of course—"

Of course, thought Roger.

"—a clay surface, in an amphitheater, about eight thousand wounded boys, I'm told, plus the usual brass—you've played in front of crowds, no nerve problems or anything?"

Roger? Nervous?

"No, sir," he said. "I played in the finals of the Ivies and I made it to the second round at Forest Hills in '44."

Fielding was not impressed.

"Yes, well, I hope not. Anyway, I usually give the boys a little talk, using Frank as a model, show them the fundamentals of the game. The idea is first to entertain these poor wounded kids but also to sell tennis. You know, it's a chance to introduce the game to a whole new class of fan."

Yeah, some class, most of 'em just glad they didn't get their balls blown off in the fighting, but he nodded intently.

"Then you and Frank will go two sets, three maybe, depends on you." Roger did not like *at all* the assumption here that he was the sacrificial goat in all this. "Then you and I, Frank and Major Miles, our regular Army liaison, will go a set of doubles, just to introduce them to that. Agreeable?"

"Whatever you say, Mr. Fielding. Uh, I saw you at Forest Hills in '31. I was just a kid—" Oops, that was a wrong thing to say.

Fielding glowered. "Not a good tournament for me."

"Quarters. You played Maurice McLaughlin."

Fielding's face lit up at the memory of the long-ago match; he was just coming off his prime then, his golden years, and still had great reserves of the good stuff, the high-octane tennis, left. "Oh, yes, Maurie. Lots of power, strength. But somehow lacking . . . Three and love, right?"

He remembers?

"That's right, sir."

"Yes, well, I hope you've got more out there than poor Maurie," said Fielding disgustedly.

"Uh, I'll sure try," said Roger. Fielding was certainly blunt.

"All right. You've got transportation out to Auteuil, I assume."

"Yes, sir, the Special Services people have a car and—"

Fielding was not interested in the details. "Fine, Sergeant, see you at one," and he turned and began to stride forcefully away, the circle opening in awe.

"Uh. Mr. Fielding," said Roger, racing after. His heart was pounding but once out at the Stade, he'd never have a chance.

"Yes?" said Fielding, a trifle annoyed. He had a long nose that he aimed down almost like the barrel of a rifle. His eyes were blue and pale and unwavering.

"Frank Benson. He's good, I hear."

"My protégé. A future world champion, I hope. Now if—"

"I'm better," blurted Roger. There. He'd said it.

Fielding's face lengthened in contempt. He seemed to be turning purple under the tan. He was known for his towering rages at incompetence, lack of concentration, quitters, the overbrash, the slow, the blind, the halt and the lame. Roger smiled bravely and forged ahead. He knew that here, as on the court, to plant your sneakers was to die. Attack, attack: close to the net, volley away for a kill.

"I can beat him. And will, this afternoon. Now I just want you to think about this. Continuing this tour with someone *second-best* is gonna kinda take the fun out of it, I'd say."

The silence was ferocious.

Roger thrust on. "Now if I bury him, if I pound him, if I shellac him—" He was prepared to continue with colorful metaphors for destruction for quite some time, but Fielding cut him off.

"What is it you want?"

"Simple. In. In *fast*."

"The tour?"

"Yes, sir."

Fielding's face confessed puzzlement. "The shooting's over. Why now, all of a sudden?"

Roger could not explain—maybe even to himself—about the bodies at Dachau, the vista of wormy stiffs.

"Just fed up, is all, sir. Like you, I was put on this earth to hit a tennis ball. Anything else is just time misspent. I did my duty. In fact my unit just took part in what will probably be the last airborne operation in the ETO, a night drop and a son of a bitch, you'll pardon me." And it had been, sitting back at 82d Airborne Ops, running low on coffee and doughnuts. Roger tried to look modest. "And finally, well"—tricky this, he'd heard Fielding couldn't abide bootlickers—"finally there's *you*: a chance to apprentice under Fielding, under the best. I knew I'd better give it my best serve, flat out, go for the line, or always wonder about it." He looked modestly—or what he presumed to be modestly—at his jump boots.

"You're not shy, are you?" Fielding finally said.

"No, sir," admitted Roger, "I believe in myself. Here, and on the court." Roger realized with a start, He hasn't said No.

"Words before a match are cheap. That's why I never had any. Frank is my protégé. Ever since I discovered him at that air base in England, I've believed he had it in him to be the world's best, as I was. You want in, do you? Well, this afternoon we'll see if your game is as big as your ego. Or your mouth."

He turned and walked out off the terrace.

Roger thought, Almost there.

But before Roger could insert Dachau into his file of might-have-beens there was Benson to play, Benson *to beat*, thinking positively, and Roger knew this would not be so easy. He'd done a little research on the guy, No. 1 at Stanford, '39 and '40, made the third round at Forest Hills in '41, a Californian with that Westerner's game, coming off those hard concrete courts, serve and volley, Patton-style tennis, always on the attack. But he'd shelved the tennis for four years, Air Corps, done twenty-three trips over Germany as a B-17 bombardier (D.F.C. even! another hero like Leets), survived the slaughterhouse over Schweinfurt the second time somehow, and only picked the game back up as a way of relaxing, cooling down near the end of his tour, when the reflexes go bad, the nerves sticky, the mind filling with hobgoblins and sirens and flak puffs and other terrors. When Fielding came to the air base in the fall of '44, first stop on his first tour, somehow Benson had been urged on him. It was love at first sight, 6–love, 6–love, for Benson. Fielding, whose game was off but not *that* off, saw in the thin swift Californian something sweet and pure and deadly and knew that here was himself twenty years ago, poised on the edge of greatness.

Fielding wanted Benson right away; he got him, even two missions short of twenty-five.

Benson was tall, thin, a ropy blond with calm gray eyes and marvelous form. He moved fast slowly, meaning that he had such effortless grace that he never seemed to lunge or lurch, rather glided about the court in his white flannels—for his eccentricity was to stick to the pleated flannel trousers of the Twenties and early Thirties, unlike the more stylish Rog, who'd been wearing shorts à la Riggs and Budge since he was a kid. Benson hit leapers, all that topspin, causing the ball to hiss and pop, even though the *Cour Centrale* was a porous clay-type composition, not quite en-tout-cas, but very, very slow. It was like playing on toast. The surface sucked the *oomph* from those slammed Western forehand drives, but to Roger, across from him, hitting in warm-up, the guy looked like seven skinny feet of white death, methodical, unflappable, unstoppable.

Still, Roger specialized in confidence, and his had not dropped a notch since his get-together with the Great Man this morning. He'd taken on big hitters before: it demanded patience, guile and plenty of nerve. Mainly you had to hold together on the big points, perform when the weight of the match squashed down on you. If you could run down their hottest stuff, these big hitters would blow up on you, get wilder and fiercer and crazier. He'd seen plenty like that, who fell apart, quit, hadn't that hard, bitter kernel of self-righteousness inside that made victory usual.

The *Cour Centrale* at Roland Garros sat in the center of a steeply tiered cement amphitheater which was now jamming up with uniforms. A flower bed along one side of the court, under the boxes where Important Brass now gathered, showed bright and cheerful, new to spring—the orderly German officers who'd played here during the Occupation had kept them up. Lacoste had owned this place with its soft, gritty-brown surface, along with his equally merciless sidekicks Borotra and Cochet; they'd called them the Three Musketeers back during their heyday, and only Fielding, with his power and control and, most of all, his guts, had been able to stand up to them here. So Roger wasn't just a player; he was a part of history, a part of tradition. He felt absorbed into it, taken with it, warmed by it, and now the ball seemed to crack cleanly off the center of strings. Was it his imagination or was even this audience of shot-up youngsters beginning to throb with enthusiasm? Pennants snapped in the wind. The shadows became distinct. The lines of the court were precise and beautiful. The balls were white and pure. Rog felt like a million bucks. This was where he belonged.

"Okay, fellows," said Fielding, calling them in.

They sat down to towel off as Fielding, to a surge of applause that grew and grew, lifting swiftly in passion as he moved out to the center of the court, stood to face the crowd, a microphone in hand. He smiled sharkishly.

"Hi, guys," he said, voice echoing back in amplification.

"Bill, Bill, Bill," they called, though most were too young to have remembered with clarity the three years, '27, '28 and '29, when he'd dominated tennis—and the larger world—like a god.

"Fellas," Bill allowed, "I know all this is kinda new to some of ya," a Midwestern accent, Kansas corn belt, flattened out the great man's Princeton voice, "but let me tell ya the truth: tennis is a game of skill, guts and endurance; it's like war . . . only tougher."

The soldiers howled in glee. Roger sat mesmerized by their pulsating animation: one mass, seething, galvanized by the star's charisma.

"Now today, we're going to show you how the big boys play. You've seen DiMage and the Splendid Splinter? Well you're going to see the DiMage and Ted Williams of tennis."

Fielding spoke for about ten minutes, a polished little speech in which he explained the rules, showed them the strokes as demonstrated by the blankly flawless Frank Benson, worked in a few amusing anecdotes and continually compared tennis—flatteringly—to other sports, emphasizing its demands of stamina, strength and courage, the savagery of its competition, the psychological violence between its opponents.

And then he was done.

"And now fellows," cheer-led Fielding, "the big boys: Captain Frank Benson, Stanford, '41, currently of the Eighth Air Force, twenty-three trips over Germany; and Technical Sergeant Five Roger Evans, Harvard, '46, now of the United States Army, attached to the Office of Strategic Services, veteran of several behind-the-lines missions—"

Yeah, *our* lines though. Good thing Leets wasn't around to hear that little fib.

"—and now," continued Fielding, mocking another game's traditions, "play ball!"

* * *

They'd already spun, Benson winning and electing to serve, but still he came to net and sought out Roger's eyes as Roger had guessed he would.

"Good luck, Sergeant," he said to Roger.

"Same to you, Chief," said Roger.

Roger was an excellent tennis player, definite national-ranking material, and though he'd not played hard and regularly in the year he'd been in the Army, he'd worked to maintain his edge, drilling when he couldn't find a partner, staying in shape, pursuing excellence in the limited ways available to him. But in the first seconds he knew he was seriously overmatched: it was the difference between skill and genius. Benson hit out at everything, fiery and hard: the white ball dipped violently as it neared the baseline and its spin caught up to and overpowered its velocity, pulling it down, making it come crazily off the court at him, faster than sin. Benson's forehand especially was a killer, white smoke, but when Roger, learning that lesson fast, tried to attack the backhand, deep, Benson rammed slices by him. He felt immediately that he couldn't stand and hit with the bastard from the backcourt and so at 1–1, after squeaking out a lucky win on his serve, which the Californian hadn't pressed seriously, he decided to angle dinks wide to the corner—now they are called approach shots but the terminology then was "forcing shots"—and come in behind them. Catastrophe followed thereupon: he didn't have enough punch on the ball to hold it deep and as he dashed in to net, Benson, anticipating beautifully, seemed to catch each shot as it dropped and hit some dead-run beauties that eluded Roger's lunge to volley by a hair.

Roger stood after fifteen minutes at 3–3, only because his own serve had finally loosened and was ticking and because the toasty composition scoured the balls, fluffing them up heavy and dull, letting Rog reach two shots on big points he never would have under normal conditions, *American* conditions, and he put both away insolently for winners, his two best strokes of the match.

But this equilibrium could not last and no one knew it better than Roger, who sensed his confidence begin to slide away. He felt a tide of self-pity start to rise through him.

On serve, with new balls, he fell behind fast on two backhand returns that Benson blew by him like rockets. He was looking at love–30, felt his heart thundering in his ribs.

He served a fault, just long, ball sliced wickedly but just off the back line.

He glanced about, a bad sign, for it meant his concentration was evaporating. The ranks of soldiers seemed to be glaring at him. A pretty nurse looked viciously unimpressed. Fielding, on a lawn chair just behind the umpire's seat, had a blank expression.

Roger felt the vise screwing in on the sides of his body. He could hardly breathe.

He double-faulted, going to add out, and quickly double-faulted again, down one, serve lost.

He sat on the bench during the change, toweling off, feeling sick. Humiliation lay ahead. He felt sick out there, knowing he'd quit. Dog, pig, skunk, jerk. He deserved to lose. Self-loathing raced through him like a drug, knocking the world to whirl and blur. He almost wanted to cry. Exhaustion crowded in.

Someone was near him. Roger couldn't care less. The unfairness of it all was overwhelming. The stands, the court, the net all shimmered in his rage. But through this rage, there came a voice, low and insistent. At first he thought it was his conscience, Jiminy Cricket-style, but . . .

"Kid," the voice whispered, "you don't belong out there. I'm carrying you."

Benson, close by, seemingly tightening his laces, was talking in a low voice, face down and hidden from the crowd.

"It ought to be done now, at love."

Roger didn't say anything. He stared bleakly ahead, letting the man mock him. He felt the sweat peel down his body inside his shirt. He knew it was the truth.

"But Christmas comes early this year," Benson said.

The oblique statement, it turned out, referred to a present: the match.

Roger ran the next three games for the set, Benson holding them close, but crapping out at key points. He could hit it an inch outside the line as well as an inch inside. Then Roger ran five more into the second set until Benson, still playing the feeb, broke through, but Roger triumphed in the seventh game for the set and the match, and the noise of the crowd, their adoration, broke over him like a wave, though he knew it was a joke, a prank, that he was unworthy, and he felt curiously ashamed.

"Congratulations," said Benson, his calm gray eyes full of malice and sarcasm. "Just stay out of California till you learn to volley" —with a most *sincere*, humble smile on his face—"and have fun with your new buddy."

Eh? What could—?

Benson, eyes down, pushed his way past Fielding.

"Frankie, Frankie," implored the old star.

Benson sat down disgustedly.

Fielding turned: his face was a mass of wrinkles beneath the lurid tan. He smiled broadly at Roger, eyes dancing, a leathery, horrible old lizard, with yellow eyes and greedy lips.

"My boy!" he said. "You did it. You did it." He clapped an arm around Roger, squeezing so that Roger could feel each of the fingers press knowingly into the fibers of muscle under his skin, kneading, urging.

"You'll be my champion," said Fielding, "my star," he whispered hoarsely into Roger's ear.

Oh, Christ, thought Roger.

XIX

Shmuel led, for he was in his own territory.

There was only one way to penetrate the barbed wire and the moat that formed the perimeter, and that was through the guardhouse. This took them under a famous German slogan, ARBEIT MACHT FREI, work makes one free.

"The Germans like slogans," Shmuel explained.

Once beyond the guardhouse, they arrived in the roll-call plaza, traversed it quickly and turned down the main camp road. On either side stood the barracks, fifteen of them, as well as additional structures such as the infirmary, the morgue and the penal blocks. Into each had been crammed two thousand men in the last days before the liberation. There had been corpses everywhere, and though they had now been gathered by the hygiene-minded American administrators, the smell remained awesome. Leets, with Shmuel and Tony, kept his eyes straight ahead as they walked the avenue. Prisoners milled about, the gaunt, skeletal almost-corpses in their rotten inmate's ticking. Though massive amounts of food and medical supplies had been convoyed in, the aid had yet to make much impression on the prison population.

Finally, they reached their destination, the eleventh barrack on the right-hand side. In it, once near death but now much improved, was one Eisner. Shmuel had gone in alone the first day and found him. Eisner was important because Eisner was a tailor; Eisner had worked in the SS uniform workshops just beyond the prison compound. Eisner alone knew of the SS Tiger jackets; Eisner alone might help them penetrate the mysteries of the last shipment to Anlage Elf.

They went in and got the man. It was not at all pleasant. They took him from the foul-smelling barrack to an office outside the compound in one of the SS administrative buildings.

Eisner was somewhat better today. His body was beginning to hold a little weight and his gestures had lost that slow-motion vagueness. He was finding words again and was at last strong enough to talk.

However he was not much interested in Dachau, or Tiger coats, or the year 1945. He preferred Heidelberg, 1938, before *Kristall-*

nacht, where he'd had a wonderful shop and a wife and three children, all of whom had been sent *Ost*. East.

"That means dead, of course," explained Shmuel.

Leets nodded. In all this he felt extremely dumb. This was their third day in the camp and he was getting a little bit more used to it. The first day had nearly wrecked him. He tried not to think about it.

Shmuel began slowly, with great patience. He had cautioned them, "It will be very difficult to earn this man's trust. He is frightened of everything, of everyone. He does not even realize the war is nearly over."

"Fine, go ahead," Leets said. "He's all we've got."

Shmuel spoke Yiddish, translating after each exchange.

"Mr. Eisner, you worked on uniforms for the German soldiers, is this not right?"

The old man blinked. He looked at them stupidly. He swallowed. His eyes seemed to fall out of focus.

"He's very frightened," Shmuel said. The old man was trembling.

"Coats," Shmuel said. "Coats. Garments. For the German soldiers. Coats like the color of the forest."

"Coats?" said Eisner.

He was trembling quite visibly. Leets lit a cigarette and handed it to the old man. He took it but his eyes would not meet Leets's.

"Mr. Eisner, can you remember, please. These coats?" Shmuel tried again.

Eisner muttered something.

"He says he's done nothing wrong. He says he's sorry. He says to tell the authorities he's sorry," Shmuel reported.

"At least he's talking," said Leets, for yesterday the man had simply stared at them.

"Here," Shmuel said. He'd taken from his field jacket a patch of the SS camouflage material, out of which the coats had been made.

But Eisner just stared at it as if it came from another planet.

Leets realized how Shmuel had been like this too, in the first days. It had taken weeks before Shmuel had talked in anything beyond grunts. And Shmuel had been younger, and stronger, and probably smarter. Tougher, certainly.

It seemed to go for hours, Shmuel nudging, poking gently, the old man resisting, looking terrified the whole time.

"Look, this just isn't getting us anywhere," Leets said.

"I agree," Shmuel said. "Too many strong young men in uniforms. Too many Gentiles."

"I think he's telling us to go for a stroll," said Tony. "Not a bad idea, actually. Leave the two of them alone."

"All right," said Leets. "Sure, fine. But remember: records. It's records we're after. There's got to be some paper work or something, some orders, packing manifests, I don't know, something to—"

"I know," said Shmuel.

Tony said he had a report to file with JAATIC, and so Leets found himself alone at Dachau. Unsure of what to do, too agitated to return to his billet in the town for sleep, he decided to head over to the warehouse and workshop complex, to the tailor's shop. He walked through the buildings outside the prison compound; here there was no squalor. It could have been any military installation, shabby brick buildings, scruffily landscaped, mostly deserted, except for guards here and there. Litter and debris lay about.

After a bit he reached his destination. The place was off limits of course, for the liberators had seen immediately that such a spot would become a souvenir hunter's paradise and in fact some elementary looting had occurred, but Leets had a necessary-duty pass that got him by the glum sentry standing with carbine outside the building.

It was a popular stop on the Dachau tour, a must along with the gas chambers and the crematorium and the pits of corpses and the labs where the grisly human experiments had been performed. Usually it was crowded with open-mouthed field-grade officers, reporters, VIP's, of one sort or another, all eager for a glimpse into the abyss—somebody else's abyss, as a matter of fact—but today the shop was empty. Leets stood silent at one end of the room, a long dim chamber lined with mirrors. Bolt on bolt of the finest gray-green material lay about and bundles of silk for flags and banners and wads of gold cord for embroidering, and reels of piping in all colors and spool on spool of gold thread. Tailor's dummies, their postures mocking the decaying dead outdoors, were scattered about, knocked down in the first frenzy of liberation. The odor was musty—all the heavy wool absorbed the peculiar tang of dust and blood and the atmosphere was tomb-like, still.

Leets found himself troubled here. The tailor's workshop was packed with the pomp of ideology, the quasi-religious grandeur of it all: swastika, slashing SS collar tabs, flags, vivid unit patches, the stylized Deco Nazi eagle, wings flared taut, preying, on shoulder tabs. Leets prowled edgily through this museum, trying to master its lesson, but could not. At one point he came upon a boxful of the silver death's-head badges that went on SS caps. He jammed his hand in, feeling them heavy and shifty and cool, running out from between his fingers. They felt in fact like quarters. He looked at one closely: skull, leering theatrically, carnivorous, laughing, chilling. Yet the skull was no pure Nazi invention; it was not even German. The British 17th Lancers had worn them on their trip to the Russian guns at Balaklava, last century.

He moved on to a bench on which the tailors had abandoned their last day's work, the sleeve bands worn on dress uniforms. These, strips of heavy black felt, had been painfully and beautifully embroidered in heavy gold thread, Gothic letters an inch high, with the names of various Nazi celebrities or more ancient Teutonic heroes; it was a German fashion to commemorate a man or a legend by naming a division after him or it: REINHARD HEYDRICH, THEODOR EICKE, FLORIAN GEYER, SS POLIZEI DIVISION, DANMARK, and so forth. The workmanship was exquisite, but by one of history's crueler ironies, this delicate work had been performed by Jewish hands. They'd sewed for their own murderers in order to live. A few, like Eisner, actually had survived.

Leets passed to a final exhibit—a long rack on which hung five uniforms for pickup. He hoped their owners had no need of them now. But they loved uniforms, that was certain. Perhaps here was a lesson, the very core of the thing. Perhaps the uniforms were not symbolic of National Socialism, but somehow *were* National Socialism. Leets paused with this concept for several seconds, pursuing it; a religion of decorations and melodrama, theater, the rampant effect, the stunning. But only a surface, no depth, no meaning. There were four of the gray-green Waffen SS dress uniforms, basically Wehrmacht tunics and trousers, dolled up with a little extra flash to make them stand out. The fifth was different, jet black, the uniform of RSHA, the terror boys. It was a racy thing, the uniform Himmler himself preferred, cut tight and elegant, with jodhpurs that laced up the legs. With shiny boots and armband it would form just about the most pristine statement of the theology of Nazism available. Hitler had been right about one terrible thing: it *would* live for a thousand years, if only in the imagination. Leets felt its numbing power to fascinate and not a little shame. He was embarrassed that it mesmerized him so. He could not look away from the black uniform hanging on the rack.

Yet the uniform signified only one face of it. He'd seen the other elsewhere. Another spectacle was intractably bound up with this one. Standing there alone in the dim stuffy room, the black uniform before him, he remembered.

The weather had turned cold, this three days earlier, but the gulf between then and now seemed like a geological epoch.

They were in an open Jeep. He sat in back with Shmuel, and pulled the field jacket tighter about himself. Tony was up front, and where Roger should have been, behind the wheel, another glum boy sat, borrowed from Seventh Army. They'd just bucked their way through the crowded streets of the thousand-year-old town of Dachau, quaint place, full of American vehicles and German charms, among the latter cobblestones, high-roofed stone houses, gilt metalwork, flower beds, tidy churches. Civilians stood about and American soldiers and even a few clusters of surrendered *feldgraus*.

And then they were beyond and then they had stopped. But feeling the Jeep bump to a halt, he looked up.

"Hey, what's going on?" he asked.

"Welcome to KZ Dachau," said Shmuel.

Seemed to be outside a yard of some sort. A wall of barbed wire closed it off, filthy place, heaps of garbage strewn all over, smelled to the heavens. Had some toilets backed up? He couldn't figure it out. The Germans were usually so tidy.

A rail yard, was that it? Yes, tracks and boxcars and flatcars standing idle, abandoned, their contents probably looted, tufts of hay and straw and the cars seemed full of . . . what, he couldn't tell. Logs? Pieces of wood perhaps? The thought of puppets came suddenly to mind, for in a peculiar way some of the forms seemed almost shaped like small humans.

He finally recognized it. In the picture Susan had forced him to look at in London so long ago, it had all been blurred, out of focus. Here, nothing was out of focus. Most of them were naked and hideously gaunt, but modesty and nutrition were merely the first and least of the laws of civilization violated in the rail yard. The corpses seemed endless, they spilled everywhere, tangled and knitted together in a great fabric. The food spasmed up Leets's throat and he fought against the gag reflex that choked him at that instant. An overwhelming odor, decomposition shot with excretion, those two great components of the Teutonic imagination—death and shit—blurred the air.

"You think you've seen it all," said Tony.

The driver was out vomiting by the tire of the Jeep. He was sobbing.

Leets tried to soothe him. "Okay, okay, you'll be okay."

"Jesus, Jesus, Jesus," said the boy.

"That's okay," Leets said. But he felt like crying himself. Now he'd seen what they were doing. You could look at it in pictures and then look away and it was all gone. But here you could not look away.

Leets in the tailor's shop reached out and touched the black uniform. It was only cloth.

"Jim?"

He turned.

It was Susan.

XX

Repp awoke when the sun struck his eyes. The sudden dazzle decreed into his head an edict of confusion: all he could feel was the raw scratch of straw against his skin. As he moved a leg experimentally, a high-pitched piping protested; he felt the scurry of something warm and living nestled in close to him.

Rat.

He coiled in disgust, rolling away. The rat had gotten under him, attracted by the warmth, and worked its way into his pack. He stared at it. A bold droll creature, cosmopolitan and fearless, it stood its ground, climbing even to its haunches, eyes peeping with glittery intelligence, whiskers absorbing information from the air, pink tongue animate and ceaseless. There had been rats in Russia, huge things, big as cows; but this sophisticated creature was Swabian and sly and mocking. Repp threw his rifle at it, missing, but the clatter sent the rat scampering deeper into the barn.

Repp pulled himself out of the straw and collected his equipment. The rat had gnawed through the canvas and gotten to the bread. A chunk was left, moist and germy, but Repp could not bring himself to put it to his lips. Revolted, he tossed it into the shadows of the barn.

He'd come upon this place late last night, an empty farm, fields fallow, house deserted and stripped, livestock vanished. Yet it had not been burned—no scorched earth in the path of the advancing Americans—and, desperately tired, he'd chosen the barn for refuge.

Repp had decided to move across country these days, avoiding the roads until he was as far from the site of the unpleasantness with the "Das Reich" Field Police as possible. In the desolate countryside, along muddy farm lanes, there was less chance of apprehension —either by SS or, worse, by the Americans.

Yet now, thinking of them, he became nervous. How close were they, how long had he slept? He checked his watch: not yet seven. Looking outside, he saw nothing but a quiet rural landscape. He'd heard cannon and seen flashes last night after dark: the bastards had to be close.

In the barnyard, Repp took a compass reading, and set himself a southward course. He knew he was already below Haigerloch, but just how far he wasn't sure. But south would take him to the great natural obstacle of the Danube, and he thought he'd cross at the little industrial town of Tuttlingen. Though the prospect of a bridge frightened him as well: for bridges were the natural site for the SS to establish checkpoints.

The fields were deserted under a bright sun, though it remained chilly. No planting had been done and the careful plots of farm-land in the rolling land lay before him dark and muddy. He strode on, alone in the world, though keeping alert. At one point he made out two fast-moving low shapes off the horizon and got into some trees before they saw him, two big American fighter-bombers, out hunting this spring morning. Their white stars flashed as they roared overhead and not long afterward he heard them pounce, some miles off to the east. Presently a lazy stain of smoke rose to mark their success.

But Repp moved on, uncurious, and did not see another human form until late that afternoon. He came suddenly to a concrete road that headed south. He paused for a moment, wishing he had a map. There were no road signs. The landscape was flat and empty. He vacillated, fearing he hadn't made enough distance on his slog through the mud. Either way, the road looked deserted. Finally, he decided to risk it for a few miles, ready to drop off and dis-appear at the first sign of danger.

This damned job is making a coward of me, he thought.

The freedom of the road filled him with a kind of liberation: after the mud that sucked at his boots, clotting heavily, this firm-packed surface seemed a paradise. He plunged on at a furious pace.

He heard the *Kübelwagen* before he saw it; turning, he was astonished at how close the small dun-colored car was.

Now where did that bastard come from? he wondered.

The damned thing was too close for him to hide from; they'd seen him but the first thing he noticed as the car drew closer was that it was jammed with a pack of sorry-looking regulars, as gray in the face as in their greatcoats.

The car didn't even slow up for him. It barreled by, its sullen cargo uninterested in one more fleeing soldier. Repp, emboldened, hurried on. Several more vehicles passed, some even with officers, but all jammed with men. There wasn't room for him if they'd tried—and they were all regulars too, no SS men.

One of them slowed.

"Better get a move on, brother. Americans aren't too far behind."

"I'm fine, thanks," Repp said.

"Sure. You've got surrender written all over you. Well, good luck, all's lost anyway."

The car sped up and soon was gone.

Just at sunset Repp came upon some old friends. Sergeant Gerngoss and the whiner Lenz and the others of the engineer platoon waited by the road.

They hung neatly from branches in a copse of trees. Gerngoss looked especially apoplectic, outraged, his immense form bowing the limb almost to the snapping point. His face was purple and white spittle ringed his lips. Eyes open, booming out of the fat face. The sign on him read: "THIS IS WHAT HAPPENS TO SCUM." Lenz, nearby, was merely melancholy.

The spectacle had drawn a small crowd of other stragglers. They stood in awe of the bodies.

"The SS did it to 'em," somebody explained. "The fat one there really put up a fight. The SS boys said they'd shot some of their pals up near Haigerloch."

"The SS shits only knew it was an engineer platoon, and here was an engineer platoon."

Repp slipped away; he was working on the next problem: the bridge. The Danube here was young, formed not fifty kilometers to the west at Donaueschingen, from two converging Schwarzwald streams, the Breg and Brigach, but still it moved with considerable force through a picturesque but enclosed defile of steep cliffs. He could not swim it this time of year, for it was swollen with winter meltings; he didn't think he had time to hunt up a boat. He walked on down the road and went around the few houses—an unnamed hamlet—that stood on this side of the Danube from Tuttlingen. Cutting through backyards and over stone walls, he came soon to a road and beyond it a stand of trees. He penetrated this growth and found himself staring shortly into yawning space. He was at cliff's edge. He wished he had binoculars.

Still, below, he could make out the ribbon of water, smooth and flat and dark, bisected neatly by a six-arched stone bridge. A road led down the cliff to it and, looking carefully in the falling darkness, he was able to detect two Mark IV Panthers dug in next to the bridge. Dappled *Kübelwagens* and a few motorcycles were ranged along it. He thought he could see men laboring just beyond the bridge to dig defensive positions. And wasn't that a raft of some sort moored to one of the center arches, and two soldiers struggling to plant explosives? Repp realized the mess in a flash. Of course. The engineers who'd been sent south to blow the thing had been executed.

He knew that if he headed down there with his vague story and obsolete papers, he'd either be shot out of hand as a deserter or thrown into the perimeter. These boys were sure to make a fight of it when the Americans arrived, have some fun with their antitank gear, and then fall back across the bridge and blow it to pebbles in the Ami faces. He envied the fellow whose job it was—a real war to fight, not these games—and briefly wondered about him; an old hand, probably, from the cleverness of the arrangement, not one to panic in the face of fire. He wished him luck, but it wasn't his business. His job was merely to get beyond, to keep moving south.

But how to get beyond?

He felt the press of time. How soon would the Americans arrive? Damn, he had to get across before they showed. He didn't want to give them another crack at him: one had been enough. Yet to head farther east along this bank was no solution; if anything the river became more of an obstacle. There were certain to be other bridges and other battles.

Repp pondered, crouched at the edge of the cliff.

"Enjoying the scenery, soldier?" a harsh voice demanded.

Repp turned; the man had approached quietly. He knew what he was doing. In the fading light, Repp recognized tough features and unsympathetic eyes: an SS sergeant in camouflage tunic, cradling an STG, stood before him. Over the sergeant's shoulder back through the trees, Repp could see a half-track out on the road, its cargo a crowd of soldiers.

"Yes, Sergeant," Repp replied. His hand had edged cautiously inside his tunic.

"You're another wanderer, I suppose. Separated, but still trying to join up, eh?" Rich amusement showed in his eyes.

"I have papers," Repp explained.

"Well, damn your papers. Wipe your ass with them! I don't care if you've got a note from the Führer himself, excusing you from heavy duty. We're preparing a little festival for the Americans down at the bridge and I'm sure you'll be happy to join us. Everybody's invited. You'll fight one more battle and fight it as an SS man, or you'll taste *this*," the STG.

Repp stood. Should he shoot the man? If he did, the only way out was down, fifty meters, the face of the cliff.

"Yes, sir," he said reluctantly.

Goddamn! he thought. What now?

He bent to pick up the rifle.

"Leave that, my friend," the sergeant said sweetly, as if he were delivering a death sentence. "It's no good against tanks and tanks are on the menu tonight. Or had you thought I'd turn my back and you'd let me have it?"

"No, Sergeant."

"Major Buchner said round up bodies, and by God I've done it. Sorry, stinking cowardly bodies, but bodies just the same. Now move your butt," and he grabbed Repp and threw him forward contemptuously.

Repp landed in the dirt, scraping his elbow; as he rose, the sergeant kicked him in the buttocks, driving him ahead oafishly, a clown. Repp stood, rubbing his pain—some of the men in the half-track laughed—and ran forward like a fool, the sergeant chasing and hooting.

"Run, skinny, run, the Americans are coming."

Repp scurried to the half-track. Hands drew him in and he found himself in a miserable group of disarmed Wehrmacht soldiers, perhaps ten in all, over whom sat like lords two SS corporals with machine pistols.

"Another volunteer," said the sergeant, climbing into the cab of the vehicle. "Now let's get moving."

That Repp had been taken again and was about to fight in what must certainly be counted a suicidal engagement was one of his great concerns; but another, more immediate one was this Major Buchner, who, if his first name was Wilhelm, had served with Repp at Kursk.

"Okay, boys," the sergeant yelled when the half-track, after a descent, halted, "time to work for your suppers. Sir," he called, "ten more, shirkers the lot, but charmed to join us just the same."

"Good, they're still trying to get this damned thing mined," replied a loud voice from ahead somewhere in the dark—Willi

Buchner's voice? "Now get 'em digging. Our friends will be here, you can bet on it." His voice seemed to come from above and Repp realized, as his eyes adjusted in the night, that the officer stood atop the turret of one of the Panthers.

He turned to his fellows, who lounged around the informal barricade of vehicles at the bridge. "I promise you some fun before sunrise, boys, party favors and all." A chorus of laughter rose from around him but someone close to Repp muttered, "Christ, another crazy hero."

"Here, friend," someone said without troubling to veil his hostility to Repp, "your weapon for the evening." It was a shovel.

"Now come on, ladies, let's get moving. You're SS men now and the SS always stays busy." Repp and the other new arrivals were directed to the approach where others were already digging under the machine pistols of patrolling SS troopers.

"I'd dig if I were you. When the Americans come in their big green tanks, you'll want a place to stay."

Repp saw the implication of the arrangement in a fraction of a second. The SS men would be clustered around the dug-in vehicles at the barricade with the heavier weapons—he'd seen a 75-millimeter gun as well as the two tanks, and several MG-42's; the rest of them, the new recruits rounded up at gunpoint, would be out here in the open in holes. At the last moment they'd be armed with something —Panzerfausts, Repp supposed, but their main job was merely to die—to attract some fire, knock out a tank or two, confuse the invaders, impede their progress for just a moment while the Panthers and the gun took their bearings to fire. Then the SS boys would fall back across the bridge on the time bought by the conscriptees, and blow it, and wait out the end of the war in Tuttlingen; for the Wehrmacht there'd be no retreat, only another Stalingrad.

"Herr Sergeant," a man next to Repp protested, "this is a mistake. I've got leave papers. Here. I was in the hospital—Field Number Nine, up near Stuttgart—and they let me out, just before the Americans came. I'm no good anymore. Blown up twice in Russia and once in—"

"Shut up," said the SS man. "I don't give a shit what your papers say. Here you are and by God here you stay. I hope you can work a Panzerfaust as well as you do that tongue of yours." He stalked away from the fellow.

"It's no fair," said the man bitterly, hunkering down next to

Repp to dig. "I've got the papers. I'm out of it. I did my part. Pain in my head, bad, all the damn time. Headaches just won't stop. Shake so bad sometimes I can hardly piss."

"Best dig for now," Repp cautioned. "That doesn't count a bit with these shits. They'd just as soon shoot you as the Americans. They hanged a bunch of engineers back a way."

"It's just no fair. I'm out of it, out of the whole thing. I never thought I'd get out of Russia but somehow—"

"Keep down," Repp whispered, "that sergeant just looked over here." He threw himself into the shoveling.

"You know what this is about, don't you?" the man said.

"I don't know anything except a man with a gun says dig, so I dig."

"Well, it's nothing to do with the war. The war's over. What I hear is the big shots are escaping with the Jews' gold. That's right, all the gold they stole from the Jews. But the Americans want it. They're going for the Jews' gold too. Everybody wants it, now the Jews are finished. And we're caught right in the middle. That's what it's—"

"To hell with fancy talk, Professor," Repp said. "You can't argue with a man with an automatic."

They dug together in silence for a while, Repp working hard, finding a release in the effort. He squared his part of the pit off, packing the dirt into a rampart on the lip, sculpting a firing notch. Around him he could hear the clink of shovels going into earth and men quietly groaning, resigned. SS troopers prowled among them. Meanwhile, back among the vehicles on the bridge, other SS men moved about, arranging sandbags, tinkering with their weapons, uncrating ammunition. Now and then a single detonation sounded in the distance, and once a long sputter of automatic weapon fire clattered out.

"We ought to build a grenade trap," said Repp, sweating profusely in his labor, his skin warm in the cool night air. He was half worried about blisters that might throw off his shooting, but he couldn't take the possibility too seriously. If he didn't get through tonight somehow, there'd be no shooting.

"Yeah, you're right," said the professor. "In case the bastards get in close."

They bent to the bottom of the pit to scour out an angled hole into which to kick grenades to contain their blast, and suddenly the professor whispered into Repp's ear, "I think we ought to make a break for it. Not now, but later, when the holes are all dug and the SS bastards are back by their tanks. We can move on down the river, get away from the fighting. When the Americans wipe out this bunch, we can—"

"Never make it," Repp said. "Man on the turret has a machine gun. He'd have us cold unless we could fly like one of those fancy jets. I checked it out, first thing."

"Damn! Come on, friend. It's death here for sure. That's what they got us here for—to die. They don't care a shit for us; in fact they never did. They just want to take a few more Ameri—"

But Repp was listening to the officer—Buchner? perhaps—as he said to the sergeant, "Get me a driver and a machine gunner. I'm going to take a *Kübel* up the hill and see what's keeping our visitors."

"Sir, I could get some of the fellows—"

"I'll do it myself," said Buchner, typically. Yes, it *was* Buchner. In the East he'd quickly picked up a reputation for exposing himself unnecessarily to fire.

"I'll blink my lights when I'm coming in. Got it?"

"Yes, Herr Major."

He was gone then, and Repp waited with the professor in the trench.

"We can't wait until the fight begins. We'll never get out then. We'll just get the Amis good and mad and they'll blow our brains out," the professor said. "They smell that gold."

Heavy firing broke out ahead. The American column must have run into some resistance in the hamlet. Repp could hear machine guns and tank cannon. Whoever was left up there was putting up quite a fight.

"We're right in the zone of that gun," Repp replied. "He'd just chop us down. He'd make sausage of us. There's no point to it. Relax for now. Do you have a cigarette?"

"I don't smoke. I was hit in the throat and lost my taste for it."

"Okay, you men," the sergeant called out. "Be alert. Any minute the show begins."

"I can't see a goddamned thing," said the professor. "They must really want that gold. They usually don't like to advance in the dark."

"Now don't get excited, fellows," crooned the sergeant from back at the vehicles, low and gentle, "just take it easy."

"We don't have any guns, you bastards," someone yelled from nearby.

"Oh, we haven't forgotten the Wehrmacht."

Repp could hear MP-40 bolts snapping. A report almost made him flinch—one of the Panthers kicking into life so there'd be power for its turret. The other joined and the smell of exhaust floated down, and over the engine purr came a deeper moan as the turrets tracked, aligning their long 75-millimeter barrels down the approach.

A man suddenly leaned over the edge of their hole.

"Here," he said, his breath billowing foggily in the cool, "ever use one of these rocket things? Line up the target through the rear sight against the pin on the warhead. Trigger's up top, the lever, crank it back to arm it, jam forward to fire. She'll go like hell and blow anything the Amis make to smithereens."

"Jesus Christ," moaned the professor, "that's all you're giving us, *Panzerfausts?*"

"Sorry, brother. I do what I'm told. Go for the tanks first, then the half-tracks. But watch them too, they're more than just troop carriers. Some of them mount four half-inch machine guns on a kind of wire frame. Devilish things. And remember, no firing till the major gives the word."

He was gone into another hole.

"We're cooked," said the professor. "This is suicide." He held up the *Panzerfaust*, a thirty-two-inch tube with a swollen five-inch bulb at one end. "One shot and it's all over."

The firing up ahead picked up in pitch. Light flashed through the night.

"Goddamn. I didn't want to end up in a goddamn hole with American tanks in front and SS tanks in back. Goddamn, not after what I've been through." He began very softly to cry, and put his head against his arm at the edge of the trench.

The firing stopped.

"All right," Repp said quietly. "Here they come. Get ready, old friend."

The professor leaned back in the trench. Repp could see the wet track of tears running down his face, but he'd come to some arrangement with himself and looked at least resigned.

"We should have at least tried," he said. "Just to die like this, for nothing, that's what's so shitty about all this."

"I think I see them," said Repp, peering ahead. He cranked back the arm on the trigger lever to arm his *Panzerfaust*, and put it over his shoulder. It was slightly front-heavy but he braced it through the notch in the rampart he'd built. The sight was a primitive thing, a metal ring that lined up with a pin up at the warhead.

"Here they come," he said flatly.

"Jesus Christ, that's the major. He just blinked."

"Easy, men, the major's coming in," the sergeant yelled.

"Here they come," said Repp. He was really concentrating. His two right fingers tightened on the trigger lever.

"Are you crazy?" the professor whispered harshly. "That's the major."

"Here they come," said Repp. He could see the *Kübelwagen* clearly now, its pale-yellow-and-sand camouflage scheme lighter against the blackness, as it ripped along the road at them, trailing dust. Its lights blinked once again. Willi Buchner stood like a yachtsman in the cockpit of his craft, hands set on the windscreen frame, hair blowing against the breeze, a bored look on his face.

Repp fired.

The *Kübelwagen* ruptured into a flash, concussion instantaneous and enormous. The vehicle veered to rest on its side, flames tumbling out its gas tank.

"Jesus," said the professor in the moment of silence that followed, "those poor—"

"*Who the fuck fired, goddamn I'll kill you!*" bellowed the sergeant. But then everybody opened up. Two or three more *Panzerfausts* flashed out and detonated, a machine gun back on the barricade began to howl, rifles barked up and down the line, and in exclamation point the Panther 75 boomed, a long gout of flame flaring out from its barrel.

Repp grabbed the professor savagely and pulled him close.

"Come on! Now's the time. Stay close and you might live."

He flung him back and slithered over the edge of the trench and began to crawl toward the bridge. The shooting mounted and he could hear the sergeant arguing with it, yelling, "Goddamn, you fools, cease firing!"

In the confusion Repp made it to the barricade, feeling the

professor scuttling along behind him. He stood boldly and stepped
between a *Kübel* and a cycle out onto the bridge itself.

The firing died.

"Who fired? *Who fired?* Oh, Christ, that was Major Buchner,"
yelled the sergeant up front. "Goddamn, I'll kill all of you pigs
if you don't tell me!"

Repp gestured "Come on" with his head and strode forward, bold
as the *Reichsführer* himself.

A trooper materialized out of the dark, rifle leveled at Repp's
middle.

"Where are you going, friend?" he asked.

Repp hit him with the shaft of his *Panzerfaust*, a murderous
blow against the side of the head, just under the helmet. The jolt
sent vibrations through his arm, and the trooper fell heavily to
one side, his equipment jangling on the bridge.

"*Run*," Repp whispered, grabbing the professor and half hurling
him down the bridge. "Hurry!"

The professor took off in lumbering panic and seemed to gain
distance.

"There he is! There he is!" Repp shouted.

By that time several others had seen him and the firing started
almost immediately.

As the blizzard of lead seemed to tear apart the world through
which the professor fled, Repp eased down the incline under the
bridge and made it to river's edge.

He found the raft the demolitions detail had left tied to one of
the piles, and threw in the pack and helmet, and then slipped into
the icy water and began to drift through the blackness, clinging
to the raft. He was almost across when the Americans arrived and
the battle began, and by the time he got out of the water, shivering
and exhausted, the Ami tanks had gotten the range and began to
blow apart the barricade in earnest.

Repp crawled up the bank. Behind him, multiple small suns
descended in a pinkish haze and tracers flicked across the water.
But he knew he was out of range.

And that he was still on schedule.

XXI

"What are you doing here?" was all he could think to say.

"I work here. I'm with the field hospital."

"Oh, God, Susan. Then you've seen it, seen it all."

"You forget: I knew it all."

"We never believed."

"Now of course it's too late."

"I suppose. How did you end up *here?*"

"A punishment. I made waves. I made real waves. I got publicly identified with the Zionists. Then Fischelson died and the Center died and the British made a stink, and they sent me to a field unit in a DP camp. British influence. It was said I didn't appreciate London. And when I heard about Belsen, I tried to get there. But it was in the British zone and they wouldn't have me. Then came Dachau, American. And my doc at the DP camp did think highly of me, and he knew how important it was to me. So he got me the orders. See? Easy, if you have the right connections."

"It's very bad, isn't it."

"*Bad.* That's not a terribly eloquent word. But, yes, it is *bad.* And Dachau is nothing compared to Belsen. And Belsen is nothing compared to Sobibór. And Sobibór is nothing compared to Treblinka. And Treblinka is nothing compared to Auschwitz."

They were strange names to Leets.

"Haven't heard of them. Haven't been reading the papers, I guess."

"I guess not."

"Did you see Shmuel? He's with us. He's still fine. I told you he'd be fine."

"I heard. An OSS detachment. With a Jew in an American uniform. That's how I knew."

"We're still after him. After that German. That's what we're here for."

"One German?"

"Yeah. A special guy. With a special—"

"Jim, there were thousands of them. Thousands. What's one more or less?"

"No, this one's different."

"No. They're all the same."

But Tony was not filing a report to JAATIC. He was writing
a letter to his older brother, in response to a letter that had finally
caught up with him earlier.

"Dear Randolph," he wrote.

It was of course splendid to hear from you. I am glad
Lisbon is interesting and that Priscilla is well.

Please do not believe any of the rumors, and do not let
them upset you. I realize my behavior has been difficult to
fathom of late and that it must be the subject of much dis-
cussion in certain circles. I have not surrendered to the
Americans. I do not flee my own kind. I do not think myself
Robert Graves. I am not insane, though that was not a question in your note; I still sensed it beneath your Foreign Office
diction.

I am quite well off. I am totally recovered. No, I do not
see women. Perhaps I should, but I do not. I do not see old
friends either. They are rather too kind for my somewhat
peculiar tastes. I am among Americans by choice: because,
fools all of them, they talk only of themselves. Children:
they prattle incessantly about self and city, country, past,
future, manufacturing noise from every orifice. They have
no curiosity beyond their own skin. I do not have to make
explanations. I do not get long, sad stares of sympathy. No
one inquires solicitously how I'm getting along In The After-
math. . . .

Dearest Randolph, others lost children and wives in the
bombings. Jennifer and Tim are quite gone now; I've accepted it and hardly think of it. I do not, as you suggest, still
blame myself. Things are quite chipper here. We are hunting
down a dreadful Jerry. It's great fun, most fun I've had in
the war. . . .

But Tony stopped writing. He felt himself about to begin to
cry again. He crushed the document up into a ball, and hurled it
across the room. He sat back, and pinched the bridge of his nose.
The pain would not go away. He doubted if it would, ever. He
wished he had a nip of something. But he didn't. He thought he
might try and get some sleep. Where was Leets? Should he head

back to the office, where the two Jews were? He had to do something, he knew that for sure.

The old man slept. Shmuel watched him. He lay on the cot, stirring now and again—the jab of an interior pain. His breath came shallow and dry, a rattle, and a bubble of drool inflated in one corner of his slack mouth. His skin was milky and loose and spotted, shot with a network of subtle blue veins. He'd pulled the blanket around him like a prayer shawl, though in doing so a foot fell free and it dangled off the cot. Somehow this old creature had survived, another freak like Shmuel, a meaningless exception whose only function was to provide a scale for the larger numbers of extinction.

Why couldn't the Americans have captured some nice plump SS officer? An eager collaborator, a cynic, a traitor? Or why couldn't they have arrived just a day earlier, before the warehouses had been looted? No—again, this Repp had been lucky. He'd left nothing behind, leaving them to hunt through the pale, pained memories of Eisner the tailor.

"Remember: the records," Leets had said.

But instead he remembered his own first interrogation with Leets and Outhwaithe: two hard, glossy Gentiles, eyes blank, faces impassive. Men in uniforms: was there a difference? Hard men, with guns and jobs to do, no time to let human feelings get in the way. The whole world was wearing a uniform, except for the Jews. No, the Jews had a uniform too: blue and white stripes, a jagged, dirty star clipped over the heart. That was old Eisner's uniform, that was the uniform Shmuel preferred, not this—

Startled, he looked at his own clothes. He was wearing American boots, field pants and a wool OD shirt. To old Eisner he was an American, the language made no difference.

Eisner the tailor still slept fitfully on the cot as Shmuel slipped out. He did not have far to go. Of the warehouses there were two kinds: badly looted and heavily guarded. Soldiers marked the latter, smashed doors and a litter of debris the former. Shmuel immediately found the single exception to this rule, a brick building that was not guarded, and had not been looted.

He stepped inside. It smelled musty and the darkness clamped down on him. He stood, waiting for his eyes to adjust. Small chinks of light glittered in the roof, almost like stars, and slowly in the darkness shapes appeared. Pile and pile, rank on rank, neatly arranged after the Teutonic fashion, were blue-and-white prison uniforms.

"No. This guy is different. I don't know why, but he is. He's a curious combination of valor and evil. He's very brave. He's enormously brave. He's much braver than I am. But he's—" He paused, groping.

She would not help him.

"I can't figure out how they turned out such men," Leets said. "You see, we always expect them to be cowards. Or perverts. Or nuts, of some sort. What if they were just like us? What if some of them were better even? Braver? Tougher? What if some were heroes. Unbelievable heroes?"

"You melodramatize. I've seen their work. They were grim, seedy little killers, that's all. Nothing glamorous in it at all. They killed in the millions. Men, women. The children, especially. At Auschwitz, at the end, they threw children living into the ovens."

"I asked Tony about all this. He's a very brilliant man, you realize. Do you know what he said? He said, 'Don't get too philosophical, chum. We're merely here to kill the swine.' But that's not enough, don't you see?"

"You're obsessed with this guy, that's all I see. And he's nothing, he's no concept, no symbol. He's just a pig with a gun. It's the gun that makes him special."

Shmuel, back in the office, slipped quickly into the uniform. He felt nothing; it was only cloth, with a faintly musty smell, from long storage.

He smoked another cigarette while he waited for Eisner to awake or for Leets or Outhwaithe to return. He knew better than to jerk the tailor out of his sleep. Now where *were* Leets and Outhwaithe? Though perhaps it was best they were away for so long, it might give him a chance to finally make contact here.

As he waited, a curious thing began to happen. It occurred to him that there would in fact be a future. For the first time in years he allowed himself to think of it. In the camps as an article of faith one kept one's hopes limited to the next day, not the next year. Yet in his sudden new leisure, Shmuel began to think of a new way of life. Certainly he wouldn't stay in Europe. The Christians had tried to kill him; there was nothing for Jews in Europe now. You'd never know who'd been a Nazi; they'd all say it had been others, but each time you heard a German voice or saw a certain hard set of the eyes or a train of boxcars or even a cloud of smoke, the sensation would be discomfort. The Zionists were always talking about Palestine. He'd never listened. Enough to concentrate on without dreams of a desert somewhere, Arabs, fig trees, whatever. It seemed absurd. But now—well, it was there, or America.

The old man stirred.

"You are feeling all right, Mr. Eisner, now?"

"Not so bad," said Eisner. "It's been worse." Then he saw Shmuel. "A uniform? And whose is that?"

"Mine, believe it or not. I had one like it anyway. At the camp in the East. Called Auschwitz."

"A terrible place, so I've heard. Still, it's a surprise."

"It's true."

"I thought you were with the Gentiles."

"With, yes. *Part of*, no. But these fellows are decent, not like the Germans."

"All Gentiles frighten me."

"That's why I'm here alone."

"Still after the records? I should remember records, all I've been through. Listen, I'll tell you, I know nothing of records. The civilian, Kohl, he kept the records. A German."

"Kohl?" said Shmuel, writing it.

"Ferdinand Kohl. I'll spell it if you like. It makes no difference though. He's dead. Not a bad man, but that's how it goes. The inmates caught him on liberation day and beat him to death. But there's too many other sorrows in here"—heart—"to make room for him."

"Mine's crowded as well," Shmuel said.

"But coats I remember. Battle coats. For the forest. Very fancy. We made them in the thousands."

"When?"

"Over the years. For four years; then last year we changed the pattern. First, a kind of smock, a tunic. Then a real true coat."

"A special demand? For a group. Say, a hundred to a hundred and twenty-five. Do you remember?"

"I just sewed the buttons on, that's all. A hundred and fifty coats a day, on went the buttons, that's all. Any fool could have sewn on buttons."

"But no special demands?"

"No. Only— No, nothing."

"Only what?" He paused. "Please. Who knows?"

"Kohl in early April I remember complaining about big shots and their special privileges. A German hero had his men here for special antitank training and demanded they be refitted with the coats as theirs had worn thin."

"Hero. His name?"

"If I had it then, it's gone now. So many things I forget. My boy was named David, my two girls Shuli and Rebecca. Them I remember. David had blond hair, can you believe it? I know the girls and their mother are gone. Everybody who went East is gone. But maybe the Germans spared him because his hair was their color. We thought it was a curse, his blondness, that they would take him from us. But maybe a blessing, no? Who could tell such things? A learned rabbi could maybe expl—"

"Mr. Eisner. The coats. The hero."

"Yes, yes, forgive me. Thinking, all the time thinking. Hard to remember details."

"Kohl. Mr. Kohl. He didn't want to give up the coats."

"Kohl. Yes, old Kohl. Not a bad sort, notions of fairness. He tried to say No. The boys at the front need the jackets. Not rear-echelon bastards. But the hero got his way. He had papers from the highest authority. Herr Kohl thought this ridiculous. From an opera. I heard him tell Sergeant Luntz that. Heroes from an opera a monkey wrench throwing into his shop. It was no good. My David, he'll grow up to be strong. On a farm somewhere, in the country. He was only three. He hadn't had any instruction. He won't know he was a Jew. Maybe it's better. Maybe that's the best way to be a Jew in this world, not to know. He's six now, David, a fine healthy boy on a farm somewhere in the country."

Shmuel patiently let him lapse into silence. When he was done, Shmuel saw tears star the old man's eyes and at the same time noticed that the old man wasn't so old: he was just a man, a father, who hadn't been able to do anything for his children. Better maybe that he'd died so he wouldn't have to live with their accusing ghosts in his head. The Germans: they made you hate yourself for being too weak to fight them, too civilized to demand revenge.

"Opera?" Shmuel finally said. "I missed that."

"What the fellow called it, the hero fellow. His plan. They name everything, the Gentiles. They have to name things. This from an opera, by Wagner. Herr Kohl hated Wagner. It made his behind doze, I heard him tell Luntz."

"What was the name?" Shmuel asked, very carefully.

"Operation Nibelungen," the old man who was not so old replied.

Shmuel wrote it down.

"It's funny. Us. In this place," he said.

She'd lit a cigarette. It had gotten dark now, and in the long still room with the mirrors and the hanging uniforms, he could see the orange glow.

"Why?" he asked. "Why did you come looking for me? You didn't come for my theories on German evil surely."

"No. I just wanted to tell you something."

"Okay. So shoot. Tell me anything."

"I'm divorcing Phil."

"No kidding?"

"I wrote him. I said I wanted to go to the Middle East. He wrote back. 'What, are you crazy, you think I spent all this time on a goddamned tin can to go live in some desert?' So, that was it. I won't see him again."

"I'm sorry."

"Don't be. Fischelson's dead, I told you?"

"Yes?"

"And the money's gone. It was all set up by this guy, this Hirsczowicz. A millionaire. But the money ran out. What little there was, most of it was lost somehow, in the early days of the war. So there's nothing in London anymore. And there's nothing back in the States. Not a goddamned thing but people talking about how they suffered without the meat."

"I'm sorry you're so bitter."

"I'm not bitter at all. I'm going to go to Palestine. Nothing but Jews there, Jim. It's the only place in the world where the Jews will be welcomed. That's where I'm going."

"Susan."

"That's where we'll all have to go," she said.

Her cigarette had gone out. Now, in the room, total darkness had arrived. He could hear her voice, disembodied.

"I'll talk to him. To the Jew. Shmuel. Do you know he had quite a reputation as a writer in Warsaw? I'll talk to him. He'll go too. He has nowhere else to go."

"That's all?"

"Yes. I suppose I wanted to tell you I don't hate you. I don't want you to die. I never did. I remove the curse. I hope you get your man. The German."

"I will," he said. "Or he'll get me."

The old man was tired now. Shmuel wanted him to sleep in the room but he refused.

"A nap, not so bad. But the night? I have nightmares, you see, I wake up. It helps to know where I am. Besides, the barracks aren't so bad now. They've moved the sick ones out. It's what I know."

"All right. It's all right with me. You can walk?"

"Not so fast, but I end up where I'm going."

He got the man up, and pulled the blanket around his thin shoulders against the cold. They walked in the twilight down the street to the *Lager*, the prison compound. It was warm, really too warm for the blanket, yet the old man clutched it around him with blue-veined fists. He leaned on Shmuel, shuffling along on frail legs. Shmuel felt the heart pulsing behind the thin bones of his chest.

A Jew, thought Shmuel. A living European Jew: the first he'd spoken to in months. It came as a shock. He'd been so long among the Gentiles. Not Germans, but still Gentiles. They didn't *know*; they couldn't *share*. Earnest, apologetic, efficient men: decent. Intelligent even, but it was as if a different kind of brain filled their skulls. They worshiped a man skewered by his hands on a lumber cross: pain and blood at the very center of it. Shmuel preferred this eternal sufferer, pathetic yet dignified, who leaned on him as they neared the guardhouse, the entrance to the compound.

When they reached it, a flashlight from an American sentry beamed onto them. It seemed to halt at their prison stripes as if those said enough and then blinked out.

"Go on," said a voice.

They walked on through the familiar geography, across the

roll-call plaza, down the street between the barracks.

"It's over there," said the old man, pointing.

"I know," said Shmuel.

Shmuel helped him to the building.

"You needn't come inside."

"No, you helped, now I help you. That's how it should be."

"You, a Jew, a yeshiva boy, you are helping them fight the Germans?"

"A little. There's not much I can do. They've got machines and guns. They really don't need me. But I can do little things."

"Good. We should have fought. But who knew?"

"Nobody knew. Nobody could have guessed."

"Maybe so," said the old man. "Maybe so."

They went into the building. Faces peered down from the tiers of bunks and voices hummed. The smell was almost blinding; Shmuel remembered through the tears that welled into his eyes. There was room for the old man near the stove. He took him over and helped him lie down. He was light and dry and fell quiet quickly. But his hand groped out once, snatching at Shmuel's wrist.

Shmuel drew back as the man's breathing deepened into regularity. He was aware that a dozen gaunt faces stared down at him, death masks, and he didn't care for the sensation. An undertang of DDT, from a recent delousing, hung heavy and powdery in the close air, causing his nostrils to flare.

Shmuel stepped to the door and out. Cool air flooded him, smooth and sweet. Above, an abundance of stars rose in their tiers, like the eyes of the men in the bunks.

There: a metaphor, drawn from the camps. "Like the eyes of the men in the bunks." Only a Jew would see stars blurry and infinite in bands from horizon to horizon and think of the white eyes of men at the point of death. Would he continue to draw on the camps for metaphors, was that how deep they'd been driven into him? Did the Germans own his imagination, a final, subtler purchase, one that would seal him off from human company, the metaphorical *Mussulman*, forever?

Yet as he in despair realized the answer was Yes, he realized also that the problem was as much literary as psychological. And from that there followed immediately the recognition that he was, for the first time in many long years, thinking of literature again.

He thought he ought to write about the camps, and that sometime, perhaps in a year or so, when one would not confuse zeal with excellence, passion with brilliance, he might in fact, if only as a private exercise.

As he walked down the street, between the mute rows of barracks, he realized what an awesome task he'd so slightly just evoked; perhaps even an impossible one. It was enormous in a thousand ways: had any man the right to try and spin stories from a tragedy so huge? What of people of ill spirit who would read such accounts purely for the extreme sensations they caused, which of course was not the point at all? What was the artist's responsibility to the gone, the lost, the unheard, the forgotten? And he saw also that in a certain way the imagination had been forever altered. The boundary of evil had been pushed back beyond the horizon on the one hand, but on the other, the capacity of the individual to withstand and triumph over the murderous intentions of the State had also been pushed back. A new form would have to be found, something that would encompass these new boundaries and at the same time convey the immensities of the act of Murder: a new esthetic for the post-atrocity world. Again, the problem of metaphor thrust itself upon him. In the camps, metaphor was everywhere: life was a metaphor, death was a metaphor. How could art be spun from a reality already so charged with elemental symbolism, the vision of hell the Germans had labored so mightily to construct on this earth: satanic sparks, the flames, the awful stench, the dogs straining on their leashes, fangs glistening? Perhaps it was beyond the reach of the artist.

You'd have to concentrate on something small: a parable; panoramas were incomprehensible. Concentrate on one man: how he lived, with as much dignity as the times permitted, and how he died, senseless perhaps, one more sliver of ash in a whirlwind dank with clouds of ash, but convinced somehow that his life had had some meaning.

No, he thought, I could never write that. I simply am not good enough. Face it, as a writer you weren't much, a few pitiful essays in long-forgotten Yiddish journals in a city that no longer existed. What positions had he attacked, what had he defended? He could not even remember.

Had he been a Marxist, a poet, a historian, a novelist, a philosopher, a Zionist? No, not a Zionist, not even in the last days before the war had come, that hot August of '39 when Zionism flared like a contagion through the Quarter, and even the richest of them, the most assimilated, had been consumed in its vision. But that had been dreams, absurd, out of scale, the problems so immense. Next year in Jerusalem! Insane! The British, the Arabs, thousands of miles to travel. He hadn't bought it then—just more dreamy Jews getting on with their own destruction.

But now he saw the dream wasn't so outsized. It was prosaic, a necessity. For where else was there to go? *Eretz Yisrael*, the land of Israel. Home of the Jews. Now that would be something, wouldn't it? That would be worth—

An immense pleasure spread through him. *Look at me*, he thought, *I am thinking again.*

He did not see them until they were quite close and then he had not time to display surprise. They seemed to materialize from nowhere, though in a splinter of a second he realized he hadn't been able to make them out against the looming bulk of the guardhouse. And yet there was a familiarity about them, as though old fears had taken on a familiar guise, and so he absurdly was not frightened and if there was to be any mercy in the next several seconds it was that one: that Shmuel was not frightened as the rushing forms closed on him and held him down.

"SS shit," he heard in Polish, "SS shit."

"I—" Shmuel started and then something enormous crashed into his skull. He felt his head inflate in pain and it seemed the abundance of stars had come down to crush him and they hit him again and again and again.

XXII

He expected trouble at the *Rheinbrücke* and hid in a stand of trees a few hundred yards down the road. The guards on the bridge appeared to be regular Army troops, not Waffen SS men, loafing in the sun. Repp studied them for some time, wishing he had binoculars to bring them up, see their procedures and moods. He tried to keep himself calm and his mind clear: only the bridge, its sentry post, and three lazy soldiers stood between him and safety. Once across, he had only a few blocks or so through the city to negotiate.

He'd feared a massive jam-up here, a refugee column, farmers' carts heaped with furniture, frightened children; officers' staff cars honking, the wounded hanging desperately on the backs of tanks; grim SS men patrolling for deserters. Instead, only this pleasant still scene, almost trafficless—occasionally a truck crossed, and once a sedan, but mostly farmers' wagons heaped with hay, not furniture, and pedestrians. From his vantage point, Repp could also see the Bodensee over the rail of the bridge, stretching away, glinting in the May sun, its horizon lost in a haze: the Lake of Konstanz, a true inland sea. There seemed no war here at all. Was he too late? Since Tuttlingen, he'd traveled mostly by night, staying away from main roads, moving south, always south, across fields and through scraggly forests: out of touch, on his own, fugitive from his friends now as well as his enemies.

The sergeant in the sentry booth watched him come, but said nothing. Repp recognized the type, tired veteran, laconic of speech, economical of gesture, face seamed with hard knowledge. No need to yell when Repp was already approaching.

"Say, friend," the sergeant finally said, unlimbering himself from the stool on which he sat. He picked up his MP by the sling, toting it with the easy motions of overfamiliarity.

"And where might you be headed? Switzerland, I suppose. Don't you know that's for big shots, not little fishies like you or me?"

Repp smiled weakly. "No, sir," he said.

"Then what's your sorry story? Running *to*, or running *from*?"

Repp handed him his papers.

"I was separated from my unit," he explained as the sergeant scanned them. "A big American attack. Worse than Russia."

"And I suppose you think your unit's on the other side of the bridge?" the sergeant asked.

Repp had no answer. But then he said, "No, sir. But my mother is."

"You've decided to go on home then, have you?"

"I'll find an officer to report to after I've seen my mother," Repp said.

The sergeant chuckled. "I doubt there's a sober one left. And if you find one, I doubt he'll give a damn about you. Go on, damn you. To mother. Tell her you're home from the wars."

Repp drew in a deep gulp of the cool air and tried to keep himself calm as he walked across the great Romanesque bridge between the Lake of Konstanz's two basins, the vast Bodensee to the east, and the Untersee, the more picturesque with its steep wooded shores, to the west. At the end of the structure, he passed under a medieval tower and stepped into the old city. It was a holiday town, cobbled and quaint, exactly the kind of place Repp didn't care for. It had no purpose beyond pleasure, with its casino and boat tours and green lakeside park. It had never even been bombed and seemed uneasy in a military role, as if it were wearing an outlandish costume. The soldiers who clustered in its narrow streets seemed wildly out of place against the cobbles and arches and turrets and timbers and spires. Repp slid anonymously among them; they paid him no attention, shouting instead at women, or lounging about drunk before the Basilica of the Münsterplatz. Even the officers were in bad shape, a sullen, loutish crew; clearly they'd already surrendered. *Kübels* and trucks had been abandoned around the Platz and Repp saw rifles already piled in the square. Repp felt himself filling with anger as he pushed through them but he kept it to himself, one straggler adrift in a crowd of stragglers.

Repp turned off the Münsterplatz and headed down Wessenbergerstrasse. Here, in the residential sector, there were no soldiers, only an occasional old woman or man whose questioning eyes he would not meet. He turned up Neugasse, where the houses were shabbier still, looking for No. 14. He found it soon, a two-story dwelling, dirty stucco, shuttered. Quickly, without looking up or down the street of almost identical houses, and without hesitating, he knocked.

After a time, the door opened a sliver.

"Yes?"

He could not see her in the shadow. But he knew the voice quite well. She sounded tired. Unlike the other times.

"It's me."

The door closed, a chain was freed, and then it opened.

He stepped into the shadowy foyer, but she was not there. He went into the living room beyond. She stood against the wall, in the dark.

"Well, at last I'm here," he said.

"So I see. They said a man. I should have known."

"Ah," he said, haltingly. The truth was, he felt a little unsure of himself.

"Sit down, sit down," she urged.

"I'm filthy. I've been sleeping in barns, swimming rivers. I need a bath."

"The same Repp: so fastidious."

"Please—a bath."

"Yes. Of course." She led him through a shabby living room, hushed in draperies and blinds, flowers grimy on the wallpaper, and up some decrepit stairs. The house stank mildly of must and disinfectant.

"I'm sorry it's so awful. But they said it had to be a house, definitely a house and this is all that was available. It's outrageously expensive. I rented it from a widow who's said to be the richest woman in Konstanz. It's also said she's a Jew. But how can that be? I thought they took all the Jews away a long time ago."

"They did," Repp confirmed. "You've got the documents?"

"Of course. Everything. You needn't fear. Tickets to Switzerland."

They walked down a short hall into the bathroom. The tub stood on claws like a beast. The plaster peeled off gray walls and the plumbing smelled. Also, the mirror was flaking off and there were water spots on the ceiling.

"Not the Grand, is it?" he said.

But she seemed not to remember. "No."

She had been ahead of him all this time and now, in the gray bathroom, she turned and faced him fully.

She searched his eyes for shock.

He kept them clear of it.

"So?" he finally said. "Do you expect me to say something?"

"My face isn't like it was, is it?" she asked.

"No, but nothing is."

The scar ran vividly from the inside corner of her eye down around her mouth to her chin, a red furrow of tissue.

"I've seen far worse in the East," he said. "They'll fix you up after the war. Make you pretty again. Make you prettier, I should say. You're still quite attractive."

"You're trying to be kind, aren't you?"

Yet to Repp she was still a great beauty. She was the most beautiful woman he'd ever seen. Her blond hair was short now, but her body had that same suppleness and grace to it; she was thin, rather unlike the ideal Aryan woman, her hips too narrow for easy childbirth, but Repp had never been interested in children anyhow. She wore a pinstriped gray skirt and a flower-print blouse and had dark stockings on, which must have been very old, and high-heeled shoes. Her neck was long and blue veins pulsed visibly under her fair skin and her face seemed porcelain or some equally delicate thing, yet fragile though it appeared her eyes were strong and rather hard.

"I think there's hot water," she said. "And civilian clothes are in the bureau in the bedroom."

"I must say, Margareta, you don't seem terribly happy about all this."

"I'll go fix some supper. You must be very hungry."

They ate in awkward silence in the dim, small kitchen, though the food she fixed was very good—eggs, black bread, cheese—and he felt much better after the bath.

"That's the best meal I've had in a long time."

"They gave me so much money. Your people. The black market is extensive here."

"Yes, it certainly must be. So close to Switzerland."

"Sometimes you can get pork and even beef and veal. And sausage of course."

"Almost as if there's no war."

"Almost. But you always know there's a war. Not from all the soldiers around, but because there's no music. No real music. On the radio sometimes they play Wagner and that terrible fellow Korngold. But no Chopin, no Hindemith, no Mahler. I wonder what they have against Mahler. Of all our composers, his work sounds the most like battles. That's what they like, isn't it? Do you know? Why won't they allow Mahler?"

Repp said he didn't know. But he was glad to see her talking so animatedly, even if he didn't know anything about music.

"I like Chopin so much," she said.

"He's very good," Repp agreed.

"I should have brought my Gramophone down. Or my piano. But it was all so rushed. There was no time, even for a Gramophone. The piano, of course, was out of the question. Even I realized that."

He said nothing.

Then she said, "Whom have you seen recently? Have you seen General Baum at all? He always made me laugh."

"Dead, I think. In Hungary."

"Oh. A shame. And Colonel Prince von Kühl? A delightful man."

"Disappeared. In Russia. Dead, I suppose, perhaps taken prisoner."

"And—but I suppose it's useless. Most of them are dead, aren't they?"

"Many, I suppose. The sacrifice was gigantic."

"Sometimes I feel like a ghost. The only one left. Do you ever think about it that way?"

"No."

"It's so sad. All those young men. So handsome. Do you remember the celebration of the *Julfest* in 1938? I first saw you there. I'm sure you don't remember. I'd just given up the piano. Anyway, the room was full of beautiful young people. We sang and danced. It was such a happy time. But of all those people, almost all are dead, aren't they?"

"Yes, I suppose."

"But you haven't thought of it?"

"I've been rather busy."

"Yes, of course. But at that party, do you know what I sensed in you? Spirituality. You have a spiritual dimension. To be a great killer must take spirituality."

Killer: the word struck him like a blow.

"Did you know how attractive that is? At that party, you were like a young priest, celibate and beautiful. You were very attractive. You had a special quality. Repp, Repp was different. I heard others speak of it too. Some of the women were wild for you. Did you know that?"

"One can sense such things."

"Oh, Repp, we're two peculiar birds, aren't we? I always knew you'd be one of the survivors. You had that too, even way back then."

"I prefer to think of nicer times we had."

"Berlin, the '42 season? When you were the hero of the hour."

"A pleasant time."

"I suppose you'll want to sleep with me now."

"Yes. Are you turning into a nun? You used to be quite eager, I recall. Dirty, even. At the restaurant on the Lutherstrasse."

"Horcher's. Yes. I was very evil." She had touched him under the table, and whispered a suggestion into his ear. They had gone back to the Grand and done exactly as she had suggested. It was their first time. It was also before the terror raids had come and Berlin turned into a ruin, and her face along with it.

"It won't be the way it was though," she said. "I just know it won't. I don't know why, but I can tell that it won't be very good. But I suppose it's my duty."

"It's not your duty. It has nothing to do with duty." Point of honor: she had to want him.

"It's not out of pity though. You can assure me of that?"

"Of course not. I don't need a woman. I need shelter. I need to rest. I've got important things ahead. But I *want* you. Do you see?"

"I suppose. Then, come, let's go."

They went up to the bedroom. Repp made love to her with great energy and after a while she began to respond. For a while it was as good as it had been. Repp did most things well, and this was no exception. He could feel her open to and accept him and his own ache surprised him, seeming to spring from outside, from far away.

Afterward, he put on some wool flannel trousers and a white shirt and some blunt-tipped brown shoes—whose? he wondered— and took his private's uniform and equipment into the garden out back. There, working quickly, he buried it all: tunic, boots, trousers, coat, rifle even. He stood back when he was finished and looked down at the rectangle of disturbed earth under which his soldier's identity lay. He felt quite odd. He was out of uniform for the first time since—how long? years and years, since '36 at least, that first year in the *Totenkopfverbände* at Dachau.

"You should have let your hair grow. It's cropped too closely around your ears," she said in the kitchen, matter-of-factly, "though since you've the proper papers, I suppose you could look like the Führer and the Swiss wouldn't care."

"What time is the broadcast?"

"At six. Nearly that now. There used to be music on all the time. Now there's only announcements."

"There will be music again soon. Don't worry. The Jews will put music on again."

"Do you know, someone said there were camps out East where we murdered them. Men, women and children. That we murdered them in the millions with a kind of gas or something. Then burned the bodies. Can you imagine that?"

Repp said he couldn't. "Though they deserve everything they get. They started the whole thing."

"I hope we did it. I hope it's true. Then we've got nothing to be ashamed of. We'll have done some good for the world after all."

"But there's always more. No matter how many they got out East, there's always more."

"Attention. Berlin calling. Berlin calling," a voice crackled through the radio. Repp fiddled with the dial to bring the signal in better, but it was never clear. "The heroic people of the Greater German Reich continue in their struggle against the monstrous forces of International Jewry which threaten on all sides. The Red armies have been driven back in flight to the Baltic by Army Group North. In Hungary, our loyal SS troops stand fast. Since the death of our leader, we have cont—"

Repp turned the radio off.

"He's gone?"

"Yes. They announced it several days back. Where were you?"

Hiding in a barn. Shooting brave men dead. Murdering them. Blowing Willi Buchner up.

"I had a hectic time reaching here."

"But it seems to go on. The war. It seems like it's been here forever. Even now I can't believe it'll be over."

He turned the radio up again. "—in the south, Munich is an

inspiration to us all, while Vienna continues to—"

"Damn them!" he shouted angrily. "The Americans walked into Munich days ago. Why don't they tell the truth?"

"The truth is dreadful," Margareta said.

Another day passed. Repp stayed indoors, although he did go into the garden around noon. It was beautiful out, though still a bit chilly. May buds had begun to pop and the sun was bright. But he could take no joy in it. She'd told him the neighbors were harmless sorts, a retired grocer on one side and a widow on the other, but still he worried. Maybe one of them had seen the scruffy private come hobbling down the Neugasse to the Berlin lady's. It was the sort of possibility that bothered him the most because he had absolutely no control over it. So many of the big problems had been mastered—begin with Vampir itself, but go on to the escape in the middle of the American attack, the dangerous hundred kilometers from Anlage Elf to Konstanz across a wild zone, the final linkup here, not half a kilometer from the Swiss border. It would be a crime now to fail on a tiny coincidence, the wagging tongue of a curious neighbor.

"You are like a tiger today," she said. "You pace about as if caged. Can't you relax?"

"It's very difficult," he said.

"Then let's go out. We can go down to the Stadtgarten. It's very pretty. They don't rent boats anymore but the swans are back and so are the ducks. It's May, it's spring."

"My pictures were in *Signal* and *Das Schwarze Korps* and *Illustrierter Beobachter*. Someone might recognize me."

"It's unlikely."

"I don't care if it's unlikely. I cannot take the chance. Stop bothering me about this, do you understand?"

"Sorry."

He went up to the bedroom. She was right about one thing. The waiting was making him crazy. Locked up in a shabby little house on the outskirts of Konstanz, his whole world a glimpse down a street from an upper story or a stroll through a tiny garden out back, and the radio, dying Berlin squawking from its ashes.

Repp was not used to being frightened; it suddenly occurred to him that he was. In war, in battle, he was always concerned, but never particularly scared. Now, with the entire heritage of the

Waffen SS on his shoulders, he knew fear. He would not let them down, but it seemed so far away, so helplessly futile. I will not let you down, he thought, I swear it. The oath began, however, *I swear to you, Adolf Hitler* . . . yet Adolf Hitler was dead. What did that mean now? Was the oath mere words? Did it die with the man to whom it was addressed?

Repp knew it did not. He knew his thinking was bad for him. Doubts, worries, something other than the will to pure action began in self-indulgent thought. A man was what he did; a man was what he obeyed.

He went instead to the dresser, yanked open the drawer and pulled out the Swiss passport, painstakingly doctored, well worn, stamped a dozen times, identifying him as Dr. Erich Peters, of German-speaking Bern, a lawyer. All fine. The difficult thing was the story.

He'd rehearsed it like an actor, trying to get the accent right, a little softer, slower. "Yes, legal business in Tuttlingen, a client's will named his half-brother executor and to gain power of attorney we needed the half-brother's signature. He couldn't come to me!" This had been designed as a joke, to lessen the tension of the confrontation with a smile. "Terrible, the bombing, the devastation, just terrible."

It should work.

He looked at himself in the mirror, searching for one Herr Doktor Peters. The dark double-breasted suit certainly would help, as would the tie and the Homburg and the briefcase. Still, a haggard, desperate man looked back at him, cheeks sunken, hardly a lawyer who'd lived fat and smooth these past seven hard years. His eyes seemed lusterless, his skin pale. Perhaps he ought to give himself color and health with Margareta's makeup when he tried the border.

And when would that be? *When?*

"Repp," she said behind him, scared.

"Yes?" He looked around.

"They're here." She pointed to the window. He peered out. A small open vehicle moved slowly down the street, four wary infantrymen in it.

"Damn!" he said. "We thought they'd pass this place."

For a third time, the Americans had arrived.

XXIII

There was no time to mourn. But Leets insisted on something. He wanted to carve the name into the trunk of a tree, or engrave it on a stone.

"So that he won't be anonymous. So that he'll have his name, his identity. Repp couldn't take that from him." For Leets believed that Repp had done the killing—not literally, of course, but at least on the metaphorical level. It was a Repp operation: at long distance, in the dark.

An American doctor less prone to melodrama had another explanation: "Just before liberation, a few trapped SS men broke into the warehouses and put on prison jerseys. They tried to mingle with the inmates. But it didn't work. Because of the faces. That thin, gaunt KZ face. They didn't have it; they were recognized right away, and beaten to death. And your friend—well, he'd been among us. All that American meat and potatoes. He'd filled out. They saw him in the prison compound and took him for an SS man. Who do you blame? Just one of those terrible things."

So Leets felt his own emotions sealed up inside himself. He could not let them escape. He stared at the corpse. The head had been smashed in, the teeth broken off. Bright blood lay in the dust of the Appellplatz where he was found.

"Go with him to the pit or something, if it makes you feel better," Tony said coldly. "Take his hand. Touch him. He's only dead, after all, and you've seen the dead before."

Leets knelt by the body, feeling a little ridiculous now. In fact he did take the hand, which felt cold and hard.

He could feel Susan accusing him once again in the dark.

He turned back to the dead Jew.

What did you expect from us? What do you people want, anyway? We had a war to win, we had to worry about the big picture. I had no idea this would happen. I had no idea. I didn't know. I didn't kn—

Leets felt the piece of paper in the cold hand. He pried the fingers roughly apart. Something in Hebrew had been written in pencil on a scrap. He stuffed it into his pocket.

After a while, two conscripted Germans came by for the body. Leets would have liked to have hated them, but they were elderly civilians—a banker and a baker—and the weight of the body was nearly beyond them. They were apologetic with the stretcher— it was too heavy, they were too weak, it wasn't their fault. Leets listened to their complaints impatiently, and then gestured them to get going. After much melancholy effort they got Shmuel over to the burial ground, a pit that had been bulldozed out, and there set him down. They would not look into the wide, shallow hole. The stench of decomposition, though somewhat controlled by great quantities of quicklime, still overpowered, an inescapable fact. Delicately the two old men coughed and averted their eyes from the hundreds of huddled forms resting under a veil of white on the pit's floor. Leets felt like kicking their asses.

"Go on, beat it, get the fuck outta here!" he yelled, and they ran off, terrified.

Awkwardly he got Shmuel up off the stretcher. Once he had him in his arms, he was astonished at how light he was after the groans of the pallbearers. He climbed into the pit and a cloud of lime dust swirled up over his boots, whitening them. The chemical stung his nose and eyes and he noticed most of the men around had masks on.

"Hey, Captain, you'll want out of there. We're shoveling 'em under now." It was another officer, calling from the far side. An engine gunned into life. The bright blade of a bulldozer lurched into view over the pit's edge, pushing before it a liquid tide of loose earth.

Leets laid Shmuel down. Any place in here was fine. He put him down in a long row of nearly fleshless forms.

Leets climbed out and brushed himself off and waved all clear. The dozer began to muscle the earth in and Leets watched for a second as it rolled over them.

"And that's it? That's all?"

He turned. Susan was standing there.

"Susan, I—it just—" and he ran out of words.

She looked at him blankly. Behind him the dozer lurched and tracked and flattened the soft earth.

"It just happened," he said. "I'm so sorry."

She continued to stare.

"There was nothing any of us could do. I feel responsible. He'd come so far."

In the sunlight, he could see how colorless her face had become. She looked badly in need of sleep. Her work with the dying, with the victims, must have been gruesome and dreadful; it must be eating her, for she looked ill. A fine sheen of bright sweat stood out on her upper lip.

"Everything you touch," she said, "turns to death, doesn't it?"

Leets had no answer. He watched her walk away.

There was the note, of course.

He had not forgotten it; but it took awhile to find a man among the prisoners who could read it.

Leets had a headache and Tony was impatient, and the translator, a bright young Polish Communist, played them for two packs of Luckies before delivering.

"That's not much," said Leets, handing over the cigarettes, feeling cheated.

"You asked, I answered," the man said.

"It's not much to die for."

"He didn't die for it. He got caught in a bad accident. Accidents are a feature of war, don't you see?" Tony said. "It must be some sort of code name."

Leets tried to clear his head. They were in the office where the interrogations had taken place. He still saw the rail yard full of corpses, Shmuel smashed to nothingness in the dust, the huddled forms laid out under the chemical snow, Susan in her nurse's uniform glaring at him, eyes vivid with accusation.

He looked again at the word. It had to have some significance, some double meaning. It wasn't arbitrary.

"Don't they have an SS division called 'Nibelungen'?"

"The Thirty-seventh," confirmed Tony. "A mechanized infantry outfit. Third-rate, conscriptees, the lame, the halt, somewhere out in Prussia against the Russians. But that's not it. This has been a *Totenkopfdivision* operation the whole way. Repp and the Anlage Elf defenders. *Totenkopf* is old Nazi—part of the elite, among the first of the Waffen SS formations. They go way back, to the camps, to the very beginning. They'd have no truck with second-raters like the Thirty-seventh."

"No, I suppose not."

"Actually, it's quite a common name in Germany. The street between this lovely spot and the town of Dachau is in fact Nibelungenstrasse. Isn't that interesting?"

"I wonder if—" Leets began.

"No: it's nothing to do with that curious coincidence. I guarantee you. No, there's a joke in this. There's some hammy German humor. I see the touch of a Great Wit, a jokester."

"I don't follow."

"It's rather too clever, actually," Tony pointed out.

Leets, way behind, requested clarification. "So what's the punch line?" he demanded.

"It's an opera."

"Oh, yes, Wagnerian, huh? Some huge thing, goes on for hours. Has to do with a ring."

"Yes. *Ring of the Nibelung.* A great hero named Siegfried steals it from them. That's the joke. Repp's Siegfried."

"Who are the Nibelungen?" Leets asked.

"I'm getting to that." He smiled. "The Nibelungen, my friend, are a tribe of dwarves, in the oldest stories. Living underground. Guarding a treasure."

XXIV

Where was she?

He checked his watch. Two hours, she'd been out two hours!

He was upstairs. He peeled back the curtain from the window and looked down the street, as far as he could see. Nothing. He'd done this a dozen times in the past few minutes, and each time his reward had been the same, nothing.

He felt warmly damp in his civilian clothes. He could not get comfortable in them. The shoes were no damned good either, blunt-tipped bluchers, pebble-grained, with cap toes, yet they rubbed a blister onto his left heel. Now he walked with a limp! Locked in this stuffy little house, he was falling apart; he hobbled about in another man's clothes with a headache and digestive problems, and a short temper and a blister on his heel. He woke up at night in cold sweats. He heard sounds, jumped at shadows.

He really was not cut out for this sort of business, the polite waiting in an untouched residential section.

He sat back, pulled out his pack of cigarettes.

He looked again out the window, even though it had been only a few seconds.

He saw the truck swing around the corner.

It was a military vehicle, moving slowly down the Neŭgasse toward him. Big thing, dark green after their fashion, about the size of an Opel Blitz, a white star bold on its hood. Soldiers seemed crowded in the back: he could see their helmets bobbing as the truck rumbled along.

Repp drew back from the window, and had the P-38 in his hand.

He threw the slide on the pistol . . . he felt very cool all of a sudden. It seemed a great weight had been drained away. His headache vanished. He knew he had seven rounds in the pistol. All right, if it was worth six of them to take him, then six it would be. He'd save the last for his own temple. Briefly, he wished he had his uniform. Better that than this silly outfit, banker's pants, white shirt, shoes that did not fit, like a common gangster.

He was breathing heavily. He crouched at the stairway. He heard the truck outside, nearly up to the house. His finger moved the safety on the grip of the pistol to off. The weapon felt cold and big in his hand. His heart pounded heavily. He knew the truck would stop shortly, and he'd hear the running feet as one squad headed out back. He was all ready. He was set.

"ALL CIVILIANS ARE WARNED THAT CURFEW IS 6 P.M. REPEAT ANNOUNCEMENT: ALL CIVILIANS ARE WARNED THAT CURFEW IS 6 P.M. YOU WILL BE DETAINED IF FOUND OUTSIDE AFTER 6 P.M."

The speaker on the truck boomed like an artillery shell as it drew even with the house, vibrating through the wood, causing the windows to rattle. It continued on, growing fainter, until it finally went away.

XXV

It began appearing in odd places.

"Yes, here, by God," shouted Tony, "mess records. March eighteenth and nineteenth, meals in the SS canteen, a hundred and three men, charged not to a unit but to one word: Nibelungen."

Nibelungen: April 11, supplies from the central storage facility at Dachau dispatched: rations, equipment, replacement, fuel allotments.

February 13: Ammunition requisition; 25 crates 7.92 mm X 33 kurz; 25 crates 7.92 mm belted; *Stielhandgranate*, Model 44, 3 crates.

March 7: More food, a wire requisition, construction supplies.

The total mounted. A hundred scraps of information providing for the creation and nurture of Operation Nibelungen, *GEHEIME KOMMANDOSACHE!!!*, highest Reich secrecy order and priority.

"It was higher than the rocket program even. My God," said Leets.

Roaming through the CIC Documents Center, a clearinghouse the Army investigative unit had established at Dachau, Leets and Outhwaithe in one frantic day seemed to succeed wherever they touched. The files here were jumbled, immense, confusing stacks and tiers of paper; yet always, on the buff folders, one stamped word, whatever the category: NIBELUNGEN.

"We were so lucky," Leets said. "If Shmuel hadn't gotten to the old man. And if he hadn't written it down. And if I hadn't picked up—"

"We've been lucky all the way through. And yet we're still no closer. I find that quite a bothersome thing."

Leets scored. "Here," he hooted, "under 'Construction and Supply,' the original site preparation order. Sixteenth of November '44, orders here for a construction battalion to prepare a site for experimental purposes. In the Schwarzwald. Code name Nibelungen. Chalked off to WVHA. And a list of specs, required equipment."

"Special transportation orders, these. Moving some solid-state testing gear down from Kummersdorf, the *WaPrüf 2* testing facility up near Berlin. These instructions mandate special care to be taken with the delicate instrumentation. Date fourth of January, the very beginning of the thing."

"We're really cooking," Leets crowed. "Goddamn, now we're getting somewhere."

Leets's fingers pawed through the drawers and vaults of the files. He worked quickly, but with thoroughness, and did not stop for lunch or dinner. He would have stayed busy late into the night on his prowl through the paper labyrinths of the Third Reich but there came a moment when a shadow fell across the face of the document he was examining and in that same second a mousy voice, full of self-recrimination and humility, spoke up.

"Uh, sir. Captain Leets. Sir?"

Leets looked up through a cloud of cigarette smoke.

"Gad, he's back," said Outhwaithe.

Roger stood shyly before him.

And Roger was some help, this time. He would not talk of Paris, or explain; he was not full of his match or himself. He even, for a day or so, worked hard as they continued their hunt through the paper work. And he came up with some possibly pertinent material: a Nibelungen-coded requisition for wind-tunnel data on projectile performance from the *Luftfahrt Forschungsanstal,* the Air Force research establishment at Braunschweig; and a record of marks for enlisted personnel taking part in the Dachau antitank course in mid-March, including 103 names identified as *Totenkopfdivision*—Nibelungen.

But still piles and piles of material remained to be gone through. Leets's frustration took the form of a headache, and it increased as that afternoon wore on. At one point, late, he looked up and around the Documents Center and took no pleasure from what he saw: they were alone in the place, the CIC clerks having taken off for the day, and all around there seemed to be stacks and cartons of German documents. It reminded Leets much of the office back in London where, months ago, this had all begun. From this similarity he extrapolated a single message: they had not made any progress, any real progress, into the middle of the thing.

His frustration was amplified by news that Roger had brought from the outside—that the war seemed finally to be winding down. It was certainly in its last phase, and this made Leets uncomfortable. He had decided that Repp's strike was tied to the end of things, somehow, in some form; it was a part of the process of the death of the Reich. The Russians were now said to be in Berlin—Berlin!—and German forces had capitulated up north, in Holland, northeast Germany and Denmark. Meanwhile Patton's sweep had carried him all the way into Czechoslovakia—Pilsen, the last reports said.

Everybody was doing so *well*; he was doing *lousy*.

He slammed down the sheet he had, some nonsense on Nibelungen-coded mess receipts. Mess receipts! Damn it, the Reich should have ground to a halt back in '43, its gears jammed tight on the tons of paper it produced. The Germans should have dropped paper bombs which killed by sheer weight with as much effectiveness as high explosives. They recorded everything in triplicate and the more they recorded, the more evidence accumulated, but the harder it was to put one's hand on anything specific.

"Damn it, this just isn't getting us anywhere," he complained.

Tony, similarly immersed in documents at another table, looked up and said, "You'd rather be perched on a roadblock somewhere? Or knocking on doors with the boys in the trench coats?"

Of course not, Leets told himself. But more manpower would have been some help, to prowl these acres of paper. And even then, would that have done it? It was clear now that Nibelungen was built, maintained and controlled out of Dachau; all the documents pointed to it. But that was it: they pointed to Anlage Elf and Leets already had Anlage Elf. What he needed was another direction, another step in the chain, higher up on the ladder. To Berlin, perhaps. To WVHA headquarters at Unter den Eichen but the Russians were there. Would they cooperate? How long would it take? What shape were the WVHA files in anyway?

"Aspirin?" he asked.

"Huh? Oh, I got some in my bag, just a sec," Roger said. "What's a *Schusswunde*? Gunshot wound, right?"

"Yes," Leets said, but then noted the folder Roger was reading. "Hey, what the hell is that?" he barked.

It was marked *Der Versuch*.

"Uh, file I picked up."

Der Versuch meant experiment.

It was at last too much. Leets's headache would not go away and Roger was pouring time down the drain, and Susan was even more unreachable than before and Shmuel was dead and Repp was closer to his target.

"Goddamn it, you little son of a bitch, I ought to kick your rich little ass to Toledo. That has nothing to do with our stuff. What the fuck, kid, you think this is some kind of reading room, some fucking Harvard library or something?" he spat out venomously.

Roger looked up in horror. Even Tony was shaken by the black rage in Leets's words.

"Jesus, Captain, I'm sorry," said Roger. "I was just—"

"Listen, we're all running without a lot of sleep and these last days have been unpleasant ones," Tony pointed out. "Perhaps we'd best close down the shop for today."

"Suits *me*," said Roger sullenly.

"Ah," Leets snorted, but saw at once that Outhwaithe was right.

Roger stood and gathered up his materials wearily and began to stuff them into a drawer.

But then he paused. "Look, this is pretty funny here, if I'm reading it right."

Nobody paid any attention. Leets still hadn't taken any aspirin and Tony was consumed in tidying up. Tony was a tidy sort, always had been.

Roger lurched on. "Funny-ugly," he said. "They used this Dachau as headquarters for a lot of testing. Block Five, it was called. All kinds of terrible—"

"Get to the point," Leets said coldly.

"Okay," and Roger held up the bulky file. "Full of freezing, pressure-chamber stuff, gas, injections, water—*deaths* I'm talking about. How people die. How long it takes, what the signs are, what their brains look like afterward, pictures, stuff like that. And this—"

He pulled a folder out.

"It's not like the others. Different forms entirely. Didn't come out of Block Five. It's a report on *Schusswunde*—gunshot wounds, twenty-five of them, complete with autopsy pictures, the works. It's been sent down to a Dr. Rauscher—the head SS doctor here. Sent down for his collection on how people die. It's dated—this is how it caught my eye—it's dated the eighth of March. A couple of days after Shmuel made his breakout."

"Let's see," said Leets.

The folder consisted of several typewritten pages of wound descriptions and several grisly pictures, shot with too much flash, of naked scrawny men on slabs with great orifices in their chests or portions of their heads blown away, eyes slotted and blank, feet dirty, joints knobby. Leets looked away.

"Maybe it is them," he said. "No way to tell. Shmuel could tell. But even if it is, so what? The way I make it is they must have autopsied the corpses Repp hit at Anlage Elf. Wanted to see what that fat slug does, more data to help him in the shooting. Then they ship those data back to—back to we don't know where. WVHA, I guess. Or SS HQ, someplace, Berlin. Then"—he sighed, weary with the effort, for he could see the approach of another dead end—"someone up there sends it on down to this Dr. Rauscher. For his collection. And you find it. Looking where you're not supposed to be. But it doesn't mean a thing. We know they've got a big, special gun. We know—"

"Yet it's not Nibelungen-coded," Tony said.

"Well, it had really nothing to do with the guts of the mission. It was just an extra curiosity they'd dug up and thought to send somewhere it might do some good. Their idea of 'good.'"

"You miss the point," Tony said. He'd ceased tidying and was over at Roger's, pushing his way through the papers. "If it hasn't gone out under the code, then it's not top secret. It's not *Geheime Kommandosache*. That means it hasn't been combed, scrubbed free of connections, examined closely from the security point of view. It's pure."

Leets wasn't sure what he was getting so excited about.

"Big deal, nothing there to be top secret. We don't even know if those are the same twenty-five guys. They could be twenty-five guys from any of the camps."

"Hey," said Roger, off in a corner with one of the sheets. "There's a tag here. I didn't see it. It's some kind of—"

Leets had it, and took it into the light.

"It's a file report, that's all," he said. "It says these came from some guy's file, some guy in some department, Amt Four-B-four, some guy I never heard of. Jesus, this is nothing, goddamn it, I'm getting tired of all this—"

"Shut up," said Tony.

"Look, Major, this is—"

"Shut up," Tony said. He looked hard at the tag. Then he looked at Leets, then to Roger, then back to Leets.

"Remember your German, Captain. In German, the word *Eich*?"

"Huh?"

"It's oak. *Oak!*"

Tony said, "Remember: it wasn't Shmuel who heard of the Man of Oak, but someone else, a *shtetl* Jew, who spoke Yiddish. He knew some German words, the common ones, but he was scared and didn't listen carefully. He heard 'Man of Oak.' *Mann.* And *Eich.*"

Tony continued, "It has nothing to do with Unter-den-Eichen, Under the Oaks. We were wrong. We stopped short. We didn't follow it hard enough. The Jew was right. It *was* Man of Oak."

Leets looked at the name.

"There's your bloody Man of Oak," said Tony.

The tag said, "Originals on file Amt IV-B-4, Obersturmbann-führer Eichmann."

XXVI

"Repp?" He hadn't heard her come in. "Repp? Where are you?"

"Here," he said feebly. "What the hell took you so long?"

She came up the stairs and into the room. Today she wore a smart blue suit and a hat with a veil.

"My God," she said. "You look ill. Are you all right?"

"I'm fine."

"You look as if you've seen a ghost."

"It's nothing."

"Do you want something? Brandy? I have some brandy."

"No, no. Stop it, please. Tell me what I sent you out to find."

"I have a surprise for you."

"Margareta. I have a headache. I don't have time for—"

She held out an unopened pack of Siberias. "Surprise," she said.

"Where on earth did you get those?"

"From a boy. I smiled at him. He was charmed to give them to me. He'd been in the East, I guess."

Repp opened the pack greedily, and extracted one of the cigarettes. The paper had begun to turn brown from age and, lighting it quickly, he realized how stale the thing was. Still: delicious.

"French, incidentally," she said.

"Eh? I'm not sure what—"

"It's the French. The French who've occupied us. In American uniforms with American equipment. But the French."

"Well, it's the same. Maybe worse. We never took America. We took France in '40."

"They seem very benign. They sit in the square and whistle at the women. They drink. The officers are all in the café."

"What about ours?"

"Our boys handed in their rifles and were marched away. It was almost a ceremony, like a changing of the guard. It was all very cheerful. No shots were fired. The guns weren't even loaded."

"Tell me what I sent you out for. How many are there? What are the security arrangements? How are they monitoring civilian traffic? Have they set up border checkpoints? Is there a list that you know of?"

"List?"

"Yes. Of criminals. Am I on it?"

"I don't know anything of any list. I certainly didn't see one. There are not so many of them. They have put up signs. Regulations. All remaining German soldiers and military personnel must turn themselves in by tomorrow noon on the Münsterplatz. All party uniforms, banners, flags, standards, regalia, knives—anything with the swastika on it has been collected and dumped in a big pile. Denazification they call it, but it's souvenirs they want."

"The border. The border."

"All right. I went there too. Nothing. Some bored men, sitting in a small open car. They haven't even occupied the blockhouse, though I do know they removed our Frontier Police detachment. I think the fence is patrolled too."

"I see. But it's not—"

"Repp, the border is not their central concern right now. Sitting in the sun, looking at women, thinking about what to do when the war's over: those are their central concerns."

"What travel regulations have they posted?"

"None, yet."

"What about—"

"Repp, nothing's changed. Some French soldiers are now sitting around the Münsterplatz, where yesterday it was our boys. Our boys will be back soon. You'll see. It's almost finished. It won't last much longer."

He sat back.

"Very good," he said. "You know they offered me an Amt Six-A woman, a professional. But I insisted on you. I'm glad. It was too late for strangers. This is too important for strangers. I'm so glad they convinced you to help."

"It's difficult for a German to say No to the SS."

"It's difficult for a German to say No to duty."

"Repp, I have something I'd like to discuss, please."

"What?"

"A wonderful idea really. It came to me while I was out."

She did seem happier than yesterday. She wasn't so tired for one thing and she looked better, though maybe he had only grown used to the imperfectly joined face.

"What?"

"It's simple. I see it now. I knew there was a design in all this. Don't go."

"What?"

"Don't do it. Whatever it is, don't do it. It can't matter. Now, so late. Stay here." She paused. "With me."

"Stay?" A stupid thing to say. But she had astonished him.

"Yes. Remember Berlin, '42, after Demyansk, how good it was? All the parties, the operas. Remember, we went riding in the Tiergarten, it was spring, just like it is now. You were so heroic, I was beautiful. Berlin was beautiful. Well, it can be like that again. I was thinking. It can be just like that, here. Or not far from here, in Zurich. There's money, you have no idea how much. You've got your passport. I can get across, I know I can, somehow. All sorts of things are possible, if you'd only—"

"Stop it," he said. "I don't want to hear this."

He wished she hadn't brought it up; but she had. Now he wished she'd drop it; but she wouldn't.

"You'll die out there. They'll kill you. For nothing," she said.

"Not for nothing. For everything."

"Repp, God knows I'm not much. But I've survived. So have you. We can begin with that. I don't expect you to love me as you loved the pretty idiot in Berlin. But I won't love you the way I loved the handsome, thick-skulled young officer. It'll be fine. It'll be fine."

"Margareta—"

"Nobody cares anymore. I could see it on their faces. Our boys' faces. They didn't care. They were glad it was over. They went willingly, happily. To die now is pointless. My brother and father are dead. All the men I've loved are dead. To join them would be insane. And you did more than all of them put together. You've earned your holiday."

"Stop it."

"These French seem all right. They're not evil men, I could tell. Not Jews, or working for Jews. Just men, just soldiers. They got along quite well with our boys. It was a touching scene."

"You sound like you're describing some kind of medieval pageant."

"There's no disgrace in having lost a war."

How could he tell her? What words could there be? That he

was part of a crusade, even if no one remembered or would admit it. He was all that was left of it. If he had to give his life, he'd give it. That he was a hard man, totally ruthless, and proud. He'd killed a thousand men in a hundred wrecked towns and snowy forests and trenches full of lice and shit.

"We lost more than a war," he said. "We lost a moment in history."

"Forget what's been or what might have been," she said. "Yes, wonderful, but forget it, it's over. Get ready for the future, it's here, today."

"There's not even any choice in it. There's no choice at all."

"Repp, I could go to the French. I could explain to their officer. I could say Repp, of Demyansk, the great hero, is at my house, he'd like to come in. I could get him to guarantee that—"

"He can only guarantee a rope. They'd hang me. Don't you see it yet, why I can't turn back? I killed Jews."

He sat down by the table and looked off into the corner of the kitchen.

"Oh, Repp," she finally said. "I had no idea." She stepped back from him. "Oh, Christ, I didn't know. God, what terrible work. You must have suffered so. It must have been so hard on you."

She came beside him and touched him gently, put her fingertips against his lips and looked into his eyes.

"Oh, Repp," she said, and then was crying against him. "It must have been so hard on you."

XXVII

At last it was a simple proposition.

"To get Repp," Leets told them, "we have to find this Eichmann."

"Yeah, but, Captain, if we can't find one *Obersturmbannführer* in the SS, how the hell are we going to find another?" Roger wanted to know.

And Tony said, "The possibilities must be endless. The man may be dead. He may have made it out of the country. He may be hiding as a private in a Luftwaffe anti-aircraft battalion. He may have been captured by the Russians. He may be in Buenos Aires."

"And if he's any of those things, we're out of luck. But if he's been captured, then maybe we can find him. Just maybe."

"So I guess we have to go on the assumption he's been taken," said Roger. "But still . . ."

"We've got no other choice."

"And if we get him, then we gotta make him talk," Roger said.

"I'll make him talk," said Leets. "Don't you worry about that."

But Roger did worry; for he did not like the look that crossed the captain's face when he spoke.

If this Eichmann was a prisoner, then he'd be property of the Army Counter-Intelligence Corps, for interrogation intelligence was a CIC initiative. So early the next day they took off for Augsburg, where Seventh Army CIC had decamped at Army Headquarters on an old estate just beyond the ruined city. Army took up the main house and the CIC unit one of several hunting bungalows spread over the rolling hills.

It took them quite some time to see a Major Miller, the CIC exec officer, and Leets found this wait the hardest thing yet, worse even than rushing into the German fire at Anlage Elf or watching the doctor open up the week-dead kid at Alfeld, for at least in those episodes he'd been able to do something. Now he simply sat. The minutes ticked by and suddenly it turned into nighttime. Darkness came and sealed off the windows.

"What's the German word for night?" Leets asked Tony.

"Come on, chum. You know it."

"Yeah. *Nacht*. Sounds like a rifle being cocked."

Presently Miller showed up, dead tired, in his GI overcoat, a pale, freckled man in his late thirties.

"Jesus, sorry I'm late. How long you guys been waiting?" he asked by way of introduction.

"Hours, sir," said Leets. "Look, we need some help, that's why we're here."

"Sure, sure. Listen, if I'd of known—"

"German prisoners. SS prisoners, especially. Over the rank of major. Specifically, the rank of Obersturmbannführer Eichmann, out of a department called Amt Four-B-four."

"That's Gestapo."

"Gestapo?" said Leets.

"Under the RSHA. Central Security Department. Eichmann, huh?"

"You know him?"

"No. But we're beginning to see how RSHA was set up."

"Well, where would he be? I mean, if you had him. Where would we look for him?"

"Long way off. A castle. Sorry, classified location." Leets felt his mouth drop open in stupefaction. "Is it access you want?" the major continued. "Oh, sure. It can be arranged. Get OSS upstairs to write a fancy letter to Seventh Army CIC. It'll reach me in a week or two with twenty-six different qualifications attached from the brass and then—"

"Major," Leets interrupted. "We need to see this guy tonight. Tomorrow might be too late."

"Look, fellows, if I could help, believe me I would. But I'm powerless. Look." He held up his hands from underneath his desk, wrists joined in a pantomime of bondage. He smiled weakly and said, "They're tied. See, those officers are an intelligence source of the first magnitude. We've got 'em at an interrogation center, a castle, like I said. Later, there's some talk of establishing a Joint Services interrogation center. But for now, we've got 'em. See, a lot of them operated against the Russians. Look, let's face it, this war's over and the next one's about to begin. And those guys fought its first battle. They've got all kinds of dope on the Russians, on Communist cells in Europe in Resistance groups, on hundreds of intelligence operations. They're a treasure. They're worth their weight in gold. I mean, they are—"

"Major," Leets spoke very quietly, "there's a German operation that's still hot. So hot it smokes. Now. Today. There's an officer named Repp, Waffen SS, top man with a rifle. He's going to put a bullet into someone. Someone important. This is the last will and testament of the Third Reich. He's the executor."

"So who?"

"That's the hard part. We don't know. But we believe this Eichmann must, for we found his name on a crucial file down at the Dachau admin center."

"I'm sorry. I'd like to help. I just can't. There are channels. It'd be my ass. You just have to go through channels."

"Look, Major, we may not have time to go through channels. Someone could be on the fucking bull's-eye while we're filling out forms."

"Captain Leets. There's just no—"

"Okay, look. Let me give you the real reason you ought to give this guy to us: he's simply ours. We bought him. You didn't. You stumbled onto him and don't even know if you've got him. But we bought him with lives. Thirty-four paratroopers checked out on this thing in the Black Forest, twice as many again wounded. And eleven guys in the Forty-fifth Division got nailed back in April. Then there were twenty-five KZ inmates this Repp used up for practice. And finally, an operative of mine, another KZ survivor. He's at Dachau, in a pit full of stiffs and lime, lovely spot. He deserved better, but that's what he got. So when I say this Eichmann is mine, because he's going to give me Repp, then that's what I mean."

"It's not a question of deaths. Men die in this war all the time, Captain"—but not your sort, Leets thought—"but still we've got to stick to our procedures. I can't just . . . there's just no way . . . it's ridiculous. But—" And then he stopped.

"Oh, hell," he finally said. He looked away and seemed to breathe deeply. "How old are you?" he finally said to Roger.

"Nineteen, sir," said Roger.

"A paratrooper. I can see by the boots."

"Uh, yes, sir," said Roger.

"Any combat jumps?"

"Six," Roger lied.

"Young and crazy. Crazy-reckless. Everybody tried to talk you out of it, I bet."

"Yes, sir," said Roger.

"But you went anyway, had to show 'em how tough you were, huh?"

"Something like that, sir," said Roger. "Sicily, the Boot. Into Normandy. The big Holland screw-up. A nasty spell in Bastogne, the Bulge. Some Christmas. Finally the Rhine drop. Varsity, they called it. March."

That's only *five*, Roger, Leets thought. Nobody jumped at Bastogne.

"Oh, and the drop, uh, Captain Leets and Major Outhwaithe mentioned, um, sir, you know, the one—"

"That's quite a record. Nineteen and six combat drops. What's it like?"

"Oh, well, um, scary, sir. Real scary. Normandy was the bad one. We came down way off the zone, half the guys in my stick went into water, Germans, see, had flooded the place, pictures didn't, um, show it, and they drowned. Anyway, I was one of the lucky ones that hit on high ground. Then: confusion. Lots of light, flares, tracers. Big stuff going off. Like the Fourth of July, only prettier, but more dangerous—"

Jesus Christ, thought Leets.

"—but then we got formed up and moved out. First Germans we saw were so close you could smell them. I mean, there they were, right on top of us. I had one of those M-threes, you know, sir, the grease gun they call 'em, and *BADDDDADDDADDAAA-DDDAAA!* Just knocked 'em down, never knew what hit 'em."

"You know," the major said, leaning back in his chair, staring absently off into space, "sometimes I don't feel I've actually been in the war at all, the real war. I suppose I should be grateful. And yet in ten years, twenty years, people will talk about it, ask questions, and I won't have the faintest idea what to say. I don't think I ever even saw any Germans, except for the prisoners, and they just look like people or something. I saw some ruins. Once I did take a look through somebody's binoculars at the Ruhr pocket. Real enemy territory. But mainly it's been a job or something, paper work, details, administration, just normal life, except there are no women, the food's lousy and everybody's dressed the same."

"Major—" started Leets.

"I know, I know. What's your name, Sergeant?"

"Roger Evans."

"Roger. Well, Roger, you've packed a lot into your nineteen years, I salute you. Anyway, Captain Leets, this is my war. I can see you have no respect for it. Fine, but still somebody's got to do the paper business. So while you won't understand and won't respect it, nevertheless let me tell you I'm about to do a very courageous thing. Fact is, the CIC brass hates you OSS types. Don't ask me why. So when I tell you where the officers are, I want you to understand how brave I'm being. No, it's not a combat jump, but it's a big risk in its own right. Name of the place is Pommersfelden Castle, outside Bamberg, another sixty or so clicks on up the road. Schloss Pommersfelden, in German. A very ornate place, on Route Three, south of the city. I'll call them and tell them you've got approval. If you leave in the morning, you should get there by late afternoon. The roads are terrible, tanks, men, just a mess. Columns of prisoners. Terrible."

"Thank you, sir. Would that mean—"

"Yes, of course. Eichmann. We picked him up in Austria last week. If you can get anything out of him, fine, swell. We tried and came up with nothing except the remarkable fact he was following orders. Now, please. Get out of here. Don't hang around. Okay? God help me if they ever find out about this."

The drive the next morning was murder. The tanks were bad enough, and the convoys even worse, interminable lines of deuce-and-a-halfs, sometimes two abreast, struggling southward to keep up with the rapidly advancing front; but worst of all were the Wehrmacht prisoners. There were thousands of them, men in Chinese numbers, marching—rather, meandering sluggishly—to the rear in battalion-sized formations, usually guarded by one or two MP's at either end in a Jeep. The Germans were surprisingly rude, considering their position, insolent, sullen crowds who milled in the road like sheep, stunting progress. Roger again and again had to slow the Jeep to a crawl, honking and cursing, while Leets stood in the back shouting "*Raus, raus*," and waving madly, and still they refused to part except at the nudge of a fender. At one point, Leets pulled his Thompson submachine gun from the scabbard mounted slantwise off the front seat, and made a dramatic gangster's gesture out of tossing the bolt; they moved for *that*, all right.

Finally, beyond Feuchtwangen, the prisoners seemed to thin, and Roger really belted the Jeep along. Yet Leets was not at all happy.

He had the terrible sensation of heading in the wrong direction, for if, as they had speculated, Repp's target had to be to the south, beyond the reach of the Americans, here they were slugging their way north, putting themselves farther and farther out of the picture.

"I hope this is right," Leets said anxiously to Tony.

Tony, morose lately, only grunted.

"We don't really have a choice, do we?" Leets wanted reassurance.

"Not a bit of it," Tony said, and continued to stare blackly ahead.

They had to swing in a wide arc around the ruined city of Nuremberg and that ate up more time. It lay in the distance under a pall of smoke, though it had not been bombed in months. Ruins were not so remarkable, yet the scope here was awesome. But Leets paid no attention; he used these hours to meditate on Repp.

"You're talking to yourself," said Tony.

"Huh? Oh. Bad habit."

"You were saying Repp, Repp, Repp over and over again."

At that moment a fighter plane, a P-51, screamed low and suddenly over them, a hundred or so feet up, almost blowing them off the road, Roger letting the Jeep slew a bit before regaining control. The plane rolled over in a lazy corkscrew turn at 380 miles an hour, star white, flaps trim, bubble sparkly with sunlight, whooping kidlike in the pale German sky.

"Jesus, crazy bastard," yelled Leets.

"He almost strafed us," yelled Roger.

"Bastard, ought to be reported, I just may report him, flying like that," Leets muttered in heated righteousness.

"Hey: we're *here*," Roger announced.

"On a wing and prayer," said Tony.

They pulled into the grounds of Schloss Pommersfelden.

At the end of a long road through the trees sat the castle. Even the American military vehicles parked around it, dingy green with peeling, muddy stars, could not detract from its eighteenth-century purity.

"Willya look at that," Roger suggested, dumbfounded.

Leets preferred not to, though the thing was impressive: a fantasy, an elegant stone pastry, foolish, insanely overelaborate, but proud in its mad grandeur.

Leets and Outhwaithe hurried into the place after Roger stopped, and found themselves in a theatrical stairwell four stories tall, embellished with arcaded galleries, stone nude boys holding lanterns, wide steps of marble that could have led to heaven, all under a painted ceiling.

Their boots crunched dryly across the tile toward a PFC orderly. MP's with automatic weapons stood at each of the many doors leading off this area.

"Leets. Office of Strategic Services." He fished for some ID. "This is Major Outhwaithe, SOE. A Major Miller of Seventh Army CIC said he'd call down and set up a chat with a guest you've got here."

"Yes, sir. The Eichmann thing."

"That's it."

A phone call was placed; a captain, in Class A's, appeared. He looked them over.

"Eichmann, eh?"

"Yes."

"I don't know why. Doesn't know a thing. Most of them are talking like canaries. Trying out for new jobs. This guy's the sphinx."

"He'll talk for me," Leets said.

The captain took them up to the second level and down a hall. Tapestries and portraits of men and women three hundred years dead in outlandish outfits with fat glossy German faces hung on the walls. Finally, they reached doors at the end of the hall and stepped through. The room except for table and three chairs was empty.

"He's in the detention wing. He'll be here soon. Look, Miller's a buddy of mine, I know this thing's kind of unofficial. Glad to help out, no problem, no sweat. But we don't go for any rough stuff, you know. I mean, Leets, it bothered me what you just said."

"I won't harm a hair on his head," Leets said. "Neither will the major."

"We British are quite gentle, hadn't you heard?" Tony asked.

A roar rose suddenly; the windows rattled as it mounted.

After it died, the captain said, "That's the fifth one in the last half an hour. Those guys are really feeling their oats today. There's an airfield at Nuremberg, not too far. Mosquito squadron there too, Major, not just our boys going goofy."

"Glad to hear it," Tony said. "We try and do our bit."

The door opened. Two MP's with grease guns and helmet liners brought a third man in between them. Leets was immediately impressed at how unimpressed he was: a wormy little squirt, pale, watery eyes, thinning hair, late thirties. Glasses askew, lips thin and dry. Scrawny body lost in huge American prison fatigues.

"Gentlemen," said the captain, "I give you Obersturmbannführer Karl Adolf Eichmann, late of Amt Four-B-four, Gestapo, Number One Sixteen, Kurfürstenstrasse, Berlin. Herr Eichmann"—the captain switched to perfect brilliant German—"these fellows need a few moments of your time."

The Man of Oak sat down across from them. He looked straight ahead and smelled faintly unpleasant.

"Cigarette, Herr Obersturmbannführer?" Leets asked.

The German shook his head almost imperceptibly, clasped his hands before him on the table. Leets noted he had big hands, and that the backs of them were spotted with freckles.

Leets lit up.

"I understand, Herr Obersturmbannführer," he said, speaking in his slow German, "you've been uncooperative with our people."

"My duties were routine. I followed them explicitly. I did nothing except my job. That is all I have to say," the German said.

Leets reached into his pocket, and removed something. With a flick of his fingers, he set the *draydel* to spinning across the surface of the table. Impelled by its own momentum, it described a lazy progress over the wood. Leets watched the man's eyes follow it.

"Your colleague Herr Repp left that for me at Anlage Elf. Now, dear friend, you are going to tell me about Operation Nibelungen. When it started, where it's headed, who its target is. You're going to tell me the last secret. Or I'll find it out myself, and I'll find Repp. And when I find Repp, I'll tell him only a little fib: I'll say, Eichmann betrayed you, and let him go. Then, Herr Obersturmbannführer, as well you know, you are a very dead man from that second on. Herr Repp guarantees it."

Roger leaned against the fender of the Jeep out in front of the castle—*castle?* it was more like a big, fancy house!—enjoying the freedom of the moment. No fun, the ride down, two raw nerves in back for cargo. They'd jumped the Jeep while it was still rolling and headed straight for the great doors, as if there were free money inside, instead of some Kraut.

He popped a piece of spearmint into his mouth. He had no dreams of the future and no memories of the past; he was determined to extract the maximum pleasure of that exact instant. He worked the gum into something soft. Sure was a nice day out. He assumed a Continental grip on an imaginary racquet and slow-motioned through a dozen topspin approach shots to the background corner. The trick was to keep your head down and follow through high. It was a shot he'd need to *own*, lock, stock and barrel, if he hoped to stay with the Frank Bensons of the world in the years to come.

And then he saw a woman.

She was just a silhouette preserved momentarily between the window through which he glimpsed her and what must have been another window or set of doors behind her. Just a profile, blurred, moving down a corridor between wings of the castle, gone in a second.

Women! Here? It had been weeks since he'd pulled out of London and that mix-up in Paris hadn't amounted to anything. Women. He explored facets of the problem. Now what would women be doing here? Wasn't this some kind of prison or something?

Still, that had definitely been—

Jesus Christ!

The roar seemed to flatten him. He fell back in momentary confusion, looking for the source of this outrage, to see a P-47 maybe fifty feet above him flash past, more shadow than substance at over 400 miles an hour. He could see its prop wash suck at the trees, pulling a cloud of leaves off them in its wake. It rolled majestically as it yanked its nose up—crazy bastard, he was going to get in real trouble that way, Roger thought—and he followed the fighter-bomber as it climbed.

He was dumb struck. The sky was jammed with planes. He'd noticed contrails earlier, but the sky was always full of contrails on the rare, clear European days. Now, staring, he saw them jumbled, tangled, knotted even, tracing corkscrews and barrels and loops and Immelmanns and stall-outs. He could make out the planes themselves, fighters mostly, specks at the head of each furry, swooping track. Must have been fifty, sixty. What a show.

One last giant dogfight? Maybe the Germans had saved up for an aerial Bulge, a last go, all their stuff in the air, jets, rockets, ME's,

Focke-Wulfs, and a Stuka or two if any were left, and all the experimental stuff everybody said they were working on. One last shoot-out at 25,000 feet: all guns blazing, take on the entire Eighth Air Force, some kind of *Götterdämmerung*, or maybe a crazy kamikaze thing, like Japs, just crashing into their targets?

But if this were a battle, wouldn't there be puffs of flame up there, and long jags of smoke from crashing ships, and wouldn't there be other columns of smoke on the horizon from planes that had already gone down?

Yes, there would.

This was—*fun!*

Another plane, a two-engine British job, howled overhead, slightly higher than the Jug but just as loud. He ducked.

What the hell's going on? Rog wondered.

He looked about and saw nobody in the house. No guards, no officers, nothing. He did notice a path off to one side in the trees and thought to head out back, dig somebody up. The path turned quickly into a kind of sidewalk, though of fine, tiny pebbles set between metal rails of some sort. Very fancy, it reminded him of the kind of arrangements he'd seen in Newport. He followed it through some tricky turns, and at last found himself in some sort of garden, low hedges arranged like a geometry problem around flower beds that were beginning to show signs of waking up. Beyond lay a vast rolling carpet of grass and behind, though shielded by a screen of tall, thin trees, was the castle. But Roger picked up something more interesting immediately: standing on the grass, by a bench of some sort, back turned, looking up at the aerial circus, was a girl. A WAC or something.

He advanced warily, unsure whether she was an officer. She was in some kind of uniform all right, but not an officer, for there was no gleam at her collar. He stepped forward.

"Uh, pardon me, have you got any idea what's going on, miss?"

The girl turned. One of those clear, guileless Midwestern faces organized around big eyes, blue, a pert nose and even freckles. A kind of strawberry complexion, hues of pinkness, and it all made him think of freshness, a kind of innocence.

Hey, would I like to pork *that!* he decided.

Then he noticed she was crying.

"Gee, what's wrong? Bad news, huh?"

She came into his arms—he could not *believe* his famous luck again—and began to sob against his shoulder. He held her close and tight, muttering, "Now, now," stroking her hair.

She looked up, soft and blurred, and he thought she wanted a kiss and so he pressed his lips into hers.

At last Eichmann spoke.

"What guarantees can you offer? Repp is very dangerous. You insist that I betray him, or you'll let it be known I betrayed him. Yet without a guarantee, the first possibility does not exist."

"We have a way of remembering our friends. We've that reputation, don't we? Give us a chance to live up to it. That's all I can say."

"I'd need to disappear. Understand, it's not the Americans who frighten me. It's Repp."

"I understand," said Leets. "All right. I'll see what I can do."

"A bargain then. Eichmann for Repp?"

"I said I'd see."

"Eichmann for Repp. How that would sicken him." He laughed.

"Herr Eichmann," Tony said, in better German than Leets's, "let us proceed with our business."

The *draydel* had run out of energy, and sputtered to a stop, lurching spastically on the table. Eichmann picked it up in his blunt fingers—an anatomical oddity, hands so big on such a skinny man—and began to talk.

"Operation Nibelungen: I was in on it from the beginning. It was Pohl's actually, Pohl, of the Economic and Financial Office, WVHA, but he brought me into it, and together we sold the *Reichsführer*. It was nothing personal, the business with the Jews, you understand that. It was just our way, our job. We had to do it. The policies were set from the very top. We only did what we were—"

"Get to the point," Leets instructed.

"Operation Nibelungen. The point of Operation Nibelungen is a Special Action."

"A 'Special Action'?"

"With a rifle."

"Special Action means murder."

"Call it what you will. It can be justified morally from a World Historical perspective which—"

"Who?" said Leets, surprising even himself at how uninterested he sounded after so many months of sawing on the same question.

"You must realize. I am not against the Jews. I respect and understand them. I myself am a Zionist. I believe it would be best for them to have their own country. All this was forced upon us by our superiors—"

"Who? When?"

"When, I cannot say. I was taken off the project and sent to Hungary on special emergency assignment before the final planning took place. But soon. If not already."

Leets said, "Who, Herr Obersturmbannführer Eichmann? For the last time, *WHO?*"

His yell seemed to startle the little man.

"No need to yell, Captain. I'm about to tell you."

"Who?"

"A child," Eichmann said. "A six-year-old boy. Named Michael Hirsczowicz. Now I think I might have one of those cigarettes."

Roger put the tip of his tongue through the girl's lips.

She smashed him in the face, open hand.

"What?" he said. "Hey, I don't get it."

"Fresh," she said.

"You kissed *me*! I just walked around the corner and here's these *lips*."

"You made it dirty. You spoiled it."

"I'm sorry, I'm sorry." She was knocking him out. He was in love, or half in love at any rate.

"Look, I really didn't mean anything bad. It was just a friendly gesture."

"Tongues are more than just friends," she said.

"Oh, well, you get carried away, is all. Heh, heh. My name's Rog, Rog Evans. What's yours?"

"Nora."

"Well, Nora, how are you? Nice to meet you. Do you play tennis, by any chance? Where'd you go to school?"

"Prairie View."

"Prairie View, yeah, think I heard of it. Women's school out west, California, isn't it? A real good school, I hear."

"It's a high school in Des Moines. I doubt if you've heard of it. I didn't even go to a college yet."

"Oh, yeah, well, college is pretty much a waste of time. Even Harvard, where I go, is not really for serious people. Are you a WAC?"

"The Red Cross Women's Auxiliary."

"A civilian?"

"Yeah. But we're still supposed to call officers sir and all."

"Must be real interesting," he said.

"I hate it. It stinks. They watch you like a hawk. You never get to *do* anything."

"Yeah, well, that's the service. Speaking of *do*ing something, I was wondering, you tied up or anything tonight?" Get the date first, then worry about dumping Leets and Outhwaithe. "See, I don't know the area too well. I'm OSS—Office of Strategic Services . . . high-level intelligence, that sort of thing. Anywhere it's hot, that's where you'll find us. But I was wondering if you could sort of—"

"How can you think of *that* on a day like *this*?"

"And what's *this* day?" he finally asked her.

Eichmann smoked and explained.

"In the last days before the war, a wealthy, assimilated Warsaw Jew named Josef Hirsczowicz seemed to convert to Zionism. Naturally, there were ramifications."

Leets thought of just one of them: the shabby little office in London, the old man Fischelson, and all the grim, dark, weeping women. And Susan Isaacson, American, from Baltimore, Maryland, who'd lost her soul there, or perhaps found it.

"We viewed this with some concern. First, we felt the Hirsczowicz fortune to be ours, by right of biological superiority. Second, an accumulation of capital such as this fellow's is not without its influence. And that much money in the hands of Zionist agitators, anarchists, Socialists, Communists, what have you, could create considerable problems for us. Incidentally, Major, in this respect we are not so much different from your own government, which, in the Mideast at any rate, recognizes the World Jewish Conspir—"

"Get on with it," Tony said.

"Thus it was imperative that the man Hirsczowicz and his family and heirs be added to the list of Warsaw intelligentsia marked for special handling. And so it happened." Eichmann left to their imaginations the full meaning of the euphemism.

"But imagine our dismay and surprise," and here the German allowed himself a prim, wicked smile, "when our accountants discovered in an audit of the Bank Hirsczowicz that his fortune had disappeared. Disappeared! Vanished! A billion zlotys. Five hundred million Reichsmarks."

One hundred million bucks, thought Leets.

"Discreet inquiries were made. Naturally so large a sum cannot simply become invisible. A hundred rumors were tracked, a thousand interrogations launched. Obergruppenführer Pohl made it his special project. He was experienced in financial matters and saw the power of the fortune. He scoured Europe, when he was not busy running his concentration camp empire. And finally, he had success. In the middle of 1944, a source in Zurich was able to prove that the Jew had actually gotten his funds into the country, to the Schweizerschaft Banksellschaft. And that he had gotten something else out."

"The boy. The heir," said Tony.

"Yes and no. Again the Jew had been clever, very clever. The boy was not the heir. The boy was to be provided for, of course, but the fortune would not be his."

"Who would get it?" Leets asked.

"The Jews," said Eichmann.

"The Jews?"

"Yes. I told you the man was a Zionist. He had decided that his people's only salvation lay in a Jewish state, an Israel. Privately, I agree with him. Thus the money was held in escrow for several groups. Zionist groups. Refugee groups. Propaganda outlets. All dedicated to this idea of a new country."

"I see."

"But he was too clever, this Jew. Too clever by half. He of course worried about the son."

"Any father would."

"And so he made an arrangement with one of the fiery young Zionists. That the boy should be raised as one of them, as a first-generation Israelite. And know nothing of the fortune. But the father was terrified for the boy. And so he had written into the document for the transfer of the money a special complication. He did it on the last day, in an emotional state. We believe it to be a reenactment of one of their rituals. *Pidyon Haben*. The redemption of the firstborn son. May I have another cigarette, please? Thank you. What does that say? A Lucky Strike? Finding me has indeed been a lucky strike for you, hasn't it?"

"Get on with it."

"The arrangement holds that the boy must survive the war. He is to be delivered to the bank and identified by fingerprints. It made sense, because the boy would be raised in Palestine, far from any battles. It was only to make sure the boy didn't get somehow lost in a shuffle."

"But the war broke out," Leets added. In his mind he could see the Zionists stuck in the middle of Switzerland, in the middle of Nazi territory, with the boy who was the key to their future. "And so they left him there."

"You have grasped the essence."

"Kill him and there's no money for the Jews."

"No. And this is how I was brought into it. I was considered an expert in finding Jews."

"I see."

"I supervised the search team. It was not easy. It was very difficult. An agent of ours, one Felix, operated under my direct control. Painstakingly we tracked the rumors, the lies, the missing trails."

"And again, success."

"He heard of a place, a convent, the Order of Saint Teresa, in the canton of Appenzell in the foothills of the Alps, in northeastern Switzerland. There were said to be Jews there, Jew children, whose parents had somehow gotten them out. But the nuns were very frightened. Very secretive. It took us more weeks until . . . until this."

He held up the *draydel*.

"Felix got it from the caretaker, an alcoholic old man. In exchange for a small sum of money. It's very old, unique. It had been passed down in their family for generations, father to son. It was identified by an inmate in the concentration establishment Auschwitz, a former member of the Hirsczowicz household. It proved to us the child was there. It made our operations feasible. Both of them."

"Both?" said Leets, feeling his stomach begin to grow cold. Was there some aspect they had no idea of, some part of it they'd not come across, that was this very second beginning?

"There is another man, a German agent in Spain. A long-term

chap. He has wonderful papers. Authentic papers, in fact, and neighbors to vouch for him and a whole set of references, a most impressive documentation. All identifying him as Stepan Hirsczowicz. A cousin. Long lost. The papers are quite real; they were taken from a real Stepan Hirsczowicz, who died at Mauthausen."

Leets saw it now: the final twist.

"And so you get the money."

"Yes. Early on, the plan was to bring it straight into the Reich, a matter of simple transfer, no difficulties. But then we began to see how the war would turn out. It was the *Reichsführer*'s idea, quite brilliant. All that money, clean, untouched, money that had never been in the Reich, never been associated with it. And he knew that after the war it could have its uses. All kinds of uses. It would be for the SS men who had gotten out, or were in hiding, or for this, or for that. It was a wonderful opportunity. It was really wonderful."

And Leets understood how important it was to them: he saw now how a modern state, as it died, could totally invest its resources into the murder of one child. It wasn't astounding at all, really; he felt no sense of anticlimax, of being let down.

He fingered the *draydel*: what a route it had traveled, what a long, sad journey. From the father, Josef, to the boy, Michael: a symbol of a father's love. It's all I can give you. I have no other, here. I would give anything, everything, to save you, but I have only this. Then it had gone to the caretaker, and then to the killers. To Felix and then to this smarmy creep here in the room with them and then to the big cheese Himmler, and Pohl's greasy little fingers had probably gotten onto it. Then, finally, to Repp's cold hands. A great miracle has happened.

"A bomb would be chancy, I suppose," said Outhwaithe. "Any kind of elaborate commando mission difficult to mount in a neutral country. Thus it's got to be one man, one good man."

"And there was a special problem that made Repp the inevitable selection," Eichmann explained bloodlessly. "The nuns keep the children in the cellar all the time."

"They must bring them out at night."

"For half an hour in the courtyard at midnight. . . . It's behind a wall. But a man with a rifle could reach it from the mountain.

"There would be twenty-six of them, right? In all?"

"Yes, Captain."

"So he doesn't have to worry about hitting the right one."

"No, Major. That's the beauty of it. He doesn't have to know. He'll kill them all."

"What do they call it? The gun, I mean."

"Vampir."

"Vampire," Leets said in English.

"They had great trouble with the weight. Vollmerhausen worked very hard on the weight. It had to be light, because Repp had to carry it around the mountain. There were no roads."

"How did they solve it?"

"The technical aspects I'm not sure of. It has to do with the sun. He exposes a plate to sunlight, and it makes the light-sensitive elements more potent. Thus he needs less power, and can carry a smaller battery. It's very ingenious."

"How much money will Repp get?" Tony asked.

"How did you know?" Eichmann said.

"Come now, we're not that stupid. If there's all that money at stake, he's not going to be the only chap risking his neck and do it for the pure ideological pleasure."

"He was coy. He pretended not to be interested. He said it was his bequest to the fallen. The German fallen. And so the *Reichs-führer* pressed him. He did not have to press hard."

"How much?"

"A million. Million, U.S. If he succeeds, he gains the world." He sat back.

"There. That's it. I sold you Repp. That's everything."

"Not quite. When?"

"I said I didn't know."

"You know," said Leets. "Everything you've told us is meaningless unless you tell us when."

"I have violated every oath I ever took this afternoon."

"I don't give a fuck for your oaths. When? When?"

"It's a trump card. I want a letter, saying how helpful I've been. Address it to the commandant here. Already, certain groups have been sent back to a large PW camp, where surely they will be set free at first convenience. I only want to go there. I've done no wrong."

"You were playing for this. To bring us all the way, except for this, weren't you?"

The German officer gazed at him levelly. "I'm not a stupid fellow either." He even had a pen and paper ready.

"I wouldn't," Tony said. "We don't know what this bird's up to. We'll find out soon enough. There's got to be records—"

But Leets scrawled a brief note To Whom It Concerned, testifying to the German's outstanding moral character. He handed it over, signed, dated.

"Thank you," said Eichmann.

"Now: when?"

"A night when he can move with absolute freedom. A night when countermoves are impossible. A night when nobody is thinking of war."

Leets stared at him.

Roger burst in, shrieking. He danced past the German, knocking him to one side, and grabbed Leets up in a wild do-si-do and in a croaking babble informed them the sky was full of airplanes, the booze was gurgling, the laughter building.

"Reams. Reams," he cried.

Reams of what? Paper? Leets thought in confusion.

"I got a date," Roger shouted, "a real pretty girl."

"Roger," Leets yelled.

"It's over, fucking World War Number Two, over, they signed the surrender at Rheims, we missed it on the road."

Leets looked beyond the boy to Eichmann, who sat, composed and grim, and then beyond Eichmann, and out the door, and in the wall there was a window. Tony was rising beside him urgently, calling for the MP to take the German back, and Roger said he was in love, he was in love, and out the window Leets noted the setting of the sun and the coming of the German night.

XXVIII

Repp came out of sleep fast: gunfire.

He rolled from the bed and moved quickly to the window. A glance at his watch told him it was still before nine. Margareta, her blond hair unkempt, one thin bare leg hanging out, stirred grumpily under the covers.

Repp could see nothing in the bright light. The crackle of guns rubbed raggedly against his ears again, a messy volley. A battle? He recalled something about the German soldiers turning themselves in today. Perhaps a few had decided on more honorable action, and war had come at last to Konstanz. But then he realized what must be happening: a cold finger pressed for just a second against his heart.

He snapped on the radio. Nothing on Radio Deutschland. Broadcast not scheduled till noon. He fiddled with the dial, picking up excited jabber in English and Italian, which he didn't understand.

Finally, he encountered a French-speaking station. He knew the phrase from 1940. He'd seen it chalked on walls then, a fantasy, a dream.

À nous la victoire.

To us, victory.

They were playing "The Marseillaise." He turned it off as Margareta lifted her head, face splotchy from sleep. A breast, pink-tipped and vague, swung free as she rose from the covers.

"What is it?" she asked.

"It's time to go," he said.

He was eight hours ahead of Leets.

Repp checked the mirror once again. Gazing back at him was a prosperous, sleek civilian, freshly bathed and shaved, hair brilliantined back, crisp carnation of breast-pocket handkerchief, neat tie on glossy white shirt under exquisitely tailored suit coat. He had trouble recognizing this image as his own, the cheeks so rosy, the eyes set in a pink bland face.

"You look like a cinema star," she said. "I didn't realize how handsome you were."

Yet he could see the lights playing off his forehead where the sweat had begun to accumulate in beads, high and moist. The border was coming up, the nightmare passage.

"Repp. One last time," she said. "Stay. Or get across and go somewhere safe. But best, stay with me. There's some kind of future here, somewhere, I know there is. Children even."

He sat down on the bed. He felt exhausted. He tried to press images of prying border guards and intensive interrogations out of his mind. He noted that his hands were trembling. He knew he had to go to the toilet.

"Please, Repp. It's all over now. It's done, finished."

"All right," he said weakly.

"You'll stay?" she said.

"It's just too much. I'm not meant for this kind of thing, for playing other people. I'm a soldier, not an actor."

"Oh, Repp. You make me so happy."

"There, there," he said.

"So gallant. So damned gallant, your generation. You had so much responsibility, and you carried it so well. Oh, God, I think I'm going to start crying again. Oh, Repp, I also feel like laughing. It'll be fine, I know it will, it'll work out for the best."

"I know it will too, Margareta," he said. "Of course I do. It'll all be fine."

He went to her.

"I want you to know," he said, "I want you to know an extraordinary thing. The most extraordinary thing in my life: that I love you."

She smiled, though crying.

She dabbed at her messy face.

"I look so awful. All wet, hair a mess. Please, this is so wonderful. I've got to clean up. I don't want you to see me like this."

"You are beautiful," he said.

"I must clean up," she said, and turned and stepped for the door.

He shot her in the base of the skull and she pitched forward into the hall. He himself felt awful, and he was trying to be kind.

She didn't know, he told himself. Not for one second did she know.

Now all the trails were dead and there were no links between Repp and the private and Herr Peters.

Repp moved her to the bed and delicately put the sheets over her. He threw the pistol in the cellar and washed his hands. He checked his watch. It was almost nine.

He stepped bravely out, blinking in the sun.

The French private, glum because his comrades were drunkenly shooting up central Konstanz, demanded Repp's passport. Repp could see the boy was sullen, presumably stupid, and would therefore be inclined to mistakes. He handed over the document, smiling mildly. The boy retreated to a table where a sergeant sat while Repp waited near the gate. Here, the German side, the arrangements were more imposing, a concrete blockhouse, gun emplacements and sandbags. But this formal military layout seemed a little idiotic now that it was manned only by a few Frenchies rather than a platoon of German frontier policemen.

"*Mein Herr?*"

Repp looked up. A French officer stood there.

"Yes? What is it?" Repp demanded.

"Could you step over here, please?" The man spoke bad German.

"Is something the matter?"

"This way, please."

Repp took a deep breath and followed him over.

"I have a train to catch. The noon train. To Zurich," he said.

"This will only take a moment."

"I'm a Swiss citizen. You have my passport."

"Yes. The first I've seen. What business did you have in Germany?"

"I'm a lawyer. It was a matter of getting a fellow's signature on a document. In Tuttlingen."

"And how was Tuttlingen?"

"Loud. The Americans came. There was a battle."

"At the bridge, yes."

"It was very frightening."

"How did you get from Konstanz to Tuttlingen?"

"I hired a private car."

"I thought petrol was all but impossible to find."

"The man I hired took care of that. I paid a fortune, but I don't know anything about it."

"Why do you look so uneasy?"

Repp realized he wasn't doing well. He thought his heart would burst or shatter in his chest. He tried not to swallow or blink.

"I don't care to miss my train, Herr Hauptmann."

"Use the French, please. *Capitaine*."

Repp said the French word awkwardly.

"Yes, thanks."

Repp knew he'd been a hair from calling the man *Sturmbann-führer*, the SS word.

"May I go now?"

"And what's your rush? Hurrying to get to the wonderful Swiss climbing?"

"There are avalanches this time of year, Captain."

The captain smiled. "One other thing. I notice a curious designation on your passport. It's the first Swiss one I've seen. Here, it says 'R-A.' What can that mean?"

Repp swallowed. "It's an administrative category. I know nothing about it."

"It means 'Race—Aryan,' doesn't it?"

"Yes."

"I didn't know you Swiss went in for that sort of thing."

"When you are a little country next to a big country, you try and make the big country happy."

"Yes. Well, the big country is not too happy these days."

How much longer would this last?

"But the Swiss are. The Swiss win every war, don't they?"

"I suppose so, sir," said Repp. His mouth tasted sour.

"Go on. This is ridiculous. Pass, get out of here."

"Yes, sir," Repp said, and scurried off.

It was like a sudden transit to wonderland: People pink and gay, crowding, chunky, prosperous. Just a few miles, a fence, a bitter officer overzealously guarding his gate and this, a whole other world—Kreuzlingen, Konstanz's Swiss suburb. Repp struggled in the dangerous intoxication of it. He tried to locate deep within himself a primordial sense of righteousness, or abiding moral discontent. But he was too bedazzled by surface charms: goods brightly wrapped in shopwindows, chocolates and all kinds of foods, beautifully dressed women who were totally oblivious of their appearance, fat kiddies, banners flapping out of windows, private autos purring down the street. A holiday air prevailed: had he blundered into some quaint Swiss festival?

No, the Swiss were celebrating war's end too. Repp darkened as this knowledge made itself clear to him. A fat mama with two children seemed to materialize out of the crowd along the sidewalk.

"Isn't it wonderful, *mein Herr*? No more killing. The war is finally done."

"Yes, wonderful," he agreed.

They had no right. They weren't a part of it. They had not won a victory, they had not suffered a defeat. They had merely profited. It made him sick, but though he felt like a pariah among them, he pressed ahead, several blocks down the Hauptstrasse, into Kreuzlingen's commercial center, then took the Bahnhofstrasse toward the station. He could see it ahead, not a huge place like the Berlin or the Munich monstrosities before the war, but prepossessing on its own scale, with glassed-in roof.

Glass!

All that unbroken glass, glittering whitely among the metal girders, acres of it. He blinked stupidly. Were there trains there that actually chugged through a placid countryside without fear of American or English gangsters swooping down to rain death from the sky? Almost in answer to this question, a whistle shrieked and a puff of white smoke rose.

A block yet from the Bahnhof itself, he arrived at an open-air café, the Café München.

They'll change that name by noon, he thought.

A few tables were unoccupied. Repp chose one and sat down.

A waiter appeared, a man in white smock with attentive eyes. "*Mein Herr?*"

"Ah," a little startled, "coffee, I think," almost having said "real coffee." The man withdrew instantly and reappeared in seconds with a small steamy cup.

Repp sat with it, letting it cool. He wished he could stop feeling nervous. He wished he could stop thinking about Margareta. All the hard business was over, why couldn't he relax? Yet he could not seem to settle down. So many of the little things of the world seemed off: the Swiss were fatter, cheerier, their streets cleaner, their cars shinier. It was impossible to believe that with the money he'd be a part of all this. He could have a black shiny car and dress in a suit like this and have a thousand white shirts. He could have ten Homburgs, two hundred ties, a place in the country. He could have all that. What lay ahead was only the operation itself, and that was what he was best at.

He tried not to think of After. It would come when it came. If you looked too far ahead you got in trouble, he knew for a fact. Now, there was only room for the operation.

Across the street, he saw a small park, green under arched elms, and in it benches and gym apparatus for children. Strange that it was so green so early; but then, was it early? What was the date? He'd been keyed to the surrender, not the date. He thought hard: he knew he'd crossed the bridge into Konstanz May 4; then he'd been sealed up with Margareta—how long? It seemed a month. No, only three days; today then was May 7. Yet the pale sun had urged bud growth out of the trees and lay in pools on the grass, which itself was green and not the thatchy stuff of earlier.

In the park, two blond children played on the teeter-totter. Repp watched them idly. Surely they were Swiss: but for just a moment he saw them as German. Uncharacteristically, he began to feel morbid and sentimental about children. Today of all days. Yet these two beauties—real Aryan stock, chubby, red-cheeked— really represented something to him: they were what might have been. We tried to give you a clean, perfect world, he told them. That awesome responsibility—a major cleaning action, *Grossauberungsaktionen*—had fallen to his generation. Hard, difficult work. But necessary. And so close, so damned close! It filled him with bitterness. So much accomplished, then *pfft*, gone up in smoke. The big Jews had probably finally stopped it. Repp almost wept.

"A pretty boy and girl, eh, Herr Peters?"

Repp turned. Was this Felix? He hadn't used the approach code. Repp looked at a man about his own age, with acne-pitted face, in a pinstriped suit. Felix? Yes, Repp had been shown a picture of the same fellow in Berlin. Felix was just the code name; he was really a Sturmbannführer Ernst Dorfman of Amt VIa, SD Foreign Intelligence.

"Hansel and Gretel," said Felix. "A fairy tale."

"Yes, beauties," agreed Repp.

"May I sit?"

Repp nodded coldly.

"Oh. Forgive my manners: did you get the Tuttlingen Signature?"

"Without difficulty."

"Excellent." Felix smiled, and then confided, "A silly game, no? Like a novel. In Berlin, they think business like that is important." His cool eyes showed amusement. But the man's cavalier attitude bothered Repp. "And how was the trip?"

"Not without difficulties."

"Yet you made good time."

"The schedule was designed around maximum time allowances. I came through in minimum."

"And how was the woman?"

"Fine," he said.

"Yes, I'll bet you had pleasant hours with that one. She was pointed out to me once. You aces, you always get to go first-class, don't you?"

"The car?" Repp asked.

"Christ, you're a firebreather. Still trying to make *Standartenführer*, eh? But this way."

Repp did not at all like to hear the word *Standartenführer* thrown so casually into a public conversation, but there were in fact no other customers within earshot of the table. He stood with Felix and pulled some money out of his pocket. But he had no idea how much to leave.

"Two francs would do nicely, Herr Peters," Felix said.

Repp stared stupidly at the strange coins in his hand. Now what the hell? Finally, he dumped two of the big ones on the table and followed Felix.

"That's quite a tip you left the fellow, Herr Peters," said Felix. "He can send a son to *Kadettenanstalt* on it."

They crossed the street and walked along some shop fronts and then turned down a smaller street. An Opel, black, pre-war, gunned into life. Its driver turned as they approached.

Repp got in the back.

"Herr Peters, my associate, Herr Schultz."

He was a young man, early twenties, with eager eyes and an open smile.

"Hello, hello," said Repp.

"Sir, I was with SS-Wiking in Russia before I was wounded. We all heard about you."

"Thanks," said Repp. "How far to Appenzell?"

"Three hours. We've got plenty of time. You'd best try and relax."

They pulled from the curb and in minutes Schultz had them out of the town. They took Road No. 13 south, following the coast of the Bodensee. It shimmered off to the left, its horizon lost in haze, while on the right tidy farms were set far back from the road on rolling hills. Occasionally Repp would see a vineyard or a neatly tended orchard. They soon began to pass through little coastal towns, Münsterlingen with its Benedictine nunnery, and Romanshorn, a larger place, with a ferry and boatyards; beyond, a fine view of the Appenzell Alps, blue and brooding, was disclosed; and then Arbon, which boasted a castle and a fancy old church—

"The Swiss could do with an autobahn," said Felix.

"Eh?" said Repp, blinking.

"An autobahn. These roads are too narrow. Very funny, the Swiss, they won't spend a penny unless they have to. No grand public buildings. Not interested in politics at all, or philosophy."

"I saw them dancing in the streets," said Repp, "because the war was over."

"Because the markets will be open, rather," said Felix, "and they can go back to being the clearinghouse of nations. They do not believe in anything except francs. Not idealists like us."

"I assume we can chat as if we are at a reception following a piano concert because all the necessary details have been attended to," Repp said.

"Of course, Herr Peters," said Felix.

"The weapon is—"

"Still in its case. Unopened. As per instructions."

"You're not known to British or American Intelligence?"

"Oh, I'm known. Everybody in Switzerland knows everybody else. But as of the thirtieth I became uninteresting to them. They expected me to politely put a bullet through my skull. They'd rather pay attention to their new enemies, the Russians. That's where all the activity is now. I'm a free man."

"But you were nevertheless cautious in your preparations?"

"Herr Obersturmbannführer, an incautious man does not last any longer in my profession than in yours. And I've lasted since 1935. Here, Lisbon, Madrid during the Civil War, a time in Dublin. Buenos Aires. I'm quite skilled. Do you want details? None of our part of the operation was set up through code channels; rather it was all done via hand-carried instructions, different couriers, different routes. Lately, I haven't trusted the code machines. And I had a ticket to B.A. out of Zurich last Saturday. Which I took. I got as far as Lisbon, where another agent took my place. I returned, via plane to Italy and then train through the Brenner Pass. I haven't been in Zurich for nearly a week. We've been staying in the Hotel Helvetia in Kreuzlingen, on Swiss passports such as yours. All right?"

"My apologies," said Repp.

Repp lit a cigarette. He noticed that they'd turned inland. There was no more water to be seen and now, ahead through the windshield, the Alps seemed to bulk up majestically, much nearer than when first he'd observed them.

"The last town was Rorschach, Herr Peters," said the young driver. "Now we're headed toward St. Gallen, and then to Appenzell."

"I see," said Repp.

"Pretty, the mountains, no?" said Felix.

"Yes. Though I'm not from mountainous territory. I prefer the woods. How much further in time?"

"Two hours, sir," said the driver. Repp saw his warm eyes in the mirror as the young man peeked at him.

"I think I ought to grab some sleep. Tonight'll be a long one."

"A good idea," said Felix, but Repp had already dozed off into quick and dreamless sleep.

"Herr Obersturmbannführer, Herr Obersturmbannführer."

He awakened roughly. The driver was shaking him. He could see that the car was inside something.

"We're here. We're here."

Repp came fully awake. He felt much better now.

The car was in a barn—he smelled hay and cows and manure. Felix, in the corner, labored over something, a trunk, Repp thought.

"Vampir?"

"Yes."

"Good."

Repp walked to the barn door, which was ajar, and looked out. They were partially up a mountain, at the very highest level of cultivation. He looked down across a slope of carefully tended fields and meadows and could see the main road several miles away.

"It seems desolate enough," he said.

"Yes, owned by an old couple. We bought it from them at an outrageous price. I tell you, I never worked an operation with such a budget. We used to have to account for every paper clip. Now: you need a farm, you buy a farm! Somebody sure wants those little Jew babies dead."

Repp walked out of the barn and around its corner, to follow the slope upward. The fields ended abruptly a few hundred meters beyond, giving way to forest, which mantled the rest of the bulk of the mountain, softening its steepness and size. Yet he still knew he was in for some exercise. The best estimates, based on aerial survey photos, put the distance between himself and the valley of the Appenzell convent roughly twenty kilometers, rough ground through mountain forest the whole way, up one side of it, around, and then down the other. He flipped his wrist over to check his watch: 2:35 P.M. Another six or seven hours till nightfall.

Repp shook the lethargy out of his bones. He had some walking to do, with Vampir along for the ride. He calculated at least five hours on the march, which would get him to his shooting position by twilight: vitally important. He needed at least a glimpse of the buildings in the light so that he could orient himself and calculate allowances on his field of fire, the limits to his killing zone.

Repp stabbed out his cigarette and returned inside.

He took off the tie, threw it in the car, and peeled off the jacket, folding it neatly. He changed into his mountain boots, a pair of green-twill drill trousers and a khaki shirt. Then he put on the Tiger jacket, the new one, from the workshops at Dachau, its crisp patterns, green on paler green, flecked with brown and black. But Repp had vanity too: against regulations, he'd indulged in one of the traditions of the Waffen SS and had the German eagle and swastika sewn onto his left sleeve.

Against whose regulations? he wondered. For now not only did he represent the Waffen SS, he *was* the Waffen SS: he was what remained of thirty-eight divisions and nearly half a million men, heroes like Max Seela and Panzer Meyer and Max Simon and Fritz Christen and Sepp Dietrich and Theodor Eicke; and Totenkopf, and Das Reich and Polzei and *Liebstandarte* and Wiking and Germania and Hohenstauffen and Nord and Prinz Eugen, the divisions themselves, Frundsberg and Hitlerjugend: gone, all gone, under the earth or in cages waiting to be hanged by Russians or Americans: he alone was left of this army of crusaders, he was chief of staff and intelligence and logistics and, most important, the men, the dead men. It was an immense legacy, yet its heaviness pleased him. Better me than most. I can do it. A simple thing now, move and shoot. After Russia all things have seemed easy, and this last mission will be easiest of all.

"Herr Obersturmbannführer?" The young driver stood looking at him as he snapped the last of the buttons.

"Yes?"

"Sir, wouldn't it be safer to travel in civilian clothes, in hiker's kit? That way, if—"

"No matter what I'm wearing, I'll have *that*"—he pointed to a table, on which Felix now had arranged the weapon components, gleaming with oil—"which no hiker would carry. But I won't run into anybody. Dense forest, high in the mountains, far from climbing and hiking trails. And this is a day of celebration, people everywhere are dancing, drinking, making love. They won't be poking about."

"But the boy has a good point," called Felix, "after all—"

"And finally, this is no SD operation. It's the last job of *Totenkopfdivision*, of the Waffen SS. I'm no assassin, gone to murder. I'm an officer, a soldier. This is a battle. And so I'll wear my uniform."

"Well," said Felix wearily, "it's your funeral, not ours."

"No," said Repp. "It won't be my funeral."

He went over; he could see smudge marks from Felix's fingers on the sheen of the cool, oily metal of the rifle components; these somehow bothered him.

"Of course it has not been opened until just now?"

He knew Felix was giving the driver a look of disbelief, but he heard the voice ring out, though without conviction, "Just as we were instructed."

Repp assembled the rifle quickly, threading the gas piston, operating handle and spring guide into the receiver, inserting the bolt camming and locking units, forcing the pin into the hinge at the trigger unit pivot, and locking the whole together. It took seconds. Then, without ceremony, he loaded each of the six magazines, thirty rounds apiece, with the special subsonic ammunition with the spherical bullet heads. He set the rifle and clips aside, and checked off the connections and wiring in the electro-optical pack. Finally, after examining it closely for defects and finding none, he locked the night scope itself with its infrared lamp to the zf.4 mount on the receiver of the STG-44, using the special wrench. Turning the bulky weapon sideways, he edged a magazine into the housing, feeling it fit into the tolerances; then with a sharp slap from the heel of his palm he drove the magazine home, hearing it snap in as the spring catch hooked.

"You look like a doctor getting ready to operate," said Felix.

"It's just a tool, that's all, a modified rifle," Repp responded, uneasy at the man's apparent awe of the equipment. "Now help me with this damned thing."

He put on the battle harness, with canteen and pouches for the magazines, and over that fitted the instrument rack. Felix and the youngster helped lift the thing into position, and he stepped into it like a coat, pulling the straps tight. He stepped away from them, taking the full weight.

"Christ, that's a heavy bastard. Will you make it?" asked Felix.

"I'll make it all right," said Repp grimly, as he looped the sling on the rifle over his shoulder. One last glance at his watch; it was 2:45 P.M.

"Sir?" The driver. He held something bright out. "For you. For afterward."

Repp took it: Swiss chocolate, wrapped in green foil.

"Thanks. Breakfast. A good idea." He dropped it in the pocket of the Tiger coat, then stepped away from the table, taking the full heft of the rifle for the first time. He felt the blood drain from his face with the effort. A hand touched his shoulder.

"Are you all right?" Felix asked.

"And if I'm not, you'll go?" Repp said. "No, I'm fine, just have to get used to the weight. I've been living too soft lately."

"Too many *Fräuleins*," said the irritating Felix.

Repp left the barn, into the sunlight, blinking. Already he could sense his body growing used to the weight.

* * *

Quickly the trees swallowed Repp. He moved among them in plunging, deliberate strides, a manifesto of purposefulness. But already the straps cut into him. Sweat broke out on his skin. His muscles became warm and fluid in the effort and he knew—from Russia—that if one pushed hard enough, if one had enough resolve, enough need, enough concentration, one reached a stage beyond pain, where great feats of endurance and stamina were possible. Repp knew he needed greatness today; he needed everything he had, and then more, and he was prepared to offer it. He was quite cheerful at this stage, full of confidence, hungry for the test, alert and content.

He forced his way through the underbrush, not looking back at all. He knew that higher, where the air was thinner, this rough new forest of elm and oak and a thousand tangles would give way to an ancient one of virgin pine, somewhat like the interior of the Schwarzwald. The travel would be much easier then, through solemn ranks of trees on pine-needle-packed dust which would billow up in great clouds, catching in the slanting sunlight as he rushed along. But that was hours away still; now, only this thick green stuff, sticky with sap and gum, every step of the way urging him to slow. He felt himself moving through screens and curtains, each one yielding finally to another; the visibility was limited and the air moist and close. The leaves were all wet; steam seemed to rise here and there. He felt he was in jungle. But he knew he'd be all right if he just stuck to his compass bearing, ignoring the paths he now and then passed, leaping over them, feeling clean each time he avoided their temptation. He aimed to reach the spine of the mountain and there stick to it for a long session of even-keel walking, before dipping down on the other side. He'd begin the descent long before reaching the severe peak that loomed above the timberline 5,000 meters or more.

He forged ahead, fighting the increase in the incline, sidestepping where possible, climbing over where not, the clumps of rocks that began to sprout in his way. As he rose along the mountain the forest began a gradual change; he almost didn't notice it and could pick no one moment when it had one character and another when it had a different one; or perhaps a cloud, far above, had sealed off the sun. At any rate, it ceased soon to be a jungle; the trees, though more majestic, were farther apart; denseness gave way to longer, gloomier perspectives; that sense of tropical green light, opaque chlorophyll in the sun, vanished in a darker pall. He felt as if he were in a cellar, clammy cool, tubed and catacombed, a jumble of ambiguous shadows, pools of abstract blackness, sheer thrusts of light at unexpected points where a gap in the canopy admitted the sun. The trees grew huge and gnarled. The undergrowth remained but now it fought its way through a carpet of decomposition, matted leaves, vegetable matter returning to the gunk of creation. There was a splendor in this dark vision, but Repp was in no frame of mind to enjoy it. He concentrated on movement, on pace, though once in a while reached with relief a flatter place where the mountain itself seemed to pause in its race upward.

In one such he himself seized a moment for rest. He was alone in the trees. He could hear his own breathing, ragged and forced, in the gloom. He was uncomfortably warm. He still hadn't reached pines. Nothing seemed familiar; it was like no forest he knew and he knew plenty of forests. He actually wished he'd hear a bird hoot or an animal cry: sign of some animate thing. His eyes scanned ahead: only massed-together trunks, white or gray scars of rocks standing out among them, some mossy and dull, and utter silence. The rifle sling was taut against his shoulder and the straps from the pack knifed deeply into him. He ignored a dozen or so other small agonies—scratches, a twisted ankle, sore joints, the beginnings of a cramp—but the straps really bothered him. Yet he knew to fuss with the damned thing now would be a mistake. He bent and tried to get the thing higher on him, so as to carry it more with body than with shoulders. Painful as it was, he took some sustenance in remembering how close they'd been to going operational at over fifty kilos. Under those conditions he'd be exhausted now. That strange little geek Hans the Kike really got the job done: the man deserved a medal. Right now Hans the Kike was a bigger hero to Repp than any of them. Thank God the Germans could produce men like him.

Wearily, he began his march again. The rocks had become quite troublesome by now, and he had to pick his way through defiles and up sudden smooth slopes. At one point he came even with a break in the trees and could see out: in the far distance a kind of blue haze. Actually, since he was facing north, and visibility was good, it might actually be Germany he could see. But what difference did it make? He pushed himself on. Ahead, nothing but the steady rise of the mountain, blanketed in trees and dead leaves and scrawny bracken and thistles. No pines yet, not easy travel. He feared he was losing time. He didn't even want to stop for water, though his throat was parched. His boots occasionally slipped in the treacherous footing and once he went down, badly banging a knee on a stone. It throbbed steadily. He felt also as though he had a fever. He felt unnaturally hot. He'd imagined it would be much cooler up here. Why was it so warm?

Where was he going? Did he even know? Yes, he knew. *Wir fahren nach Polen um Juden zu verschlen.* He was going to Poland to beat up the Jews. He'd seen it chalked on the sides of the troop trains in 1939, next to grotesque profiles of heavy kike faces, beaked nose, primitive jaws, almost fishlike: a horrible image. He was going to Switzerland to beat up the Jews: it was the same thing, the same process, the same war. He was going to beat up Jews.

The pain in his shoulders increased. He ought to slow or even rest, but he knew he couldn't. He was obsessed with failing light. If he didn't get there before dark he was lost.

He was going to beat up some Jews.

Jews.

You killed them. Messy, disturbing work. No one liked it, and in Berlin they were wise enough to see that those few who did should not have been on the firing line. It was a responsibility, a trust, a commitment to the future.

Repp had asked for the special duty.

He'd been wounded after Demyansk and though the wound wasn't serious—a crease across the thigh, healing quickly—his blood count was so low, they had wanted to put him on less rigorous duty. But Repp wanted to be a part of the other business, the other war. It was simple duty: no one forced him, and he did not enjoy it. It was simply part of the job, a bad part, but one had to get through the bad parts too.

The day that swam to his mind now was in October, 1942, at Dubno Airport in Volhynian Province in the Generalgouvernement. Why this day? It was not so terribly different from most days. Perhaps it was the cigarette and the girl, or more precisely the odd congruence of the cigarette and the girl.

It was a Siberia. It tasted wonderful, filling his head with a most pleasant buzz. He was only then learning of the joys of these fierce Russian things that tasted like burning villages and left him just a bit dizzy. He sat at the edge of a pit on a cool sunny day. Everybody was being very kind, because the business could get messy and difficult and hard on everyone. But today things were going quite nicely. A lot of people were around, civilians, relaxing soldiers, some with cameras, smiling, security policemen.

The gun across his legs was a Steyr-Solothurn, designated an MP-34. It was a wonderful old weapon, beautifully crafted though quite heavy. It had a fine wood stock and a perforated barrel and a horizontal magazine feed system. Repp loved it: the Mercedes-Benz of machine pistols, too elegant and precise for wartime production. The barrel had finally cooled. He nodded to a black-uniformed security policeman. The man disappeared behind a bulwark of earth that had been gouged out to form the pit, and Repp for just a second was alone with his morning's work: there must have been five hundred of them by that time, filling half the excavation, most of them lifeless, though a cry would now and then rise. They did not look so bad; he'd seen many worse bodies on the Eastern front, their guts blown out, shit and legs and shattered skulls all over the place; these people were neatly slumbering, though there was a great deal of blood.

The policemen got another group into the pit. An old man with a child, a mother and father and several young children. The mother was crooning to them, but the father did not seem to be much help. He looked terribly scared and could hardly walk. The children were confused. They were talking that infernal language of theirs, almost a German dialect, yet hideously deformed, like so many things German they touched. Yet Repp could not hate them, naked women and men and children, walking daintily into the mud, as though they wanted to keep their feet clean. There were several other women, the last of them a girl in her twenties, young and dark and quite pretty.

As Repp wearily stood, hoisting the gun up with him, he heard the young girl say, to no one in particular, "Twenty-three years old."

What a remarkable thing to say! He thought about it later. Curious: what had she meant? I'm too young to die? Well, everybody's too young to die, miss.

Repp engaged the bolt, braced the weapon tightly against his ribs, and fired. The bullets thudded neatly across the bare backs and they fell quivering. They lay, one or two convulsing. It was

odd: you never saw the bullets hit or the blood spurt and yet
before they were still they seemed doused with it, red, thin, pouring
from every orifice. A child moved again, moaned. Repp fingered the
selection switch back to single shot and fired, once, into the skull,
which broke apart.

Then he changed magazines.

Everybody was happy when Repp did the shooting. He was
quick and efficient. He didn't make mistakes or become morose
after a while as so many of the others did. He even came to believe
that it was best for the Jews too. "Better me," he said later that
day, drinking coffee, "than some butcher."

Repp saw light ahead. At that same moment a new sensation became apparent to him. He was moving without trouble, through
clean, flat forest floor. He'd reached the high virgin forest. He
rushed on to the light. He stood at the crest, amid pine and fir, in
cool air. He looked about, his eyes tracing the ridge he was on
to a peak, stony and remote. Across the way, he could see other
mountains, their shapes softened in trees, and beyond that the true
Alps, snowy and heroic.

But Repp's vision was drawn downward. His eyes followed the
carpet of forest sliding away for thousands of feet down the slope
of the mountain, until finally it gave way to cultivated land,
checkerboarded, but much of it green, the Sitter Valley in the
Canton of Appenzell. He could not see the town—it was in another
leg of the valley—but there was the convent, a medieval church,
high-roofed with two domed steeples and a jumble of other subsidiary buildings, walled off from the world. He could see the
courtyard from here too.

He knelt swiftly and peeled the rifle from his shoulder. He
braced it on the bipod and stood for just a moment, freed at last
from a part of the burden, though of course the bulky pack on his
shoulders still hurt. But then he was back down, sliding the hatch
off the opaque face of the Vampir apparatus. He saw the light
strike it. Did it glitter, seem to come alive; or was that his imagination?

Whatever, Obersturmbannführer Repp allowed himself a smile.
He had quite a distance still to go, but downhill, through the virgin
pine, and he knew he'd make a shooting position well before dark.

XXIX

"He's already there," said Tony. "On the mountain. Over the convent. With Vampir."

"Yeah," said Leets, tiredly. He sat back, put his feet up on the table and with two fingers pinched the bridge of his nose. "Christ, I've got a headache," he said.

Beyond, music lifted, American, popular, from off the Armed Forces net. He could hear laughter, the sound of women's voices. Women? Here? Laying it on a bit thick, weren't they?

"We could call the Swiss police," said Roger brightly. "They could get some people out there and warn the—"

"No lines," said Tony, "not in the middle of a war. End of a war. Whatever. You can't just ring up the operator, eh?"

"Okay, okay," said Roger quickly, "here's what, I got it, I got it, we'll radio OSS in Bern or Zurich. They could get in contact with the Swiss police. There's just a chance that—"

"There's no chance at all," said Leets. "We are now in the middle of the biggest celebration in three thousand-odd years of European history. They knew all along."

"I suppose we can rationalize our failure," said Tony. "We could argue that it's really none of our business: one lone German criminal and some stateless Jews in neutral territory. We did give it a very good effort. Nobody can say we didn't try."

"Anybody got any aspirin?" Leets asked grumpily. "Jesus, it sounds like a goddamned *party* out there. I keep hearing women. Are there women out there, Roger?"

"Some Red Cross girls," Roger said. "Look, another thing we could try is the legation. There's bound to be a night duty officer. Now he could—"

"I sure could stand to get laid," Leets said. "I haven't gotten laid since—" he trailed off.

"And of course there's a political dimension to be considered too," said Tony. "All that money going to Zionists. It seems quite possible that some of those funds might be diverted into ends other than those best for King and country, eh? Let's fold up here and go find ourselves a pint, and enjoy the celebration."

"Captain, we—"

"All right, Roger."

"Captain, we can't just—"

"All right, Roger," he said. "Boy, do I have a headache. I always knew this would happen. Right from the start. I could feel it, I *knew* it was in the cards. Goddamn it."

"I suppose I did too," said Tony, rising wearily. "It certainly has got dark fast, hasn't it?"

"What're you guys talking about?" Roger asked, fearing the answer.

"Roger, go get the Jeep," said Tony. "And tell me please where the bloody phone is in this mausoleum."

"Hey, what—"

"Roger," Leets finally explained, "it's come down to us. You, me, Tony. Only way. Go get the Jeep."

"We can never *drive* there," said Roger. "We're hundreds of miles away. It's almost eight. Not that far in so short—"

"We can probably make it to Nuremberg in two hours. Then, if we're lucky, real lucky, we can promote an airplane. Then—"

"Jesus, what is this, dreamland? We'd have to get landing clearances, visas, stuff like that. Permission from the Swiss. Find another car on the ground. Drive to, what was it, Applewell or whatever, *then* find this place. Before midnight. That's the craziest thing I—"

"No," Leets said, "no cars, no visas, no maps. We jump in. Like Normandy, like Varsity, like Anlage Elf."

"Where *is* that damned telephone?" said Tony.

Tony found his phone—a whole abandoned switchboard full of them, in fact—in the great monumental stairwell around which Schloss Pommersfelden was built. But the space began to fill with people, drawn out of offices and billets, or drawn off the road by the blazing lights. It was one of those rare nights when no one wanted to be alone; no one was moody or unhappy. A future had just opened up for them.

Women began to appear. From where? Wasn't this place really a kind of prison? Red Cross girls, newspaper correspondents, WAC's, a few British nurses, some German women even. The stairwell jammed up with flesh. Everybody was rubbing, grinding, bumping, stroking. Liquor, looted from somewhere in the castle, began to appear in heroic quantities. Nobody had time for glasses;

one-hundred-year-old Rhine wines in black dusty bottles were sucked down like Cokes by GI's. A radio provided music. Dog-faces and generals rubbed shoulders in crowded orbits around the girls. Leets thought he heard the German officers singing in the detention wing—something schmaltzy and sentimental in counter-point to the Big Band jangle from the radio.

A girl kissed Leets. He could feel her tits squash flat against his chest. She put a boozy tongue in his ear and whispered something specific and began to tug at him, and then someone ripped her away.

Meanwhile, Tony worked the phone. Leets could not help but hear.

"I *say*." Tony especially the stage Englishman, David Niven, for Christ's sake. "Major Outhwaithe here, his Majesty's Royal Fusiliers, hello, hello, is this Nuremberg, Signal Corps, could you talk up, please, yes, much better, I'm told a British Mosquito squadron is about, at the airfield of course, can you *pos*sibly buzz me through, old fellow, must be an Air Officer Commanding about, no, no, English chap, funny talker like me, right, Limey, at least a group captain, what you chaps would call a colonel, yes, it sounds like a lovely party, we're having quite a one at this end ourselves, but *do* you think you could arouse Group Captain Manville? I see, yes, pity, then is it possible you could patch me through to that bunch then, yes, RAF, yes, hello, hello, are you there, Group Captain Manville? Yes, another Brit, Outhwaithe, of MI-six, or SOE actually, you're not Sara Finchley's cousin, ah, yes, thought so, believe I laid eyes on you in '37 at Henley, the regatta, you were the coxswain in the number-two boat, yes, bit of a hero, weren't you, Magdalen man, eh? and didn't you football as well, thought so, no, not Magdalen, Christ Church, '30, languages, got me into this spy business, yes, cushy, I agree, a few times, France, scratches though, yes, wonderful it's over, but I've heard Labour will win the next general, boot poor Win-ston out on his arse, yes, drinks awfully, heard the same myself, stay *in*? Good God, *now*? done my bit, time to get back though it'll be all different, every little thing'll have changed for the worse though I fancy in a year or so or ten or twenty, we'll look back on all this and think it great fun, highlight of our days, though right now it seems bleak enough, yes, sad in a way that it's over, they *were* mighty days, weren't they? and how is dear Sara, really, that common little Welshman Jones, Ives, *Ives*, both legs, she's marrying him anyway? why, how splendid, sounds like a novel, Arnhem, heard it was a throw of the dice all the way, Red Devil, those were brave lads, those were, make the rest of us look like sodders, quite a show, quite a show, Frost's adjutant? and how is Johnny? glad to be free, I'll bet, now, by the way, Group Captain, Tom, Tom is it? Tony here, yes, Antony, a major, they weren't so generous with the rank in our backwash department of the war, hope it doesn't hold me back after I'm demobbed, no telling how the records will count, yes, anyway, now, Tom, dear fellow, I'm in a bit of a pinch, yes, not a real bother, but time-consuming nevertheless, need an airplane, a Mosquito actually, yes, good ship, the Mossie—" Tony looked up at Leets, covered the speaker and said, "The beggar's completely sozzled," and returned without missing a beat. "—all wood, I know, I always wondered how they stood up to Jerry flak, flew *between* it, ho ho ho ho, *very* good, Tom, now, Tom, we've got to get to Switzerland in rather a dash, I know it's the best party since Kitchener reached Khartoum and God knows we've all earned it, and it's rather a *chunk* of a favor I'm asking, but it seems to be on the urgent side, a loose Jerry end we need to tie down, time's a-wasting and I haven't got time to call the right people upstairs, and of course the Yanks, *as usual*, would rather play rub-my-bum with the Russians than listen to us, but as I say, it would be awfully nice if I could hitch a ride to, well, I'm glad you realize the importance, yes, Tom, yes, yes, about two hours, yes, I understand, yes, quite, quite, of course, best to Sara, best to her fellow Jones, *Ives*, sorry, Ives, wonderful girl, so brave, tally-ho," and at last he laid the phone down in its cradle.

"He said No?"

"He said Yes. I think. So drunk he could hardly speak, the music was quite loud. But there'll be a Mosquito on the field at ten at Grossreuth Flughafen. God." He stood.

Leets and Outhwaithe pushed their way through the celebrants, and out into the night, where Roger waited with the Jeep and the Thompson submachine guns.

Repp, at 400 meters out, had an angle of about 30 degrees to the target zone. It was his best compromise, close enough to put his rounds in with authority, yet high enough to clear the wall.

He half crouched now behind an outcrop of rock. The Vampir rifle lay before him on the stone, on its bipod, the bulky optics skewing it to one side. Repp had removed the pack and set it next to the rifle so that its weight wouldn't pull his shooting off.

Enough light lingered to let him examine the buildings beneath and beyond him. Built five hundred years ago by fierce Jesuits, the buildings had been walled and somewhat modernized early in the century when the order of Mother Teresa took them over as a convent. It looked like a prison. The chapel, the oldest building, was not impressive, certainly nothing on the scale of the Frauenkirche in Munich, a true monument to papism; it was a utilitarian stone thing with a steeply pitched roof, two domed steeples with grim little crosses atop them. But Repp steadied his binoculars against the other, larger edifice, the living quarters of the order that fronted on a courtyard. Patiently in the fading light he explored it until he found, not far from the main entrance with stairway and imposing arches, an obscure wooden door, heavily bolted. The children would spring from there.

There would be twenty-six of them, and he had to take them all: twenty-four, twenty-five even, simply wasn't good enough. The SD report said they came out every night at midnight and played in the yard for about forty minutes. Repp calculated that they'd be bunched in the killing zone, that is, outside the door but not yet dispersed enough to prevent a clean sweep of the job, for about five seconds. He'd take them when the last one had stepped out the door. Fantastic shooting, to be sure, but well within his—and Vampir's—capabilities.

And what if twenty-seven targets came out, or twenty-eight, or twenty-nine, meaning a nun or a novitiate or two had come along to watch and help? It was entirely possible, even probable. In Berlin they'd been vague and half-apologetic. Perhaps even the *Reichsführer*, who'd sent millions East, felt queasy about ordering him to shoot a Swiss nun. Yet they chose Repp for his strength as well as his skill and he'd resolved to make the difficult decisions. If a nun had to die in the cause of making the world *Judenrein*, clean of Jews, then so be it. He'd kill everything on the scope.

Repp laid down the binoculars as the last of the light died. He clapped his hands, and pulled his jacket tighter. He was cold and afraid of fatigue, which could take his edge. And he was strangely uneasy about all this: so simple, everything had whirred into place. He knew enough to distrust such ease. He shifted an arm and looked at his watch. Almost nine.

Three more hours.

It was almost nine. The drunken lieutenant was explaining but his words kept dissolving into giggles. He was under the impression Roger was an officer and he seemed to think the more he giggled the more trouble he was in, which meant that he giggled even harder.

"The tank carrier, sir, uh, he stripped his gears trying to get her outta the mud, uh, or he *thought* he would, uh, sir, he put her in reverse and she jumped the road and—" The remainder of the communiqué was lost in a seethe of giggles. The lieutenant was trying to explain why the flatbed truck, designed to transport tanks, lay angled across the road ahead, garish in the light of a dozen purple flares. Around it clustered a group of Americans—they'd drawn duty on VE night and someone had a bottle and whatever they were supposed to do just wasn't going to get done.

It had been like this most of the way since Schloss Pommersfelden. Nuremberg still lay somewhere in the distance, mythical like Camelot, and to get there they'd have to pass through more of what they'd already seen: drunken joyous men of all nationalities, accidents, honking horns, flares, small-arms fire. And women. In the small town of Forchheim—"Fuck-him," in GI argot—through which they'd just pushed their way, the nonfraternization law had broken down totally, and young officers were the most audacious offenders. College boys mostly, with no real military careers on the line, they'd turned the town into a fraternity party or prom night. The Jeep had been laid up at a corner behind a column of stalled vehicles before Leets, in a frenzy of rage, had gone forward to find two staff cars hung up on each other in a minor crash, and in the back seat of each a couple necking hotly while around them MP's argued and screamed. Leets went back and they'd pulled out of line to try an alternate route, but almost ended up in the Regnitz River and did in fact become lost until a studiously inebriated British major of the Guards, elaborately polite, had pointed them back in the right direction.

"Well, Jesus, how long, Lieutenant?" Leets demanded, leaning across Roger. Something in his voice must have startled the youngster. He stepped back abruptly and began to speak in an oppressive imitation of sobriety. "There's a maintenance vehicle from the motor pool in Nuremberg on the way, uh, sir."

"Christ," said Leets in disgust.

He climbed out of the Jeep and pushed by the lieutenant to the truck. The fucking thing was hopelessly locked in, its double-axled set of rear tires having slipped off the roadway into a culvert, hooking there, and as the driver had pulled to free himself, he'd actually twisted the huge flatbed up and out into the air; it looked like a drawbridge stuck halfway, blocking the road completely. It would take a heavy tow truck or perhaps a crane to move the thing.

Up ahead loud voices clashed off one another. Leets looked into the circle of vivid pink light from the flare and saw two men facing each other. They were about to begin throwing punches.

"Hey, what's going on here?" he yelled.

"Asshole here dumped his fucking truck in the middle of the road, now he won't move it so I'm gonna move *him*," said one.

"You just go on and try it, sucker," said the other.

"Knock it off, goddamn it," Leets ordered.

"There's broads up in that Fuck-him place," said the first man, "and goddamn I mean to get a piece of ass tonight."

"All right," said Leets.

This son of a bitch and his fuckin' tru—"

"*Knock it off, goddamn it!*" Leets shouted.

"Captain," said Roger.

"Shut up, Roger, goddamn it, I got enough—"

"Captain. Let them have *our* Jeep. We'll take *their* car. Everybody's happy."

"What are you driving?" Leets asked.

"Ford staff car," the man said sullenly. "I'm General Taplow's driver. But, hey, I can't let anything happen to that car."

"More pussy in Fuck-him than you ever saw in one place in your life," said Roger. "Some of them German women are walking around *bare-tit.*"

"Oh, Christ," said the man weakly.

"Harry, you're gonna get us all in a lot of trouble."

"Bare-tit?"

"Some of 'em even have these little pasty things on."

"Oh, Jesus. That I gotta see."

"Harry."

"Look, you'll take real good care of that car, won't you?"

"You know where the Nuremberg airport is, Grossreuth Flug-hafen?"

"Yeah, sure."

"That's where the car'll be. All locked up."

"Fine," the man said, "fine and fine again." Then his excitement beached itself. "Uh. Didn't see you was an officer. Uh, sir."

"Forget it. No rules tonight, that's the only rule."

"Yes, sir."

"Get the major and our stuff," Leets told Roger, who'd already started.

The two groups of men filed by each other in the fading light of the flares. One of the drunken GI's suddenly looked up at the three fellows passing him, and saw them grave-faced, a trifle solemn, grumpy with their automatic weapons. "Jesus," he said, stunned at the vision, "you guys know where there's a *war* or something?" But he got no answer.

As Leets climbed into the Ford staff car, he forced himself to check his Bulova. He didn't want to but there were a lot of things he didn't want to do that night that he knew he was going to have to do anyway, and the easiest of them all was to look at the watch.

It was almost ten.

It was almost eleven. Repp felt sluggish from his long wait in the cold rocks. During this time he had closed his mind down with his extraordinary self-control: he had willed out unpleasant thoughts, doubts, twinges of regret. He'd put his mind in a great dead cold place, letting it purify itself in the emptiness. He wasn't exactly sure what happened in this trancelike state and he'd never spoken of it to others. He simply knew that such an exercise in will seemed to do him a great deal of good, to generate that icy, eerie calm that was the bedrock of the great shooting, the really fantastic shooting. It was something he'd learned in Russia.

But now it was time to bring himself up, out of the cold. He began with exercises, pedantic physical preparations. He rolled to his belly and entwined his fingers, clamping them behind his neck, elbows straining outward. Then, slowly, he lifted his torso from the ground, chin thrusting high on the strength of his stomach. He rocked, stretching, feeling the pain scald as the muscle tension rose; then, sweetly, he relaxed. Up, hold and relax: three sets, ten each.

Then the shoulders and upper chest: this was difficult—he didn't
want to do a classic press-up because he didn't want to deaden his
touch by putting his weight on his palms. He'd therefore evolved
an elbow press-up, planting them on the ground, gathering his fists
before his eyes. Then he'd force the fists down, levering his body
on the fulcrum of his elbows—a painful trick that soon had the
girdle of muscles around his shoulders, chest and upper body singing. But he was hard on himself and pushed on, feeling at last the
sweat break from his body and its warmth come bursting out his
tunic collar.

He lay on his back and thrust his arms out above him; he twisted
them, clockwise, then back, each as far as he could, forcing the
bones another millimeter or more in their casings of gristle and meat.
He could feel his forearms begin to throb as the blood pulsed
through and enlarged his veins. He struggled against the pain,
knowing it to be good for him. His hands he opened and closed
rapidly, splaying them like claws until he felt them begin to burn
and tremble.

Repp lay back, at last still. His body felt warm and loose. He
knew it would build now in strength and that when his heart settled down it would be deadly calm. He stared up through the
canopy of firs at the stars blinking coldly in the dead night. He
stared hard at the blackness above him. It was impenetrable, mysterious, huge. Repp listened for forest sounds. He heard the hiss
of the wind among the needles, forcing them to rub dryly against
themselves. He felt it to be an extraordinary moment: he felt he'd
actually become a part of the night, a force in it. A sensation of
power unfolded in him like a spasm. He felt himself flooding with
confidence. Nothing could stop him now. He envisioned the next
few minutes. In the scope, the buildings would be cold and blank.
Then, a moment of blur, of blitz almost, as the warmth from the
door opening dissipated in the cool night air, molecules in the tril-
lions swirling as they spread. A shape, shivering, iridescent, would
tumble across the screen, almost like a one-celled creature, a germ,
a bacillus, a phenomenon of biology. And another, and another, out
they'd tumble, buzzing, swarming, throbbing in the inky-green
color Vampir gave them, far away, and Repp would count . . .
three, four, five . . . and with his thumb slip off the STG's safety
and begin tracking . . . thirteen, fourteen, fifteen . . . Vampir's
reticule was a black cross, a modified cross hair, and he'd hold it

on the lead shape . . . twenty-four, twenty-five, twenty-six . . .
And then he'd fire.

The sound of an airplane rubbed the image from Repp's eyes.
He rolled over to his stomach and slithered up the rock to the
rifle. He felt calm and purposeful, a force of will. He did not want
to draw the rifle to him yet and have to hold the shooting position
too long.

The airplane had faded.

He glanced at his watch.

It was almost midnight.

Plenty of time.

It was almost midnight. They'd been in the air nearly an hour
now and Roger may have been more miserable in his life but he
wasn't sure when. In the first place, he was scared. He'd never
been scared like this before because he'd never jumped into battle
before. He was so scared it hurt to breathe.

Following close upon this terror, indeed making it keener, richer,
was his bitterness. He was ferociously bitter. *The war was over!*
That fact linked up with the other one: *he was going into combat!*

Next, working down his taxonomy of misfortune, he was uncomfortable. He squatted in the hull of the Mosquito, which was
rocketing along at about 408 miles an hour but a Mosquito, a
twin-engine fighter-bomber noted for speed and maneuverability,
was a three-man kite, and Roger, after the pilot and Outhwaithe
beside him in the bubble cockpit up top and Leets forward in the
Perspex nose cone, was the fourth man. All they had for him was
a crappy little seat, typical British junk, wedged into the tunnel
between nose and cockpit, and he had to squat like some nigger
shoeshine boy. He was also jammed with equipment which made
the small space harder to bear, the parachute for one, a supremely
ridiculous M-1 Thompson submachine gun, eleven pounds of gangster's buddy, for another. Worst of all, the hatch, through which,
sometime soon, they'd all take the Big Step, didn't seem sealed too
well and rattled around loosely just a foot away from him, cold air
just crashing through. But then what didn't rattle in this crate? It
really *was* wood—plywood, glue and canvas, just like the Wright
Brothers' Dayton Flyer or a Spad. And just as cold. And it smelled
of gas, and the engines, big enough to drive a fucking PT boat,
were hung off the wings just outside the hull on either side, Rolls-

Royce 1680's, and they pulsated crazily, filling Roger's young bones
with dread. He had a headache and no aspirin. He felt a little sick
and not too long ago he'd peered down the tunnel to Leets—it
wasn't far, six feet—and seen, over Leets's hunched shoulder, *white*.
White? Snow, you dope. Then he'd felt the plane banking and
sinking, his stomach floating for just a second, and he'd realized they
were in the Alps. They were knifing through the Alps.

Suddenly, Tony hung down and then was beside him, having
descended from his perch in the bubble. He roughly butted young
Rog aside as though he didn't count for bloody much, and sprang
the hatch. Cold night air rushed in, inflating under Roger's coat.
Goose pimples blossomed on his pale skin and he began to shake.

What's going on? he wondered.

His nigger's place in the aircraft wasn't even equipped with an
intercom jack. The three big shots must have been merrily chatting
away all this time, and here he was in this dark tunnel in the guts
of the plane, unable to see, not knowing what was going on, and
suddenly this: hatch open, Outhwaithe checking his gear. Roger
realized they must have found it. He felt Leets, who'd crawled
down his tunnel, next to him. Leets gestured wildly. He seemed
unhealthily excited. Roger felt numb, even tired, under his fear,
disgust and chills.

Leets pressed Tony's earphones onto Roger and spoke into his
own throat mike.

"Rog, we think we've found it. We're going around again, he's
going to try and put us down in a field just west of the place. Tony
first, then me, then you. When you land, you'll see it off behind a
wall, very ornate, four stories—"

"Chickies, chickies, Mama Hen here, thirty seconds off your
drop," said the pilot, a calm steady young voice, over Leets.

"He'll be shooting from the mountain beyond, down into the
courtyard. Around back from where we're coming in. Thing to do
is to get into that courtyard before those kids get there. Got that?"

Roger nodded weakly.

"We'll be going out at six hundred. And don't forget you gotta
pull the rip cord on that chute, no static lines."

Roger, in horror, realized that though he was jump-qualified he'd
never pulled a rip cord in his life, there'd always been a nice panic-
proof static line to pop the chute for him. Suppose he froze?

"Ten seconds, chickies."

Tony looked at them. His face was smeared with paint. His wool commando watch cap was pulled low over his ears. He gave them a thumbs-up, a very WWII gesture. But WWII was over.

"Go, chickies, *go!*"

Tony pitched forward. Leets followed.

Roger stole a glimpse at his watch. It was still almost midnight. It occurred to him for just a fraction of a second that he could sit tight and go back to Nuremberg with the guy up there. But even as he was considering this delicious alternative, his legs seemed to acquire a heroic will of their own and they drove him to the hole in the bottom of the plane. He fell into silence.

It was time to shoot.

Repp was very calm, as always, now when it was only himself and the rifle. Its slightly oily tang, familiar amid the odor of the forest, rose to meet his nose, and he took the sensation as reassurance. His breath came evenly, smooth as soft music, feeding his body a steady flow of oxygen. He felt marvelously alive, focused, his nerves tingling with joy. A great yearning had passed.

He set himself on his elbows, belly, loins pressing against the rock, legs splayed for support, and drew the rifle to him. He laid the butt-stock against his shoulder. He palmed the pistol grip; the metal and plastic, cold as bone, heated quickly in his hand.

He rocked the weapon on its bipod, feeling its quick response to his guidance. It seemed alive, obedient. Repp had a special feeling for weapons; in his hands they were animate, almost enchanted. With his other hand, he reached up and plucked the lens cap off Vampir. He clicked on the auxiliary battery. He let his trigger finger search the curve of the trigger; then, finding it, drop away.

Repp eased the bolt back. It slid through oily stiffness, making a show of resistance; then he felt it yield with a snap and he freed it to glide home, having taken the first of the subsonic rounds off the magazine and seated it in the firing chamber, simultaneously springing open the dust cover on the breech. A whole system orchestrated itself to Repp's will—gas piston, operating rod and handle, bolt camming and locking units, pieces moving and adjusting within the weapon itself—and he took great pleasure in this, seeing the parts slide and click and lock. He checked the fire-control switch: semi-automatic. He thumbed off the safety.

* * *

A kind wind took Tony. Leets felt like he was descending in molasses and could see the Englishman a hundred feet below and three hundred feet away, his white canopy undulating in the wind, and he could see nothing else. The Mosquito drone was a memory. Leets fell in heavy silence, still a minute from touchdown when he saw Tony's chute collapse as it hit the ground.

Leets landed in a bundle of pain. Lights flashed behind his eyes on impact and his leg began to throb. He'd tried to favor it, a mistake, throwing himself off, and he hit on his butt and shoulder and lay there for a second in confusion, senses shaken by the hit. He could make out Tony's silk flapping loosely across the field, unconnected to any other thing. Climbing to his feet—leg hurt like hell but seemed to *work* okay—he popped his own harness toggle, and felt it fall away. He shook himself loose of it.

"Shit!" someone said close by, concurrent with the thud of meat and earth colliding. He looked and could see Roger scrambling up, struggling with his shrouds.

Leets unslung his Thompson. He could see he was in a meadow in a valley, ankle-deep in grass, low hills looming around. A quarter-mile or so away he thought he could see a building and a wall closing it off.

"This way," he hissed at the still befuddled young sergeant, and began, in his slow and painful way, to run. He could not see Tony.

Tony ran. He seemed to be closing the distance fast. There ·was some pain, but not so much. He wasn't sure about the gun, he'd lost that when he hit. Still, the place seemed a long way off.

He just kept running. Someone else in his body was breathing hard. He wanted to cough or stop. A footrace. Didn't they realize a certain type of gent doesn't run vulgarly and blindly across fields, almost to the point of vomiting, his own sweat burning hotly on his skin? A gentleman never *sweats*. The boots were impossibly heavy and the grass slowed him. He felt perfectly lucid.

Repp flicked on the scope and finally, last step, braced his free hand on the stock, just behind the receiver. He fit his shooting eye against the soft rubber cup of the scope.

The world according to Vampir was green and silent.

He felt very patient and helpful almost. He felt not that he was a part of history, but that he was History, a raw force, reaching

out of the night to twist the present into the future. Savage, perhaps, in immediate application, but in a much longer run Good
and Just and Fair.

A smear of light radiated across the scope as a trillion trillion
swirling molecules spilled out the opening door.

Right on time for their appointment with destiny, Repp thought.

A blurry splotch of light jiggled out, barely recognizable as a
human shape. And another.

Repp tracked it against the reticule of the sight, as other splotches
paraded helpfully along behind.

"There, there, my babies, my fine babies, come to Papa," Repp
began to croon.

Leets was almost dead with exhaustion. He was no runner. He
wanted to throw himself onto the grass and suck in great quarts
of cool oxygen. Roger was running next to him. He'd caught up,
all that idiotic tennis making him strong and fast, but Leets wouldn't
let him get beyond. Wasn't that Tony ahead at the gate?

The gate!

A sick feeling burned through Leets, almost a sob.

How could they get through the gate?

Tony hit the door in the wall. It didn't budge.

Repp had nineteen, now twenty.

Repp's finger was on the trigger, taking the slack out.

Repp had twenty-one, twenty-two.

Leets tried to get there. He'd never make it. He had a terrible premonition of the next several seconds. "Tony!" someone
screamed, himself.

Old Inverailor House gimmick, from the first days of SOE training up in Scotland. The man was an ex-Hong Kong police inspector,
knew all kinds of tricks of the trade, of which this was but one:

"Now if you've got a lock in a door and you want in and you're
in a bit of a hurry, say Jerry's coming along, take your revolver,
just like a chap in a Hollywood cowboy picture, and shoot—but
not into the lock, flicks are all wrong about that. You'll just catch
the slug on the bounce in your own middle. Rather, at an angle,

into the wood, *behind* the bloody lock. That big four fifty-five makes a wonderful wrench."

Funny how it came back, swimming up through five years of complicated past, just when he needed it.

Carefully, holding the Webley snout at an angle two inches from the ancient brass lock plate, Tony fired. The flash spurted white and blinding.

Repp had twenty-five. There was no slack in the trigger. But what was going on?

"*Kinder*," yelled Tony, German perfect, "the bad man can see in the dark, the bad man can see in the dark."

He could see their white faces stark in the night, and eyes white as they fled. They were apparitions. He heard the scuffle of panicked feet across the pavement. He heard squeals and yelps. He must have seemed a giant to them, a nightmare creation. They must have thought *he* was the bad man who could see in the dark, running through the yard, breathing hard, face blackened, gigantic pistol in one hand. Another irony for his collection.

How quickly they vanished. Several brushed against his leg in their flight and yet it seemed to take only a second. They scurried like small animals. He could not see them anymore.

A woman was crying. Terrified. She didn't know.

We're good fellows, madame, he wanted to explain.

He heard Leets yelling. What *did* the man want?

Repp fired.

Leets reached the gate. He heard them screaming and running. He fixed on fleeing figures that seemed to career through the darkness. Someone was crying. A woman's voice, pitched high in uncontrollable fear, unfurled. "*Bitte, bitte*," please, please.

"Go away, dearest God, go away."

The bullet had taken most of Tony's head. He was on the ground in the middle of the courtyard, in a dark pool spilling out across the pavement.

Then Repp shot him again.

Part Three

Endlösung

(Final Solution)

Dawn, May 8, 1945

XXX

Leets finally stopped being insane near dawn. He'd really gone nuts there for a while, yelling up at the mountain after Repp shot Tony. Leets even fired off a magazine, spraying tracers hopelessly up to disappear into the dark bank of the hillside. Roger had hit Leets with his shoulder behind both knees, and Leets screamed at the blow and went down; then Roger pinned him flat in the arch of the open gate and, using every fiber of strength he had, dragged him back into the protection of the wall.

"Jesus," Roger yelled in outrage, "tryin' to get yourself *killed?*"

Leets looked at him sullenly, but Roger saw a mad glint, the beam of secret insane conviction spark in his irises, werewolflike, and when Leets twisted savagely for the gun, Rog was ready and really hit him hard in the neck with his right forearm, his tennis arm, big as an oak limb, stunning him.

"Out there it's death," he bellowed, deeply offended.

Then Leets had insisted on recovering the body.

"We can't leave him out there. We can't leave him out there."

"Forget it," Roger said. "He doesn't care. I don't care. Those children don't care. Repp doesn't care. Listen, you need a vacation or something. Don't you see? You *won!*"

No, Leets didn't see. He looked across the courtyard to Outhwaithe. A hundred streams of blood ran out of him, across the stones of the yard, catching in cracks and hollows. His head and face were smashed, an eye blown out, entrails erupting with gas, spilling out. Repp, in uncharacteristic rage, had fired a whole magazine into him. Then he'd turned his weapon on inanimate things and in a spooky display of the power of Vampir he'd shredded the door through which some few of the children had disappeared, then methodically snapped out windows, sent a burst of automatic across a plaster saint in a niche in the church, and finally, in a moment of inspired symbolism, shot the crosses off the two domed steeples. A real screwball, thought Roger.

Now, hours later, a chilly edge of dawn had begun to show to the east. Leets had been still, resigned finally, Roger figured. He himself was quite pleased with his coolness under fire. His friend Ernest Hemingway would have been impressed. He'd even

saved the captain's life. You saved your CO, you got a medal
or something, didn't you? What's a captain worth? A Silver Star?
At least a Bronze Star. For sure a Bronze.

Roger was wondering which medal he'd get—which to *ask* for,
actually—when Leets said, quite calmly, "Okay, Rog. Let's take
him."

Repp would have to train himself to live with failure. It was
another test of will, of commitment; and the way to win it was
to close out, ruthlessly, the past. Put it all behind. Speculation as
to how and why he had failed were clearly counterproductive.

He explained all this to himself in the dark sometime in the long
hours of the night after the shooting. Still, he was bitter: it had
been so close.

Repp had killed one, he knew. Now the question was, How
many remained? And would they come after him? And other
questions, nearly as intriguing. Who were they? Should he flee
now?

He'd already rejected the last. His one advantage right now lay
in Vampir. It had run out, but they didn't know that. They only
knew he could hit targets in the dark and they couldn't. It would
be foolish to surrender that advantage by racing off into the dark,
up a steep incline, through rough forest with which he was unfamiliar. A misstep could be disastrous, even fatal.

They wouldn't come, of course, in the dark. They'd come in
the light, at dawn, when they could see him. They'd come when
the odds were better.

If they came.

Would they? That was the real question. They'd won, after
all, they'd stopped him, they'd saved the Jewish swineboy and
the money and perhaps even the Jews, if there were any left.
Sensible men, professionals, would most certainly not come. They'd
be pleased in their victory and sit back against unnecessary risks.
In their position, he'd make the same decision. Go up a strange
mountain after a concealed marksman with one of the most sophisticated weapons in the world? Foolish. Ridiculous. Insane.
Impractical.

And that's when he knew they'd come.

Repp felt himself smile in the dark. He felt happy. He'd reached the last step in his long stalk through the mind of his enemies; and he'd realized just how much now, when it was all over, all finished, when as a species the SS man was about to disappear from the earth, he realized how much he wanted to kill the American.

Roger blinked twice. His mouth felt parched dry.

"Now just a sec," he said.

"We'll never have a better chance. We can do it. I guarantee it."

"Money back?" was all Roger could think to say.

"Money back." Leets was dead serious.

"H-h-h-h-he's long gone." *Damn* the stutter.

"No. Not Repp. In the night he thinks he's king."

"I'm no hero," Roger confessed. He felt a tremor flap through him.

"Who is?" Leets wanted to know. "Listen close, okay?"

Roger was silent.

"He can see in the dark, right?"

"Man, it's *daytime* out there for him."

"No. Wrong. Eichmann said they thought they were trying to work out a way to make this Vampire gadget lighter. So Repp could carry it."

"Yeah."

"He said it was some kind of solar-assist unit. The thing would take some of its power from the sun."

"Yeah."

"You see any sun around here?"

"No."

"It's run-down. It's out of juice. It's empty. He's blind."

Oh, Christ, thought Roger. "You want us to go out there and—"

"No." Leets was very close, though Rog could not see him. But he could feel the heat. "I want *you* to go out there."

Repp was blind now. These were rough hours; lesser men, alone in the night and silence, might have yielded to the temptations of flight.

He was thinking, marvelously alive, taking sustenance from the intricacies of the problem that now faced him.

The chief dilemma was Vampir itself. Now that it was dead,

it was forty kilos of uselessness. In a fire fight, things happened fast. You needed to be able to move and shoot in fractions of seconds. Should he remove the device?

On the other hand, it was unique. It might be worth millions to the proper parties—perhaps even the Americans. It also might make a certain kind of future more feasible than others.

A running gunfight, if such a thing were to occur in the next few hours, might push him all over the face of this mountain. If he dismounted Vampir and hid it, he might never find it again, or he might be hit and unable to get back to it.

The decision then came down to his confidence.

He decided for Vampir.

"No, Roger," the captain repeated. "You. *You're* going out there."

"I, uh—"

"Here's how I've got it doped out. He doesn't know how many we are. But mainly he doesn't know we know Vampire's out of juice. So he's got to figure that if we come, we come at first light. So this is how I figure it. A two-step operation. Step one: Rog goes fast and hard for the mountain. You've got nearly an hour till light. Work your way up, keeping out of gullies, moving quietly. Nothing fancy. Just go up. His range at Anlage Elf was four hundred meters. So to get in range with your Thompson you've got to get at least two hundred, two hundred fifty meters up the slope. You got it?"

Roger couldn't think of a thing to say.

"Step two: at seven-thirty A.M. on the fucking dot, I'm coming up the stairs. Wide open, flat out."

Roger, for one second, stopped thinking about himself.

"You're dead," he said. "You're flat cold dead. He'll drill you after the first step."

"Then you kill him, Rog. You're close enough so when that subsonic round goes off you can get a fix on it. He doesn't know you're there. Now the key point in all this is wait. *Wait!* As long as you're still, you're fine. You start moving around and he'll take you. It's how these guys work, patience. After he fires, there'll be at least half an hour, maybe an hour. It'll be rough. But just wait him out. He'll get up, Roger. You may be surprised at how close he is. He'll probably be wearing one of those camouflage suits, spotted brown and green. Now, aim low, let the rise of the gun carry the rounds into him. Five-, six-round bursts, don't risk a jam. Even when he's down, keep shooting. When you use up that first magazine, put another in. Shoot him some more. Don't_ fuck around. Try and get some slugs into the brains. Really blow them all over the place."

Roger made a small noise.

Leets had taken the boy's weapon and was checking it over. "You've fired a Thompson, I suppose? Okay, that's a thirty-round mag in there. I've set it on full auto, but no round in the chamber. Now this is the M-one, the Army model. The bolt's on the side, not on the top like the ones you see in the gangster movies. Just draw it back, it locks; you don't have to let it go forward again, it fires off the open bolt."

He handed the weapon back.

"Remember, wait him out. That's the most important thing. And that shot of his, it won't sound like a shot. It won't be as loud, like a thud or something. But you'll hear it. Then wait, goddamn it, how many times do I have to say this? Wait! Wait all day, if you've got to, okay?"

Roger stared at him, openmouthed.

"Your move, Rog. Match point coming up."

He wants me to go *out there*? Roger thought in horror. The distance from the corner of the wall to the mountain seemed immense.

"Remember, Rog. It all starts happening at seven-thirty."

Leets clapped the boy on his shoulder and whispered into his ear, "Now go!" and sent him on his way.

The light was growing. He could see the convent seem to solidify magically before and below him out of gray blur. Quiet down there, a body in the courtyard, otherwise empty.

Repp pressed the magazine release catch and a half-empty magazine slid out. He reached into his pouch, got out a full one, and eased it into the magazine housing.

He cocked the rifle and, leaning over it, peered down the slope through the trees. The light was rising now, increasing steadily; and birds were beginning to sing. Repp could smell the forest now, cool and moist.

The night was ending.

If there was a man, he would come soon.

Repp waited with great, calm patience.

Leets knew it was nearly his turn.

He crouched in the shadow of the wall of the convent, breathing uneasily, trying to conjure up new reasons for not going. It was quite light by now and the second hand of his Bulova persisted in its sweep, pulling the two larger hands along with it. Roger had made it but Leets couldn't think about Roger. He was thinking about the long one hundred yards he had to cross before he reached the cover of the trees. A fast man could make it in twelve seconds. Leets was not fast. He'd be out there at least fifteen. One Mississippi, two Mississippi, three Mississippi . . . out there forever, fifteen Mississippis, which was nearly forever. He figured he'd catch it about the sixth or seventh Mississippi.

He'd peeled off his jacket and rolled up his sleeves, but he was still hot. He'd checked the laces and straps of his boots—tight— and tossed aside his cap and taken the bars off his collar. There wasn't much else to do.

He checked his watch again. The seconds seemed to drain away. They seemed to fall off the Bulova and rattle to the grass. He tried to feel good about what would probably happen next. Instead he felt puke in the bottom of his throat. His breathing came hard and his legs were cold and stiff and his mouth was dry.

He glanced about and saw the day opening pleasantly, a pale sun beginning to show over the mountain, a pure sky. A few fleecy clouds unraveled overhead. He knew he could catalog natural phenomena until the year 1957 if he didn't watch himself. *Goddamn it*, he was thirsty.

He looked at the Bulova again and it gave him the bad news: almost time to go. Seconds to go.

He eased his way up to a crouch, checking for the thousandth time the tommy gun: magazine locked, full auto, safety off, bolt back. The forest was a long way off.

Don't blow it, Roger, goddamn you, he thought.

And he thought of Susan once again. "Everything you touch turns to death," she'd said. Susan. Susan, I didn't mean to hurt you. I didn't mean it. He did not hate her. He wished she were here and he could talk to her.

And he thought of Repp, behind his rifle in the trees.

The Bulova said it was time and Leets ran.

Repp watched the American break from the wall. He'd picked him up minutes ago—the fool kept peering out, then withdrawing. He couldn't make his mind up, or perhaps he was enchanted with the view.

It didn't matter. Repp tracked him lazily—such an easy shot— holding the sight blade just a touch up, leading him, drawing the slack out of the trigger. A big, healthy specimen, unruly hair, out of uniform: was this the chap that had been hunting him these months? He wobbled when he ran, bad leg or something.

Repp felt the trigger strain against his finger.

He let the fat American live.

He did not like it. Too easy. He felt he could down this fat huffing fellow anytime. He owned him. The man still had 400 meters of rough forest climb ahead of him, and Repp knew he'd come like a buffalo, bulky and desperate, crashing noisily through the brush. At any moment in the process, Repp could have him.

But as the American perched at his mercy on the sight blade, it occurred to him that he'd been blind for hours. Suppose in that time another American had moved into the trees? It turned on their knowledge of the flaw in Vampir. But they had consistently turned out to know just a touch more than he expected them to. Thus: another man.

A theoretical enemy such as that could be anywhere down the slope, well within machine-pistol range, grenade range, waiting for him to fire. Once he fired, he was vulnerable. So he recommitted himself to patience. He had the fat one off on his left, coming laboriously up the hill. He could wait.

Now, as for another fellow. Where would he be? It seemed to him that if such a fellow in fact existed, then he and the fat one would certainly make arrangements between themselves, so as not to fall into each other's fire. So if the big one was to his left, then wouldn't this theoretical other chap be on the right? He knew he had four or five minutes before the big man got dangerously close.

He began methodically to search his right front.

* * *

What now? wondered Roger.

Guy must be gone. He would have plugged the captain for sure.

From where he was, he'd had a good view of Leets's slow, lumbering run. He'd seen him go and turned back quickly but couldn't see much, the dense trees fighting their way up the slope, stone outcroppings, thick brush.

Leets had been so positive the German would fire. But nothing. Roger scanned the abstractions before him. Sweat ran down his arms. A bug whined in his ears. Looking into a forest was like trying to count the stars. You'd go nuts pretty soon. The patterns seemed to whisper and dazzle and flicker before his eyes. Shapes lost their edges and melted into other shapes. Fantastic forms leapt out of Roger's imagination and took substance in the woods. Stones poked him, filling him with restlessness.

Should he move or stay put? Leets hadn't said. He'd said wait, wait, but he hadn't said anything about if there was no shot. He probably ought to still wait. But Leets hadn't said a thing. Repp was probably gone. What the hell would he be hanging around for? He was no dope. He was a tough, shrewd guy.

On the other hand, why would he have taken off when he held all the aces in the dark?

Roger didn't have any idea what to do.

Leets had gotten well into the trees, deep into the gloom. He rested for a moment, crouching behind a trunk. The slope here was gentle, but he could see that ahead it reared up. The footing would be treacherous.

Squatting, he tried to peer through the trees. His vision seemed to end a few dozen feet up: just trees woven together, trees and slope, a few rocks.

He hoped Roger had the sense to stay put. Surely he'd see that the game hadn't changed, that it was still up to Leets to draw fire.

Don't blow it, Roger.

He'll kill you.

Leets gathered his strength again. He wasn't sure there'd be any left, but he did locate some somewhere. He began to move up the slope, tree to tree, rock to rock, dashing, duck-walking, slithering, making more noise than he ought to.

* * *

Roger looked around. A few shafts of sunlight cut through the overhanging canopy. He felt like he was in an old church or something, and light was slipping in the chinks in the roof. He still couldn't see anything. He imagined Repp sitting in a café in Buenos Aires.

Meanwhile, here I sit, breaking a sweat.

If only I could see!

If only someone would tell me what to do!

Cautiously, he began to edge his way up.

The other American was perhaps 150 meters downslope, rising from behind a swell in the ground, half obscured in shadow. But the movement had caught Repp's experienced eye.

He felt no elation, merely lifted the rifle and replanted it on its bipod and drew it quickly to him.

The American was just a boy—even from this distance, Repp could make out the callow, unformed features, the face tawny with youth. He rose like a nervous young lizard, eyes flicking about, motions tentative, deeply frightened.

Repp knew the big man would be up the slope in seconds. He even thought he could hear him battering through the brush. Too bad they hadn't climbed closer together, so that he could take them in the same arc of the bipod, not having to move it at all.

Repp pressed the blade of the front sight, on the young man's chest. The boy bobbed down.

Damn!

Only seconds till the big one was in range.

Come on, boy, come on, damn you.

Should he move the gun for the big one?

Come on, boy. Come on!

Helpfully the boy appeared again, cupping his hands to shade his eyes, his face a stupid scowl of concentration. He rose right into the already planted blade of the sight, his chest seeming to disappear behind the blurred wedge of metal.

Repp fired.

A split second may have passed between the sound of the shot and Leets's identification of it: he rose then, hauling the Thompson to his shoulder, and had an image of Roger—Roger hit—and fired.

Fire again, you idiot, he told himself.

He burned through the clip. The weapon pumped and he held the rounds into that sector of the forest his ears told him Repp's shot had come from. He could see the burst kicking up the dust where it hit.

Gun empty, he dropped back fast to the forest floor, hands shaking, heart thumping, still hearing the gun's roar, and fumbled through a magazine change. Dust or smoke—something heavy and seething—seemed to fill the air, drifting in clouds. But he could see nothing human in the confusion.

Leets knew he had to attack, press on under the cover of his own fire. He scrambled upward, pausing only to waste a five-round burst up the slope on stupid instinct, and twice he slipped in the loose ground cover, dried pine needles woven with sprigs of dead fern, but he stayed low and kept moving.

A burst of automatic fire broke through the limbs over his head, and he flattened as the bullets tore through, spraying him with chips and splinters. Again bringing his submachine gun up, he fired a short burst at the sound, then rolled daintily to the right, fast for a big man, as the German, firing also at sound and flash, sent a spurt of fire pecking through the dust. Leets thought he saw flash and threw the gun back to his shoulder but before he could fire it vanished.

Then seconds later, to the left and above, his eyes caught just the barest flicker of human motion behind a tangle of interfering pines, and he brought the gun to bear, but it too vanished and he found himself staring over his barrel at nothing but space and green light and dust in the air.

But he'd seen him. At last, he'd seen the sniper.

Repp changed magazines quickly. He was breathing hard and had fallen in his dash. Blood ran down the side of his face; one of the machine-pistol slugs had fragmented on a stone near him and something—a tiny piece of lead, a pebble, a stone chip—had stung him badly above the eye.

Now he knew safety lay in distance. The machine pistol had an effective range of 100 meters, his STG 400. It would be ridiculous to blaze away at close range like a gangster. Too many things could happen, too many twists of luck, freaks of chance, a bullet careening off a rock. Repp thought for just a second of the Jewish

toy he'd played with back at Anlage Elf: you set it spinning and
when finally it stopped a certain letter turned up. Nothing could
change the letter that showed. Nothing. That was the purest luck.
He wanted no part of it.

He'd get higher and take the man from afar.

The sniper climbed.

Leets too knew the importance of distance. He pushed his way
through the trees, forcing himself on. In close he had a chance.
He knew the Vampire outfit had to be heavy and Repp would
have no easy time of it going uphill fast. He'd stay as close as he
could to the sniper, hoping for a clear shot. If he hung back, he
knew Repp would execute him at leisure.

The incline had steepened considerably. He drove himself forward, pawing at the trees with his free hand. Loose glass clattered in his stomach and he could feel the sweat washing off him
in torrents. Dust seemed to have been pasted over his lips and his
leg hurt a lot. Several times he dropped to peer up under the
canopy of the forest, hoping to see the sniper, but nothing moved
before him except the undulating green of the trees.

Vampir was impossibly heavy. If he'd had the time, Repp would
have peeled the thing off his back and flung it away. But it would
take minutes to get the scope unhitched from the rifle, minutes he
didn't have.

He paused in his climb, looked back.

Nothing.

Where was the man?

Who'd have thought he could come on like that? Must be an
athlete to press ahead like that.

Repp looked up. It was quite steep here. He wished he had
some water. He was breathing hard and the straps pinched the
feeling out of the upper part of his body.

He and this other fellow, alone on a mountain in Switzerland.

It occurred to him for the first time that he might die.

Goddamn it, goddamn it, why hadn't he ditched Vampir? To
hell with Vampir. To hell with them all, the *Reichsführer*, the
Führer himself, the little Jew babies, all the Jews he'd killed, all
the Russians, the Americans, the English, the Poles. To hell with
them all. He pushed himself on, breathing hard.

* * *

A stone outcrop loomed ahead. Leets paused as he came to it. It looked dangerous. He peeped over it, upward. Nothing. Go on, go on.

He was almost over, slithering, straining his right leg to purchase another few inches.

Here I am, a fat man perched on a rock in a neutral country, so scared I can hardly see.

He had the inches and then he didn't; for the leg, pushed to its limit, finally went, as Leets all along knew it must. One of the last pieces of German steel that neither doctors nor leakage had been able to dislodge ticked a nerve. The fat man fell, as pain spasmed through him. He thought of it as blue, like electricity, and he corkscrewed out of balance, biting the scream, but then he felt himself clawing at the air as he tumbled backward.

He twisted as he fell and hit on his shoulder, mind filling with a spray of light and confusion. His mouth tasted dust. He rolled frantically, groping for his weapon, which was somewhere else, flung far in the panic of his fall.

He saw it and he saw Repp.

The sniper was 200 meters up, calm as a statue.

He'd never make the gun.

Leets pulled his feet under him, to dive for the Thompson.

Repp shot him and then had no curiosity. He didn't care about the American. He knew he was dead and that made him uninteresting.

He set the rifle down, peeled the pack off his back.

His shoulder ached like hell, but seemed to sing in the freedom of release. He was surprised to notice that he was shaking. He wanted to laugh or cry. It had seemed seconds between first shot and last; clearly it had been minutes.

It had been extremely close. Big fellow, coming on like a bull. You and I, we spun the *draydel*, friend. I won. You lost. But so close, so close. That bullet that spattered on the rock near his head, what, an inch or so away? He shivered at the thought. He touched the wound. The blood had dried into a scab. He rubbed it gently.

He wished he had a cigarette, but he didn't so that was that.

The chocolate.

The driver had given him a piece of chocolate.

Suddenly his whole survival seemed a question of finding it. His fingers prowled through pouches and pockets and at last closed on something small and hard. He removed it: the green foil blinked in the sun. Funny, you could go through all kinds of things, running, climbing, shooting, and here would be a perfect little square of green foil, oblivious, unaffected. He unwrapped it.

Delicious.

Repp at once began to feel better. He had settled down and was again under control. He did not feel good that Nibelungen had failed but some things simply weren't to be. *He* hadn't failed; his skills hadn't fumbled at a crucial moment.

And pleasures were available: he'd been magnificent in the fight, considering how hard he'd pressed to make the shooting position, the long sleepless night that followed. For a short action, it had been enormously intense.

Repp noticed for the first time where he was. Around him, the Alps rose in tribute to him. Solemn, awesome, like old men, their faces aged with snow, they seemed especially grave in their silence. Far below, the valley looked soft and green.

He realized suddenly he had a future to face. It frightened him a little. And yet he had a Swiss passport, he had money, he had Vampir. There were things one could do with all three.

Smiling, Repp stood. His last duty was now to return. He pulled the pack again onto his back. It did not hurt nearly so much now. Thank God for Hans the Kike and his last ten kilos. He swung the rifle over his shoulder.

He pushed on for several minutes through the forest, not unaware of the beauty and serenity around him. After a time he came out of the trees into a high Alpine meadow, several dozen acres of grassland. The grass rolled shadowless in the sun.

Above, clouds lapped and burled against diamond blue, hard and pure. The sun was a cleansing flare. A cool wind pressed against his face.

Repp walked across the meadow. He took off his scrunched *feldgrau* cap and rubbed a sleeve absently across his forehead, where it felt a prickle of heat.

He walked on, coming at last to the end of the meadow. Here

the grass bulked up into a ridge before yielding again to the trees. The ridge stood like a low wall before him, unruly with thistle and bracken and even a few yellow wild flowers.

He turned back to the field. It was empty and clean. It was so clean. It had been scoured clean and pure. It looked wonderful to him. A vision of paradise. Its grass stirred in the breeze.

This is where the war ends for me, he thought.

He knew he had a few more kilometers of virgin pine; then he'd be up top for a long, flat walk; then finally, that last plunge through the gloomy newer trees.

It was only a matter of hours.

Repp turned back to his route and started to trudge up the ridge. More yellow buds—dozens, hundreds—opened their faces to him. He paused again, dazzled. They seemed to pick the light out of the air and throw it back at him in a burst of burning energy. The day stalled, calm and private. Each mote of dust, each fleck of pollen, each particle of life seemed to freeze in the bright air. The sky screamed blue, its mounting cumulus fat and oily white. Repp felt giddy in the beauty of it. He seemed to hear a musical chord, lustrous, rich, held, held, ever so long.

Strange energies had been released; they bobbed and sprang and coiled about him, invisible. He felt transfigured. He felt connected with the order of the cosmos. He turned to the sun which lay above the ridge and from its pulsing glare he sought confirmation, and when two figures rose above him, on the crest line, drenched in light, he took it at first for the benediction he'd demanded.

He could not see them clearly.

He blocked the sun with one hand.

The big one looked at him gravely and the boy had no expression on his pretty face at all. Their machine pistols were level.

Repp opened his mouth to speak, but the big one cut him off.

"Herr Repp," he explained in a mild voice, "*du hast das Ziel nicht getroffen,*" using the familiar *du* form as though addressing an old and dear friend, "you missed."

Repp saw that he was in the pit at last.

They shot him down.

Roger edged down the ridge, changing magazines as he went. The German lay face up, eyes black. He'd been opened up badly in the crossfire. Blood everywhere. He was an anatomy lesson. Still, Roger crouched and touched the muzzle of his tommy gun gently as a kiss against the skull and jackhammered a five-round burst into it, blowing it apart.

"That's enough, for Christ's sake," Leets called from the ridge.

Roger rose, spattered with blood and tissue.

Leets came tiredly down the slope and over to the body.

"Congratulations," said Roger. "You get both ears and the tail."

Leets bent and heaved the body to its belly. He pried the rifle off the shoulder, working the sling down the arm, at the same time being careful not to break the cord to the power pack.

"Here it is," he said.

"Bravo," said Roger.

Leets pulled out the receiver lockpin and the trigger housing pin. Taking the butt off and holding the action open, he held the barrel up to the sun and looked through it.

"See any naked girls?" Roger asked.

"All I see is dirt. It's a mess. All those rounds he ran through it. All that pure, greasy lead. Each one left its residue. The grooves jammed. It's smooth as the inside of a shot glass in there."

"Yeah, well, he nearly threaded my needle."

"Must have been your imagination," Leets said. "At the end the rounds were veering off crazily as they came out the muzzle. No, the Vampire rifle was useless in the end. It amounted to nothing. A man with a flintlock would have had a better chance this morning."

Roger was silent.

But something still nagged Leets. "One thing I can't figure out. Why didn't Vollmerhausen tell him? They were so good at the small stuff. The details. Why didn't Vollmerhausen tell him?"

Roger knitted his features into what he imagined was an expression of puzzlement the equal of Leets's. But he really didn't give a damn and a more rewarding thought presently occurred to him.

"Hey!" he said in sudden glee. "Uh, Captain. Sir?"

"Yeah?"

"Hey, uh, I did okay, huh?"

"You did swell. You were a hero." But he had other heroes in his mind at that second, dead ones. Shmuel the Jew and Tony Outhwaithe, Oxonian. Here was a moment they might have enjoyed. No, not really. Shmuel hated the violence; no joy in this for him.

And Tony. Who ever knew about Tony? Susan? No, not Susan either. Susan would see only two beasts with the blood of a third all over them.

"Well, now," said Roger, grinning, "you think I'll get a medal?" He was supremely confident. "I mean it was kind of brave what I did, wasn't it? It would be for my folks mainly."

Leets said he'd think it over.

ACKNOWLEDGMENTS

A good many friends and colleagues assisted the author in the preparation of this manuscript, though they are in no way responsible for its excesses. But they should be thanked nevertheless. They are James H. Bready, Curtis Carroll Davis, Gerri Kobren, Henry J. Knoch, Frederic N. Rasmussen, Michael Hill, Binnie Syril Braunstein, Bill Auerbach, Joseph Fanzone, Jr., Richard C. Hageman, Lenne P. Miller, Bruce Bortz, Carleton Jones and Dr. John D. Bullock. Two special friends deserve their own sentence: Brian Hayes and Wayne J. Henkel. Lastly, the author would like to pay tribute to two extraordinary people: his wife, Lucy, and his editor, Maria Guarnaschelli, of William Morrow, without whom all this would not have happened.

ABOUT THE AUTHOR

Stephen Hunter was born in 1946 in Kansas City, Missouri. He grew up in the Chicago area and graduated from Northwestern University in 1968. He spent the next two years in the United States Army and in 1971 joined the staff of the *Baltimore Sun*, where he is book review editor.

Mr. Hunter and his wife and son live in Columbia, Maryland.